NEARLY ROADKILL

a novel

QUEER LOVE ON THE RUN

KATE BORNSTEIN
+CAITLIN SULLIVAN

GENEROUS PRESS
AN IMPRINT OF ROW HOUSE PUBLISHING
BELLINGHAM, WA

Because we at Generous Press and Row House Publishing believe that the best stories are born in the margins, we proudly spotlight, amplify, and celebrate the voices of diverse, innovative creators. Through independent publishing, we strive to break free from the control of Big Publishing and oppressive systems, ensuring a more liberated future for us all.

Library of Congress Cataloging-in-Publication Data Available Upon Request

ISBN 9798991642859

Printed in the United States

Distributed by Simon & Schuster

Cover design by Sara Pinsonault.

Interior design by Fritz Metsch and Neuwirth & Associates, Inc.

Photo of Kate Bornstein by Jess Dugan. Photo of Caitlin Sullivan by Erika Lerfald Photography.

First edition

To the fearless queer pioneers for their bravery and perseverance in creating a community we could all live in safely. Thank you for your vulnerability, kindness, and fierce dedication to taking up space in the world.

WARNING

This book contains instances of alchemy, baiting, compassion, corn, corporate greed, dominance, fascism, gender dysphoria, gender questioning, government oppression, heteronormative assumptions, humor, idealism, ideas, inclusiveness, kindness, misgendering, noir sex, police actions, police ineptitude, queer everything, queer sex, rebellion, romance, sarcasm, sex, speculation, straight sex, submission, suspense, teasing, unidentifiable political stances, witchcraft, and zest.

Dear Reader,

If you're of a certain age, you'll recall the sound and feel of '90s dial-up internet: the beeps, the buzzing, the wild sense of possibility. This was the World Wide Web, the Information Superhighway, a newfangled means of connection through chat rooms and electronic mail; it is the neon-bright, erotically charged, and pixelated backdrop of this very special book. Kate Bornstein and Caitlin Sullivan have tapped back into that old buzz to create a new kind of magic entirely.

When the first edition of *Nearly Roadkill: Queer Love on the Run* was written (original subtitle: *An Infobahn Erotic Adventure*), homophobia was a cultural norm and AIDS was killing people on a massive scale. Enter the internet, a place where desire could be joyfully explored, no-holds-barred. Caitlin recalls, "How fun was it to use this technology for hot, wicked sex (after you dialed up on your giant tower computer)? *So fun*."

Sex was just one of the acts of queer resilience this new technology made possible. Back then, trans people didn't gather in public. Kate says, "Trans identity was completely about our bodies, then—and most of us were too ashamed or afraid to go out in public, so there was no way to practice embodying the genders we wanted so badly to be. There was no way to meet and share information, to encourage or warn one another. The dawn of virtual reality made it possible for us to learn what words to say, how to flirt, and importantly: how best to say no." Kate speaks lovingly of The Gazebo, a chat room on America Online founded in 1994 by trans elder and cyberspace superstar Gwendolyn Ann Smith. "The Gazebo was open 24/7 and provided a safe space for trans folk from around the world to gather and talk. That was the beginning of the trans movement—we grew up in cyberspace, and spilled over into real life."

There was a parallel blossoming for Deaf people who had previously used TTY machines, if they were available, to communicate electronically. As an ally, Caitlin says, "The Deaf community's online revolution was a joy to behold." For many marginalized people, the dawn of the Internet marked an end to isolation.

The authors used real chat room culture as inspiration for the 1995 edition of this book but added their own speculative twist, asking, *What if the internet was government-surveilled? What if gender identity was policed and commodified for corporate gain*? Such imaginings are, of course, eerily prescient today. But Kate and Caitlin's more hopeful visions have borne fruit too: Since the '90s trans and queer communities have iterated and blossomed, online and off, not into utopian lockstep but into a vital, creative, and ongoing conversation. A conversation that is crucial as LGBTQ+ rights, immigrant rights, racial justice rights, disability rights, and reproductive rights are threatened or stripped away. A conversation not unlike the one begun by *Nearly Roadkill*'s lovebirds, Scratch and Winc, back in 1995, and continued by D.I. Drew reporting to us from 2025.

While *Nearly Roadkill* isn't a time-travel story, this 30th anniversary "reboot" does bend the laws of time and space, pulling that old dusty ethernet cord as far as it can go, reaching backward from that giant tower computer and forward through the decades to let you know you're plugged in, you're part of the big picture, you're worthy of love. By "you" we mean you, Reader: queer or straight or cis or trans or nonbinary beauty, rebellious lover or lonely heart, enthusiastic or fed-up surfer of Wi-Fi, seeker of justice and joy in a time of great global sorrow. Just like those chatrooms Scratch and Winc can't stay away from, you have a place here if you want it, whoever you are.

Now, buckle up—the Information Superhighway is a twisting road, and you're in for a ride.

With love,
Elaina Ellis & Amber Flame
Generous Press

NEARLY ROADKILL:
QUEER LOVE ON THE RUN

To: Editor, They/Them magazine
From: D.I. Drew Sparrow
Subject: Nearly Roadkill aka Queer Love on the Run aka The Ballad of Scratch and Winc

Hi Asa,

Thank you so much for the go-ahead on this story. I am excited! Since we originally talked last year, I've done some serious sleuthing. I found witnesses, developed reliable online sources, and made deep dives into archival material. I've been surprised and moved by what I've found; I think you will be too.

The story unfolds over the months and weeks leading up to the infamous "day the Internet went silent" in March of 1995. Of course, the shutdown on that infamous day has been covered—I don't know about you, but I've been hearing about it my whole life (my dad used it to lecture me about online safety)—but no one has ever told the personal story of the two folks who first called for the worldwide Internet strike. Nope, Scratch and Winc have been reduced to footnotes. Why? Who were they? Who were they to each other?

Here's my elevator pitch: The story of Scratch and Winc is a love story, a queer love story, one of the great love stories of the age.

The bad news is, I haven't been able to find a trace of Scratch or Winc in the 21st century. Are they dead? Still running? No one knows. It's well-documented that they ran from the law and initially escaped. But what happened after they limped off into the sunset?

The good news is, the amount of material I have found is staggering: original logs, emails, reports, direct messages, and corporate memos. I scored a ton of internal archives, phone logs, and confidential reports from the Federal Bureau of Census and Statistics. It took me a full year to find and patch it all together into the right order. Now the players can tell their own story of queer love on the run.

There's no way I can duplicate the experience of reading/living their words live onscreen. This was back in the wild and woolly days of the Internet frontier. No TikTok or Instagram. People actually talked with each other in chat rooms, live chat, direct messaging, you name it. I've formatted the manuscript to mimic, as much as possible, how it was coming down in real time.

The entire collection of archival material is book-length, but I've broken it into chapters with the idea of *They/Them* publishing it as a monthly serial. Can't wait to hear what you think!

All the best,

Drew Sparrow aka D.I. Drew

To: D.I. Drew
From: Editor, They/Them magazine
Subject: Re: Nearly Roadkill aka Queer Love On The Run . . .

Hi Drew!

Wow, this is a cool concept! I remember our initial conversation and wondered what became of your idea. We'd love to see more.

Can you send some pages?

Thanks,

Asa

To: Editor, They/Them magazine
From: D.I. Drew
Subject: Floppy what?

Hi Asa,

Sweet! I'm so glad you're interested. I've attached a few chapters.

A few things for context:

The most reliable narrative I've come across is written by a kid named Toobe. At the time he was a 15-y.o. computer whiz who kept a digital diary. He's not the center of the love story, but he plays a special role—he documented the adventures of Winc, Scratch, and other Internet misfits.

Have you ever seen a floppy disk? Toobe backed up his own journals and chat logs from his friends onto about a million of them. Which is what I had to work from. Nods to SERVERPRO for their restoration tech. Toobe's million floppy disks ended up on a 1TB flash drive!

The other logs I got from various sources as mentioned above; Scratch and Winc were very protective of Toobe and made sure he had no access to their explicit sex scenes. Noting this just in case you're concerned about a teenager lurking online with grown-ups doing adult activities. They interacted with each other as part of a chosen family.

Note that there were no cell phones at the time, let alone smartphones or any kind of wireless Internet connection. Toobe would have to go to a huge "tower" computer just to write an email or join a chat room. Different times.

Right then, here we go!

Cheers,

D.I. Drew (she/they)

P.S. I think it might blow readers' minds when this series gets published: queers (although they didn't widely call themselves that) were already "refusing to submit to pronouns" in 1995. Pretty radical. Maybe it's romantic of me to think this, but I see Scratch & Winc as the early disruptors who led to the wave of pronoun-talk and genderqueer/agender identification that's been growing for decades. Even now, walking through the world as a nonbinary femme AFAB, it's hard for most to grasp my fluid use of she/they. But in 1995, these folks are using "hir." Wild, right?

01
THE LONG HELLO

1995 JOURNAL ENTRY BY TOOBE IF ANYBODY CARES

You can pretend it's the future if you want to. I don't give a rat's furry behind what you need to believe. You can say this kind of stuff doesn't exist yet, or that it's really close, like tomorrow, but not today. No such thing as the kind of shit I'm writing, you can say, if that makes you feel better. Heh heh heh. G'head.

There's all this insidious shit with the govt and electronic invasion. And my two friends are apparently at the heart of this mess. Real revolutionary material: One's confused and one's a ditz. They act like damn porpoises on some kind of perpetual cyberwave. Cuz they're moony for each other.

But they've always been serious about one thing in particular: gender! What's a man, what's a woman, why do you have to be one or the other? Why do we care? That sort of serious. Both of them, so it's inevitable that they met, I guess. They refuse to submit to regular pronouns. It's some kind of thing with them.

People get really pissed when those two refuse to answer what gender they are. Or even gay, straight, or whatever! Talk about doubling your chances if you swing both ways—I guess they swing every which way they can.

But this is where I always get confused. Who does what to who and in what body seems kinda important—doesn't it? Then Scratch goes into hir "what is gender anyway?" rap. ("Hir" is how they reject gender pronouns altogether.) And I start sputtering, cuz "what's gender?" is a stupid question, but it's not as simple as I think. What kind of fool would ask you what gender is?

Gender is the only thing we know, goddammit. But Winc says it's the only thing we're told from birth on out. We don't really know gender; no one even explores or questions it. Ze says ("ze" is another anti-pronoun) that gender gets assigned when you're born, but we never choose, not like we choose our clothes, jobs, cars, or lovers. Especially in this country, where you think you can choose anything, except the one thing that determines how you'll be treated the rest of your life you don't choose, so fuck your gender anyway. Can't argue with that one.

Things are coming down, and I have a feeling the media is gonna have their usual field day with those two, so I'm making sure there is a true record. And I'm backing up everything.

Me? I'm not really important, but Winc would kill me if ze heard me saying that. I live with my dad in a little apartment in a big city, and I'm not a nerd, but I'm not the school president either. Scratch says it's normal that I feel this whole life is a huge mass of water pulling down into a drain and I'm trying like hell not to go with it. It's pulling me to be a boy, which is mostly okay, but there's parts of me, well . . . I just don't tick all the boxes all the time. And then there's being pulled to be a grown-up, pulled to be socially adjusted, pulled to all this stuff I don't have a clue about. And apparently I have to choose. Naw. I don't want to be any one thing, but I don't have an alternative. Scratch sez I will be something, that I'll have to choose. Winc sez I won't have to choose, that I don't have to make up my mind ever and that even if I choose, I can change my mind and choose again later. Sometimes that's a comfort, sometimes it just makes me more confused.

I like to think that somebody will find this journal, and it'll be all poignant like Anne Frank's Diary.

The first time Scratch and Winc met on America Online (AOL), they were hot for each other. Still are! They wouldn't tell each other what they are, I mean what sex they are, or anything else for that matter, like how old or what color. It's a game now with them. I'm not sure anything could make them reveal themselves. It drives me crazy, but they seem to like it.

They used to trip out on whether they might be falling for someone of the "wrong" gender, but once they got over that, they got a little compulsive if you ask me, about making sure they didn't find out. Like taping a football game and not wanting anyone to tell you the final score.

They made up the "ze" and "hir" thing—well, they ripped it off like they rip off so much other stuff, so I use it to write about them, to protect their identities. Or nonidentities. Oh man, I'm confused again.

THE EYES ARE HERE TO HELP YOU

Oh, that reminds me. Can you believe that pop-up arrived just as I was writing in my own journal? Yep. I was online, and this online service promises "complete privacy," but as you can see . . . the Eyes found me. The Eyes are a new thing, well, a new term for an old concept.

See, we're all connected via computers. You can send email or chat messages, very cool. For a long time, it was all chaos and everyone was connected, hopping on- and offline as they pleased, but then the govt got wind of it, and the ad agencies, too, and they said, "Unregulated? No way!" So they started doing little things to make sure everything is "monitored." (Censored. Protected. Told you it was an old concept.)

So the Eyes are like online beat cops. You can say anything as long as it's not subversive. ::rolls eyes:: So if they catch you at anything (whatever that is), then the Eye notes that, "for everyone's own good."

PERHAPS SOME
ASSISTANCE HERE?

No thanks, Eye, signing off soon.

EYE READ YOU LOUD AND CLEAR, TOOBE. SLEEP WELL.

EYE HAS LEFT THE LOG.

Fuck that noise. It's creepy how they know my name without me telling them.

Back to my point: Scratch and Winc met online, which means they had no idea who the other was: tall, short, Black, white, whatever. They claim their "real" identities don't matter, even if they ever meet in real life. But I say they will matter.

Here's an early email from Winc, kinda shows what ze's like. Ze cracks me up but also makes me wanna hug hir.

To: Toobe
From: Winc
Subj: IS THIS WORKING?

HEY DUDE, GOT MY MODEM HOOKED UP AND I MADE IT ONLINE. WOW OH WOW OH WOW THIS IS A WAY COOL WORLD. HOPE I'M SENDING THIS RIGHT AND THAT YOU GET IT.

HUGS TO YOU,

—WINC

So I wrote back:

To: Winc
From: Toobe
Subj: Read you LOUD and Clear

Got your message. Welcome to the Net! One little note: don't write in ALL CAPS okay? That means you're shouting when you're online. And here's a hug from me to you!

{{{{Winc}}}} means I'm hugging you. The more {{{{{{}}}}}}}, the bigger the hugs. A lot of people use them but they're too cutesy. But I might give you a few sometimes. Or you can put stuff in double colons, like this: ::hugging you:: Anything in a double colon means an action, not what you're actually saying. And if you want to emphasize something, just put an asterisk around the word; you may have noticed there's no *italics*.

Have fun. I'm glad you're here.

Your pal,

—Toobe

To: Toobe
From: Winc
Subj: Ohmigosh!

::shaking my head in amazement::

I am having so much *fun* here, Tooberoo! Sorry for the all caps, I'd never shout at you!

My mind is boggling at the possibilities of stretching who/what I am in this space.

—Winc

Winc always makes me feel good. Just when I think ze's a major flake, ze comes through. Ze's a friend, a real one. Doesn't treat me like a kid. I'm glad ze doesn't have to go to an office for work, which would kill hir like it kills most people.

A couple of weeks later, ze sends me this:

To: Toobe
From: Winc
Subj: Ohmigosh!

This is amazing! 'Drag Queen' is a mighty popular thing, I discovered. (Did you know this already?) Thank you thank you for introducing me to all this! And you've been traveling in this world all this time? You are one wise cookie, don't you ever forget that, you hear me?

{{{{{{{{Toobe}}}}}}}}

This online stuff: I can explore different ways of relating with people. I can be brave one night, timid the next. I can saunter or mince, attract or pursue.

Know what I mean, bean?

—Winc

I totally get what ze means, and I have no idea why ze knows I would, but I'm glad. Even if I act like a shit sometimes, ze still keeps talking to me like I understand, and so . . . I do.

END TOOBE ENTRY

To: Editor, They/Them magazine
From: D.I. Drew
Subject: Journals and privacy

Now onto your first excerpt from Winc's journal, which I got from . . . never mind where, I have my sources. I was relieved to learn that anything in Scratch and Winc's journals were for their eyes only, no Toobe allowed!

This next log by Winc seems to be from about when ze first started to record hir online encounters, conversations, etc. No one dated anything, dammit, so no embedded dates, but I'm guessing this was maybe late 1994?

Cheers,

Drew

WINC JOURNAL ENTRY

The bottom line here seems to be sex, yay! So that's where I started.

Last night in a chat room I used a couple of different names, right? (Thanks to Toobe for teaching me *that* one.) I went into one room called the Flirt's Nook, and this guy said, Wanna go private? and I said, Sure (no idea what it meant), so he gives me the name of this room.

So I go there, and he starts *taking off his clothes*! I mean, online he does. He used that double-colon thing, ::I'm stripping off my shirt:: etc. It's amazing! So ::blush:: we have sex right there! He asks me what I look like, what I'm wearing, and it's kind of like the phone sex work I do only better, because there's even *more* to the imagination!

So he has his way with me ::grin:: and then he just *signs off*! Poof, he's gone. ::wryly:: Guess he came, huh? That's what guys do on the phone line, too, they come, then they hang up.

At that point, I figured in for a penny, in for a pound. So I signed off, then signed back on as, get this, a major macho dude! HAHAHAHAHAHA! And I had *more* sex—with some women this time! *Then* I signed off and signed back on as a DRAG QUEEN!

And I had all this sex with straight boyz and gay boyz AND straight girlz.

All of this is like when I'm working my phone line, being someone else for some guy. Only, online it's really *me*, a different aspect of me. *For* me. Not for some guy who's payin' me to be his fantasy.

I want to learn to do *that* in the real world. My dream come true!

END WINC ENTRY

To: Editor, They/Them magazine
From: D.I. Drew
Subject: New character

Hi Asa,

Have I got a treat for you today!

Enter a character called Jabbathehut, apparently a friend of Toobe. Toobe calls Jabba "she," so I will too. Jabba writes the technical and legal accounts of the story in a kind of narrative. Reminds me of a smoky film noir scene. Enjoy.

Let me know if you have questions about this next batch of materials—

Cheers,

Drew

NARRATIVE ENTRY, JABBATHEHUT

Green walls. Darker green trim. Wherever one might glance from the vantage point of Wally Budge's well-worn government issue swivel chair, there's some shade of green. The brightest green is the monitor into which Wally Budge is now peering: it's positively glowing green. The lone window in his office is a pale brown-yellow: layers of nicotine obscure nature's one shot at adding some real green to Wally Budge's life at the Federal Bureau of Census and Statistics. Wally Budge couldn't describe the color of his office walls if you paid him. He's 46 years old, and the best he can come up with is: "The same color I went to school with."

Cigarette wedged between his fingers, he reads the daily reports offered by the FBCS's twin Cray supercomputers; he's sucking at a hole in his teeth, an annoying habit, but Budge has no one left in his life to annoy. Three failed marriages and two lost custody battles, so no one to care about his three-pack-a-day cigarette habit, no one to wince at the soft sucking sounds his tongue makes as it pokes the well-traveled cracks and crevasses of his teeth. His nicotine-stained fingers are, ironically, well-manicured; they now dance clumsily across the worn and battered keyboard of one of the Bureau's oldest desktop computers as he adds information to his spreadsheet. He peers up at the screen from time to time in search of a clue, a pattern. And for someone outside a pattern.

Wally Budge knows that once you have a pattern down, criminals show up outside it; criminals will inevitably break the patterns laid down by the law. He begins humming a mangled version of "London Bridge is Falling Down." Good sign for him, bad sign for some poor sap trying to escape the length of this particular lawman's long arm.

His monitor beeps, and on his screen flashes:

To: FBCS Investigations
From: DevilsOwn
Date: (transmission garbled)
Subj: Think about this, my fine-fettered friend . . .

"Of course the entire effort is to put oneself

Outside the ordinary range

Of what are called statistics."

—Stephen Spender

Budge snorts once and hits SAVE. The hackers are getting downright poetic. At first he'd been alarmed by the ease with which some of these people could read his files, but he's learned there is nothing you can do about them except collect what they send you, save their electronic signatures, and build a profile—those files are getting fat. Who knows, they might come in handy some day. He has, however, the persistent suspicion that the hackers are only letting him collect what they want him to collect.

It was easy enough to spot patterns in the old days: the object of everyone's desire had been money, and money had very few possible pathways—into and out of banks, or into and out of the black market. Follow the money, and eventually you'd find your criminal. But money is on the way out, and the world is beginning to trade in information.

Information, Budge quickly discovered, can come from anywhere and can go anywhere else, be it cyberspace or real space. And there is no clearly defined black market for information. Well, none that the Registration Enforcement Task Force is aware of. That's why Budge is humming happily: he's discovered a pattern, and it's finally starting to pay off.

Not that any of his supervisors had wanted to hear about it. A month ago, he'd tried to explain it to them:

"Most people sign onto the Net with whatever name they're given by the system or whatever name pops into their head at the time," he'd said to the roomful of FBCS brass. "They tend to go to more or less the same areas of the Net time after time."

His audience had looked at him blankly. He was used to it.

"Okay," he continued gamely. "Let's say some Joe out there is going online using the name JoeBlow, and let's say you're going to find him night after night in a corner of the Net called, say, Flirt's Corner. One guy, one name, one place to hang out and shoot the electronic breeze. With me?"

Heads nodding tentatively. The word *flirt* had made most of the men nervous.

"Right," Budge continued, buoyed slightly.

"Then there's this other type: the guy who changes his name night to night from JoeBlow to JoeCool to CoolBlue to Blue Velvet to whatever, but that's still him in that Flirt's Corner room, no matter what his name is. He's got a lot of names, but only one personality, like a core identity. He's no different, really, from the first guy."

The half-dozen faces bore the unmistakable look of "Yeah, so?" But Budge was on a roll.

"Finally, there's the guy who keeps changing not only his name but also his entire identity—he doesn't have a single, unshakable identity."

His audience had looked decidedly uncomfortable with that one. Single, unshakable identities were, after all, the basis of any social grouping and key to their profiling techniques.

Budge forged ahead. "These folks might hang out in Flirt's Corner one night, Bible Talk the next night, and Love My Puppy the next. If they're doing that online," he'd concluded triumphantly, "they'll do that offline too. Those are the folks who will refuse to Register their identities with you all."

It was the undersecretary of the Bureau who'd broken the uneasy silence.

"Even if that is true," she'd said quietly, "how do you propose to find them? Follow every person on the Net to see how many names each of them has?"

"No, ma'am, no, we don't have to follow these . . . what do we call these people? Criminals? Rebels? Freaks? Nah, they're going to announce themselves to us loud and clear when they fill out their own profiles."

He thought it was so clear, but nothing but blank stares.

A memo flashing on his screen shakes Budge out of the memory of that meeting.

To: FBCS Investigations
From: Inspections&Reports
Subj: quotas

It has been noted that several departments have not submitted a projection on the status of Registration evaders. To complete the Divisional report, we need:

1. A projection (in percentile figures) of Registration evaders in your online sectors;
2. A summary of the tactics you plan to employ to identify the evaders.

Kindly respond by day's end.

—RR

He shakes his head. Right. Good plan.

But in that meeting, he'd tried so hard to make things clear:

"So, Ol' Joe, he keeps going into Flirt's Corner . . . well, pretty soon he's going to be targeted for breath fresheners, time-share condos in the islands, and adult videos. Fits a pattern. But if someone changes identities all the time, they'll get ads for everything from—" and here Budge had paused, glanced down at a printout, smiled, and said, "mutual funds to skateboard insurance. So all you gotta do is watch who's getting more than their fair share of ads."

He might as well have been speaking Klingon.

"Look, there's that whole marketing group, Allied Consumer Industries. They represent virtually every company that spends more than a nickel a year in advertising. Right now they keep records of who gets which ads and sort that by zip code. Right?"

Heads nodding slowly.

"Right! But now, with the Net, you can flip a switch and you will know exactly which individuals are getting which ads. All we have to do," he'd pointed out, "is find someone who shows up in one too many marketing windows."

More blank stares, but Budge ignored them. He was on a roll. He had a pattern, and he'd found some folks he suspected were breaking it.

"Those are the ones who won't register an identity, the ones who don't have an identity to begin with. Those are the folks who are telling us about themselves right now, three months before the Registration deadline."

They'd looked at him with polite smiles, dismissing him without really saying a word. He'd seen that look before: they were giving him just enough rope to hang himself. Well, perhaps he would.

That was four weeks ago, before two names practically fell onto his screen, right out of one too many marketing windows. And now he stares at the printout again:

Scratch \\\ Winc
a.k.a.: (no alternates located)

"What's W-I-N-C stand for?" he says out loud to his empty office with the green-green walls. "It's an acronym for something, right?"

END JABBA NARRATIVE ENTRY

To: T. Sparrow
From: Drew
Subject: Chat rooms

Hi Dad,

Still working on my dang opus. It's a ton of work, but I'm INSPIRED. It's like I'm directly meeting my queer ancestors.

Speaking of back in the day, maybe next time we talk you could tell me more about chat rooms. From what I can tell, there were tons of chat rooms on America Online, and people actually used them to chat! i.e., have long conversations with one another. No one talks online that way now. We argue in the comments section or do private messages, but that's different—right? Can you tell me more about that? It seems to me those spaces had a lot of freedoms that we don't have now.

When I was reading chat room logs, it seemed freakin' sad that they didn't even anticipate that someday you'd be able to . . . well . . . become a troll and dox people with death threats on social media.

Thoughts?

Love,

Yer kid Drew

TOOBE ENTRY

You can give yourself any name you want online. Then you can set up "rooms": little virtual places where people chat about whatever. Or you can go into some room called Love of Christ with the screen name of SatanDear, and then you might have a little trouble. That's why it's fun to come back five minutes later as ChristOnACrutch or something. . . .

Anyway, one time Scratch chose a name that had "bere" in it cuz it's Irish, but people took it as a misspelled "bear." So in the pagan room they thought it meant that Scratch's totem was a bear. In the Love My Beastie room, they thought that Scratch was being a teddy bear. In the gay room, the men thought it meant ze was a gay, hairy guy.

Winc sez I have no blinders on, like they left them off at the baby factory. Scratch sez I have no idea what's taboo or not, and I'm mostly just curious, curious, curious. I don't know what Scratch looks like in the real world, I only know hir online. I used to care what sex ze is, but now I talk to hir without thinking about that.

Scratch can get into these loops where it's hard to get hir out. Ze starts spiraling down some helix that I can't follow all the time. But one loop was pretty cool:

To: Toobe
From: Scratch
Subj: Online

I just got off the phone with my brother and he doesn't get why people spend so much money to talk to strangers or have more email than they can handle. Stumped me for a minute, but then I got a theory. Ready for another one, ol' pal?

It used to be you could talk to people on the street. You could chat about the weather or the news and then you'd go your separate ways. But you might have to worry that they're psycho or they're gonna ask you for something, or that they'll think *you're* weird. So we've shut ourselves down. We size somebody up in a second and we cross the street, either literally or figuratively. We judge people by how they look, of course, but it's a complex assessment—in a flash!—based on so many little things that it takes up too large a portion of your brain.

The thing is, people still want to connect. You know when people do good deeds spontaneously, like keeping a whale alive when it's washed ashore or helping somebody out during a fire or something? They all feel so fucking good, and they can't quite explain it.

So in cyberspace, they're talking to people again! They don't have to worry that somebody's gonna pull a gun if they say the wrong thing. And even if someone *is* acting like a shithead, nobody has to "see" each other again. And for women! Whoa! Suddenly they can tell assholes to fuck off without getting killed, or be really sexy in a way they would never be normally and just enjoy it in safety. Which leads me to another theory, which is why so many men pose as women online. It's like cyber-crossdressing. They give up the male role for a while, for the sheer relief of giving it up. Or pretend they're lesbians. What cracks me up is that they're probably doing it with other guys pretending to be women too! I got off the track. But do you know what I mean?

—S.

Before I met Scratch online, I wouldn't have been thinking about this kind of stuff. But now, yeah, I know what ze means.

Here's more about the word *hir*: I found out in English class that the English language used to have gender assigned to nouns, just like German and most other romance languages have. We still have some of that left-over, like ships are "she," and Mother Nature is "she," and of course, everything else is "he." And in Chaucer, there's the word *hir*. That's how they used to say the possessive when they didn't know the gender of the noun, or it was a neutral noun. Way back then! So it would be "The person sat down at hir computer and began to type." (It was pronounced "here" sort of, with an English accent so who really knows. Ancient English is as dead as ancient Greek.) That's why S&W use a word that they didn't even make up!

Scratch and Winc don't really know this yet, but they keep running into each other online, no matter who they're being at the time. They'll be in a room called Fooling Around and maybe Scratch has chosen for hir persona a big strapping hunk of a sexist pig, and sure enough Winc will have chosen tiny damsel in distress, and they'll play it out, and then one of them will recognize the other's "style" or something and they'll crack up. Then one of them will say, "I know you're a woman now," and the other one will ask "How do you know?" and off they go again.

I'm a chronicler, I guess. And I'm a guy. I call myself "Toobe" (pronounced tube) cuz it sounds cool, and it's a lot better than my real name.

They really challenge people about this, which I never thought of before. So here's an example of Scratch messing with some poor dude who thinks ze's a girl.

Forwarded Chat Log:

Scratch--->TOOBE

AWESOME: You a guy or a girl?

Scratch: Does it matter?

AWESOME: I'm pretty loose about most things, but I don't fuck dudes.

Scratch: Ah, that's a shame, hon. You'd probably enjoy it if you loosened up. That's OK, I'm not anything tonight.

AWESOME: I take it you enjoy watching guys together. No, I don't think I would enjoy it, and yes, I am pretty loose.

Scratch: I enjoy lots of things, like guys who can be receptive, as it were. :)

That little :) symbol is a smile (turn it on its side and you'll see). I don't use them, way too cute for me. Scratch doesn't usually, either, but I guess ze was "in character."

AWESOME: I can be very receptive to certain things. But I enjoy it more when I do the giving.

Scratch: Ain't that sweet. And rare . . .

AWESOME: So do you just naturally have a fucked-up attitude, or is this your way of weeding out certain people?

Scratch: What the fuck do you know about my attitude, dude. ::firing up weedwhacker::

AWESOME: Somehow I get the impression you're a guy. If that is the case, bring the weedwhacker over here and I will demonstrate on you how it is used properly . . . ha ha. Your attitude is all fucked up. LOL.

Scratch: I don't give a fucking shit in hell what gender I am . . . I try to leave it in the car with the windows rolled up as much as possible.

I like when Scratch and Winc send me stuff. It makes me more brave.

END TOOBE ENTRY

To: Editor, They/Them magazine
From: D.I. Drew
Subject: Scratch and Winc's first chat

Hi Asa,

From everything I've been able to put together, the following is a true narrative of the first time Scratch and Winc hooked up online. Look at this dance and how it gets so steamy fast. Love it!

Then I found a gold mine: an entry from Scratch hirself about the first time ze met Winc. It was a themed chat room that was monitored so you could kick out trolls. Sigh. So nice to have.

Not only was that the first time Scratch and Winc met, it shows how long the two of them could keep a conversation going (if a "conversation" can include sex—and why not, right?). Does a long convo even happen these days? Where? Seriously, I'd like to know. Maybe we can ask people to let us know in the comments of an online version.

Cheers,

Drew

PS: There's a lot of great sex in this. Not sure if *They/Them* can publish it all. You'll let me know, right?

NARRATIVE ENTRY, JABBATHEHUT

There's a "pub" in the virtual world, which, despite the unlimited possibilities of description, the "patrons" have chosen to create as a slightly tacky lounge for more than tacky people to frequent. It's all there—the polyester, the smoky haze, the blender drinks, and the elevator music. At any given time, day or night, this bar can be full of people, with a wide range of handles reflecting their status—usually heterosexual, married, and restless. They come because there are others like them; this is their first tentative step onto the worldwide connection to the Net.

It is here that Scratch has found hirself, bored out of hir mind but unable to sleep. Ze has signed on as Scratch, without a gender, waiting to see if someone else will fill in that blank. As ze fends off the third of a series of polyester advances, ze realizes wryly that ze must be giving off the scent of someone female, and muses on the invisible cues cyberspace somehow allows. Pissed off but curious, ze decides to give them what they want, but takes time crafting hir profile. Ze can see out hir window: riot grrls with backward baseball caps, combat boots, and skirts. They're scary, angry, frenetic, and beautiful. Funny how even in this androgynous new generation, there is still a gender uniform for girls and boys.

"Okay," ze says to hirself. "You want girl, I'll be girl."

Into this bar skateboards Winc, oblivious of the hour, the patrons, the atmosphere. He (for that's the pronoun chosen at the moment) shakes the rain out of his long, dark hair like a puppy, again clueless of the startled stares his presence provokes. He turns on his "All Messages" option, allowing him to receive not only Private Messages from the other patrons, but also the news, public service announcements, and advertisements. In this virtual world, he sits down at the bar, orders a beer, and surveys the place.

"Cool," he says. Onscreen is a lottery game, inset with a football broadcast, which he idly watches. He has a small waterfall tattooed under his right eye. His body is lithe, boyish, and he's added a bit of mascara tonight.

Meanwhile, Scratch puts the final touches on "her" transformation. Unsuspecting souls checking her profile would see:

Member Profile

Name: Scratch
Occupation: Fully
Quote: Fuck your gender
☐ click here to read more

Of course, the "more" part is what Scratch is still working on. Immediately after creating her profile, Scratch starts receiving advertisements. Since she elected to receive more info about fragrances, she has been pelted with pleas from the fashion industry for her attention, her time, her body fat, her virtual crow's-feet. It's helping. Her profile is getting more solidly centered in "pissy." By the time a pastel-colored layout urges her to buy the latest PMS medication, she's in full swing: young, female, angry. She hits the REFUSE button hard, almost breaking her mouse. She recovers by surfing the other patrons' profiles, whose scintillating conversation is revealed:

Online Host

***** You are in room "The Tavern" *****

FredMan: Hey, honey, come sit closer to me.

Scratch: No thanks, I'm fine right here.

Tomgun: Don't mind Fred, he's harmless. But I'm not. ::grin::

FredMan: Not that harmless.

Scratch: Winc, how long is your skateboard?

Winc: Oh, it's not a long one, it's about average.

Azazello: LOL, Winc, tell her it's huge!

Winc: ::startled:: huh? What do you mean?

Scratch: I'm sure it's long enough, babe.

Hanzoo: Scratch wants your body, man.

Scratch: Thanks, Han, but you can go do yourself now.

Winc: ::to Scratch:: So I missed that one, eh? You want my body?

Scratch: Why don't you come with me and see?

Winc: ::gazing at Scratch from beneath hooded eyes:: What's in it for me?

Hanzoo: Go, Winc!

Scratch: ::shrugging:: Suit yourself, cautious one.

A soft chime sounds in the background. Everyone in the bar instantly becomes "quiet" and listens—no one is typing.

A Public Safety Announcement
from
the United States Government
Bureau of Census and Statistics

presented with the cooperation of your local Net service provider

Only three more months left until New Year's Eve.
One more month to Register!

Registrants are still eligible for the following benefits:

- Entry by invitation to special areas of the Net
- Harassment insurance and protection by the Eye network
- Personalized advertisements which focus on what *you* want!
- A chance to win our SIX MILLION DOLLAR LOTTERY!

Tonight's winners will be announced in 32 minutes.
All new registrants will be awarded a double chance to win tonight's drawing.
So send those entry forms in now now now!

We apologize for interrupting your service temporarily, and we thank your local service access provider for their assistance in making this public safety announcement available to you.

End: PSA #3724

The silence continues until the last of the announcement fades from the screens of The Tavern attendees. Then gradually, the room's ambience begins to return.

FredMan: I know someone who won last week's lottery.
Hanzoo: Wow, what I could do with $6 million!
BarBun: You do, Fred, really? ::pouting:: I suppose I should Register.

FredMan: It wasn't six million, Han, that's only the grand prize. You haven't Registered, Bun?!

Hanzoo: You haven't Registered, BarBun?! Get with it, woman!

BarBun: I know, I know, it's just all those questions they ask you!

Winc: I'm with you, BarBun. Major ick!

Hanzoo: The questions aren't so bad, BarBun . . . just the standard age, sex, race, income, stuff like that . . .

Winc: ::whispering the name of a private room to Scratch::

Azazello: Yeah, and what else . . . simple stuff like sexprefs, brandprefs, zip, zip-plus, famzips . . . it's not hard.

Scratch: Got it, Winc . . .

BarBun: All right, all right, you guys, I'll fill out the forms now. Geez!

Winc: ::waving::

FredMan: If you win, BarBun, take me to the islands! I have a time-share condo, but no way to get there!

Scratch: No Reg for me. Too intrusive. Plus Reg messes up what's so great about this place. We're all the same, we can be whatever identity we want, the playing field is leveled.

Hanzoo: Leveled how?

Scratch: Huh?

Hanzoo: Don't you think the default is white, and probably male?

Scratch: Well yeah in the world, but not here.

Hanzoo: Are you sure?

Scratch: ?

Hanzoo: When you're *not* a white person, you can tell what the vibe is in the room—real life or online—

Scratch: Oh.

Hanzoo: You probably assume everyone is white because you're white.

Scratch: Right. But it doesn't matter to me!

Hanzoo: To you. But for me, I need to know where I can have a good conversation and not be treated like shit. Let's just say you won't find me in the "Confederate flags for Jesus" chat room.

Scratch: Oh.

Hanzoo: And, ::very gently:: it's usually white people who say the playing field is level.

Scratch: Oh.

Hanzoo: ::laughing:: It's okay, hon.

Scratch: No it's not.

Scratch: Yeah, sorry. Got a long way to go.

Hanzoo: Oh don't we all. Just go with BarBun and register!

END JABBA NARRATIVE ENTRY

SCRATCH'S ONLINE JOURNAL

The first time I met Winc was unbelievable. Perfect that ze was there. If I'd heard another stupid line I would've thrown up right into my keyboard. I captured most of it:

Member Profile

Name: Winc

Age: 28

Occupation: hahahahahahahaha!

Hobbies: Skateboarding, it's my life.

Quote: jus' wanna be yer cherrybomb!

But just as I was to join the Winc dude in a private room, I get one of those Private Messages. . . .

Private Message from Thesman

Thesman: Um, Scratch, just being friendly here, but if any member of this service catches your profile (you wrote: "the F-word your gender") it will mean a quick end to your online days. You might want to take that offending word off and replace it with something more mainstream.

Scratch: Thanks, oh my goodness! I'm taking out my frustrations with Winc. Catch you next time.

Thesman: Leave him in one piece OK? See ya later . . .

Scratch: If he wants it. ;) bye.

Thesman: I'll remember that . . . have fun . . .

Ah yes, self-policing—way more effective than actual law. As always.

I didn't even care what this guy Winc was or if he was a guy. I was trapped in "girl," with all these lounge lizards around me. Thought some cybersex would be nice. I gave him a whole lot of attitude, but he stuck around anyway.

You are in Private Room "Apt. 3G"

Scratch: Warning: I'm pissy and I'm horny and I want . . .

Winc: Yeah? ::grinning:: What is it you want?

Scratch: I don't care what sex you are, I just wanna fuck. If that's too rough for you piss off.

Winc: ::leaning forward, putting my hands on your shoulders:: Do your stuff, Scratch.

Scratch: ::crotch zing:: I like that in a partner. Gotta know about your hair. Long or short?

Winc: ::laughing, turning away, tossing long hair out of my eyes::

Scratch: <--- likes long hair.

Winc: You?

Scratch: Short, bristle, you have to ask to touch it.

Winc: What if I don't wanna ask first? ::turning and walking back closer to you::

Scratch: Then you get a kick in the balls.

Winc: ::stopping short:: Ah . . . well . . . With what kind of shoe?

Scratch: They're boots, dude. Bet you're pretty in that long hair.

Winc: ::dropping to my knees, pressing my cheek against your boot:: ::purring:: I'm as pretty as they come.

Scratch: ::grabbing hair:: ::pulling face up to look at me:: Stay with me, though . . .

Winc: ::jerking to my feet::

Scratch: ::kissing your neck, pulling hair::

Winc: mmmmmmmmmm . . . nice, very nice . . .

I'll summarize a bit: It's a bare room, mattress on the floor, but we're nowhere near it. I can practically hear our voices echoing, it's so real. I'm horny as hell, urgent, with a kind of intensity I've never felt before. Like I don't care what he wants. I'll use him anyway, I'm not obligated to his rhythm.

I push him against the wall, and he gasps.

"You like it rough, huh girl?" he asks.

My hands are hungry, rough on him, rougher than I wanna be, but now I understand that phrase "I can't help it." He shudders, I bring my hands to his chest, squeezing his nipples. I squeeze them hard, and his eyes go wide. It makes me laugh softly. I've pegged him; his hardness turns me on, but it's the way he yields that takes me over the top. I've never been here before, it's not some bitch in high heels with a whip I'm being, but I'm definitely running this thing. I can feel my own desire take over, spill out, let it guide my fingers on the keys, my hands along his body. I lift his shirt, suddenly impatient.

"I want it off!"

He tosses his head, making his hair whip my face a bit.

"Make me," he says.

He still doesn't get it. He's describing himself, and I begin seeing him. Lithe boy body, soft hair on his belly, sinewy. I ease up to his chest, kittenish, unassuming, kissing his chest, but then bite his nipples hard. He gasps.

"Shirt off," I repeat. He's breathing hard but pauses, maybe in confusion, maybe still impudent. "Off!"

He pulls his torn T-shirt over his head. He folds his arms across his chest: I pull his arms down, knead his chest with my hands. He gasps, and I press myself fully against him, kissing him deeply.

He lifts his arms up and around my shoulders. I lean into him, suddenly grateful for his strong body, his boy strength.

"Yes," I say, "hold me strong."

He opens his mouth wide for me, pulling my tongue deep inside. I press against his pelvis, and he moans into my mouth. My hands are around his back, digging in.

Winc: ::pushing hard against you, kneading your shoulders with long strong fingers . . . my cock harder now::
Scratch: ::Hand drifting absently down to the top of your jeans::
Winc: ::whimpering::

I tug on his jeans; he shivers. I rub his bulge through the jeans.

Winc: Oh
my
gosh
Scratch: ::backing up, pulling off my shirt::

I turn him around, rubbing my breasts on his back. His back is warm, and a moan escapes, startling us both. He pushes his ass back against my crotch, as I wrap my arms around his belly.

Winc: ::sighing::
Scratch: ::sliding my hands down to your hips, pulling you against my crotch, pushing you hard, bending you over::
Winc: ::lifting my hands above my head, against the wall::
::turning my head to face you . . . questioning::

I push him into the wall, crotch pressed against his ass.

"Questioning what, boy?"

He gasps, shakes his head. "What are you doing to me?"

"Gonna take you, boy, are you complaining?"

"No . . . not complaining, no."

I pull away from him, lean against the wall next to him. And suddenly look at him, a grin on my face. I have my hands across my chest.

Winc: ::breathing hard . . . looking in your eyes:: ::softly:: I want you . . . please.
Scratch: I know . . . stand up.
Winc: ::standing up . . . shakily::

Scratch: ::coming over to you, putting fingers on top of your jeans::

Winc: ::cock throbbing in my jeans::

Scratch: ::Pulling first button slowly, plup!:: ::watching cock::

Winc: Ahhhh. ::not moving . . . watching you closely::

Scratch: There, all free now? ::smirk:: Or do you need more buttons undone?

Winc: ::head of my cock peeking out over undone top button::

Scratch: ::pressing against you, feeling tip of cock on my belly::

Winc: M-m-more, I think.

His tentative desire makes me laugh. His arms go up around me, I grab his hair with one hand, buttons with the other. Plup, plup, plup, and he's free. The odd thing is, while I'm typing that, he's typing this:

Winc: ::cock springs free from my jeans::

It keeps happening, this kind of simultaneous post, what Winc and I have come to call "simulpost" where despite the delay of online time, we're in sync.

He leans forward, burying his face into my neck. I grab his cock, squeezing gently. I feel the hair around his balls. He sighs happily, licking my shoulder and throat. I slide my hands around his ass, under his jeans, pressing against his cock, squeezing his ass. His hands work up and down my bare back. My crotch is throbbing, the wetness warm against my clothes.

He pushes his hips hard against me, I pull his hand to my breast. I slide my hand back around to his cock, pushing his jeans down. He's squeezing my breasts softly, kneading. His jeans are down to his knees. I push him to the floor.

Winc: ::startled . . . falling back::

Scratch: Yeah. I like that. Don't move.

Winc: ::looking up at you . . . hungry::

Scratch: ::Walking around you, stopping behind your head, looking down at you::

Winc: ::wiping hair out from in front of my eyes::

Scratch: ::Pulling off my own jeans::
Winc: ::moaning::
Scratch: ::Standing straight up, straddling your head, bending over from the waist::
Winc: Oh yes!
Scratch: ::Cunt hair wet::
Winc: ::pushing my face forward, inhaling you::
Scratch: ::placing my hands on either side of you, I lower my mouth down to your cock::
Winc: ahhhhhhhhhhhh
Scratch: ::Licking, once, twice, a few soft swipes with my tongue::
Winc: ::licking up and down your cunt lips gently::
Scratch: ::Lowering my cunt to just a few inches from your mouth lower, lower:: ::moaning as I feel your tongue, licking your cock::

I suddenly stand up, walk away from him; he cries out.

Winc: ::falling back onto the floor::

I walk back to his side, grasping his cock with my hand, bringing my mouth to it.

Winc: Oh!
Scratch: ::Other hand on my pussy, rubbing juices around. Rubbing juices on your cock::
Winc: ::my hands go to your breasts . . . tweaking your nipples, pinching harder::
Scratch: ::moaning::

I bring my mouth back up to his . . .

Winc: ::hungry mouth meeting yours::

. . . slap his hand, kiss him hard, bite his lip.

Winc: ::crying out, tasting my own blood::

Scratch: ::Pulling your jeans all the way off:: Turn over.

Winc: Huh?

Scratch: Turn the fuck over.

Winc: ::mumbling, confused:: . . . OK. OK . . .

Scratch: You want a bed or something? Turn over.

Winc: ::turning over:: ::looking at you over my shoulder::

Scratch: ::Pressing you into the floor:: ::Straddling you::

Winc: Oh!

Scratch: ::Sitting on your ass, my cunt on your butt bone:: ::Rubbing, rocking back and forth::

Winc: ::pushing my ass back to meet you::

Scratch: ::moaning::

Winc: ::moving my ass side to side against you::

Scratch: oh, gawd . . . yes . . . ::pressing your cock into the floor::

Winc: ::pushing back harder, twisting against you::

Scratch: Does it hurt, does it hurt, boy?

Winc: ::crying out:: YES!

Scratch: ahhhhhhh

Winc: Hurts realllll good!

I bite his neck, pushing against him.

Winc: ::tears spring to my eyes, twisting against you::

I rub my juices on my hand, rubbing his ass, squeezing. It's so nasty, this wetness all over him, not caring what it does to him. I can smell myself, sweet and tangy, wafting up to me. I circle two fingers closer to his hole.

Winc: ::gasping:: ::clenching my asshole tight::

Scratch: ::Teasing, entering just a little, coming back out::

Winc: ::shuddering::

Scratch: ::Sliding one finger all the way in, wet with my juices::

Winc: ::moaning:: ohyesohyesohyes ::pushing up against your finger::
Scratch: ::Reaching around you with my other hand, grabbing your cock:: That feels good in my hand.
Winc: ::moaning:: ::clenching, unclenching around your finger::

I can feel his own wetness on the tip of his cock, as I slide another finger in hard, deep.

Winc: ::whimpering::
Scratch: ::Pushing both fingers deep inside you::
Winc: YAHHHHH!

I slide his cock up and down in my hand.

Winc: ::rotating my ass back against you::
::shuddering::
oh geez
Scratch: ::Sliding around to the side of you, turning you slightly::
I want you, I want you, boy.
::Turning you over again, on your back::
Winc: ::looking into your face . . . tears in eyes, bloody lip::
Want you to take me, grrrl.

I rub his blood all over my breasts.

Winc: Want you real bad.
Scratch: Want more of that.

I watch his cock, swelling at the head. He pushes forward, hungrily, licking his blood off my breasts. I squeeze his balls in my hand, pinching his nipples, kissing him with my teeth.

Winc: ::leaning back, arching my neck back:: Bite me . . . bite me hard. Please!

At the same time, I type what he's just said:

Scratch: ::biting you on the nipples hard, feeling blood on my tongue::
::biting you up to your neck, bites all the way up your chest::
Winc: ::crying, laughing:: Oh yes!

I pin both his arms to the floor.

Winc: ::startled . . . looking up at you::

I slide up his body, straddling his cock, just above it. I dangle my cunt hairs, teasing his cock.

Winc: ::lifting my hips up to meet your cunt::
Scratch: uhhhhhh . . . ::pushing your cock against my clit::

END SCRATCH JOURNAL ENTRY

WINC JOURNAL ENTRY

This wasn't my first round of cybersex, not by a long shot. But it sure was the best.

Winc: ::wriggling my cock back and forth against you::
Scratch: ::sliding in a little, then back out to my clit, rubbing.
::moaning:: yessss
Winc: ::moaning:: oh yes!
Scratch: ::sliding down hard on your cock, taking it deep inside me::
Winc: ::urgently pushing up against you::
::gasping . . . feeling you wet and hot around my cock::
Scratch: ::Feeling you stirring inside me::
Winc: ::pumping my hips hard into you::

Scratch: ::sliding off you abruptly again, bending down to your cock with my mouth::

Winc: ::crying out:: OH!

Scratch: ::sly smile::

Whatsa matter, huh?

Winc: ::shuddering::

Pleeeeeeease!

Scratch: Please what? What do you want? Say it. Say the nasty words, boy.

Winc: Want you so bad!

Want you on top of me . . . fucking me . . .

please!

Want your cunt swallowing my cock!

Want you dripping juice all over me!

Scratch: Good boy, good good boy.

Yup. Good boy, that was me! She grabbed my cock with both hands, pulling it hard, up and down. Then, just as suddenly, she stopped and said:

Scratch: No.

Winc: Ohhhhhhhhhhhhhhhhhh!

::tossing head side to side frustrated::

So then she stood up again, walked around by my head, and pulled me across the floor by my hair. I got to my knees quick enough to scramble along as she pulled me. She straddled my head, dipping her cunt to my face.

Scratch: Not ready yet.

Winc: ::on my knees in front of you . . . looking up into your eyes::

::cock throbbing::

Winc: ::precum glistening with your juices on my cock::

Scratch: Whatcha gonna do for me now, huh?

Winc: ::swallowing hard:: I . . . I want to lick your cunt . . . want to taste you, fuck you with my tongue. ::breathing hard::

Scratch: Lie back down . . .

Winc: ::not moving, looking at you::

Scratch: ::Straddling your face . . . pressing my pussy into your mouth hands on floor on either side of you::

Winc: ::moaning into your pussy::

Scratch: ::dropping my body down onto your chest::

Winc: ::kissing up and down your lips:: ::lapping you with the broad of my tongue::

Scratch: yessssss.

Winc: ::swallowing your juice:: ::flicking your clit with the tip of my tongue:: ::over and over::

Scratch: ::pulling on your cock, squeezing your balls::

Winc: ::gasping::

Scratch: ::tugging on your hairs::

Winc: ::pushing my tongue up inside you::

Scratch: ::Knees pressing into floor, hurting, sending pain straight to my cunt::

Winc: ::lapping at you like a dog::

And that's when I started to get these private messages from FoolsGold! Of course, Scratch couldn't see them, but I ended up still in the scene with Scratch, while flirting with FoolsGold at the same time. Hey, don't judge me. It happens all the time.

Private Message to Winc

FoolsGold: Look upon my garden gate a snail that's what it is.

Winc: ::gasp:: What a lovely note to send. *So* much better than "what are you wearing"!

FoolsGold: Well, I like the song and that's what I could remember of the lyrics.

Winc: ::laughing:: And what song is that?

FoolsGold: By the way, what are you wearing? Only joking.

Scratch: ::bringing my mouth to the tip of your cock. lapping at you::

Winc: ::shuddering:: ::hips pumping against your mouth::

Scratch: ::grasping your tongue with my cunt, letting my body fall completely down onto you, taking your cock all the way into my mouth::

Winc: ::moaning:: oh yessssssssssssss

Scratch: ::Juices pour out of me::

Winc: ::wrapping long arms up around you::

Private Message to Winc

> **FoolsGold:** An old song by Donovan. First there is a mountain . . . is part of the lyrics. As is the snail part.
>
> **Winc:** That's right, he made a song out of that!
>
> **FoolsGold:** I'm showing my age, I fear.
>
> **Winc:** <--- has a penchant for hippies.
>
> **FoolsGold:** Kind of a Zen feeling to it. Or Taoist.
>
> Well I used to be a hippie . . . ::wink::

Scratch: ::throat contracting around your cock. Moaning, building, pulling away from you:: ::panting:: Can't, can't stay there . . .

Winc: ::crying out:: NO!

Scratch: ::Sweat on my back, sliding your hands around my back::

Winc: ::trembling fingers kneading into your back::

Scratch: ::Coming back around to gaze at you, still playing with your cock::

Winc: ::licking my lips . . . your juice and my blood::

Scratch: ::sliding up to it, lowering myself slowly down on it, looking at you, not flinching::

Winc: ::looking at you, adoring you::

Private Message to FoolsGold

> **Winc:** The phrase "first there is a mountain, then there is no mountain, then there is," is part of an old koan. ::grinning:: I know you, don't I?

Scratch: ::holding your arms, rocking up and down, closing eyes, throwing head back::

Winc: Yesssss.

I thought this guy FoolsGold mighta been Jabba! But no, I don't think it was. ::grin:: Not J's style. Still . . . I kinda wished I had more hands.

Private Message to Winc

FoolsGold: Relating to the spiritual growth of the student and his/her perception of reality.
Winc: ::eyes widening:: Yeah . . . I *do* know you, don't I?
FoolsGold: I don't know, perhaps in a past incarnation. We might have been possums in the same pouch.
Winc: Or fishies in the same pond. Snails on the same garden gate?
FoolsGold: In fact I seem to have a vague memory of something like that, but maybe it's just the mushrooms.
Winc: ::snapping my fingers:: Shrooms! That's it! Golden Gate Park!

This double conversation was doing a number on my head. Not a bad number, mind you, but a number nonetheless. ::grin:: Meanwhile, back in Apartment 3G . . .

Winc: ::tasting your blood:: ::lapping at your shoulder, pumping my cock into you:: ::my balls slamming up under your cunt::
Scratch: ::Juice gushing down onto your cock, not caring what you do, just rocking hard pumping, using your cock in me, using you::
Winc: ::hair on my stomach rubbing against you:: ::tossing my head from side to side . . . out of control::
Scratch: ::putting a finger in your mouth:: Suck it, boy, Suck your ass . . .
Winc: ::sucking your finger my ass your finger::
Scratch: ::Cunt tightening:: ::gasping::

It was getting a lot harder to pay attention to FoolsGold, but I left off being myself and . . . splattered myself across the two simultaneous identities I was creating: the sexpassion with Scratch and the mindspirit with FoolsGold were spilling into each other.

Private Message to Winc

FoolsGold: I don't know if we have indeed met before, but I have the feeling that I would like to be acquainted with you, if that's not too forward.

Winc: ::grinning:: To be honest, I thought you were someone I know from Seattle. She surfs as a guy sometimes.

FoolsGold: I'm assuming that you are a woman, but you might be a guy. Still you seem to be a friendly creature. And I am not a woman, I'm glad to say. I have all the respect in the world for them, but wouldn't want to be one.

Winc: ::blinking:: Why not?

FoolsGold: Well, they have to put up with a lot of crap, some of it biological, and some from men.

Winc: ::nodding:: For sure!

FoolsGold: Are you a woman?

Winc: ::tasting myself on you, licking sucking::

Scratch: ::Reaching under, grasping your balls, squeezing::

Winc: ::thighs trembling:: oh yesssssss . . . yesssss ::cock throbbing inside you::

Scratch: ::feeling you swelling bigger inside me, clamping down on you::

Winc: ::balls tightening::

gonna . . .

wanna . . .

Scratch: I'm gonna . . . I'm gonna, don't you dare youmotherfucker I'm gonna

Winc: p-pp-p . . .

Scratch: ::Legs shuddering rocking against you—frenzy::

Winc: ::groaning::

I

need

to . . .

Scratch: Higher higher, Cccccominggggggyou fucker you comeyoucome

Winc: YAAAHHHHHH!

Scratch: ::shaking, shuddering:: ohhhhhhhhhhhhhh

Winc: ::pumping hot cum up inside you::

Scratch: yeah.

Winc: yeaaah.

Scratch: ::Rocking slower, slower, digging my hands into your chest::
::throbbing, cunt raw, sore::

Winc: ::panting, gasping:: ::reaching up around you:: ::pulling you tightly against me::

Scratch: ::my hand sliding up to your throat . . . tightening:: ::leaning over to kiss you deep, my hand around your throat, tight, squeezing::

Winc: ::kissing you deeply . . . no breath::

Scratch: ::Biting your lips again::

Winc: ::can't breathe, world is slowing down . . . kissing you . . . tasting more of my blood::

Scratch: ::rubbing my clit, contracting again and again around your cock::

Winc: ::relaxing into your hand around my throat::

Scratch: ::releasing your throat, putting both hands on your chest, falling down on you, sliding your cock out slowly:: ::panting:: ::sweat all over us::

Winc: ::gulping air::

I was a goner. But deeper than a casual I-love-you. How could that happen in such a short space of time? ::shaking my head:: I thought I was gonna really die. I love that. Some day I wanna die in Scratch's arms.

Scratch: ::pulling your hair gently::

Winc: ::wrapping around you:: I . . . I could die like that . . . happily.

Private Message to Winc

FoolsGold: You haven't answered me. Are you a woman?

Winc: ::blinking:: Isn't that a rather personal question? ::laughing delightedly at your need to know::

Scratch: ::smile:: ::Playing with hairs on your belly:: No hairs on your chest?

Winc: ::laughing softly:: Yeah . . . hair on my chest . . . soft hair.

Scratch: ::you could be a girl here ::touching:: and here.

Winc: yeah . . . could be.

Private Message to Winc

> **FoolsGold:** Well, I'm enjoying the conversation regardless of your sex or sexual orientation.
>
> **Winc:** ::laughing:: As am I!
>
> **FoolsGold:** Just trying to form a mental image.
>
> **Winc:** <--- tall, copper hair, green eyes, waterfall tattoo spilling down from under my right eye. Rose tattoo on right thigh (rose has a whip curled up around it).

Scratch: But not there: ::patting cock::

Winc: ::gasp:: No, not there . . . not . . . well . . .

Scratch: ::rubbing hands all over sweaty bodies:: ::rubbing my juices all over you::

Winc: ::licking your neck and shoulders::

Scratch: Shit.

Winc: ::taking your face in my hands:: What?

Scratch: Want you real time.

Winc: ::smiling::

Private Message to Winc

> **FoolsGold:** Is that how you keep guys in line? With a whip?
>
> **Winc:** ::grinning:: Perhaps. Is that your interest?

Scratch: Real hands on real crotch right now. Hate this part. I mean, real time hate this part.

Winc: Where are you? No! Don't tell me.

Scratch: What?!

Winc: Can't say stuff like where and who . . . I keep forgetting.

Scratch: Nope, you can't.

Private Message to Winc

FoolsGold: Well, I do enjoy it at times when a woman takes control, but I have my limits.

Winc: ::purring:: Everyone does, darlin'.

FoolsGold: Gee, and I thought that I was strange or something.

Winc: ::laughing:: Without limits, S/M would be limited to one session, then *poof*.

FoolsGold: Are you into the S&M scene then?

Winc: S/M, or SM, not S&M darlin' . . . Yeah, guess I am.

Scratch: You're a nice guy. Too bad.

Winc: ::kissing you all over your face:: ::chuckling:: Tonight I'm a nice guy, yeah.

Scratch: What? Nice or a guy?

Winc: ::eyes sparkling:: Both. Neither.

Scratch: Hey! You fucking with me?

Winc: Always. Never!

Private Message to FoolsGold

Winc: ::grinning:: Yeah, I really think either/or questions should be answered yes or no.

FoolsGold: LOL, you seem to maintain a bit of an air of mystery, but that's an attraction too. You're keeping me guessing.

Winc: ::blinking:: Mystery? Moi?

FoolsGold: What can I say.

Winc: ::biting my lip, thinking of a *lot* of things he could say::

Scratch: ::grabbing pants, stepping a few feet away from you::

Winc: Hey! Hey, wait. I'm sorry . . . I . . .

Scratch: ::coming back to you, giving up::

Winc: I . . . this . . .

Scratch: ::pulling you up . . . climbing into your lap::

Winc: mmmmmmmmmmmm.

Scratch: ::sitting facing you:: ::rocking with you::

Winc: ::touching your cheek:: I like you. A lot.

Scratch: Winc . . .

Winc: mmmmm?

Scratch: Don't. And no I can't get email.

Winc: ::face falling::

Scratch: Well, do you get email? How long do you stay at an address?

Winc: Wait . . . you signed on with a bypass, didn't you?

Scratch: Maybe I did, maybe I didn't.

Winc: Are you CRAZY?

Scratch: OK, OK, I did.

Winc: ::fiercely:: Grrrrrl . . . you make sure of it next time. I don't want them arresting you, and me having to bring you a file baked into a cake.

Private Message to Winc

FoolsGold: I'm 6'1" with brown hair (what's left of it) and about 190 lbs, and a full beard.

Winc: ::laughing delightedly:: Now tell me you live in Bolinas, CA!

Scratch: How did we know neither of us were Registered? ::smiling::

Winc: Whoa. True. Just assumed.

Scratch: Hey, you ever get it on with an Eye?

Winc: Huh??

Scratch: Did it with someone who turned out to be an Eye?

///7990F0 909I//

Winc: No, I hate them. You can always tell when it's an Eye.

Scratch: Oh, yeah?

Winc: Oh shit. You see that garble?

Scratch: That's not me, you know . . . line's frazzing.

Winc: ::carefully:: Not so sure about that.

Scratch: Anyway, I fixed him up, though, threatened to go public, he's never bothered me since.

Winc: ::laughing, shaking my head:: That is so cool! So who are you? I want to know.

Private Message to Winc

FoolsGold: I'd guess that you are a bit younger, early 20s (a wild stab).

Winc: ::leaning forward, kissing you gently on the cheek:: You're really sweet . . . but I've made a solemn vow not to talk gender or age online. ::grin:: Makes life interesting! ::brushing my lips with my fingertips from where your beard tickled::

Scratch: I'm a me. What the fuck is it to you? Who are you?

Winc: Me? ::straining brain to come up with best description::

Scratch: Wait! Don't tell me.

Winc: Huh?

Scratch: I don't wanna know. It doesn't matter. But I know you're a guy.

Winc: ::laughing:: Oh do ya, now.

Scratch: ::shy:: well, yeah . . . We could be anything.

Winc: ::reaching down between my legs, stroking my cunt:: Yes, we could. ::impish grin::

Private Message to Winc

FoolsGold: Would you care to exchange email?

FoolsGold: You still there??

I couldn't tell FoolsGold I was on an illegal bypass, or that I had just had this great sex with someone else, and that we were starting to lose contact. He could have been an Eye; though why I trusted Scratch is a mystery. . . .

///3999 —-444///

THIS LINE IS SECURE. THIS IS NOT A PUBLIC LINE.
YOU ARE WARNED¢_76

Scratch: Is your numbers key stuck?

Winc: I didn't write that!

///SAFE PASSAGE IS NOT ABLE¶¶¶///

Scratch: I didn't either! Outta here.

Winc: Wait! I wanna see you again! I like you!

Private Message to FoolsGold

Winc: Eeeeeeep . . . sorry, I was super tied up . . .

FoolsGold: ::chuckling:: Literally? I thought I'd lost you.

Winc: Not a chance, mister! Anyway, there's lots of places, especially in the Bay Area, that are filled with opportunities to explore S/M.

FoolsGold: That is not my only interest in you. It only came up late in our conversation, but it is an interest of mine, I fear.

Winc: ::putting my hands on your shoulders:: I know it's not your only interest. And there's nothing to fear . . . well, almost nothing. ::wicked chuckle::

Scratch: We'll meet up again, we will, I know it. ::giving you a real look:: Feel it. Bye.

Private Message to Winc

FoolsGold: You still there? Are you getting my messages?

///JI U9K JIOPJH]\///

Scratch has left "Apt 3G"

Winc: Noooooo! Oh major rats.

I never did find out what happened with FoolsGold, but that was it with Scratch. ::sighing happily:: Was it ever! Scratch says it took "her" longer, but I don't believe hir. I think ze was as in love as I was. It can happen. ::grin:: Cool, huh?

END WINC JOURNAL ENTRY

NARRATIVE ENTRY, JABBATHEHUT

And in a decidedly green office, a message flashes on the screen:

To: FBCS Investigations
From: Jabbathehut
Date: (transmission garbled)
Subj: Sex, Sex, Sex—is that all??
Re: file Scratch and Winc

You're reading their sex logs? These are the ones you're calling outlaws? ::rolling my eyes:: Surely you jest!

—J.

Sucking at his teeth, Wally Budge mutters out loud, "Son of a gun. Does this joker know everyone I'm lookin' for?"

(To this bit of expected incredulity I cannot help but add: Of course I do, I am all-powerful, nothing escapes my notice.)

02
THE FOOL AND THE FOOLISH

To: Editor, They/Them magazine
From: D.I. Drew
Subject: Old tech, new tech

Hi Asa,

I rumbled through a ton of sources for this installment, most of them private and anonymous. I have to rant: It's just so unsettling how folks back then worried about exactly what is plaguing us now. No privacy, government interference, corporate interference, etc.

Cheers,

Drew

TOOBE ENTRY

I just found a Chinese wall, a bathroom stall, a place everybody writes random stuff in no particular order: an electronic graffiti board. I grab anything new that's popped onto the Net. It's completely disorganized when it comes in, then I arrange it like a collage. Some of the postings are like a bulletin board, some more urgent, like the walls in a ghetto where you can see lines being drawn, rage or sorrow vented.

FUNNY OF THE DAY

Where are the baby pigeons? Has anyone *ever* seen one? No! You just see grown-up ones . . .

—*P.*

That's all there was today. I didn't say they were real deep or anything. Although it's true, I've never seen a baby pigeon.

I'm not sure I've mentioned Jabba before. Jabba is a genius, and although I always thought ze was a guy, hanging around with S&W I realize how stoopid that was. I have to admit I've never seen a pronoun. I'm gonna say *she*, just to balance it out. I've known her forever, through my dad. As far as I know, they've known each other a long time.

Jabba never comes out of her hole and has banks of computers all over the place. It's freezing inside, and that's why she has fish. They can take the cold. The lights from the computers weave a magic stream through the tanks, rippling patterns all over the ceiling and walls. The water bubbles through little chugging pumps in the tanks, scattering ultraviolet and dark green pockets around the room. And the computers hum, of course. It's really cool. Feels like a safe, green cave with water escape routes.

I saw it only once, when I went over a long time ago to pick up a disk. Jabba was there, but she didn't come out of the other room until I left. I always picture it when I write with Jabba. Here's something I got today.

To: Toobe
From: Jabbathehut
Subj: Handwriting

My quick little friend, I need a favor of you. A distribution point, if you will. I won't begin to tell you my thoughts on the proud forces of government, but you may have been following the news re: Registration.

Where there is a new rule, there are new rule breakers.

Our men in Washington are attempting, in their usual slipshod way, to organize that which cannot be organized. But what they do have on their side is the slowness of Time. In other words, those who don't go along with the program will simply be put in a category called Other, where they will languish until they figure out what to do with them.

As it stands now, if you don't Register, you don't get to play where you were able to play before. In an unusual burst of compassion, I have come up with some bypass codes. They are quite simple and easy to use. You, who seem to have the attention span of a gnat (as a teenager you can be forgiven this, but not for long), are the perfect letter carrier for me. You may never light long but you do light everywhere. If you would, please offer your acquaintances these codes (discreetly of course) in your wanderings. Would much appreciate.

Fighting God,

—J.

PS baby pigeons grow incredibly fast and reach adult size in the blink of an eye. So yes, my featherless friend, you've seen plenty of baby pigeons.

No, I don't know what Fighting God means, and I'm afraid to ask.

To: Jabbathehut
From: Toobe
Subj: On the wall

"Burst of compassion" my nuts. Just how much are you charging for these, may I ask? Don't tell me you've put a virus on them so they stop working if people don't pay?

To: Toobe
From: Jabbathehut

Subj: Exactly

Of course, my little schmendrik. At least I don't require real names, as the Registration mavens do. Will upload package within the hour. You, of course, may simply fill out yours with your screen name, free of charge.

To: Jabbathehut
From: Toobe
Subj: Ah, I see

Gee, thanks. No, seriously, does this mean I can go anywhere?

To: Toobe
From: Jabbathehut
Subj: Indeed

Yes, but do Register anyway. You won't be bothered again by cheap govt suits. They haven't been thorough and refuse to see the inevitability of the mess soon to be on their hands.

So I've just handed out Jabba's bypass codes like candy. Can't believe how many people don't want them, they're worried about breaking the law. The majority of people actually said no. Scary. Everybody's having Reg parties like it's some goddamn gift they've been given, and not the equivalent of willingly signing up for all the junk mail you've ever received, and your neighbor's too.

But the government's working with Bizness on this one. People are all stirred up. Here's a good one: If you don't have a computer, the govt will give you one when you Register. Who could resist?

I got a hysterical note from a law freak who found Lexis (a deep law library). He's racked up hundreds of dollars looking through tits and torts, and he claims he didn't know he'd be charged for all that time. Poor doode had to pay anyway. On top of that, the phone company charges BY THE MINUTE, which costs you ON TOP of the gateway fee.

I bet if I wait a bit, Jabba's little toyz will look a lot better to these folks. But here's another twist: When you fill out all the profile crap, you'll start getting advertisements and product samples just for you! How exciting. This one friend of mine went on as a girl in the lesbian room (he's a guy—they always figure him out, but he keeps trying), and he got tampon ads. His mail's flooded with them. If he tries to stop them, they change to menopause stuff. Cracks me up. But if you Register right, you'll get just what you "need." It's seductive.

Of course, I could be flooded with crap about computer toys and skateboard gear if I'm not careful. There's hope: some people are figuring things out.

ZINE EXCERPT

PISSED OFF, NOT GONNA TAKE IT ANYMORE

> Some of us have noticed that we're not all getting the same information since Registering. Nothing obvious, just this or that product isn't offered to everyone. I almost missed a concert because I wasn't in the right demographic to receive the invitation. I went anyway. Next thing you know you won't be allowed into a concert if you weren't prescreened.

This all started cuz the businesses cooperated for once (I think a phone company's behind it), and people are believing anything and panicking. They're really freaked about missing out. There's just enough differences in what Registered people get, and what you miss if you don't Register. It's like cable TV, people without it miss all the cool movies, so after a while everyone thinks they should have cable. Here's what came out today:

Registration Will Curb Criminal Activity

by Thomas Fulton

The Internet, and the so-called 500-channel television, have become out-of-control monsters. So said spokespersons for Allied Consumer Industries at a press conference yesterday. No one can find what they want on the Net anymore; consumers complain that they can't buy the brands they want because they can't find them; indeed, the choices are too many to justify the exhaustive hunt-and-peck a simple "shopping trip" has become.

Although the government's Registration plan will ultimately make the process smoother, at present there are several million more users of a highly sophisticated information system with no clear way to navigate. Veteran users are skeptical that an interface can be created to accommodate the average computer user, but plans move forward to organize.

Add to this mix the goals of Internet Intelligence, and the need to organize the system becomes crucial.

"The criminal element has made inroads into most of the major electronic bulletin boards," says Federal Bureau of Census and Statistics Undersecretary Margaret LaBouchere. "They are distributing illegal information, false advertising campaigns, and worst of all, porn, all over the Internet system." Once everyone is Registered, says LaBouchere, only criminals will be unregistered. It will be virtually impossible to conduct illegal activity, "because all the users can be traced back to their Registration numbers."

While it is doubtful all criminals will be forced offline, the effort so far is working and has met no real resistance. New Registrants agree their Net sessions are easier to manage. As consumers indicate their preferences, they are saved into a profile, so an algorithm based on the user's demographics (age, sex, income, location, etc.) can find and offer points of interest.

What's more, buying and browsing preferences are noted so that the range of services offered to them will grow narrower, thereby thinning out the traffic on the Internet.

Matching the consumer with his or her interest will become a quick and easy process for the new, streamlined, and technically savvy marketing departments of the private sector, with little interaction needed by the consumer at all, says ACI. Users will simply point and click to their interest icon, and the information will appear.

Yeah, right. But if you want to go outside the lines, you have to wait forever. So most people just stick with what they've got and don't explore. Which I think is the point. Old Net users are furious, the ones who started it some time in the '70s, when it was an exclusive Pentagon and MIT system. But they seem to agree that at least the traffic won't be as bad in the areas they're in, cuz nobody knows how to get there.

Oh, got some email this morning. Scratch thinks too much.

To: Toobe
From: Scratch
Subj: Not gonna

Hey pal, option means option. I'm not Registering for the same reason I don't have a driver's license. I don't need paper to travel around, especially on the Net. I can't even get past the first few questions on that sign-up thing (like "Sex") they have. I tried to fill in "Yes," but it will only take one answer or the other. I tried to write "N" for neither but it wouldn't take that either. Look at this #@!*&%!!&*:

Sex? (M) or (F)?

Yes

Very funny. Sex? (M) or (F)?

No

Very funny. Sex? (M) or (F)?

?

Very funny. Sex? (M) or (F)?

WHY?

Very funny. Sex? (M) or (F)?

EXIT

Very funny. Sex? (M) or (F)?

CANCEL

Very funny. Sex? (M) or (F)?

QUIT

Really want to quit the Registration Process?

NO!

Sex? (M) or (F)?

This is an invasion of privacy! What the hell does my gender matter in cyberspace?

I know you think I go in for conspiracy theories too much, and you may be right. But people who create forms don't think about the questions they ask. This is a computer form; you can't go to the next question unless you fill it out right. That's scary, Toobers. I mean, there isn't even a human to argue with.

—S.

Here's a small part of the form. Ever since Scratch and Winc have been talking to me I can't look at it without seeing what they mean.

Registration Information

Name:

Credit Card #:

Sex:

Social Security #:

Income Level (round off to nearest ten thousand):

Address:

Phone:

Age:

Spouse's Name:

Spouse's Work Phone:

Ethnicity (choose one): Caucasian/Black/Hispanic/Asian/Other

Sexual Orientation (choose one): Heterosexual/Homosexual

Number of Children, and Their Ages:

Computer:

Occupation:

Employer's Name:

Work Phone Number:

Number of People in the Household:

Names of Other Residents:

Brands:

(Registrants must fill out the Product Survey Questions 1–125.)

That isn't even all of it! Doesn't that seem a little weird? That's a lot of info; where's it going? There's more on the form, like what kinds of toothpaste I use, how much I watch TV. It took me almost an hour to finish the whole thing. If I try to skip a question, it says I haven't completely filled out the form. I emailed Jabba again, and she said to put fake answers in as many boxes as I can. I wonder if she's Registered.

I'm trying to understand Winc's thing about losing your gender. Or rather, choosing it. Consciously. Ze sez everybody's obsessed with guessing what people really are behind their screen names. Ze sez ze's found, without exception, that once people's covers are blown, they can't seem to keep going with the fantasy-persona. They revert back to their real identity and get self-conscious.

Winc saves some samples under the entry: "A perfectly good conversation ruined by gender." Hah! Ze says they'll be funny in the future.

END TOOBE ENTRY

WINC JOURNAL ENTRY

Playing with these guys is so fun!

Private Message to Winc

Daisy: Hello.

Winc: Hello yourself, whassup?

Daisy: Just looking to get off. I'm slowly hiking my skirt.

Annnnnnd, there's your first clue. When they talk about getting off, that's pretty much it.

Winc: ::slowly lifting aviators off my eyes to see you better::

Daisy: ::slowly pursing my lips::

Winc: ::twirling the stem of my sunglasses on my tongue::

Daisy: ::panties at my ankles:: ::wishing u were under my desk::

And that would be clue number two.

Winc: ::chuckling:: If anyone is gonna be under anything, darlin', it's you. Keep talkin'.

System will go offline in 30 minutes for maintenance.

Private Message to Daisy

Winc: hmmmm . . . we have thirty minutes. Want to go to a private room?

Daisy: Yes. Which one?

Winc: ::slow smile:: What place would be the most embarrassing for you to have sex in?

I thought that was a way good question; it embarrassed me just to read it.

Private Message to Winc

Daisy: My grandparents' room . . .

Winc: ::nodding approvingly:: Good girl. I'll be in private room called Grandparents Rm.

Daisy: ::getting wet::

Winc: Tell me . . . what kind of sex or position would be most embarrassing for you?

Daisy: I like it all, baby . . .

Winc: That's not what I asked.

Daisy: My ass.

Winc: What about your ass?

Daisy: I like only certain things there.

Winc: What *wouldn't* you like?

Daisy: Thick dicks.

And the clues just keep on dropping.

Winc: ::laughing softly:: I think you're a guy. It doesn't really matter, OK? But I appreciate a good acting job, and there are some flaws in yours, that's all.

Online Host

***** You are in room "Grandparents Rm" *****

System going down in 20 minutes=

Daisy has entered the room.

Winc: ::tapping my foot:: you kept me waiting. ::walking over to you slowly::

Daisy: ::shrugging:: Sorry.

Winc: ::purring:: Don't move . . . wanna look at you. Lift your skirt for me.

Daisy: ::wanting to touch you::

Winc: ::smiling, sensing your needs::

Daisy: Here you go baby slowly.

Winc: ::taking your chin in my hand::

Winc: ::shaking my head::

Winc: No . . . I'll tell *you* where we're going, right?

Daisy: Don't have a skirt, I like it nasty.

Calling Continuity! "Her" skirt was on and last seen as hiked.

Winc: ::laughing:: Describe this room for me.

Daisy: Which one?

Winc: Your grandparents' room.

Daisy: Lots of old dressers, six-shooters, a trunk, family portraits staring at u.

Winc: mmmmmm . . . nice. ::taking you in my arms:: ::leaning you back, kissing you hard on the mouth::

Daisy: ::slowly using one finger right now:: What are you wearing?

Winc: ::suddenly letting you go, walking to the other side of the room:: ::lighting a cigarette, staring at you:: So, who are you? Describe yourself to me. ::inhaling slowly . . . eyes never leaving you::

Daisy: 5'8, 34-24-34, aerobics instructor, firm ass, great tits and love to play.*

Winc: ::blinking:: I see. ::blowing smoke rings:: And . . . a guy?
It's OK with me if you are . . . I'm just curious.

Daisy: Nope I'm legit.

Daisy: Are you?

Winc: ::chuckling:: Like I said, it's OK if you're a gal or a guy . . . cybersex is cool either way, but you come across as a guy. Am I what?

Daisy: I'm asking you, are you a guy.

Winc: ::laughing:: nope . . . not this lifetime.

Daisy: lol.

Winc: Where are you on your cycle?

Daisy: Nope. Are you?

Yep, that was his undoing.

Winc: ::chuckling:: Reread my question. It wasn't a yes or no.

Daisy: No.

Winc: ::softly:: no . . . what? What do you think I'm asking?

Daisy: YOU ASKING IF IT'S MY TIME OF THE MONTH RIGHT. If not I'm lost.

Winc: ::shaking my head:: You're lost.

System going down in 10 minutes

Winc: I asked *where* on your cycle you are, not if you're bleeding.
::glancing down:: I'm bleeding now, though. Just curious where on your cycle you are.

Daisy: 2nd week.

Winc: ::blinking:: You're a guy. ::running a finger up inside me, then licking my blood off my finger::

Daisy: OK, how figure?

Winc: ::smiling:: First off, no woman I know knows her measurements. Or if they do, they don't give them out.

Daisy: Got it flaunt it baby.

Winc: ::shaking my head:: nope . . . men do that. ::leaning back, watching you::

Daisy: Us Californians are like that . . .

Winc: Do you like being a woman online?

Daisy: We think we have it all.

Winc: ::shaking my head:: you forget, I'm from California too.

Daisy: I know. Read your profile.

Winc: Women *know* they don't have it all, darlin'.

Daisy: This one does.

Winc: ::mild applause::

Daisy: How's that finger?

Winc: ::sniffing:: Nice.

System going down in 5 minutes

Daisy: You think you know it all, hon.

Winc: ::laughing:: I know I don't!

Winc: System's gonna go down any minute. Sigh. Wish you'd open up a bit.

Daisy: OK, OK, I'm a guy, happy?

Winc: ::nodding:: Yep. ::softly:: Thank you so much. Really. ::leaning forward, kissing you gently::

Daisy: You're god.

Daisy: Whoops, I mean good.

Winc: ::laughing:: nice slip there, mister.

::wrapping my arms around your neck::

Ohhhh, I could make you a pretty girl.

Winc: Still there?

Daisy: Guess my age.

Winc: You really want me to?

Daisy: Yeah.

Winc: 20. 21? Too young for me, if I'm honest.

Daisy: No.

Winc: ::laughing:: then ya got me!

Daisy: 19. Close enough, I guess.

Daisy: What do you mean, make me a pretty girl?

System going down in 2 minutes

Winc: ::smiling:: you're very sweet . . . Thank you for being honest with me. And since you're still a kid I'll just give you a huge hug.

Daisy: How come all the ladies can tell I'm a guy?

Winc: ::smiling:: We just run into so many guys being girls, it gets easy . . .

Daisy: I'm really known as "dabug" onscreen.

Winc: In the future, don't put all the emphasis on sex, rather, get to know people. That's what girlz do . . .

::grin::

LOL

Daisy: Steven Langley from Madison.

Winc: Pleased to meet you, Steven.

My name is in fact ::grin:: Winc.

Daisy: Okay here's one for you, Winc

Daisy: Bet you think I'm white, don't you

Daisy: Hey Winc, cat got your tongue?

Winc: No, no omigosh. Yes, I've been thinking—Oh man, I've been *assuming* you're white. Ummmm . . . ?
Daisy: Why thanks for asking. Nope I'm Black but people online think I'm white until I tell 'em, if I ever do.
Winc: Whoa.
Daisy: Yeah, so maybe next time don't assume. Hah hah. Bye, Winc.

SYSTEM CLOSING, ALL CONTACT TERMINATED

Nice diversion on a Sunday afternoon. Glad things didn't escalate—no minors for me. Poor li'l guy, trying so hard!

END WINC JOURNAL ENTRY

To: Drew
From: T. Sparrow
Subject: re Scratch and Winc Website?

Hey Kiddo,

In answer to your questions: yes, sure there were websites back in the period you're researching. And of course I remember all the hoopla surrounding Scratch and Winc. As far as I know they never had a website that I can remember; nothing I can find using all the magical wizarding tools at my disposal here at Apple. Websites were really hard to build back then. You had to use HTML only.

BUT—good news—my search for a website dredged up the attached chat room log from a very early Gay Pride meeting. Hope it's helpful.

You know, I'm so proud of you for tackling this story. And you also know I have to ask, are they paying you enough for this? Still got your night job at the bakery?

Love,

Dad

To: T. Sparrow

From: Drew

Subject: re re Scratch and Winc Website?

Well damn the dead end on a possible website of theirs but wow the gay pride chatlog you found is SO HELPFUL. I'm totally using it.

And it's perfect that the queers in that room can see how dangerous the tech would be for them, including the backlash. I needed that perspective.

Oh and jackpot! The Luvboyz and DigQueer in this chat were aliases of Scratch and Winc!

Thanks, Dad!

love you big,

Your kid Drew

PS—yup, I'm still baking the finest on-demand caricature cookies in the city. Sigh. But hey, we're making some pretty chic dog biscuits as well. I'll bring you some for Monstro.

Chat room log: "Gay Pride meeting"

Minutes: The Coalition

Topic: Registration

Attendees: 104

Participants principally concerned with how Registration impacts solidarity. Majority in agreement that the Reg process serves to divide us.

Many are refusing to answer sex pref. cuz then aren't we telling everyone in the whole wide world that we are gay?!?!?

Some bisexual attendees objecting to either/or choice homo/hetero.

Many confused as to whether to list spouse for Significant Other, etc.

Miss Doris Fish as usual objects to either/or choice male/female.

Digqueer: Cooperation = Death!
Tom: That's Silence, you turkey! This is really about do we list our partners in the spouse box, and do we ask them before we do?
Sharina: Point is, do we make our stand right here, right now by just saying no to the whole fucking form? Or do we infiltrate, work from the inside by Registering along with everyone else?
Digqueer: Maybe some of us could do one, and some of us could do the other?
Tom: Fuck no, all or none.
Dick: All of us have to sign, or none of us do.
Harry: One for all, all for one. Solidarity above all.
David: yknow, if we Register now we're proving we're just like everyone else.
Sharina: Fuck that shit! We're not like everyone else and proud of it!
Digqueer: God I am so sick of that phrase being used by queers.
David: It's not an insult! We are so just like everyone else.

Private Message from Digqueer to Luvboyz

> **Digqueer:** *No*body's like anyone else. They act like they're on the outside looking in.
> **Luvboyz:** ::sadly:: True. What made you PM me?
> **Digqueer:** Your name. At least you seem to be out of the closet.
> **Luvboyz:** ::laughing:: Oh, that I am.

Vina: OK, OK, let's table the issue of assimilation. Meanwhile, if anyone wants to go ahead and Register, do so, and let us know what happens to you at the next meeting.

Private Message from Digqueer to Luvboyz

Digqueer: Here we go again.

Luvboyz: Yup.

Digqueer: ::laughing:: splittin' hairs.

Luvboyz: Yeah. Maybe it's just a phase?

Digqueer: ::smile:: Let's hope so.

Luvboyz: Maybe this is the only way we grow?

Digqueer: I'd rather see something else grow.

Luvboyz: ::blushing::

Digqueer: Oh how sweet!

Luvboyz: Not as sweet as you think. Wanna go private?

Digqueer: Sure. I have the feeling you're not big and hard and hairy, and right now that sounds really good.

Luvboyz: You mean that's your usual M.O.?

Digqueer: Yeah, gets boring sometimes.

Vina: The government is trying to legislate our lives.

Tom: They're not fucking trying to legislate, they're trying to organize! If we cooperate, we'll be represented!

Dick: Yeah, we'll have a voice in the government.

Harry: Yeah, cooperate!

Private Message from Luvboyz to Digqueer

Luvboyz: So you do this a lot?

Digqueer: When I can't sleep, when I can't get myself off. I can say I'll try something new, but certain things are just tried and true.

Luvboyz: Yep. Right now just "hard" sounds good.

Digqueer: Hard, urgent, maybe a little sweaty.

Luvboyz: I wanna stand up with you, cup our cocks together in our hands.

Digqueer: Yeahhhhh. It's warm, arms wrapped around each other's waists.

Luvboyz: Fuck cooperation!

Brknstck: You guys and your foul mouths. Goddess!

Tom: ::rolling my eyes::

Private Message from Luvboyz to Digqueer

Luvboyz: My hair is long, I rub it all over your back.

Digqueer: Mmmmm. I bend over to feel you against me.

Luvboyz: I turn you around.

Luvboyz: Kiss you hard. Mmmm, your beard against mine feels great.

TOOBE ENTRY

Jabba found a memo from the cops!

Actually it's the cop division of the Bureau of Census and Stats, called Internet Intelligence. Scratch sez that's an oxymoron. That Scratch, har de har.

END TOOBE ENTRY

NARRATIVE ENTRY, JABBATHEHUT

The memo flashes up in front of his eyes. He hates the interruptions but obediently reads the voice from up on high.

To: All Staff, FBCS
From: Undersec'y LaBouchere
Subj: Registration Evaders

Registration window ends one week from today.

Reminder: All those not Registered must be within 24 hours of the window closing.

We want to send a message that our department is organized and efficient, and that we will enforce Registration as legally mandatory.

I know I can count on each of you to help set this nation straight.

Margaret LaBouchere

Undersec'y, FBCS

Lieutenant Detective Budge brings his seat back down hard, feet flying off the desk. What the hell are they thinking up there? Reg was supposed to be optional! And we can't even track down parking violators; how the fuck do they think we're gonna track computer users?

Reminder to self: get the wording of the law that makes Registration legally mandatory.

END JABBA NARRATIVE ENTRY

TOOBE ENTRY

I hacked their system! How cool am I!?

But ohfuckohfuck. I think I blew it. I mean, I scan police messages, but with Jabba's toyz I can get a little further in. I think she likes me even though she calls me names in Yiddish. Wait, Jabba? Jewish? Concentrate, Toobe, concentrate.

Anyway. I was so excited, I mean, proof they're gonna be real anal about catching people who didn't comply. Proof! I download that sucker, and as soon as the download starts . . . BAM!

///7990F09091///

I was too long in that area, and I think my screen name was spotted! If they ever play back activity in that area, my stupid name would be right there!

Okay, maybe they won't play it back.

Why should they play back a day's worth of cybermessages?

They won't play it back.

So who do I call?

JJJJJa-a-a-aba. . . .

To: Jabbathehut
From: Toobe
Subj: Trouble

Answer me something please? If I was reading messages on a police bulletin board and I downloaded something, could they trace me?

—T.

To: Toobe
From: Jabbathehut
Subj: in River City

Absolutely. However, chances are they won't because they have no reason to go over logs every day. As far as they know it's a Bulletin Board Service for gendarmes only. (BBS, of course.)

Young one, permit me to remind you: do NOT go into their BBS anymore. Do NOT trigger screen capture by initiating downloads. Use the backdoor for all downloads. As I've taught you.

::muttering::

Fighting God, J

Well that didn't make me sleep easier.

Just got another letter from Winc. Ze digs deep into this stuff.

To: Toobe
From: Winc
Subj: Curiouser and Curiouser

Hey, my friend, here's an interesting log for your growing pile of trivia. I'm sending you excerpts because it was an hour's worth of chat, a lot of it goofy. They offered me two choices. Sigh. I picked the name "Gyrl" ::sighing:: it was either that or "Boye." (::standing on top of The Wall Between Two Choices:: Hmmm, looks more interesting from up here!)

Have fun!

—W.

8:02:56 P.M. "GUEST SPEAKER Transcript"

Now open for recording.

There are 17 people in the room.

Webster: Hey, gang, remember I invited someone this week? She's going to talk about her experience as a phone sex hostess.

Lisa321: No duh, Webster, why do you think the whole group showed up?!

Webster: Hah! Writers Anon. has never had such attendance.

Gyrl has entered the room.

Gyrl: ::rushing into room, out of breath:: Phew! Howdy!

Webster: Had a flat on that old info highway, love?

Lisa321: "Gyrl?" I thought Webster was kidding.

Gyrl: It's me name. ::glancing down:: And let's not talk about flat here, OK? ::rueful grin::

Webster: LOL

Webster: *Good* to see you Gyrl.

Gyrl: ::purring:: Good to see you too, hon.

Genuine1: Gee, Webster, just how *did* you meet this Gyrl?

Gyrl: Ah, so we discover the first pitfall of writing, class. ::glasses slipping down nose:: The stereotype! ::glancing over at Webster, giggling::

Webster: While I have no problem with the possibility of having met Gyrl for phone sex, the truth is we ran into each other as blood drinkers in a vampire room.

Lisa321: There's a chat room for vampires?

Webster: Yep!

Webster: OK, let's start!

Webster: Welcome to GUEST SPEAKER. Our guest tonight is Gyrl. She'll be taking questions relating to sex and gender in fiction, on the phone, and in life . . .

Lisa321: If you're saying a man can be a female phone sex hostess, are you also saying a man can write a woman's character?

Gyrl: Well, I think that "Man" and "Woman" are only two of many possible genders . . .

Pico: Wow.

Gyrl: . . . and gender is simply another facet of identity, like age, race, state of body, etc. So, why can't a man write a woman's character.

Gyrl: . . . If he does the work.

Gyrl: . . . Big if, I know.

Gyrl: . . . ::bracing myself for onslaught::

Tale2Tell: Gyrl, I don't know if *you* are a man or a woman.

Gyrl: ::chuckling:: I like to keep it that way, too.

Mythter has entered the room.

Tale2Tell: ::laughing:: OK: Do you believe that gender in fiction is now passé?

Gyrl: I believe gender in the *world* is now passé.

BillJo: Gender is passé? Does that mean gender was once a trend?

Gyrl: I think so, Bill. A trend that's gone on for millennia. Gender may have been important back when we had to breed & only breed. There're more options now, maybe we don't need gender?

BillJo: You'd do away with biology?

Gyrl: We definitely need biology! But biology is sex, not gender.

Mythter: Wait a minute . . . Gyrl, are you a man or a woman?

IrishEyes: Good question!

BillJo: Right on, Mythter!

Webster: Can't dance your way out of *this* one, hon.

Gyrl: Well, the answer is both. Neither. I'm still working on it.

Tale2Tell: Coolness.

Private Message to Gyrl

Mythter: Do I know you?

Gyrl: ::eyes sparkling:: I dunno. I talk like that with lots of folks.

Mythter: I bet!

Gyrl: How many folks here have surfed in other genders?

Vick TF: ::raising hand::

Mythter: ::raising hand::

IrishEyes: I try to keep gender out of the issue online unless it's forced.

Gyrl: Has anyone ever gotten caught? In another gender, that is?

Gyrl: Caught by the person you were "fooling"?

Vick TF: Yep, I did. ::studying fingernails::

Private Message to Gyrl

Mythter: ::leaning back against the wall, thumbs through my belt loops::

Gyrl: ::walking into the schoolyard:: Young man! Recess was over 20 minutes ago!

Mythter: ::looking up lazily:: Don't you recognize me?

Gyrl: ::going pale:: You! ::sputtering:: You were expelled two months ago!

Mythter: Hee hee. Hey, you're good.

Gyrl: Takes one to know one. ::wide grin::

Vick TF: Oh, I got caught because I was being obnoxiously bubba . . .

Vick TF: ::scratching crotch::

Vick TF: I think I played BigBob69 a bit too broadly.

Gyrl: ::cracking up::

IrishEyes: Actually, that seems to be the problem acting the other gender . . . playing too broadly.

Gyrl: Definitely! Maybe that's the first step, going overly broad. After a while, you learn to tone it down. The boys who work the phone line do!

BillJo: Maybe too broad at first is inevitable.

IrishEyes: Maybe it's even necessary.

Private Message to Vick TF

Gyrl: Hey, darlin' . . . who's this Mythter?

Vick TF: ::chuckling:: What do I look like . . . Cupid?

Gyrl: ::wheedling:: Pleeeeeeeeze?

Vick TF: Mythter is good people. In fact, Mythter just asked the same thing about you!

Gyrl: REALLY?

Vick TF: ::clearing throat:: Your audience awaits you, darlin'.

Gyrl: Eeep!

Genuine1: Are we operating under the belief that your personality has something to do with or derives wholly or in part from your gender? Or . . . are we operating under the belief that every human being is first a human being and second a male or female?

Gyrl: ::slowly:: I think there's danger in thinking "we're all human." Same with saying "we have no gender" (which I do think can be true). The danger being that we overlook all the very real violence done in the name of gender . . .

Genuine1: But . . . hmmmm

Gyrl: . . . it's the danger of any humanist philosophy.

Mythter: Right. "We're all human" makes women invisible.

IrishEyes: Makes Blacks invisible.

WheelsOnFire: Makes disability invisible.

Genuine1: I can't see how gender has a particular role in violence.

Mythter: Aw, come on!

Gyrl: ::turning slowly to Genuine1:: You're a guy, right?

Catch 22: Maybe the point is that gender just IS—biologically and culturally—but we don't have to be stuck with its nuances.

IrishEyes: I like that one, Catch.

Private Message to Gyrl

Mythter: You seem to have a lot of answers!

Gyrl: ::flustered:: No, no . . . I chew on the questions. That's all.

Mythter: I like that in a gyrl/boy.

Gyrl: ::shy grin:: Thanks.

Webster: Gyrl, you have some questions sent to me by PM waiting for you. You still here?
Gyrl: Ummmm, Got lost in a couple of PMs. Sorry.

Private Message to Mythter

Gyrl: Bad bad bad bad bad! See what you made me do? ::laughing::
Mythter: ::chuckling::

Catch 22: I've begun to realize that I need a definition of "gender" from Gyrl.
Gyrl: ::laughing merrily:: How about: gender is a category.
Gyrl: A classification.
Gyrl: Nothing more than that.
Catch 22: Am I the only nut here who *likes* the distinctions of gender?
IrishEyes: Viva la difference!
Gyrl: I love distinctions in gender, Catch . . . I just think there's more than two to like, that's all.
Mythter: <---loves distinctions, just wish they were "cross" genderal, so we all could have more fun.

Private Message to Mythter

Gyrl: Cross genderal . . . way cool term!
Mythter: Something *I'm* chewing on.
Gyrl: So, you're a writer?
Mythter: ::ducking my head:: Nah, I just tell stories sometimes.
Gyrl: Tell me a story.
Gyrl: Please.o

Tale2Tell: We need more fuzzy thinkers!
Mythter: Yes, Tale2.
Tom: Wait, isn't anyone going to speak up on behalf of what's natural?

Dick: Male and Female He created them. And that comes from the best selling book of all time.
Harry: Amen, Dick.

Private Message to Gyrl

Mythter: Once upon a time . . .
Gyrl: ::settling down at your knee, listening::
Mythter: . . . in a faraway land, there lived a very beautiful gyrl.
Gyrl: ::resting my head in your lap, listening::
Mythter: Only no one knew she was beautiful because she was invisible. They only knew her voice.

Genuine1: I believe that every human being is FAR too different . . . has met with FAR too unique circumstances . . . to be able to know the mind of any others.
Gyrl: Gotcha, Gen, and I think that by calling ourselves MEN or WOMEN, we deny ourselves the uniqueness you talk about.

Private Message to Mythter

Gyrl: ::softly:: So this gyrl, all she had was a voice?
Mythter: Uh huh. And they all loved her until . . .
Gyrl: Until?
Mythter: Until one day, a child asked, "Is that a boy or a girl?"
Gyrl: Oh geez.

Tale2Tell: Actually, I've always thought that the poles of gender were like chaotic attractors, anyway . . .
Gyrl: ::wincing:: I think we need to do away with the image of opposite poles when it comes to gender.
Tale2Tell: No no, Gyrl. Chaotic attractors are different: you can orbit them, never touch.
Catch 22: Binaries will always exist.
Giant: Some people will always need labels. The rest of us just won't care.

Private Message to Mythter

Gyrl: And no one could see her.

Mythter: Right.

Gyrl: And she liked it that way.

Mythter: Right.

Gyrl: But everyone in the town *wanted* to see her.

Mythter: Hey, who's telling this story?

Gyrl: ::clamping hands over my mouth::

Mythter: They wanted to know if she was a boy or a girl.

BillJo: So, Gyrl, why do you suppose gender is such a big deal, nowadays?

Beatitudes: A time to go along, a time to question.

Gyrl: Zactly, and maybe now's just a time to question.

Mythter: And it's gonna get worse before better.

Webster: Worse?

Gyrl: Mythter's right. When folks in power hear the voices of people who've got no gender . . . there's gonna be a mighty big backlash . . . and it's not gonna be pretty.

Genuine1: {{{{{Gyrl}}}}}

Webster: I fear you're right. Backlash enough already.

Private Message to Mythter

Gyrl: Sorry, I had to jump in there big time. You were saying . . .

Mythter: You're really good, carrying on with me and with them.

Gyrl: Well you too!

Gyrl: ::gently:: OK, Genuine1 . . . do you have a gender?

Private Message to Gyrl

Mythter: The mayor and the town council convened to do something about it. They brought her to trial on charges of sedition.

Gyrl: Eeeep!

Mythter: "You are disturbing the natural order," they said to her. "You must tell us if you are a boy or are you a girl!"

Mythter: On the day of the trial, a fool happened to walk into town.

Gyrl: ::softly:: And this fool stood up to speak?

Mythter: ::nodding:: Uh huh. And the fool asked the townspeople what all the fuss was. And the townspeople said "This gyrl is an abomination."

Gyrl: ::wincing::

Mythter: "This gyrl is disturbing the natural order," they said.

Mythter: "How?" asked the fool. "She will not tell us if she is truly a girl," cried the townspeople.

Gyrl: ::curling up closer to you, listening::

Mythter: "We cannot see her!" cried the townspeople.

Mythter: And the fool said, "What's a girl?"

BeenThere: I have a comment, um, kind of long, do you mind?

Gyrl: Go for it!

BeenThere: I think reporting the news, marketing, and politicking all in black and white only is a tool to control folks by limiting their choices to only two. If I do that, I control what you choose. I may even create a dilemma in which you feel you have no choice.

BeenThere: In other words, black-and-white thinking.

BeenThere: Sorry, that was a long comment indeed.

Gyrl: Yeah, but you brilliantly summed up the whole "only two genders" problem!

Private Message to Gyrl

Mythter: "A girl is obedient to boys," proclaimed the Bishop.

"A girl bears children" said the Doctor, quite sure of himself.

"A girl is not a boy!" proclaimed the Lawyer.

"A girl does the housework," cried the Merchant.

"Well," said the fool . . .

Gyrl: Gen, what box do you fill in on govt forms?

Genuine1: I fill in the ones that have the little "m" next to them, OK?

Mythter: Gee, what a surprise.

Gyrl: Right, Gen . . . so you have a gender.

Genuine1: I have a physical gender—not a mental gender.

Gyrl: ::raising an eyebrow:: As you say, Gen.

Genuine1: :)

Private Message to Gyrl

Mythter: "It seems to me," said the fool, "that if you cannot agree on something as simple as what exactly a girl *is* . . ."

" . . . then how can you charge or sentence this person?"

Gyrl: And the mayor, who was quite wise after all, agreed, and everyone lived happily ever after?

Mythter: ::softly:: In the story, yeah, they all live happily ever after.

Gyrl: And in real life?

Mythter: ::shrugging:: In real life they listen to the herd's loudest voice, hang the gyrl *and* the fool.

IrishEyes: All gender tells me for sure is how I'm gonna have sex with them if the spark catches. ::smile::

Mythter: Right *on*, Irish!

BillJo: Imagine if there were only one, rigidly defined "Blue" in the world.

Gyrl: ::listening intently to Bill::

BillJo: We don't want to wipe away "Blue," we want to go further in describing the shades, right?

Mythter: Yes!

Gyrl: Yes!

BeenThere: Yes!

Genuine1: Yes!

Private Message to Gyrl

Tale2Tell: Ummm . . . would you like to go private with me after this?

Gyrl: ::purring:: Thanks, darlin', but ::glancing over at **Mythter::** I think I've got other plans.

Tale2Tell: ::chuckling:: Ah, yes. Scratch is a dear.

Gyrl: HUH? SCRATCH?

Tale2Tell: Whoops. I thought everyone here knew Mythter was another of Scratch's screen names.

Gyrl: Ah.

Private Message to Gyrl

Mythter: Hello? OK, so my ending was a little cynical. Sorry. Is that why you didn't answer?

Gyrl: Um, no, hon . . . I . . . oh shoot.

Mythter: ::grinning:: What?

Gyrl: It's me, Scratch. I'm Winc.

Mythter: WHAT??

Gyrl: Scratch? You OK?

Mythter: This is too weird.

Gyrl: ::softly:: Way good story. Really, way.

Mythter: Winc/Gyrl, whoever, I'm outta here . . . Yes, again. Our encounters seem to leave me looking for the exit signs.

Gyrl: Sorry!

Mythter: No! I mean, I've been thinking about . . . look, I'll see you again, OK? Just need some . . . ::no words::

Mythter is no longer online

Gyrl: SCRATCH! WAIT!

Mythter: ::muttering:: space. That's the word, space . . .

Gyrl: What's the *matter*? This is *lovely*!

Mythter is no longer online and did not receive your last message

Genuine1: I'd like to know how the topic strayed from phone sex to the role of gender in fiction to gender, period.
BillJo: Natural progression, Gen.
Genuine1: Yeah, probably was.

Private Message to Gyrl

Vick TF: Hey, what happened to Mythter? You two have a fight?
Gyrl: ::wailing:: I don't *know*! I thought it was all going so *well*!
Vick TF: ::wry grin:: Hey, don't take it personally. You probably got way close, right?
Gyrl: ::sniff:: Uh huh.
Vick TF: Don't worry. Mythter takes off fast. A trademark.
Gyrl: Oh, goody.
Vick TF: But comes back. Really. Just has to think. Hang in there.
Gyrl: ::squaring my shoulders:: I *intend* to!
Vick TF: ::chuckling:: You go, Gyrl.

Webster: We're outta time! Damn! I think we're gonna have to ask Gyrl back! A round of applause!
Gyrl: Aw shucks. OK, gotta go.
Vick TF: Gyrl, you were brilliant.
Gyrl: Awwwww, Vick . . . you see yourself in me.
BillJo: Mind-boggling, Gyrl. Still don't know if you're a man or a woman.

Private Message to Gyrl

Tale2Tell: Um . . . Mythter's not online. Do I stand a chance?
Gyrl: ::softly:: You're real sweet, hon, I'm just not there right now.
Tale2Tell: ::kissing Gyrl's cheek:: Goodnight, then.
Gyrl: G'nite.

9:07:47 P.M. Closing transcript file

Awww, Toobe . . . where did I screw up?

I'm glad Winc sends me stuff, but I gotta say I don't get half of what the heck that room was talking about. Can you believe it? Ze does this amazing interview with people asking questions I never in a million years would even think to ask, then beats hirself up for Scratch leaving.

Scratch just has to disappear sometimes.

Still worried about that memo I snarfed from the law. Maybe I should go back into that cop BBS and get me some dirt I could use against . . . Ugh . . . my stomach just answered that one. No way.

END TOOBE ENTRY

NARRATIVE ENTRY, JABBATHEHUT

Out of habit, Wally Budge of the Federal Bureau of Census and Statistics does his hourly, albeit usually fruitless, scan to find any newly created alternate screen names for Scratch and Winc.

Search Results

- 0 hits on search criteria "Winc"
- 2 hits on "Scratch" = Mythter, O'Bere

A smile spreads across the craggy face of the cyber-gumshoe, as he happily adds the names "Mythter" and "O'Bere" to his database. So, he thinks to himself, Scratch is the careless one.

END JABBA NARRATIVE ENTRY

03
FOMO

To: Editor, They/Them magazine
From: D.I. Drew
Subject: A bit more detail on Scratch

The simultaneity of their writings was a little spooky. I'd search for a journal and find that they mirrored each other's entries as well as logging chat rooms. And Jabba nailed FOMO before FOMO was a thing!

Cheers,

Drew

TOOBE ENTRY

FUNNY OF THE DAY

The cable television company that serves Columbia, SC, aimed a live camera full-time at an aquarium to occupy a vacant channel while awaiting the start-up of the Science-Fiction Channel. When they replaced the "fish channel," complaints were so numerous that they were forced to find another channel for the aquarium, which runs 24 hours a day, all year round, to this day.

—*South Carolinian News*

END TOOBE ENTRY

NARRATIVE ENTRY, JABBATHEHUT

Shaking his head in disbelief, Wally Budge reads the article one more time.

> WASHINGTON—Sources inside the Bureau of Census and Statistics today confirmed reports that "a number of warrants" have been issued for the arrest of Registration Evaders.
>
> "The only people who aren't registering are people who have something to hide," said Undersecretary LaBouchere, "and we have the full cooperation of the FBI and local law enforcement agencies to find these people and bring them to justice."
>
> All that extra muscle may not be necessary—the FBCS has been slowly building up its own enforcement arm over the past few years in preparation for yesterday's Registration deadline. Bureau officials have declined to disclose details, but officials agree "arrests are imminent."
> See Registration Benefits, p. 3

Budge puts down his paper noisily. He drums his fingers on the table, blinks once, and a smile breaks across his face. Set a thief, catch a thief. Maybe it's time to get a little help from somebody who knows the cyberstreets like I know New York City. A hacker.

Nicotine-stained fingers tap happily at the keyboard as Budge hums "London Bridge Is Falling Down." Good for Budge.

Trouble for Scratch and Winc.

END JABBA NARRATIVE ENTRY

TOOBE ENTRY

I'm trying to remember how I met Scratch. It was online, I don't know hir in real life like I do Winc. You make so many "friends" online, it's hard to remember the details, which chat room or post. But I know I told hir to fuck off after a few letters cuz ze wouldn't tell me hir age or if ze was a man or woman. I didn't know that was kind of a point of honor with hir, but I had my own reasons for being cryptic. Then ze ran into me in a teen chat room and figured it out. "I'm no predator after your ass, Toobe," ze wrote. "I'm sorry I was so insensitive." I liked that about Scratch. Ze apologized right away and didn't try to explain it away like most people do. Ze also added that ze was in the teen chat room by mistake. I believe hir. You wouldn't believe how dumb Scratch is about getting around online.

Ze said that within 10 minutes of being in that room ze saw all of us get harassed by older men. Scratch, being Scratch, did a little investigating. Checked out each one, found them out every time ze got online, and cross-referenced them with other rooms. About 2/3 of them hung out in the Christian room, all of them were married men, and a whole bunch also hung out in rooms as women. I told Scratch not to jump to conclusions about all that cross-referencing. They were probably making up the Christian part.

Scratch forwarded some of these conversations to the powers that be and got a couple of them bounced off the service. Hard to do on a private service where they're more interested in your money than civil rights. Ze didn't tell me any of this, I heard it throo da grapevine. Jabba had heard it, too, so I know it was true.

Scratch gets pissed easily. Righteous anger is hir best suit.

I just emailed Scratch asking where we met online, and ze couldn't remember either. "Left-handed Lithuanians for John Lennon, probably," ze wrote back. So helpful.

But check this out—Scratch is all excited about Winc!

To: Toobe
From: Scratch
Subj: Gender roles

Tripped out by my online adventure last night. Ran into that Winc character again. You say you know this person? Any insights into why I want to head screaming for the hills every time I run into hir? In a good way, though. I get all calm with hir one minute, hysterical a minute later.

—Scratch

END TOOBE ENTRY

WINC JOURNAL ENTRY

Rode my bike past a group of old men today. Smiled and waved to them, long legs pedaling. They loved it, I could see it in their faces how much they loved my smile, my long legs, they smiled and waved back. Maybe right now they're thinking about me, maybe they're lying in bed next to their wives and they're thinking about my smile floating past them, a butterfly they'll never catch. Some of them saw the girl of their dreams. Some of them saw a young boy.

They never see me when I sign off and sit here naked with a bug floating in my teacup. And I wonder. How do some people just get off their bikes and laugh with a stranger who seems nice? How do they move their heads just so? How do they know when to smile? Is there some secret code I've never been taught? Is it in the genes? What's wrong with my genes, then? How do they drink their tea? Without bugs, that's for sure.

Scratch, what if I'm not the right one on the bike this time? What if you need the long-haired Winc with the urgent cock, and you're that nasty riot grrl? What if you need that boy because you're a sweet young boy, too, what if I could be your strong woman, the one who would love you for your strong woman self?

END WINC ENTRY

TOOBE ENTRY

To: Jabbathehut
From: Toobe
Subj: No Fallout Yet

Hey, I haven't had any fallout yet from that police snooping incident.

To: Toobe
From: Jabbathehut
Subj: Re: I see everything

But that's not what you should be thinking about, youngster.

Registration is what you should be thinking about.

To: Jabbathehut
From: Toobe
Subj: Re: Any?

What do you mean? Why should I be thinking of Registration?

To: Toobe
From: Jabbathehut
Subj: Connection

Stretch your 10-second brain, my little cybergnat. I noted your report as to the reluctance of people to receive the bypass codes and choose Registration instead. The fear of missing out is predominant, it guides some people's every action. Ironic, because as they are struggling so hard to fill the blanks, they are indeed missing the far reaches of their own adventures, if they only had the courage.

Pardon my philosophical bent, perhaps you bring it out in me.

Now, I must ask: when you tell people about filling out Reg cards, do you also tell them to not put in their real birthdays? They will be snagged so fast their ears will freeze-dry. Note this, from one of my clients:

Forward msg. from XXXXXXX

> Dear Jabba:
>
> Thank you so much for helping me with the parental controls. You have no idea the number of children using their parents' accounts. My eleven-year-old had been approached by several older men within the first few weeks of our using this online service. I've had to keep her completely away from the thing. I've Registered her, but now the system withholds many rooms from her that her mother and I have no problem with her

> using. It's either all or nothing with the Reg restrictions. But your lockout code lets my daughter use *my* account, and now she doesn't have to bother with being assigned one of her own by the government.
>
> Nice to have the govt choose what your kids can read. Like old-fashioned book banning.

Please be sensible, my young friend.

To: Jabbathehut
From: Toobe
Subj: Understood

I'm thinking about holding one of those workshops for teenagers (and younger? Ugh) on how to avoid perverts. You can't have a teen room without all of them flocking.

To: Toobe
From: Jabbathehut
Subj: No, you're not

And what would your advice be?

To: Jabbathehut
From: Toobe
Subj: Uh uh

I can't even tell you, Jabba. With my luck (lately) the message will get intercepted and all your stupid pervert clients will find out.

To: Toobe
From: Jabbathehut
Subj: Clients

I believe I resent that remark, but do as you wish.

END TOOBE ENTRY

04
HEART AND SOUL

NARRATIVE ENTRY, JABBATHEHUT

The roach slowly makes its way across Wally Budge's desktop, looking for all the world like a miniaturized Jules Verne battle contraption. Budge shakes his head in disgust, causing the roach to stop its forward motion and neatly blend in with the coffee stain on which it hovers.

If I ignore it, it'll go away, he thinks to himself, returning to his latest memo.

To: FBCS Investigations
From: Undersec'y LaBouchere
Subj: Cough Up

Wally,

I think you'll agree I've given you more than enough time to test out your theories about Reg vaders. Well? Do you have any leads? I have the secretary himself breathing down my neck. I need names. Give me what you've got, and I'll keep the dogs away from your door.

L.

Raising his hand slowly, Budge makes to swat the invader from his domain, but with that inexplicable fore-sense they seem to possess as a species, the roach dashes for cover down the back of his desk.

Rich, dark phrases of disgust escape Budge's lips as he stabs three digits into his desk phone.

"Yeah?" comes the smoky, familiar voice into his ear.

"Shelly, I got me an infestation up here."

"You talkin' about your office or your brain, Wally?"

"Har-de-har-har, Shel. I got me some roaches."

"Yeah, well everyone's got roaches, Walls. They'll die."

"Huh?"

"They'll die. My guys put out a poison last week, great stuff. Roaches eat it, carry the poison in their bellies back to their nest, and there they die. Cannibals that they are, the other roaches eat the dead one, and they die. So don't sweat it. If you saw one roach, you saw Typhoid Mary heading back to wipe out her nest."

"Typhoid Mary. . . ."

"She was the woman who—"

"Yeah, yeah. I know who she was. Shelly, you are an amazing woman, and if the girls and boys down in programming can build it for me, I owe you a steak dinner."

"Build you what, Walls?"

But Budge just chuckles as he hangs up. Rapidly, he types:

To: Development
Via: Records, Assets, Materiel
From: FBCS Investigations
Subj: Not So Common Cold

Booker: Remember you were explaining computer viruses to me the other day? And you said they can search stuff out on the Net? Do me a favor: Put your head together with Shelly Dunlap, ask her to describe Typhoid Mary to you. Then see if you can come up with a little virus for yours truly?

—Budge

He presses SEND, and it's not five minutes later that he receives:

To: FBCS Investigations
From: P_Booker
Cc: S_Dunlap
Subj: Your wish is my . . . etc, etc.

Shel and I have been talking about this for weeks. I have a prototype, but you'll need some new hardware to accommodate it. Shel's arranging.

By the way . . . you're still using your generic department account? Haven't you Registered yet? You'll need a private account in order to work this thing I'll be sending you.

—Booker

Register, huh? Soon.

To: Undersec'y LaBouchere
From: FBCS Investigations
Subj: Coughing

Ma'am,

I've got two fish I'm playing real gentle here. They're using black market bypass codes. I traced the acquisition of the bypasses to the same distributor. No name there yet, but I'm closing in.

Looks to me like we've got an honest-to-God conspiracy going here, ma'am . . . that or first-class stupidity. I need some time to figure out which, and I don't want to scare these folks off.

—W.

Wally Budge is putting it all together. His favorite task. What had Shelly called him? A garbage hound? Yeah, and two of his wives had been only slightly kinder with "pack rat." Collect, think, catalogue, muse, compare, review, and ta-da: useful information. He loses himself happily for the next few minutes or so. It's a shock when he hears a voice behind him, and the clock says it's five hours later.

"Lieutenant Wallace Budge?"

Budge's bloodshot eyes swivel themselves onto the workman standing in the doorway. "Yeah?"

"This stuff is for you; where do ya want it?" The workman wheels in a dolly loaded with sleek dove-gray boxes, a huge monitor, and a keyboard from the future.

Budge narrows his eyes. "Whassat?"

The workman shrugs. "New workstation. Merry Christmas, I guess."

"Hold on, hold on, lemme check this out first."

The man eyes Budge's archaic desktop computer. "Sure thing, Boss. You fond of antiques or somethin'?"

Ignoring him, Budge punches numbers into his phone.

"Yeah, Walls?"

"Shel! What's with the new computer?"

A husky laugh. Then, "It's for Mary."

"Huh?"

"Typhoid Mary . . . hell of a sophisticated search engine for the Net."

"Huh?"

That chuckle. "Your virus, Wally. She's got a graphic interface, so she won't live in your old Unix box. She needs Windows at least, and a Mac at best. So I got ya an Apple PowerBook Duo, fastest machine this side of the Berlin Wall. Typhoid Mary is gonna dance before your very eyes. Speaking of which, we should go dancing sometime. Merry . . ."

". . . Christmas, yeah yeah yeah. I like my old box, Shel!"

"Oh hush. This stuff is top of the line. Wait'll you see what you can do with it! Full color, video. And you'd love to dance! I have to take you out more often. Trust me, you'll thank me for this machine."

"I trust you, Shel. I've just never trusted a computer that smiles at me when it starts up."

"Get over it. Who knows, maybe you can download some dirty pictures and bring them over to my house some night, and we can check out the pixelation."

Budge flushes despite himself. "Awright, awright."

Another chuckle. Then, "Friday night. Put your cowboy boots on. Meantime, enjoy the new toy, Wally."

Hanging up the phone, Wally looks up at the man still standing in the doorway. "Umm, I guess you can put it here, next to the old one."

The man snorts. "Not a chance. That box of junk is headed for the dump. How could you stand looking into that green screen all day, anyway?"

"I like green," sniffs Budge, pondering cowboy boots.

END JABBA NARRATIVE ENTRY

PERSONAL LOG, JABBATHEHUT

If I lacked character, I would idly scan the world's computers.

While I do so enjoy playing detective, it's time to turn my attention to other sources. The only behavior that astounds me anymore about the human race is its continued gullibility. The following is a memo about to be sent out to the general public. I like to see these things before their official release date:

> Dear Service Consumer:
> Please note you are about to be given an extraordinary opportunity. The members of Allied Consumer Industries have generously donated their time and expertise to a new Registration bonus which would allow you complete access to any area of the online world you desire. Simply Register as you normally would, but be sure to select Special Options. This will allow you special access and cost you nothing in additional fees.
> —ACI etc.

This was sent to all computer users, not any special demographic as claimed. Your bennie is being assaulted with a billion digital mail-order catalogs. And just like that, you're tracked. How about that for a special option?

END JABBA PERSONAL LOG

NARRATIVE ENTRY, JABBATHEHUT

Meanwhile, back in a certain green office:

Lt. Wally Budge is making his beefy paw guide a small plastic "mouse" that somehow attaches to the cursor on his computer screen. Now he's supposed to be able to navigate through a shifting sea of endlessly cute Macintosh icons. He clicks on one, and on his screen appears:

Congratulations!
You are now ready to open your online account.
Please enter your name in the highlighted spaces.

Budge frowns and maneuvers the mouse, but it sends the arrow skittering to all corners of the monitor. The memo now repeating itself on his screen helps neither his mood nor his coordination.

Congratulations!
You are now ready to open your online account.
Please enter your name in the highlighted spaces.

"I heard ya the first four times," Budge mutters darkly. "Is this what people go through every day just to use their computers? No wonder they try to be someone else online."

Congratulations!
You are now ready to open your online account.
Please enter your name in the highlighted spaces.

Budge manages to land his mouse in the little glowing box, where he enters his name.

Thank you, now enter your age.

Grumbling, Budge enters 43.

What is your sex?
(M) or (F)

Budge laughs ruefully, trying to think back to the last time he got laid. He types "None," receiving a disapproving beep.

Very funny.
What is your sex?
(M) or (F)

Budge laughs again, peers over his shoulder to make sure no one is looking, and types "Hopefully."

Very funny.
What is your sex?
(M) or (F)

"Screw this," he mutters under his breath, positioning his mouse to move on.

I'm sorry. Your sign-up sequence will fail to complete unless you fill out the form.

"What the hell do you need to know all this for, anyway?" says Budge aloud as he tries to maneuver his mouse to get the cursor back into the "Sex" box. Just as he lands in place, though, a roach peeks its armored head over the edge of the sleek, new dove-gray monitor.

His left hand moves slowly toward the roach, while his right hand fills in the sign-up motions indiscriminately. Left hand and right hand continue crazily until the dialogue box opens on his screen.

> You have completed the sign-up process.
> To use your new account right away, please click OK.

Budge's index finger clicks OK at the same time his left hand crashes down, missing the roach by less than an inch.

"Dammit!"

> Thank you, Ms. Budge, and welcome to your Online World.
> Would you like to take the guided tour?

"Huh?"

The message repeats itself.

"Ms. Budge?" Sure enough, when he clicks his profile, "Female" is entered firmly in the "Sex" box.

"Damned roach," he mutters, and makes to change the designation.

> I'm sorry, Ms. Budge, you may not change any information in your master account. Would you like to set up a secondary account?

"Huh?"

END JABBA NARRATIVE ENTRY

TOOBE ENTRY

I think Scratch is starting to relax a little. Keeps running into Winc, but maybe ze's getting used to it. At least when ze gets freaked out, which is pretty often, ze can just jump offline. Apparently they ran into each other in some Star Trek room. Winc plays in there all the time. Weird, though, Scratch never goes into those rooms.

END TOOBE ENTRY

SCRATCH JOURNAL ENTRY

Spoiler: Hey, what's a nonspacey like me gotta do to get a little attention around here?
Ishara Yar: Oh, something like that'll do.
Spoiler: ::slow grin::
Ishara Yar: Why "Spoiler"?
Spoiler: Oh, you'll find out ::assuming aggressive combat stance::
Ishara Yar: Will I, now? ::kicking up at your head::
Spoiler: Actually, main mission in life is getting you off . . . ::ducking::
Ishara Yar: ::slow smile, folding my arms:: Is that right? And why would that be?
Spoiler: You space aliens are so repressed. Always shooting down ships when you'd be better off fucking . . .
Ishara Yar: ::swinging, missing:: Who you callin' an alien? ::growling::
Spoiler: Hmmm, thought all you space things liked girls in every port. ::dancing sideways real fast::
Ishara Yar: That did it! ::lunging at you, tackling you at the knees::
Spoiler: Eeeeeep!
Ishara Yar: ::pulling you closer, the two of us on the ground::
Spoiler: ::Muffled:: My, what big muscles you have . . .
Ishara Yar: ::grinning:: All the better to do what must be done, my darling!
Spoiler: Ooh, your scent, it's so seductive. Wish I could see you better. ::muffled:: But your sleeve's across my face, and ::grunt::
Ishara Yar: ::straddling you, looking down into your eyes:: ::smiling::
Spoiler: Yes?
Ishara Yar: ::leaning down, my face against your neck:: ::biting gently::
Spoiler: ::squirming:: Mmmmmmmm
Ishara Yar: ::sitting back up:: ::whispering:: Next time, it's for blood.
Spoiler: ::batting baby blues:: Did you say blood?! If you say that again I'm afraid you'll wake a sleeping beast.
Ishara Yar: ::whispering:: Blood.
Ishara Yar: Wakey, wakey, sleeping beast.
Spoiler: ::batting some more:: You wouldn't want to do that, would ya?

Ishara Yar: ::holding your wrists out at your sides:: Do what, darlin'?

Spoiler: ::shoving leg over yours, flipping you over:: ::lower voice:: Bring out the bloodlust.

Ishara Yar: ::yelping at sudden move::

Spoiler: ::jumping up, grabbing phaser::

Ishara Yar: ::reaching for the phaser, getting as far as grabbing your wrists::

Spoiler: ::stopping dead still:: ::Looking down into your eyes::

Ah hah . . . ::struggling with inner demons:: Perhaps we are at an impasse.

Ishara Yar: ::looking up at you, falling into your eyes::

Spoiler: ::watching pulsing in your throat::

Ishara Yar: ::feeling the pulsing in my throat:: Ah . . . that sort of beast.

Spoiler: Mm-hmmm ::slow blink:: Would you like to get up?

Ishara Yar: ::breathing hard:: I . . . I'm not sure.

Spoiler: You do look awfully nice there, lying on the ground with your hands on my wrists . . . ::soft chuckle::

Ishara Yar: ::snarling, trying to flip you over::

Spoiler: heeheehee. You forget I have the phaser . . .

Ishara Yar: ::falling back, panting:: You'd use that?

Spoiler: ::soft murmur:: Ah, no, let me just use my words then . . .

Ishara Yar: Uh oh.

Spoiler: ::smiling:: If you provoke the bloodlust in me, you will surrender, for your blood sings loud in my ears, and you need it to break free . . . for me . . . ::soft, soft voice:: Don't you darlin'?

Ishara Yar: ::mesmerized, slowly loosening my grip on your wrists::

Yes . . . yes . . .

Spoiler: ::low:: You are such a tempting morsel . . .

Ishara Yar: ::lying back, arching my throat::

Spoiler: ::watching your pulse:: beat, beat, beat, beat, beat . . . I can hear it.

Ishara Yar: ::softly:: Do it. Please.

Spoiler: Please, what?

Ishara Yar: Please take my blood. Please open me. Please!

Spoiler: It's awfully late ::looking at cyberwatch:: Perhaps a little nibble . . .

Ishara Yar: ::holding my breath::

Spoiler: ::snick:: A light nick on your upper shoulder, my head flashing beyond quickness to drink . . .

Ishara Yar: ::crying out joyfully::

Spoiler: ::drinking the little trickle from your shoulder:: ::rocking back on my heels:: ::wiping my mouth::

Ishara Yar: ::small happy noises::

Spoiler: ::Eyes glowing red, then green, then amber, then blue again::

Ishara Yar: I . . . am . . . taken . . .

Spoiler: Yesssss.

Ishara Yar: ::eyes flashing:: This time!

Spoiler: Of course this time. Next time, we start all over again . . . Whatever you say, dear.

Ishara Yar: ::narrowing my eyes:: A gag would do you wonders.

Spoiler: But wouldn't you miss my tongue? ::stepping back ever so slowly:: And now I really must say goodnight.

Ishara Yar: ::chuckling:: I can think of some very good uses for your tongue . . .

Spoiler: ::never letting my eyes off of you:: Good night, sweet Yar.

Ishara Yar: Good night, beast.

END SCRATCH JOURNAL ENTRY

NARRATIVE ENTRY, JABBATHEHUT

She's dressed in a granny dress and moves coquettishly across his screen. Budge slaps his hand over his eyes and groans, "If this damned computer gets any cuter, I'll feed it to the roaches." But gamely he types, "Who are you?"

The onscreen coquette turns, winks at Budge who, in turn, lights another cigarette despite the two already burning in his ashtray.

"Hi there, Missy; my name's Mary. What's yours?"

Budge rolls his eyes. He'll have to remember to get Shelly to change his sex. He groans inwardly at the conversation that would entail. "My name is Budge," he types, "and you're Typhoid Mary?"

The flirt curtsies prettily and nods her head.

"Okay, then, I've got a—"

Budge's screen suddenly flashes ominous dark violet. The sound of a gong sets him coughing. Onscreen appears:

> **To:** FBCS Investigations
> **From:** DevilsOwn
> **Subj:** YOUR DISCARDED MEMO RE: REG. VADERS
>
> So, you're the folks looking for prowlers on your weeny machine, huh newbie? Someone picked up a memo you discarded. I'm enclosing the perp's tag (Screen name: *Toobe*) in case you want to put some sort of tail on him.
>
> This one's on the house, but if you want any more, I work on retainer. Wanna talk?
>
> —Devil

Toobe? Toobe? Where'd he heard that name before? He glances up to his wall charts, tracing the movements of his suspects. Swiveling back to the screen, he types out a memo from his generic department account. Damned if he's going to write some hacker as "Ms. Budge."

> **To:** DevilsOwn
> **From:** FBCS Investigations
> **Subj:** You're Hired
>
> Good work, mister. Consider yourself on retainer. Email me info on how to get $$$ to you. Don't need you at the moment, but I might.
>
> —(And I may be a "newbie," but it's Lieutenant Budge to you)

Grinning, peering into the results on his screen, he lights a fourth cigarette. Sure enough, there are almost as many meetings with this Toobe character as the many encounters between Scratch and Winc. He tries not to get excited, but if luck is with him, he's got them. Glancing back down to the screen, he sees another memo flashing:

> **To:** FBCS Investigations
> **From:** Undersec'y LaBouchere
> **Subj:** NAMES!
>
> Wally: Names. I need names. Or we're both out in the cold. We won't let it out of the bag, I promise you.
>
> —L.

Damn! Quickly he types:

> **To:** Undersec'y LaBouchere
> **From:** FBCS Investigations
> **Subj:** TOP SECRET
>
> Ma'am: OK, as close as I can tell, "Scratch" and "Winc" (see attached ident summaries) will be our first collars. They've been everywhere, I mean everywhere, and neither of them have Registered. Please keep this Eyes Only.
>
> —B.
>
> ☐ File attached

In the corner of his screen, the hippie chick in the granny dress waits, endlessly patient.

"Mary," he types, "I have someone I want you to meet."

Budge makes his way through the arcane series of icons on the screen, programming Typhoid Mary to search. "Find the Toobe character, stick to him or her like glue." He chews his lip for a moment, then calls Shelly.

Her throaty chuckle in the receiver almost wakes something inside him. But he presses on.

"So all I do now is hit 'YES,' and it goes and looks for this character? Right?"

"Nail on the head, hot stuff. And then it'll tag this person nice and pretty so they can't get away from you."

"Shel," he says, beaming broadly, "you are a peach," and hangs up the phone without waiting for an answer.

He takes a deep breath, then his thick finger darts out and stabs at YES. The hippie chick icon on his screen turns to him, winks once, and practically dances off the screen.

"I'll be damned," he mutters.

To: FBCS Investigations
From: Sgt. Harrison, Bureau Demographics
Subj: Your Request re: "Scratch" and "Winc"

Lieutenant Budge: Enclosed please find our profiles on the two . . . people you named. This is an odd collection of information. Where did you find these two? People like this could make the lives of people like me quite miserable, thank you.

Usually I come back with one name. One name, one person. But with this search, there are several names for each person. See the following, Lieutenant, and I think you may share my consternation:

SCRATCH: aka Luvboyz, MarthaW, Chicanita
WINC: aka Digqueer, Katchoo, Deth.

The multiplicity of these two is exactly why I told the powers that be that we cannot let people sign on as anything but their own names.

You can imagine the possibilities. Not a pretty world, Lieutenant.

Your Obedient etc. etc.

D.H.

Budge smiles around his cigarette, the smoke curling up into his well-watered eyes, and reads the attached profiles:

CITIZEN WINC

> According to product interest area frequency, Citizen is a young senior white Native American female male earning between $6,000 and $500,000 annually. Objects of regular perusal include, but are not limited to, *Vogue Online*, *True Romance*, *Scientific American*, *Mondo 2000*, *Tales from the Crypt*, *Urban Sportsman*, and *Girlfriends* magazines, as well as *National Enquirer*. Citizen also frequents multiple university libraries, searching for information in the field of ethnomethodology, is a regular subscriber to *The Spider-Man*, *The Batman*, *Wonder Woman*, several Vertigo comic book titles, and to a small press comic called "HotHead Paisan: Homicidal Lesbian Terrorist!!!!!" Pattern indicates Citizen is a heterosexual, homosexual, bisexual male ages 12 through 58 or heterosexual, homosexual, bisexual female ages 23 through 72.
>
> Note: Account window shows activity in sectors clearly counter-Registrational. Name is Registered but no feasible profile corresponds with the name. This indicates the user has some sort of bypass "worm technique," which inserts a name into the database without the required demographic information.

Budge takes a long, satisfying suck at an old, familiar missing tooth and scribbles down the words "ethnomethodology," "Tales from the Crypt," and "HotHead Paisan."

"Damnedest thing I ever saw," he chuckles to himself.

Flipping to the next page, he reads:

CITIZEN SCRATCH

> According to product interest area frequency, Citizen is a middle-aged senior female male African American Caucasian of Irish descent, living on several welfare programs, alternately earning up to $75,000 annually. Objects of regular perusal include, but are not

> limited to, *Black America*, *Rolling Stone*, *Wired*, *Ms.*, *On Our Backs*, *Off Our Backs*, *Tales from the Crypt*, *GQ*, *Interview*, and *Mother Jones* magazines. Citizen also frequents multiple university libraries, searching for information in the fields of psychology of mind, goddess culture, and weaponry, the latter with a focus on knives. Citizen subscribes to both *Time* and *The New Yorker*, all indicating that citizen is a heterosexual, homosexual, bisexual male ages 12 through 58 or heterosexual, homosexual, bisexual female ages 23 through 72.
>
> Note: Account window shows activity in sectors clearly counter-Registrational. Name is Registered but no feasible profile corresponds with the name. This indicates use of bypass "worm technique," which inserts a name into the database without the required demographic information.

Budge writes the words, "Tales from the Crypt" (again!), "goddess culture," "psychology of mind," and "BLADES," the last underlined several times.

"In all my years," he muses aloud, "I've never had to locate someone without at least knowing something about them. Like age, maybe? Maybe you could tell me what sex or color, hmm?" His laughter dissolves into a series of coughs.

END JABBA NARRATIVE ENTRY

TOOBE ENTRY

Scratch and Winc just had their first cyberdate. I mean, a planned one. Not just accidentally running into each other. Scratch was in hir "Fuck your gender" profile, and Winc was in hir "ain't life grand" mode, and they went on a little surfing safari. When they started, they were really pissed off—the whole intent was to flame everyone who got in their way.

I guess I should explain: You can chat in a public room or a private one. At the same time! You can even have more than one private chat going. This gets a little dizzying, but that's part of the fun.

They started with the Christian room (two rooms full up to the maximum allowed on any given night). Scratch sent me a note inviting me to join, so I dropped by.

***** You are in room "Christian Fellowship" *****

Scratch: This is my first time in this room. Can I ask a question?

Eccle: Go for it.

Ruth: Ask away, Scratch!

Scratch: I'm sure no one here is like this, but, what do you think of your fellow Christians who are so intolerant of others? Kind of bad PR, don't you think?

Luke: You're right Scratch.

Eccle: Don't have to answer to God for others . . . Just me.

Winc: ::muttering:: It wasn't God who asked for an answer, Eccle, it was Scratch.

Beatitudes: A time for hugging, and a time for pushing away.

Matthew: Scratch . . . its' just the way some peepl deal with there own lack of self esteme . . . attack others so you don't have to look at yourself.

Ruth: Yes, it's bad to be intolerant. Have you heard "love the sinner, hate the sin?"

Scratch: Yes, Ruth. But I guess I think it's up to God to hate the sin, too. Who are we to judge?

That went on forever, with both of them trying valiantly for a little dialogue. I stayed quiet. Eventually we all drowned in a sea of quasi-scripture and counter-quasi-scripture.

Private Message to Toobe

Scratch: Whoa! What a trip. I need to go to a queer room or something! Anything!

Toobe: Gotcha. I'm logging off to walk the dog but I hear the Gay/ Lesbian room is good. Have fun.

Scratch told me, at one point they went into a room and presented themselves as "nothing," no gender. I'm barely holding onto my version of "kid" and "boy." And peeking over the wall at "sexual activity," but that's too overwhelming right now.

What does "nothing" feel like?

END TOOBE ENTRY

SCRATCH JOURNAL ENTRY

Private Message to Scratch

Winc: You were good in there.

Scratch: ::heavy sigh:: Right. Thought we could talk. Out of 19, there was only one who was open. Feel like I need a shower.

Online Host

***** You are in room "Gay and Lesbian Room" *****

CJ: Age, sex check?

Sniffer: Escondido, CA.

Baubles: And you? Where were you born?

Private Message to Scratch

Winc: Uh oh, Age/Sex check!

Scratch: Yeah, sameolshit.

CJ: Sniffer: What an unusual name.

Sniffer: Gracias.

CJ: Female, 25

Scratch: Hi.

Sniffer: Scratch and sniff!

Meds: hi from boston; 26 m lifeguard/grad student looking for playmates.

Winc: ::boppin' into the room, shakin' rain out of my hair:: Evenin', all!

Baubles: Evening, Win. Raining where you are?

Winc: East Coast, Baubles. An' it's Winc. Not Win. ::grin::

Scratch: Does anyone ever converse in here, or is it all just cocktail chat, hmmm?

HardGuy: Hi all from the big Eazy.

Sniffer: Hey I've been to the Big Easy! Great town.

HardGuy: 'Specially around Mardi Gras!

Private Message to Winc

Scratch: I'm outta here. Disappointing.

Winc: Way.

Private Message to Scratch

Winc: How bout the Women's Room?

Scratch: OK, why?

Winc: Either it's full of boyz trying to be girlz, or maybe there *are* women there and the talk is good.

Scratch: We're there! But let's just try being a nothing, I mean no gender. Or whatever.

Winc: ::eyes twinkling:: Right!

***** You are in room "The Women's Room" *****

Private Message to Winc

Scratch: There's a guy named Holiday in here, I think he likes me!

Winc: Cool!

Holiday: Hey let's talk about pussy, anyone game?

Debbie: Go away Holiday.

Private Message to Winc

Scratch: Duh, something tells me I was wrong about Holiday . . .

Winc: What are you *doing* to get all these PMs?

People call the Eyes when they start getting unpleasantness from assholes, but sometimes their comments are entertaining.

Scratch: Gee, Holiday, no men in here I thought.

Holiday: So what, vibrator-head, you need one!

Private Message to Winc

Scratch: Honey, I'm in an IM storm.

Winc: What's happening?

Scratch: Dunno. I called Holiday a man, maybe?

Winc: LOL! Dastardly thing to do, m'dear.

Scratch: What is?

Winc: Calling a man a man when he's in the women's room.

Private Message to Holiday

Scratch: Gosh, Holiday, you must be about 17.

Holiday: 17 or not, you donut bumper, you have to buy a plastic electrical device to get off.

Donut bumper?! I didn't follow up that conversation, but I was falling off my chair laughing.

Private Message to Winc

Scratch: Where exactly is a "donut bumper" on the anatomy?

Winc: ::looking down:: no donuts here! ::smiling:: Nice pie, though.

Scratch: No, seriously, I—aw, forget it.

Winc: Mmph!

Holiday: Are you scared to talk about our sexuality?

Emily: What's the topic tonight?

MizMaid: Holiday, are you provoking?

Winc: "Our" sexuality, Holiday?

Debbie: Well MizMaid, I think he's trying to.

Slim: Any bi women out there?

Emily: Any single mothers here?

Minn: Any bohemians here?

Emily: All of the above!

Princess: Anyone in love out there?

Princess: That's a start. Age, sex check?

Winc: Fine/yes.

Emily: Let's talk about pathological assholes. Any practical advice on how I don't have to put up with a guy just because I had a child by him?

Princess: Homicide?

Emily: I love that suggestion!

MizMaid: LOL, Princess.

Emily: Am I the only woman here who had a child with a pathological asshole?

Janis: Does everyone in here hate men?

Emily: I don't hate men.

Princess: Some are OK.

Private Message to Scratch

> **Winc:** <---having way cool PMs with MizMaid about lies and cyberspace.
>
> **Scratch:** Just realized my name changes its meaning in different contexts. In this room I would be a yeast infection.
>
> **Winc:** STOP THAT!! :X

Minn: To call an asshole an asshole does not = hate.

MizMaid: Right, Princess.

Janis: Everyone is griping about men.

MizMaid: Trash is trash, doesn't matter the gender.

Minn: If you can't hate an asshole, then who can you hate?!

Emily: No, we're not griping about *men*, we're griping about assholes.

Private Message to Winc

> **Scratch:** And in the gun room it would be . . .
>
> **Winc:** Winc . . . chester?
>
> **Scratch:** Uh huh.
>
> **Winc:** ::winc-eing::

Private Message to Scratch

Pubes: Touch me.

Scratch: Well that's a weird one, never heard that one before . . .

Pubes: I'm surprised. With a name like that?

Scratch: Like Pubes, or Scratch?

Scratch: Question: how many here are PMing right now?
Fess up!

Winc: ::liftin' head from PMs:: Howdy, Scratch!

Scratch: Well, hell-o there, Winc! OK, Winc fessed up, anyone else?

Profile of Pubes

Screen Name: Pubes

Member Name: Rita Mae

Location: Madison, WI

Birthdate: 5-1-69

Sex: Female

Computer: 386

Hobbies: rafting

Occupation: flowers

Quote: Love the one you're with

Private Message to Scratch

Winc: ::laughing:: I think I'm having fun with MizMaid! I like hir!

Scratch: Me too! Now ze's "challenging" me! Muhahaha.

MizMaid: Yes, Win is very busy, aren't we?

Winc: ::blushing:: You could say that, MizMaid, yes.

Scratch: Ah, brave MizMaid's confessed.
You call her Win? Hmm. I call her Winc.

MizMaid: Scratch, how do you know Win is a she?

Winc: ::grinning:: MizMaid, right!

Scratch: Well, MizMaid, she's fairly clever. That's one clue. And in this room that's what you get to be. A She for a day.

MizMaid: Non, ma chérie, you get to be you.

Private Message to Winc

Scratch: I think your Maid's a guy, tho. Don't you?

Winc: Yup. I asked her about favorite books. She list=ed dead white boy authors all.

Scratch: All? Shew-w-w. She appears to be holding court right now. Bet s/he's over 50.

Winc: ::sadly:: I think so . . . how do they do that?

Scratch: "They?"

Winc: ::muttering:: men, grabbing center stage.

Scratch: I dunno, I thought it was pretty graceful.

Winc: Funny, I didn't think it was graceful. Ze prefaced going back on to the main screen with "Watch this," then took over.

Scratch: Huh. You are so hard on men sometimes. Do you realize when you're being a "straight girl" that you're not as hard on them? ::ducking::

Winc: ::eyes going wide::

Scratch: Uh huh.

Winc: That is weird. True. And weird.

Scratch: But you're neutral tonight, aren't you? Actually, what are you?

Winc: I have no idea.

MizMaid: Win, read Scratch's profile, you'll like it.
Winc: Nice profile there, Scratch.

Private Message to Scratch

Scratch: Heehee. ::blush:: you know, I'm playing darling little boy to Maid's benevolent mother. Happens every time. Feel embarrassed.

Winc: How do you know Maid's not playing you as darling little gay girl?

Scratch: Whoa.

Winc: Uh huh.

You have left "The Women's Room."

END SCRATCH JOURNAL ENTRY

PERSONAL LOG, JABBATHEHUT

I have issued a warning, as I do from time to time, to my young, energetic friend. Perhaps he will actually retain the thread of this conversation.

To: Toobe
From: Jabbathehut
Subj: Patterns

I wanted to make you aware of a stirring, my friend. Certain elements of the police persuasion are wending their way towards some truths. I have no faith in their detective powers, nor their ability to interpret.

But, they are starting to realize that many of us are not what we appear.

All this means they will be making quite a show of those who masquerade. You, of course, will not be so silly as to lose any bypasses and lead them to your lair.

In short, do not for a moment sign on casually without bypass codes; even if these detectives don't catch any aberrations, their computers automatically will.

—J.

To: Jabbathehut
From: Toobe
Subj: Whoa!

What's the big deal? So what if we sign on as different people? Jesus, don't they have anything better to do?

—T.

To: Toobe
From: Jabbathehut
Subj: Patterns

They're ostensibly after those who break laws in cyberspace, and ostensibly crimes directed towards children. But you'll learn that threats to children are always the sword held up as the first weapon of invasion. No, they're after much bigger fish, and many of us will get caught in the net, purely by accident, not by design. They won't ask questions. They'll simply arrest people.

—J.

To: Jabbathehut
From: Toobe
Subj: Goofy patterns

I've never seen you so ominus, however you spell it. But I think I could take your warning much easier if I could get around like you do. How the heck did you intercept those memos?

—T.

To: Toobe
From: Jabbathehut
Subj: Not so fast, Bub

(May I urge you to use your spellcheck tool?) All I can tell you is that you, like Dorothy, have had the power all along. But unless you know how to cover your tracks, don't go anywhere you can't immediately get out of.

Fighting God,

—J.

To: Jabbathehut
From: Toobe
Subj: Paranoid

Hey, don't worry. I wouldn't. Talk to you soon.

—T.

END JABBA PERSONAL LOG

TOOBE ENTRY

I just did a bunch of memos with Jabba about this police thing and assured her everything was cool. Then I promptly turned around and started messing around with Jabba's whole package of bypasses. What's wrong with me? I started charting her movements, working up to cracking just about every area on the Net. It was so much fun! There were Pentagon files, phone networks, universities, the works.

But did I stop there? Nope. One simple little code I had completely overlooked turned out to be this magic lamp, and boom! I was into the database of ACI, Allied Consumer Industries. Then into some police bulletin board. And that's where I acted like some addict going through a dumpster. I was just soaring around that place, reading memos and shit. Leaving a trail that might as well have said, Go find Toobe, he lives right there, and he works right here, and his friends are A-Z, and his dad does this, and everything except, thank gawd, my connection with Jabba. Of course she has a shield that protects her from such mistakes. But my connection to everyone else; I handed it all over on a fucking platter. Fuck fuck fucking fuck.

END TOOBE ENTRY

WINC JOURNAL ENTRY

To: Winc
From: Scratch
Subj: Talking

I have been thinking about you a lot. Thinking and reading Gertrude Stein if you want to know you know. You know. Thinking when there is no thinking I think of you. Thinking about talking to you makes me want. Want to meet real time to ask questions as real as we can get I mean online.

A room has been created that is I have created this room. This room is called "Woods" to which you might go.

—S.

Online Host

***** You are in room "Woods" *****

Scratch: ::Soft carpet of needles, sunlight filtering through trees::
Winc: ::kicking the leaves ahead of me as I walk:: ::inhaling pine scent from the forest . . . happy::
Scratch: OK, so my mind's been spinning. I gotta know.
Winc: ::settling down into a large pile of leaves, listening::
Scratch: I have gone a lot into the male and female roles, for lack of a better model. If you were being a girl, I stressed a lot of girl stuff. In you I mean. And yet you refer to a "third space," . . .
Winc: Well, actually, I read that someplace.
Scratch: OK. I realized I *have* made a third space, for many people, not just you. And I wonder if I've made the girl space too big, gone too far the other way I mean.

Winc: ::listening::

Scratch: If you're a guy, maybe you feel rejected that way. That part of you. When we're online, that third space seems huge, you and I both are all things. Like when I call you dude, it's not something I usually call girls.

Winc: Yes, I make that kind of space for you, too. Third, fourth, fifth . . . I dunno

Scratch: Ahhh. Point is: I don't want you to repress any of that! I mean, third space should be everything and nothing, as they say.

Winc: ::letting my fingers trail along the edges of a dead leaf . . . listening::

Scratch: Maybe you feel you have to "bring it down," restrain yourself? Like maybe you think I wouldn't like you as a boy? Because I'm a het man or a lesbian?

Winc: ::pulling my knees up beneath my chin, thinking:: I agree with you that the space we share, like right now, is very much "third" space . . . genderless as it can be . . . where each of us is talking.

Scratch: ::listening, watching you::

Winc: Yet when it comes to love, romance, sex, perhaps a little S/M . . . ::breaking leaf into little bits:: umm . . . This is hard . . .

Scratch: Yes, go on . . . I'm with you.

Winc: ::laughing:: All my life I never *really* fit into "girl" or "boy." Always felt outside, y'know?

Scratch: ::Chewing on blade of grass, nodding::

Winc: For so long, I've *wanted* to be just one or the other, some gender I can hang with full-time, but now that I *can* be whatever, here online . . .

Scratch: ::gently:: Let me guess . . . why bother choosing?

Winc: ::chewing lip, nodding:: Exactly. I don't want to get stuck in *any* of this, don't want to freeze into either. Don't want to lose any sense of myself as boy or . . .

Scratch: So you *are*—

Winc: Wait a minute. ::curling toes inside my boot::

Scratch: ::going quiet, looking up at you, soft eyes::

Winc: ::looking back, grateful:: You're still trying to find out what I "really" am, but I'm *being* who I really am! Right now. We're talking about all of us being boy and girl inside, not what we live as in the so-called real world.

Scratch: Right, sorry.

Winc: But at the risk of breaking out into song, I enjoy being a girl.

Scratch: ::softly:: What is boy? What is girl? Heehee.

Winc: Right, good point, but I'm just getting into exploring something, a softer strength, and that's *amazing* to me.

Scratch: Yes. You mean not just the sex of girl, but a feminine kind of girl?

Winc: Yes. ::softly:: I always thought I was too tall, awkward to be feminine that it'd be really, really stupid. ::looking off into the forest::

Scratch: Wow. I just realized that if you really are a girl, that sentence would fit. And if you really are a boy, it would, too.

Winc: ::shrugging:: Yeah . . .

Scratch: OK. See, what really gets me with these boxes is that people might miss out on how wonderful you are . . .

Winc: ::blushing::

Scratch: . . . because of the *packaging*. We all miss each other that way.

Winc: ::gently:: You can't prevent that.

Scratch: I feel stuck in my real-life persona, but I love exploring variations. It's so heady. I never got to be this particular form of human until now, online.

Winc: You mean, you're a guy, but you're being a particular kind of guy for once? Or you're a girl, and you're being a particular kind of girl right now?

Scratch: Yes! I can be androgynous, but I'm exploring something more specific.

Winc: ::looking up at you, questioning::

Scratch: I'm not trying to be coy. I just want to keep the discussion more abstract. As soon as we know each other's sexes, it limits us.

Winc: You mean genders.

Scratch: Oh, yeah. Sex means something else, eh?

Winc: Right, I use sex to mean biological distinction. Gender is a personal or cultural category of human.

Scratch: Sex is biology . . . gender is . . . wow. Gonna have to think about that one.

Winc: Uh huh. So what is it you're exploring?

Scratch: That lots of people respond *sexually* to this form of me. Some of them wish I would be more yang, some more yin, but there's still a sexual response! From different levels within one gender, and from different genders.

Winc: Whoa!

Scratch: Yeah! I get more yang when more yin types are around. It's weird.

Winc: ::settling back against a large tree, listening, fascinated:: You mean, if you're being a hippie boy, you get more response from hippie girls, and if you're being a gay man, you get responses from other gay men.

Scratch: Yes. But it goes deeper. Within the gay men's group, there are maybe 100 other more ways of being yin and yang. Like you just keep going down down down into the variations.

Winc: ::a bit confused:: You mean like people have to go *some* kind of yin when someone else is yang?

Scratch: Exactly! They can't help it! Even if they're really macho with one kind of person, if they met up with another macho person, they might get less macho.

Winc: So gender is interactive.

Winc: Scratch?

Winc: You still there?

Scratch: Oh, fine, you sum all that up in one perfectly succinct sentence.

Winc: ::blushing:: I've been working on it.

Scratch: Well, the more I think about it, the more I panic: whoamIwhoamIwhoamIwhoamIwhoamI . . .

Winc: Oh hon.

Scratch: If I'm talking to a guy and all of a sudden he becomes a girl, what does that make me? Especially if I'm attracted?

Winc: ::softly, slowly:: Hmm.

Scratch: And then I go to the store, to the park, a bar, to work, and I'm told: You are _____. Even though I was born as a biological male/female, I'm *supposed* to belong to one gender.

Winc: ::nodding, listening intently::

Scratch: I haven't been as willing to push, and let go, and just float ::looking around:: out here . . .

Winc: ::murmuring:: yes yes yes.

Scratch: . . . and if our two genderless spaces are attracted to each other, as they clearly seem to be, no matter the package . . . why did *we* of all people . . . immediately put them into such tight extremes of male/female?

Winc: Yes, good question. ::leaning over, kissing you gently:: Because we're frightened? Human? Because we recognize that we have to take that journey and we want to lay in provisions?

Scratch: Yeah! And because one needs traction in order to make any movement at all?

Scratch: Winc?

Scratch: Hey did I say something bad?

Winc: No no no. You said *traction*. That makes so much sense. That makes pieces come together into a whole. Gender is interactive and dependent on traction. Cool!

Scratch: Oh man. So deep. I gotta take a break. Brb.

END WINC JOURNAL ENTRY

To: Editor, They/Them magazine
From: D.I. Drew
Subject: Two Little Words, So Many Meanings

Hi Asa,

Those two words being: sex and gender. I found it interesting how early this area became a snarl in the discussion. People in 'the gender community' now have all sorts of definitions for sex and gender. But we understand those definitions differently from each other. We can't just sit down and talk and know what everyone else means by those words. Oddly, I notice the more terms we introduce, the more confusing and even restricted things get.

For example, I blithely summarize myself as a dyke, polyamorous, kinky, sometimes asexual; my gender is nonbinary (currently), and femme (mostly). And that still doesn't say much about me. I love how simple things seem to be between these two; they just love each other.

Cheers,

Drew

NARRATIVE ENTRY, JABBATHEHUT

Wally Budge is reading a full page ad in his favorite tageblatt, *The Daily News*. It reminds him of his old days as a beat cop in NYC. Nowadays, he walks his beat on a screen, in whatever race they sign him up for. He was a lot happier, he realizes, when the only pressure he got came from upstairs. Now everyone's getting into the act. To wit. . . .

A PUBLIC APPEAL FROM CONCERNED CITIZENS

In June of this year, a 12-year-old child was repeatedly assaulted via electronic mail by evil men interested in tarnishing her.

The nation's security is being compromised by the dissemination online of top security documents.

Terrorists obtain access to electronic files, which they turn around as weapons that threaten the fabric of democracy.

Yet the government, and its all-too-willing sponsor, Allied Consumer Industries, do nothing.

We concerned citizens have formed a grassroots network: Family Values Above All. We call for the immediate apprehension and severe punishment of these criminals, and a tightening of restrictions regarding the Network. And so, we pray:

God, help us care for our children. Give us wisdom to fashion regulations that will protect the innocent. Guide our Government when they consider ways of controlling the pollution of online intercourse and how to preserve one of our greatest resources: The minds of our children and the future and moral strength of our Nation. Give us the power and the might of your own arm so that we may rise up in Your Name and strike down any individual or government who opposes Your will, on earth or here in cyberspace. Amen.

Wally Budge shakes his head wearily as he scans a list of approximately 500 individuals and organizations, in 8-point type. As if that weren't enough, a fat packet of documents awaits—hard copy, no less. Replies, at last, from Allied Consumer Industries regarding his queries. Approaching perhaps his first break of the day, Budge flops his bulky frame farther back into his squeaky chair and reads the first one.

Dear Lt. Budge:

In response to your department's request for persons who fit the demographic profile of conflicting consumer patterns, I have the following match:

Onscreen name: Noh
Online service: CompuServe
Income: $35,000/yearly

This person is a white male, 25 years old, frequents Young Christians, Married but Restless, and Trivia II approximately four times a week. Mr. Noh has requested information regarding retirement funds, hemorrhoid medication, subscriptions to *TV Guide*, *PC Computer*, and *The Saturday Evening Post*. A number of adjacent advertising products have been requested relating to consumer products targeted to elder Black females, which we can forward to you if you are interested, but each seems to fall outside the parameters of your search. We are having our database checked for a programming error, as this is clearly impossible. Our apologies. Within the narrow bands of your department's request, we have come up with this name and one other. The other person's income was below $10,000 and unfortunately, we discard such persons after 3 months.

One cigarette smoking away in the ashtray, another wedged between tight lips, Budge is not pleased. Noh? Never heard of him. He scans the next memo:

Onscreen name: Deafkid
Online service: America Online
Income: unknown

Subject is 17, orders a wide range of home security products, frequents the deaf-disability forums only, and is a frequent user. We are certain this is the candidate you were seeking in regards to the profile you requested. We can release more information, if you like.

I have to ask you, will you be staging a sting operation to apprehend him?

"Someone's been reading too many action adventure novels," he mutters out loud. Deafkid, huh? Well, at least that's something. He shuffles a few memos, and plucks out another at random.

Onscreen name: Miss Thing
Online service: Renaissance Technical Institute
Income: $55,000/yearly

Miss Thing buys a wide range of products not consistent with her profile. In addition to the usual feminine hygiene products, she also requests information about tools, lawn products, and geriatric goods, rarely buying anything at all to date, but we feel confident that the target advertising will result in increased consumption shortly. Miss Thing came to our attention for the inconsistent profile you are looking for. We find it hard to believe that she is who she says she is. In addition, she has listed her occupation as welder, which is highly unlikely.

Unlikely, but consistent, Budge thinks ruefully. As he has begun to suspect, his perp is Black, female, disabled, young, old, Asian, male, gay, straight, a cross-dresser, a child, an old woman.

"How the hell am I supposed to find someone like that? How am I supposed to find someone who thinks like that?"

He slams down the sheaf of useless paper. "Oh, we're hot on that old trail now."

Idly, he flicks a dead cockroach off the edge of his desk. Shelly's poison is working.

Disgusted, he glances at his screen, hoping to find word from Typhoid Mary.

Nope.

END JABBA NARRATIVE ENTRY

SCRATCH JOURNAL ENTRY

Scratch: Different people pull different things out in me. ::quietly:: I usually don't like when the woman in me is pulled out . . . by someone else I mean. I did it once when I dressed up in drag. I mean stockings and heels. But, I hate it being yanked out by aggressive women or stupid men . . .

Winc: ::not breathing . . . listening::

Scratch: I just don't feel it! Whatever it is I'm supposed to, I don't feel it! But if there's a give and take, even if I'm being very "girl," it's quite wonderful.

Winc: ::gently:: maybe the chief thing going on with you is that you're a dominant type, no matter what gender.

Scratch: Dominant type?

Winc: ::very gently:: When we were playing het characters, when we were gay guys, you took the "lead" both times.

Scratch: True. ::Sigh:: That disappoints me. I feel like such a shape-shifter in other ways . . .

Winc: ::fingers moving through the leaves::

Scratch: ::bewildered::

Winc: ::speechless::

Scratch: Don't like being dominated.

Winc: Like when I was Yar and starting to dominate you?

Scratch: Right . . . ::wriggling uncomfortably:: Makes me claustrophobic. But I don't want to smother *you*!

Winc: But you wanted to take me down as Yar?

Scratch: Right.

Winc: And suppose you had? Then what?

Scratch: In the best of all possible worlds?

Winc: Uh huh.

Scratch: Then I'd have set you free, so you could move again. Literally and figuratively.

Winc: Do you like playing the top?

Scratch: Emphasis on top, or playing?

Winc: ::smiling:: yeah.

Scratch: A lot of the time it's unconscious . . .

Winc: Jeeze, we're so similar, well I mean we fit together. I like playing the bottom . . .

Scratch: Ah. No matter the gender?

Winc: ::nodding:: No matter the gender. I spend so much of my real life days being warrior, fighting off labels, being in third space, I *like* the traction you and I create. ::blinking:: at-traction?

Scratch: Hah!

Winc: The idea of traction has been bubbling in my brain ever since you said it. So we need traction to realize desire and that would equal . . . attraction.

Scratch: That's what I meant earlier! Maybe you need a place to *stand* in order to act on desire, to feel desire.

Winc: ::smacking my forehead with palm of my hand:: DUH!

Scratch: We were initially drawn without roles/gender, but then chose personas to act out in, like ghosts who choose bodies to be in.

Winc: Ohhhhh good one. Boo! But most people don't play from a third space either. ::shivering:: Scratch . . .

Scratch: I can't think of one sexual connection where I haven't chosen some kind of role. What?

Winc: Whenever I post something about this genderless space, there's inevitably one person who's thinking it's a space with no desire. No! If anything it's desire of . . . everything, anything, nothing.

Scratch: ::smiling:: When I fucked you online, I mean, when it got deep, so to speak, it was the closest thing to being in genderless space, while being sexually intimate.

Winc: YES . . . I was . . . I was me. ::softly:: And I knew you were you.

Scratch: I didn't want to move or talk or breathe, I didn't want to change anything. That's why I was so quiet at the end there. When you were boy and I was girl.

Winc: Yessssss. And that, my darling, is what we call desire in a third space.

Scratch: Oh, great, *now* you can explain it on Geraldo . . .

Winc: ::cracking up::

Scratch: Guess what . . .

Winc: ::smiling:: what?

Scratch: I have to go . . .

Winc: ::small voice:: no.

Scratch: Um . . . I'm excited!

Winc: Oh, Scratch, I am too. ::blushing:: Excited at what?

Scratch: These ideas! You! Me!

Winc: ::kicking leaves up in the air::

Scratch: What do you see when you "see" me? ::bracing::

Winc: Ummmmm . . . ::shy smile:: Puck.

Scratch: From *Midsummer's Night*?

Winc: Yes.

Scratch: Oh good! That fits!

Winc: ::smiling, pulling a loose grape leaf out of your hair::

Scratch: I could talk with you for hours.

Winc: ::looking up at the sky through the treetops:: Ever think about being dominated, topped while you were more in yin space?

Scratch: Oh, yes. And it's happened sometimes. But it's short-lived. Scary.

Winc: ::nodding:: As it would be if you topped me while I was more in yang space.

Scratch: So, forget your actual gender, you're saying you are more inclined to the yin?

Winc: Yes, and you to the yang.

Scratch: But I don't want to be trapped.in that either!

Winc: You can't solve everything all at once.

Scratch: Frankly, the first time I thought of your boyspace I wanted to top that. And now I don't want to always have to top everything, like some rutting dog pissing on every tree.

Winc: ::shiver:: Some of us *really* like that!

Scratch: ::shaking head:: I know. I've discovered that.

Scratch: OK, we leave together on the count of three . . . One

Scratch: Two

Winc: ::sniff::

Scratch: You say three!

Winc: thr . . . thr . . .

Scratch: You little . . . Why I oughta . . .

Winc: thr . . . . eeeeeeeee!

Scratch: Bye doll.

Winc: Doll? Isn't that a particularly female term?

Scratch: &*(_(*&%$$#

Winc: ::waving:: but is it goodbye or hello?

END SCRATCH JOURNAL ENTRY

NARRATIVE ENTRY, JABBATHEHUT

The little hippie chick is still off on her mission. Another interoffice memo flashes:

To: FBCS Investigations
From: Undersec'y LaBouchere
Subj: Profiles

We got a note that you've received several profiles. This is wonderful news! Please begin procedures to apprehend the perpetrators in connection with fraudulent misuse of Internet service. If we move swiftly and publicly, we can make an example of them, and the govt and the FBI liaison can go back to their real jobs.

Good work; that was fast!

—L.

P.S. Why are you still using your department's generic account?

P.P.S. You requested wording of the law making Registration mandatory. Attached Executive Order from the president. Note: Section 3, Paragraph 6: Enforcement, Arrest and Arraignment

Budge writes a conversation with himself on a yellow legal pad:

Who are these guys? Gals. Whatevers.
They're my perps, that's who they are.
But what exactly are they perpetrating?

He takes a deep drag on his cigarette.

Is there any criminal intent in this dance of theirs?
Doesn't matter. There's a law, and they're breaking it.

"Alright Miss/Mister Toobe," he says out loud in his best Telly Savalas, "ready or not, here I come."

END JABBA NARRATIVE ENTRY

05
ARE WE ON, BUTCH?

TOOBE ENTRY

FUNNY OF THE DAY

> My writing is as clear as mud, but mud settles and clear streams run on and disappear . . .
>
> —*Gertrude Stein, Lectures in America*

(It was Scratch who turned me on to Gertrude Stein.)

I don't see how monks wrote down everything in history without freaking out over their scrolls and spilling ink all over the place. No wonder history is all screwed up. This was in the paper today; if I were a monk writing this out, there'd be this big blot of ink messing up the screen:

"Vaders" Identified by Net Police

by Thomas Fulton

An unnamed official close to the president has indicated that the Federal Bureau of Census and Statistics is rapidly closing in on two Registration evaders, known as Vaders. Longtime abusers of the Internet, the suspects are known as "Scratch" and "Winc." Their real names were not released.

The anonymous source said that the two Vaders first came to FBCS attention because they are not Registered. In addition, Scratch and Winc are only two of many aliases used by the pair.

"Of course, that in itself is not a crime," said LaBouchere, who refused to confirm or deny that these two have been targeted, "but any extraordinary number of screen names held by a single individual is what sends our antennae up. If we discover that none of the aliases are Registered, we know we have a criminal profile."

Again, the undersecretary refused to admit that the aforementioned Scratch and Winc fall into that category, but this reporter can read the writing on the cyber-walls. Can you, Scratch and Winc?

Jesus fucking Christ! What is the crime? Hundreds of people must fit that profile. Why those two? I'm Registered, but I use lots of different personas too. I got into this stuff for more freedom, not less!

END TOOBE ENTRY

NARRATIVE ENTRY, JABBATHEHUT

Budge has been staring into the screen for the past five hours. His fingers dance across the keyboard. He's found a room entitled, "Don't Send Me Private Messages," so he can practice how to "surf" the internet. And an unwanted guest has shown up.

Private Message to Ms. Budge

GoodGuy: I just want to get to know you, that's all. I won't hurt you, really.

Ms. Budge: Dammit, I am *not* a woman, knock it off, will you?

GoodGuy: I'm not like all the rest of the guys you meet online, honest.

Ms. Budge: ::evenly:: And what if I told you I was a cop. A *male* cop, and you could be arrested for . . . *harassment*.

GoodGuy: ROTFL! That's a good one, baby. Even if you were a cop, how do you think you'd make it *stick*? Speaking of stick . . . ::chuckle::

Ms. Budge: Look, I have work to do, so piss off.

GoodGuy: Stupid bitch! You're probably a dyke!

GoodGuy has left the room.

Private Message to Ms. Budge

RamStud: What are you wearing?

Ms. Budge: Can't you read? The name of this room is DON'T SEND ME PRIVATE MESSAGES!

RamStud: Oh bite me!

The good lieutenant was beginning to see why people escape to chat rooms.

Private Message to Ms. Budge

SubRobert: Hello! I hear you're a police officer. Will you put me in handcuffs, please? I've been a very naughty boy.

Ms. Budge: If you heard I was a cop, you heard I was a man. Buzz off, faggot.

SubRobert: ::shivering:: Yes ma'am, Thank you for the insult, ma'am.

Ms. Budge: LEAVE ME ALONE!!!

SubRobert: Can I sniff your panties?

Ms. Budge: No.

SubRobert: I'll pay for the postage.

Ms. Budge: No.

SubRobert: Really. I'm being real.

Ms. Budge: No!

SubRobert: Yes ma'am, so sorry ma'am, goodbye ma'am

::leaving in tears::

::tears are real::

SubRobert has left the room.

Budge scratches at an itch halfway down his back where he can't reach.

"Poor guy," he says out loud to no one, mousing over to his desktop and selecting two files: Scratch.doc and Winc.doc

Clickety-clack-clickety-clack, and he drops both files into a folder named "Perps."

END JABBA NARRATIVE ENTRY

To: Editor, They/Them magazine
From: D.I. Drew
Subject: Folk heroes

Hi Asa,

It's scary, disorienting, infuriating, and to my cynical eye, utterly predictable that what Scratch and Winc (and Toobe) feared came to pass. Remember from the well-worn history of this part of the story that the Bureau was issuing warrants for any names they could match to unregistered users. Tracking them down in real life and imposing fines and jail time. And I found in a fast and furious archive between Lt. Budge and his boss that he was getting annoyed at this waste of resources but was beginning to question what the crime actually was. Nonconformity?

Of course it was impossible to match online users with real people. Lt. Budge closed in on our two lovebirds, and it was the moment he called them "perps" that Scratch and Winc became folk heroes. They were, as usual, oblivious!

It was fun to comb through literally hundreds of archives to find their love story instead of just focusing on the sting. Here's a tasty little exchange where they "discovered" butch and femme. Here I am all progressively polyamorous nonbinary etc but this chat gave me the flutters!

Cheers,

Drew

SCRATCH JOURNAL ENTRY

Got a letter from Winc that led to our next adventure.

> **To:** Scratch@aol.com
> **From:** Winc@aol.com
> **Subj:** Wait'll you see this!
>
> Scratch,
>
> I was prowling the bulletin boards and found this whole section called Lesbian Boards. *Finally* some intelligent conversation! But that's not the best part. There's a message board called Butch/Femme. Have you ever heard of this? I swear, it's the best thing ever! Look at this message:
>
> > **To:** Brknstck
> > **From:** Fembot
> > **Subj:** Imitating the dominant paradigm
> >
> > Dear Brknstck,
> >
> > Oh fiddlesticks! The lesbian construct of butch/femme is no more an imitation of the "dominant paradigm" than girl/girl sex is an imitation of hetsex. Butches (at least the ones *I* know, and I know quite a few) don't want to be men, as you intimate in your last posting. Nor do femmes want to "pass for straight."
> >
> > You seem to be a good woman, Brknstck. Dear heart, please hear me when I say I am *not* interested in attracting any men.
> >
> > I can't speak for butches, and I can't speak for all femmes. We all do this dance a bit differently from one another. But what *I* see as the soul of the thing is this.
> >
> > Courtship.
> >
> > ::slow smile::

Flirtation.

::blowing you a kiss::

Gallantry and graciousness.

When a butch is gallant on my behalf, it just makes my knees go weak. And if I can make a butch's eyes spin just by wearing a tight dress, you'd better *believe* I'm going to have more than a few choice tight dresses at hand!

Butch/femme is an expression of *equality,* Brknstck.

Look, in heterosexual terms, the man has all the power, and the woman is subordinate and obedient, at least that's the default setting. Oh you can dial the strength of it up or down but nobody usually bothers to change it. Butch/femme is a change. It's *sharing* of strength. I call myself a "high femme," but I know how to change a tire, and more often than not I like to be on top.

::laughing lightly::

I don't mind that you personally don't want to take on the roles of either butch or femme, but please don't censor me or any one of my brave butch or femme sisters.

Can we shake hands on that, in solidarity?

∴★ ∵★ ★∴° ★

｡☆* °☆* °☆

*★｡ *★

∵☆* LOVE ∴☆｡

°★｡ ｡★*

∵☆* *☆∵°

∵★*° ★∵ Fembot

Scratch!!! Is that cool, or what?

Can we try butch/femme?

Come on, come play with me!

::wriggling happily::

—Winc

PS Guess which one *I* wanna be? heehee.

PPS How ever did she make that heart???

To: Winc
From: Scratch
Subj: Femme/butch

Femme/butch, huh? (I reversed the names for a little equality.) You get into the weirdest things. Isn't that kind of tired? I mean, '50s lesbian thing?

What is it exactly that compels you?

—S.

To: Scratch
From: Winc
Subj: Snarls of all sorts

Tired? You're asking *me* if butch/femme is tired? ::laughing merrily:: Sounds awfully refreshing to me. In-your-face fuck you to homogeneity.

—W.

To: Winc
From: Scratch
Subj: Butch and femme

Hmm, maybe b/f is another kind of traction?

Now I've found a posting from a woman who calls herself a butch. Thank gawd you want to be femme, the butch one made more sense to me. Does this mean that in real life you're a woman and I'm a man? Sigh.

—S.

To: Scratch
From: Winc
Subj: Femme and butch

Re: you as butch. I'm so glad! Because I don't understand half the butch posts on that board. Maybe you can explain them to me. Like what's a "stone butch"? And . . .

You say, 'Does this mean that in real life we're a woman and a man?'

::stepping lightly away from you, moving toward the window where the soft breeze blows the curtains gently into the room, ze begins to dance à la Isadora Duncan, and speaks while dancing::

I'm a woman?

You're a man?

I *seem* to recall a certain

riot grrl

who had her way with a certain

skateboard dude.

::stopping dead still, looking at you deadpan::

Or had you forgotten our first evening of bliss?

::resuming hir dance::

Are we on, butch?

—W.

To: Winc
From: Scratch
Subj: Are we on

Hmm, well can we at least spin it like Bogie and Bacall?

Stone butch? I think it means "very butch" or it refers to the one who just pleases the other one but never gets off herself. Kind of blows me away, because they say butch lesbians are imitating men, but I don't think you'd see many men doing that for women. Nice contradictions there, let's do it.

—S.

To: Scratch
From: Winc
Subj: Bogie and Bacall

I love Bogie and Bacall!

What was the butch post you liked? I am *so* intrigued by this.

—W.

To: Winc
From: Scratch
Subj: B. posts

The post I saw was this:

> Yeah, I tend to hide my emotions and go for girls who wear theirs on their sleeves. 'Men's clothes' are just more

> comfortable for me. That doesn't make me male, any more than straight women who started wearing pants in the '60s were trying to be men. Too simple. The way I relate to women isn't about conquest, or trying to dominate her (unless she wants it ::grin::), but a celebration: strong, proud butch, and strong, proud femme.
>
> There just aren't words yet, I think. I know, and my girlfriend knows, what we mean. But it's hard to explain.
>
> —Spike

Kinda got to me, know what I mean?

—Scratch

To: Scratch
From: Winc
Subj: Ohhh, If *that*'s butch . . .

. . . then I like butches. You're kind of like that, you know? ::smiling:: Wonder what you would call yourself, if anything. ::raising a finger to your lips:: I'm not really asking. Well, maybe a little. But if you're ready to try it out, then let me set the scene a bit:

::stepping back quickly, ze draws a hand across hir face, as though ze were lifting a veil into position. Hir features lose their focus, soften and blend. A well-practiced smile forms on hir lips, the smile of a girl who's been around the block a few times. Her hair falls in taunting copper waves. She stands facing you, close enough to feel her breath at your shoulder. She's tall in heels, just a bit shorter than you. She smooths out her skin-tight dress, looks up at you. When she speaks, her husky voice goes right into your heart, to a place you thought you'd walled off years ago::

"Let's go to a Private room called Key Largo. Name the time . . ."

::she looks back over her shoulder::

"You know how to name the time, don't you?"

::laughing softly::

"You put one hand *here*, and the other hand *here*. I'll do the rest."

::the door clicks shut behind her, the sound of her sharp stiletto heels echoes down the hall, fades away, and she's gone::

—W.

To: Winc
From: Scratch
Subj: Key Largo

::moan:: Wow.

Um:

She glances up toward the mirror over the bar. She's got a stern, serious face, the kind of face that looks good to a certain kind of woman. She stopped wearing anything but men's clothes years ago; these duds fit her like a glove. Wide-brimmed hat pulled down over one eye, baggy pants that keep a lot to themselves, and two-toned shoes, her favorite pair. She sees the broad in the corner and shakes her head, grinning at the bartender. "Why didn't you tell me she walked in the door, Jack?" The bartender shrugs and wipes a glass. "I knew you'd notice her sooner or later, pal." In spite of her better judgment, she lifts her hat, and says in a low voice, heavily inflected with the state of New York:

"Key Largo it is, tomorrow, noon. Don't be late."

SCRATCH JOURNAL ENTRY CONT'D

I may not know much about tech, but I do know about old-fashioned greed, and Big Bizness is already worming their wormy ways into "the Net." Allied Consumer Industries (ACI) is an insidious consortium of marketing companies, just as creepy as marketing groups can be. They can't narrow down the demographic because people are being everywhere as everybody. So how do you target ads to multiple personas? People don't want to be pinned down to any one type. My kind of people. Hee hee.

Toobe tells me that there are various mysterious announcements warning people to be on the alert for me and Winc for god's sake. But a happy accident is that there are more than just one Scratch or Winc!

Random sample of rooms where people swear they saw them:

Alt.sex.fetish

Alt.noob.chat

Alt.deaf.bbs

Alt.bellybutton

Alt.movies.action

Alt.dykes.inyerface

Cracks me up. Finding a needle in a haystack of needles.

END SCRATCH JOURNAL ENTRY

NARRATIVE ENTRY, JABBATHEHUT

"I don't know what to make of this, Shel," Budge says flatly.

Reaching into his jacket pocket, he withdraws several neatly folded pages of text logs of his chat room adventures earlier that day.

"What's with this 'stupid bitch,' and 'bite me,' and, well, worse; you'll read it."

She skims quickly, mouth pursing.

"I'm a regular guy," he continues, confused. "I'm not some pervert or psycho." He quietly concludes, "Every one of those people was downright mean. And for no reason, Shel. For no goddamn reason."

"Every one of those men was downright mean," she says, her voice slow and even. "And the reason is, you weren't one of them. You were a woman."

"I don't get it," he says finally. "You know me."

"That's the trouble; there's not that many like you." Her voice gently challenging, her fingers resting on the back of his hand. "But you still haven't got a clue, have you?"

He grins despite his discomfort. "Aw, c'mon. 'All men are creeps,' is that what you're gonna say? G'head, I can take it. I'm a big boy."

She looks at him evenly for a moment.

"What do you suppose it would be like," she says, "if every time you signed online—no, every time you walked out your front door, you could expect that kind of treatment? You'd never know where or when it would come from, but you're always ready for it. Under the smile, under the come-on, even under the greatest words you've ever heard, someone's waiting to hammer you if you don't respond just how they want you to. . . ."

She can see him strain to grasp it. He's working hard.

"So you're saying that Scratch and Winc . . . they're women? That's why they keep changing, running . . ."

". . . playing," she finishes his thought. "They're playing."

That smile of hers.

"They're free. That's what they are."

"Huh?"

She continues, absently stroking the back of his hand.

"I don't know if Scratch and Winc are women or not. No one does; maybe that's why everyone's talking about them. But they could be Black men, Latina women, that guy in the wheelchair outside our building, old people. The Asians at SUNY. Gays. Lesbians. Children. Anyone who can't speak up because they're afraid of being put in their place. Or worse."

"Whatever they are, they're showing us a place where there's no fear."

Their eyes meet. He's dizzy; it's because of her, and she knows it.

END JABBA NARRATIVE ENTRY

SCRATCH JOURNAL ENTRY

Whew, Key Largo! I logged it all!

Online Host

***** You are in room "Key Largo" *****

Johnny: Hey, dollface. What'll ya have?

Frankie: ::turning:: You talkin' to me?

Johnny: Yeah, I'm talkin' to you. You see any other good-lookin' broads in here?

Frankie: ::giving you a long even look:: And how many times have you used *that* line? ::lazy smile::

Johnny: How often you give a slow turn like that? ::small twitch of lips::

Frankie: ::slow smile:: Only when I'm expectin' to see something I like.

Johnny: And did ya?

Frankie: ::nodding:: Oh, yeah.

Johnny: So, whaddya drinkin'?

Frankie: ::pulling out a cigarette:: Comfort and coke. Light on the coke.

Johnny: Comin' right up.

Frankie: ::looking deep into your eyes::

Johnny: ::looking into your eyes, lighting cigarette:: So what brings you to these parts?

Frankie: ::shrugging:: Maybe I heard the ponies are runnin' sweet . . . then again . . . maybe I'm the one who's runnin.

Johnny: You got a weakness for ponies? Or runnin'?

Frankie: ::throwing my head back laughing:: Right now, I've got a weakness for good-looking butches.

Johnny: ::ducking head:: Is that right? ::sly smile:: Kinda bold, ain'tcha sister?

///GOOD EVENING, EVERYTHING ALL RIGHT?///

Johnny: Oh, sure sure, it's all right.

Frankie: ::turning:: Hello, Eye . . . yeah, me and my . . . escort, we're fine.

Johnny: Nothin' doing here, Eye.

///FINE. HAVE A NICE ONE. LOVE THAT MOVIE!///

Eye has left the room

Johnny: Movie? Oh, the room name . . . Jesus! Must've followed ya in.

Frankie: Scratch?

Johnny: Yes, Winc?

Frankie: That's scary! ::moving closer to you, shaking::

Johnny: Yeah. Since s/he came *in* to ask, maybe the Eyes can't monitor us from outside the room.

Frankie: ::quietly:: Maybe, maybe not.

Johnny: You know, sweetheart, I might be bad news for ya.

Frankie: ::looking up into your eyes:: I've had my share of bad news.

Johnny: I bet you have.

But I'm on the run, see. You might say I got myself lost.

Frankie: ::arching an eyebrow:: Why ya runnin'?

Johnny: I got my reasons. What about you? [My screen just froze, Winc. Careful.]

Frankie: ::offhandedly:: I had a run-in with a . . . [huh? You signed on with a . . . you-know-what, right?]

Johnny: ::cupping your chin in my hand:: Maybe if it looks like an ordinary love scene, they won't bother us.

Frankie: ::pressing softly against you:: Yes.

Johnny: ::talking real low in your ear:: What's that perfume you're wearin'?

Frankie: ::laughing softly:: It's called Trouble. You like the smell of Trouble?

Johnny: No, but I can guarantee the scent will follow me.

Frankie: ::softly, almost to myself:: Trouble, spelled B-U-T-C-H.

Johnny: Maybe you should just be quiet for a minute. ::kissing you hard::

Frankie: ::struggling:: ::pulling back, breathing hard:: Pretty sure of yourself, aren't ya?

Johnny: No. I'm not. You're a new kind of trouble for me.

Frankie: ::wiping my mouth with the back of my hand::

Johnny: Sorry I got fresh.

Frankie: ::laughing low:: What did you say your name was?

Johnny: I didn't.

Frankie: ::sizing you up::

Johnny: Ladies first.

Frankie: ::smiling:: Some folks call me Frankie . . . and you're . . . ?

Johnny: Well, wouldn't ya know it? They call me Johnny.

Frankie: Just my luck.

Frankie: You know that story, don'tcha?

Johnny: There's a jukebox here. Maybe they got that song.

Frankie: ::turning, spotting the juke against the wall:: Play it, Johnny. Go ahead.

Johnny: Dance?

Frankie: Sure . . . why not. ::tugging my skirt down:: ::moving close into you, pressing my breasts against you::

Johnny: ::breathing in your scent above your head::

::pressing close to you, not speaking::

Frankie: ::pressing my lips to your white shirt, softly, leaving just a trace of red::

Johnny: ::feeling the softness of your dress:: You dance real good.

Frankie: ::tears springing to eyes, averting my face quickly::

Johnny: Hey, sweetheart, what is it?

Frankie: ::softly:: Damn. ::shaking my head:: Just keep holding me.

Johnny: No problem, doll. ::dancing out to the patio slowly::

Frankie: Maybe you're all right, Johnny. Maybe you're not like the rest of 'em.

Johnny: Oh, I probably am, sweetheart. But it looks like we got the same amount to lose.

Frankie: Tell me, Johnny . . . ::breaking away from you, gently::

Johnny: Yeah?

Frankie: You stone? ::holding my breath::

Johnny: ::stiffening:: Why ya gotta go and ask a question like that?

Frankie: ::softly:: Oh baby, c'mere. ::holding my arms out::

Johnny: What's it to you? ::slowly moving back close to you::

Frankie: ::softly:: Had to know, Johnny. It's OK.

Johnny: ::relaxing into you again:: Depends. I don't plan it, but it usually works out that way.

Frankie: ::running my fingers through your hair gently:: It's OK, Johnny.

Johnny: I ain't got no bones 'bout being a female. If that bugs you, you better buzz off now.

Frankie: ::pressing myself hard against you, taking your face in my hands:: ::kissing you hard::

Johnny: ::holding you tighter, kissing back:: ::Looking around:: Think we're really alone here?

Frankie: I hope we are.

Johnny: ::smiling:: Yeah, I know. But I want somethin' real bad, Frankie. Want it now.

Frankie: ::lazy smile:: What's that, handsome?

Johnny: You, dollface. We ain't got much time, so . . .

Frankie: ::nodding:: So . . .

Johnny: ::moving my hand lower:: So one thing I noticed about both of us bein' female . . .

Frankie: ::gasping, smiling, putting my arms up around your neck:: ::breathless:: What's that, Johnny?

Johnny: We can go to the can together.

Frankie: ::pulling back, raising a perfect eyebrow::

Johnny: ::whispering:: Come on, just for a minute.

Frankie: ::bursting out laughing:: The can?

Johnny: ::laughing with you:: Sorry to be crude. You just . . . you . . .

Frankie: ::rueful laugh:: I bring it out in ya, right? I always seem to do that with the good ones.

Johnny: Ladies Lounge is right over there, gorgeous. Join me?

Frankie: ::holding you back:: Hey, handsome . . .

Johnny: Come on, doll, let's do it before we gotta go.

Frankie: In there?

Johnny: Why not? It ain't polite to do what I wanna do out here by the bar.

Frankie: ::shrugging:: I saw some straight girls go in earlier, and . . .

Johnny: Yeah. They do get jumpy. Damn. ::moving my hands over your breasts:: Patio's deserted, I guess.

Frankie: ::whispering:: Patio's fine.

Johnny: You like stone butches?

Frankie: ::small smile:: I like butches. Stone or otherwise, I like 'em.

Johnny: Too many femmes . . . they're afraid. Don't want to touch us. Afraid we'll slap 'em down.

Frankie: ::nodding:: So then they don't touch you.

Johnny: Yeah . . . ::nuzzling your neck:: ::sliding hand down your thigh::

Frankie: ::bringing my hands up to your breasts, my eyes locked on your eyes, asking::

Johnny: Yeah. Yeah, do that.

///SORRY TO INTERRUPT, FOLKS.///

Frankie: What?

Johnny: What the fuck? What's up, Eye?

///THERE'S A SPECIAL ANNOUNCEMENT COMING OVER THE NET IN 7 MINUTES.. WE'RE SUPPOSED TO ALERT EVERYONE. DON'T SIGN OFF UNTIL YOU'VE SEEN IT.///

Frankie: Thanks, Eye.

Johnny: Thanks.

///HAVE FUN, YOU TWO. HEY . . .

WHICH ONE OF YOU IS BACALL?///

Johnny: With all due respect, sir or madam, we'd like a little privacy.

///::SHRUGGING:: JUST TRYING TO GET

INTO THE SPIRIT OF THINGS.

WHAT A GROUCH.///

Eye has left the room.

Frankie: ::breathing hard:: Maybe you shouldn't have—

Johnny: ::breathing hard for the wrong reasons::

Frankie: What's happening, Scratch? That isn't supposed to happen.

Johnny: Look, Winc, I don't want to sound paranoid, but . . .

Frankie: But?

Johnny: I think we gotta get outta here. I'll tell you by email.

Frankie: No, Scratch! Don't want you to leave!

Johnny: When the Net announcement comes, it'll stop all action anyway. ::pause:: I was so fucking turned on!

Frankie: I was so . . . you were?

Johnny: Of course! Weren't you?

Frankie: ::tilting my head, looking up at you through lowered lids:: Was I ever, handsome.

Johnny: Jesus! *Please* don't ever tell me who you really are! I mean *what* you really are.

Frankie: ::shaking my head, quiet::

Johnny: I can be anything with you! Don't tell me we finally hit your real persona: a tart from the '40s . . .

ATTENTION ALL NET USERS . . . A SPECIAL GOVERNMENT ANNOUNCEMENT WILL APPEAR IN 5 MINUTES.

Frankie: ::popping my gum:: And what if I was?

PLEASE STAND BY . . .

THE NET ANNOUNCEMENT WILL COMMENCE IN 1 MINUTE, PLEASE STAND BY . . .

Johnny: Let's go. It's rough to be kicked out. Better to saunter off on your own power.

Frankie: ::grabbing you, kissing you hard, sweet::

Frankie: Bye "Johnny"!

Johnny: Bye doll.

Somehow, another room magically popped up called Dark Corner Bar, occupied by only two people. Right. Neither of us signed off. I think we didn't feel "finished."

***** You are in room "Dark Corner Bar" *****

Frankie: ::closing my eyes, smiling, squeezing your breasts gently::

Johnny: ::sliding hand along your stockings, moving up under your dress:: ::turning your back to the lounge:: Oh, baby, you got a touch, you do.

Frankie: ::opening my legs a bit wider::

Johnny: ::sliding my knee in between your legs:: ::pushing you down on my thigh::

Frankie: Ahh! yesss.

Johnny: Ride, baby. Ride it for me.

Frankie: ::pushing down against your leg, eyes locked on yours::

Johnny: ::breathing:: You look so good. ::sliding hand in between your legs, dipping in::

Frankie: ::tossing my hair out of my face, riding your leg in time to the music::

Johnny: So nice and wet . . .

Frankie: ::riding your leg, more urgently:: ::standing up suddenly, widening my stance::

Johnny: ::sliding my fingers over your clit, one finger, then two, inside you::

Frankie: ::reaching up to your breasts, bringing my fingers around your nipples::

Frankie: Want you inside me . . . your hand. Now, please, baby!

Johnny: ::Looking around, can't resist::

Johnny: ::putting more fingers inside you . . . pushing hard::

Frankie: ::purring:: You are . . . ::gasp::

Johnny: ::rubbing your clit hard, breathing into your neck::

Frankie: ::rolling your nipples in my fingers, harder now, hips back and forth on your hand::

Johnny: ::my own wetness warm . . . ::riding the seam of my pants::

Frankie: ::bringing my hand down to between your legs::

Johnny: ::lifting you with my knee::

::pulling you to me, pushing my hand inside you::

Frankie: Everything I've got, Johnny. ::running my hand hard over your fly, squeezing down on your hand inside me::

Johnny: I'm not gonna lose it here, baby, but it sure feels good. ::dancing to the music, pushing my hand in and out::

END SCRATCH JOURNAL ENTRY (FILE CORRUPTED)

06

WHAT'S ALL THE TALK?

To: T. Sparrow
From: Drew
Subject: Sticky

Hi Dad,

Didn't you once tell me that "the Net" created revolutions for all different types of people? In those 1990s chat rooms folks felt safe enough to be themselves.

Deaf people could type, queer people could flirt, nerds could geek out . . . everyone had their own kind of safe space to find like-minded souls. And folks kind of watched out for harassment. If you did that, you were out! Am I being too idealistic about this?

Love,

Yer kid Drew

TOOBE ENTRY

To: Toobe
From: Jabbathehut
Subj: Time wasters

What have you been up to, mischievous one? Is this your doing? These are some messages I've scanned in chat rooms in the space of a single hour:

> Warrior Net: Scratch Wincs, Winc Scratches, the coolest dudes in the universe. They Rule!
>
> Cheating Husbands: Scratch is the most popular girl in our area, I cannot believe she is being pursued by cyberpolice. I wonder if we can help?
>
> Black Men on Black Men: Of course Winc's been gone for a while. Now I get it. Damn, what's he gotten himself into? Must have put it to an Eye ::evil grin::

This idol-worship is disgusting, to say the least, Master Toobe. Do these "people" not have anything better to do than speculate on the whereabouts of persons of no import?

—J.

To: Jabbathehut
From: Toobe
Subj: My friends

Those two persons are important to me, Jabba, but I get what you're saying. No, it wasn't me. It's a fucking epidemic. It's all cuz of some newspaper announcement.

—T.

To: Toobe
From: Jabbathehut
Subj: Friends

Ah, I see. (Must your prose be so purple so often? There are other words—many, in fact—in our English language.) Thank you for the explanation. How predictable.

—J.

To: Jabbathehut
From: Toobe
Subj: Swearing

I'm sorry, Jabba, I'm just upset now. Catch you later.

—T.

Well, I am. I am way freaked out. I haven't heard one word from Scratch or Winc. They don't even know what's going on out there, what with the govt going after anyone who isn't a Registered user. Worse, their names are out there! There was an announcement to turn in anyone who is known to be a Scratch and/or Winc! And what have they been doing? Playing "getting to know you."

END TOOBE ENTRY

NARRATIVE ENTRY, JABBATHEHUT

Wally Budge is getting a lot of mail, some useful, most of it not so much.

To: Investigations@FBCS.gov
From: Dgarner@hyperlink.com
Subj: Way sorry . . .

Hi Lieutenant, it's me, Winc. I want to make a deal—I want amnesty, the witness protection program thing, whatever you can give. I know how to get in touch with Scratch. I'll give hir up in exchange for leniency.

> I'll probably always hate myself for doing this. Scratch will hate me a whole lot more, but I have my reasons. So please, send an officer. I'll come peacefully. My name is Donald Garner, and I live at 3624 Baltimore Avenue, Apt. 8, in Philadelphia. Only this time, send an earthling. I *beg* you. The last officers to come to my apartment were from Alpha Centauri, and I . . .

Budge punches DELETE in disgust. Kooks, how many kooks out there are going to show up now as "Winc" or "Scratch"?

END JABBA NARRATIVE ENTRY

TOOBE ENTRY

The law may be after "Scratch" and "Winc," but all these people are "confessing" so there's no way to know who the real ones are. Poor cops are all dazed and confused (love that movie). Of course there were fakes but now it's gotten serious. People were uniting just to cause trouble—"I am Spartacus." (Jabba loves that movie)

I've been trying for days with no luck to reach Winc. When I finally heard back, ze was taking the government search about as seriously as ze takes anything.

END TOOBE ENTRY

ANONYMOUS CHAT ROOM LOG

Online Host

***** You are in room "The Tavern" *****

FredMan: No, I never met them but people aren't talking about anything else.

Frankie: Pour me a strong one, bub.

Bartender: You got it.

Frankie: ::winking at you:: Thanks.

Johnny: Make that two, barkeep.

Frankie: ::glancing over at the stranger::

Johnny: ::scratching my head:: How ya doin' doll.

Private Message to Johnny

Frankie: I am *so* discombobulated!

Johnny: Me too. Feel like I just got out of bed.

Frankie: ::purring:: Well, you did.

Ted: Me too. I've never met them. I don't know what all the fuss is about.

BarBun: Oh, I dunno, I've had a few dealings with Scratch. He's a real cutie.

Johnny: ::almost dropping drink::

Frankie: Hey, steady there, handsome.

Johnny: Thanks, doll.

Private Message to Johnny

Frankie: Scratch?

Johnny: What?

FredMan: What's the big deal, anyway? What'd they do?

Ted: They say trafficking in porn, but that's just a rumor.

BarBun: ::patting hair:: That doesn't sound like the Scratch I know.

Ted: ::quietly:: nor the one I know, either.

Private Message to Frankie

Johnny: Oh, gawd, BarBun. From some chat room . . .

Frankie: Uh, huh . . . and ::blush:: Ted's somebody I know, too.

Johnny: Winc, we gotta ask.

Frankie: ::gulp:: Go ahead, you're the butch.

Johnny: $@#%!

Johnny: ::scratching chin:: what's all the talk?

Frankie: Yeah, fill me in too.

FredMan: What?! These Scratch and Winc people, it's been all over the news.

Frankie: I steer clear of the news.
FredMan: Well, they were simply doing what we're all doing, only they got caught.
Frankie: Sounds like a government with too much time on its hands.
FredMan: You got that right.
Bartender: And they call it "breaking the law."
BarBun: Makes you want to show them how many of us "break the law."
FredMan: Yeah! What would they do if we all sent a letter to the govt, signed by all our other names!
Ted: A good idea, but I'm beginning to think they're tracing us all to our original accounts.
FredMan: ::snorting:: like they have that much time, or that many brains?

*** All private and public online services ***
A Public Safety Announcement
from
the United States Government
Bureau of Census and Statistics
presented with the cooperation of your local Net service provider
◊
This is to alert all citizens
to the presence of two suspected criminals
and known Registration evaders.
Their most common aliases are "Scratch" and "Winc."

Suspected activities constitute a grave threat to the safety of all Net users.
As true identities are as yet unknown, an all-nodes, all-database government search is underway with the full cooperation of the private sector, to affect apprehension and questioning.
Your government requests your cooperation as follows:
Forward exact date, time, and Net location of any encounter with "Scratch" or "Winc," under any alias.

Forward any and all evidence linking "Scratch" or "Winc" with illegal trafficking of Net access bypass codes, child pornography, or copyright infringement.

If you have participated in online commerce or exchange of any nature with "Scratch" or "Winc," forward details and scan your hard drive for potentially damaging computer viruses.

We apologize for interrupting your service temporarily, and we thank your local service access provider for their assistance in making this public safety announcement available to you.

End: PSA #309

FredMan: Jesus, it *is* true!

Frankie has left the room.

Johnny has left the room.

Ted: Did it say to forward our own chats with these people?

BarBun has left the room.

FredMan: It did say that. Hey, didn't you say you'd met one of them?

Ted has left the room.

FredMan: Nothing exciting ever happens to me.

END ANONYMOUS CHAT ROOM LOG

TOOBE ENTRY

To: Toobe
From: Winc
Subj: Natural born chillers

Don't worry, dude. ::throwing my head back with a pirate laugh:: har-r-r-r! They'll never take us alive! ::savage outlaw grin::

—W.

END TOOBE ENTRY

NARRATIVE ENTRY, JABBATHEHUT

Why, I ask you, why, did Toobe have to click on that strange little wiggling icon?

And now a too-cute giggle from his computer screen interrupts the detective's daydreams.

Looking up, he sees Typhoid Mary sashaying across his screen, her eyes positively aglow with a cyber-rendition of triumph.

"Hel-l-l-l-o-o-o-o-o, Missy Budge," she says brightly. "Look what *I* found!"

Before he has a chance to reply, the hippie chick opens her duffel bag and withdraws a . . . magic wand? She waves it over her head and giggles. "Presto," she says, "you are now connected." And Budge's screen is suddenly filled with a graphic image: the unfortunately bad high school photograph of Toobe.

At the same instant Budge is staring at the unbelievably young face of his only perpetrator, a similar stare-down is happening on a teenager's screen. Halfway across the world—or is it only across town?—Toobe is swallowing hard, gawking as suddenly into his own screen. For there he sees the unforgiving federal photo ID of Lieutenant Wally Budge.

Neither stirs. They stare at each other's photos, the detective and the kid, their hands frozen over their keyboards.

As one, two hands flash out toward two keyboards. The nicotine-stained finger wins, punching CAPTURE before the younger hand reaches ESCAPE.

And two photos vanish from two computer screens, leaving Budge with his jaw hanging open and an unsmoked cigarette burning between his fingers.

"He's a little kid," says Wally Budge aloud to no one. "Just a scared little kid."

"Got him, Boss," says Typhoid Mary. "Tracking sequence initiated and sustained. He can't get away now."

To: Henderson, Enforcement
From: FBCS Investigations
Subj: Top Priority/Scratch and Winc

Attaching electronic signature to this memo. Follow it down, will you? This Toobe guy? He's a minor. Keep me posted on every step. I'll have a warrant by the time you've got him.

—Wally

Lieutenant Wally Budge, senior investigator for the U.S. Federal Office of Internet Intelligence, Bureau of Census and Statistics, watches his message vanish from the screen, and whispers,

"A little kid."

A note: Predictably, law enforcement memos escalated because for a long spell, Toobe went offline. Yes. Frustrating to me as well. I will elaborate when the time comes.

END NARRATIVE JABBA ENTRY

07
SCARED

To: Editor, They/Them magazine
From: D.I. Drew
Subject: Gwynyth the Cyberwitch

Hi Asa,

So, Toobe is on the run. Enter Gwynyth, a longtime friend of Jabba's. Jabba describes her as a "cyberwitch," solitary, a brilliant thinker and engineer, albeit eccentric and entirely self-taught.

You can see how G. talks.

I love her!

—D.I. Drew

GWYNYTH DIARY ENTRY: 12TH OF MARCH

Dark of the Moon in three days.

I got a message from Jabba out of the blue. "Expect 'a friend' to stay for some time." I've made up the spare bed. Hope this visitor isn't allergic to pusscats.

Ninkip fares much better. Tossed a colossal hairball right into the center of my altar (good omen) and looked at me as though to say, "Fine now, Mom."

GWYNYTH DIARY ENTRY: 13TH OF MARCH

Dark of the Moon in two days.

Blackbird perched on the thrift store awning. Found the perfect straw hat for the coming Equinox. My Guides are having a field day.

Jabba has also requested I look out for and protect one Scratch and Winc online. Thank goddess I don't have to put them up too. But I am curious. On my way home, I passed several street vendors selling Scratch and Winc merchandise. What am I getting tangled up in? I need to find a way to lure these two into the safety of my crystal cavern.

GWYNYTH DIARY ENTRY: 14TH OF MARCH

Dark of the Moon tomorrow.

The young charge has arrived, now firmly ensconced in the spare room, directly beneath the primary gearbox. I've issued him earplugs.

He had a particularly virulent trace attached to each of his log-ons. I removed them, of course; he's quite safe now. But who would seek a child so doggedly? He has more intelligence than I gave him credit for: he asked to see my hardware. By the time we reached Room Five, his tongue was hanging out.

The new trace (who in heaven's name called it "Typhoid Mary"?) is more powerful than I suspected. Must warn that pup to stay away from logging on for the next day or two.

GWYNYTH DIARY ENTRY: NO IDEA

Who cares what day it is, the bloody Moon is dark!

?????!!!!!!! The child logged on without my knowledge or permission, using Safesmudge. If it weren't against my principles, I'd chop him up and feed him to the cats.

Note to myself: buy cat food.

END GWYNYTH DIARY ENTRY

NARRATIVE ENTRY, JABBATHEHUT

Lieutenant Wally Budge is happy: he's finally found a solid link from Toobe to Scratch and Winc.

"Gotta add corruption of a minor to the charges," he mutters almost protectively as he types. Until a message pops up:

> **To:** Ms. Budge
> **From:** Henderson, Enforcement
> **Subj:** Perp Toobe
>
> Wally,
>
> We got lucky today. The kid signed on long enough for us to trace him. The perp is in New York. You won't believe where we traced him to. We've got a network of 20 uniforms closing in, but we need you to make the collar . . .

"DAMN THEM," he roars in his empty office. Furious, he punches in REPLY.

> **To:** Henderson, Enforcement
> **From:** Ms. Budge
> **Subj:** Perp Toobe
>
> What the HELL is going on? I never authorized a close-in! This kid is directly connected to both Scratch and Winc, and you're sending UNIFORMS? What IDIOT authorized THAT? CANCEL CANCEL CANCEL the plans. We need to walk QUIET here.
>
> —*Mister* Lieutenant Wallace Budge

He stares at the screen.

And then: Wally Budge finally gets it.

"They went right over my head. I'm alone on this one.

"Time to play the cards close to my chest. Real close." He deletes the unsent memo.

END JABBA NARRATIVE ENTRY

PERSONAL LOG, JABBATHEHUT

Of course I have tapped into Budge's computer in every way conceivable, and a few ways inconceivable. Naturally I intercepted Henderson's message concerning the imminent arrest of our heroes. I must say that I am finally officially concerned. Do they think refusing government orders is a game?

END JABBA PERSONAL LOG

GWYNYTH DIARY ENTRY

Oh dear. Scratch invited Winc into the room where they were supposed to talk about the impending peril.

Guess what they did instead. Couldn't help themselves?

END GWYNYTH DIARY ENTRY

SCRATCH JOURNAL ENTRY, CHAT ROOM EXCERPT

Online Host

***** You are in room "Scared" *****

Winc: I'm starting to see that we really may be in danger based on Jabba's messages to me.

Scratch: Yeah?

Winc: ::hurriedly explaining:: Jabba sent each of us a piece of the puzzle—we need to put them together.

Scratch: Whatever the hell that means.

Winc: Steady, darling. Let's merge the files. One . . . two . . . three . . .

Scratch: ::uploading::

Winc: ::uploading::

Scratch: Oh.

Fine. That makes a whole lot of sense.

Winc: Maybe I should have picked "Confused" for the room name?

Scratch: What's this "clue" supposed to reveal, anyway?

Winc: Toobe's location?

Scratch: Oh, yeah, right.

Winc: ::puzzling over picture:: Hey! It's an erector set!

Scratch: That's all I got, too.

Winc: Wait! It's a close-up view of something.

Winc: *I* know!

Scratch: You know what it is?!

Winc: No, I mean I know what I should do!

Scratch: What?

Winc: I'm gonna go ask Jabba what it means!

Scratch: Uh, Winc? Doesn't that go against—

Winc: Let's see, I exit this room to use the #2 bypass . . . ::muttering:: Be right back!

Winc has left the room.

Scratch: Winc, don't you think we ought to try to . . . and I'm just typing to myself here.

Winc has entered the room.

Winc: I couldn't find her, but I figured it out all on my own: it's a password!

Scratch: You could warn me when you disappear, you know.

Winc: Oh, I'm sorry! I was excited! It gets us into . . .

///ANYTHING I CAN HELP YOU WITH, CYBERFOLK?///

Private Message to Winc

Scratch: Christ! It's an Eye!

Go back out for a minute.

Not many say "cyberfolk." I think I may know this one.

Please leave me to it?

Winc: ::petulant sigh:: OK.

Winc has left the room.

END SCRATCH JOURNAL ENTRY

GWYNYTH DIARY ENTRY

These are the nation's leading scofflaws? America's most wanted? Jabba has asked me to care for them. Is Jabba's heart beginning to thaw?

I shall assist, for reasons still vague to me: This is a safe haven, by Code and by Craft, and all rules will be respected. So be it.

Note to myself: Thaw out the portobello mushroom steaks for dinner.

END GWYNYTH DIARY ENTRY

COMBINED SCRATCH AND WINC JOURNAL ENTRIES

Scratch joins Marie, the Eye, in a room called "14Lounge."

///SCRATCH, LET'S GO TO 14LOUNGE.///

Online Host

***** You are in room "14Lounge" *****

Scratch: O.K. I'm here. What's the significance of "14Lounge"?

Marie: Just an EYE lounge. It's secure.

Scratch: More secure than the private rooms the rest of us use?

Marie: Let's not talk about work. I don't have much time. Want you now.

Scratch: Good. I'm running water in the tub, I'm supposed to be lovingly drawing you a bath, but . . .

Marie: I'm being bad.

Scratch: I'm taking—right. You're a bad girl. I grab you around the waist, half lifting you up, grabbing your crotch.

Marie: Y-y-y-ess.

Scratch: You're wet already, little girl.

Marie: I'm sorry.

Scratch: You've been thinking nasty thoughts.

Marie: Yes.

Scratch: My hand is rubbing your clit, my other sneaking around behind you, teasing. But I refuse to go in.

Marie: ::whimpering::

Scratch: I put two fingers just inside, but you want it—

Marie: Deeper.

Scratch: Yes, but I won't, you know, not until you open way up.

Marie: ::Opening::

Private Message to Winc

> **Scratch:** You won't believe what's happening. Guess what the "way powerful" want?
>
> **Winc:** ::dryly:: To be dominated?
>
> **Scratch:** Yep.
>
> **Winc:** Scratch? Make it short, OK?
>
> **Scratch:** Aw, don't be jealous.
>
> **Winc:** It's not that. Darling, we're in the middle of rescuing someone.
>
> **Scratch:** I haven't forgotten! Do you know how weird it is to be having sex at a time like this?
>
> **Winc:** ::patting your little head::

Scratch: Not yet. You writhe in the water, spreading your legs as far as the tub will let you. How dare you lift your ass that way!

Marie: I'm sorry, I . . .

Scratch: I climb into the tub, clothes and all, my boots tromping your bare feet, trapping you.

Marie: Please—

Scratch: I lift your ass against me, lift you high, my hand working furiously on your clit. Your cunt begins to open. I take my hand away.

Marie: Oh!

Scratch: I slide it up to your breasts, pinching.

Marie: Yessss.

Scratch: I'm straddling you, lifting your ass against me, pushing my crotch into you. I dip your head down into the water.

Marie: ::sputtering::

Scratch: Yes. I lift your head out, then dip it in again.

Marie: My pussy is pouring, opening.

Scratch: I slide my hand down your back, around your ass, to your pussy. I plunge in with three fingers.

Marie: Yes!

Scratch: I turn my hand, and slide in another finger, then cup my hand, pushing in.

Marie: ::very still, lifting my ass::

Scratch: Slowly, I lower you down back on your knees. My hand makes slower circles on your clit. I turn my cupped hand, reveling in the juices. And then, quickly, I slide my whole hand in.

Marie: Yes, please!

Scratch: I close my fingers together into a fist.

Marie: Ohhh, pain!

Scratch: Yes. I hold my hand very still.

Marie: Please, yes just a minute. Hurts. Deep, but touching me so deep.

Scratch: My thumb is tucked inside my fingers. I expand just a little.

Marie: Oh yes, just a little . . .

Scratch: My other hand concentrates on your clit. The water swells up over my boots. It laps your thighs, warm, touching you everywhere slowly as it rises.

Marie: Your hand moves inside me.

Scratch: ::laughing:: yes, moving.

Marie: It feels so good.

Scratch: ::gritting my teeth:: This isn't for you, girl, it's for me. What're you doing with your ass up in the air like that? What kinda horny girl are you?

Marie: ::whispering:: Very horny. All day, keeping it inside.

Scratch: I start slowly pumping my fist in you, turning it around inside you, fast, then slow.

Marie: Oh, god, no don't.

Private Message to Scratch

Winc: ::brightly:: How ya doin', Scratch ol' pal? ::doing a little dance on top of your computer:: Having fun, are you?

Scratch: :X

Winc: ::gleeful chuckle::

Scratch: I'm . . . sorry. To be doing this, I mean.

Winc: ::softly:: Darlin', if it's keeping us safe, go for it. This Eye may be asked if she saw us. If you're as good as ever, I think our passage will be safer now.

Go have good sex, and fun gender.

Scratch: ::softly:: That's so cool of you. Thank you.

Scratch: Yes, I will. Pushing inside, rubbing your clit. Feeling it expand and jump under my hand. My fist is sliding around in your wetness, pouring out of you. I push harder.

Marie: . . . and contract around your fist, tighter and tighter, so you can hardly move.

Scratch: I circle my other hand harder around your clit, moving all up and down your lips, and back again.

Marie: I press down, my ass hard against you, I'm tightening . . . my legs shuddering.

Scratch: I can feel you start to come. I lift you up higher, the water splashing around us.

Marie: I'm coming . . .

Scratch: Spasms against my hand, almost crushing my fist inside you.

Scratch: Marie? Fuck, are you gone?

Marie: I'm here.

Scratch: I am too.

Marie: No sap, just bye, OK?

Scratch: You sure?

Marie: Yeah. Bye.

Marie has left the room.

Scratch: But, but! ::muttering to self:: It's not like you want to see her again . . . . .

Online Host

***** You are in room "Scared" *****

Winc has entered the room.

Winc: How was your little delay?

Scratch: Kinda weird. I'm not sure she even knew she was in this "Gwynyth domain" at all.

Winc: ::chuckling:: Did you love it?

Scratch: No, I think I feel kind of used.

Winc: ::snorts:: OK, here's what Jabba gave me as a hint:

alpha %^&*#$% ())\anon

Scratch: Do you know what it means?

Winc: No. It's the kind of thing she always sends me. It's her way of saying "recipient is stupid."

Scratch: And you put up with this?

Winc: Long story. But at the end is anon. Anonymous?

Scratch: Yeah. Wait no. ::thinking:: Maybe it means "soon." Like Shakespeare language, soon. As in "See you anon."

Winc: Right! She talks like that! Another one came in.
::brightly:: OK, do you know what *that* means?
You've read more, I bet it comes from classical literature. That, or some forties potboiler.

Scratch: Literature's kind of a big area, my love. And many pots have been boiled. How long have you known Jabba?

Winc: A few years maybe. She's weird—I like her.

Scratch: So she's definitely female?

Winc: ::laughing:: Oh, it's Toobe's game of trying to balance out the "default masculine pronoun."

Scratch: By calling Jabba a she?

Winc: Right. Jabba doesn't go in for "hir" and "ze." Thinks it's stupid, like everything else. So Toobe just uses "she."

Scratch: Stupid?

Winc: She spends a lot of time being disgusted with people. They're *all* stupid. But one thing I do know, she's huge. That's why "Jabba." There are little hints I get, like she doesn't fit in the world so well.

Scratch: Kind of like us.

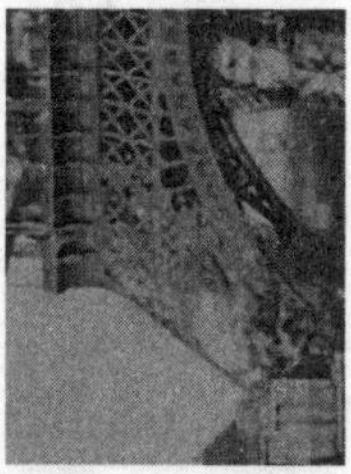

Winc: Whoa! What's that picture?

Scratch: What the hell? An erector set maybe?

Winc: Wait! ::staring at picture:: It's . . . it's sideways!

Scratch: OK sideways what?

Winc: hahahahahaha La Tour Eiffel! Well, a teeny, tiny part of the Eiffel Tower. I used to stare at that beautiful tower for *hours*. But not sideways!

Scratch: Huh?

Winc: Turn it sideways!

See? Wait a minute, let me find a picture for you. I've got it here someplace . . .

Winc: Ta-fucking-da!

Winc: Jabba's pic is way close-up. Really, way. She has amazing image editing software!

Scratch: So, Paris?

Winc: Paris was my high school graduation present. Five days and four nights. That was the view from my hotel window. I've had that same photo, or copies of it, over all my desks ever since. I sent one to Jabba a couple of months ago. But man, I never looked at it sideways before!

Scratch: How is this thing a password???

Winc: WAIT! THE HOTEL! Typing in the name of the hotel now.

> HotelEiffelTrocadero
>
> **Incorrect password**

Winc: Oh, no!

Scratch: Well, leave off the hotel part.

Winc: No, that's part of the name.

Scratch: Don't the French have accents over their vowels? Is there a . . .

Winc: Right!

HôtelEiffelTrocadèro
Entering Jabbaworld

Winc: Yowee!

Scratch: Good job! ::shyly:: Good thing we had Paris on our minds.

Winc: ::smiling at you:: Yes, good thing.

Jabbaworld message
If you're reading this past 10pm, you're either in trouble or you're lacking imagination and/or education.
My guess is the latter.

Winc: ::dryly:: I've got 10:30, how about you dear?

Scratch: 10:30 here, too.

Winc: ::shyly:: That means we're in the same time zone. I like that.

Scratch: Right! But I live in the boonies, hee hee.

Jabbaworld message
Toobe has no access to the Net, repeat none: not email, not bypass, nothing.
He is safe at present, but there is a slight possibility that the law has located him and is closing in.

Scratch: Oh no. Poor little shit.

Winc: Oh no.

Jabbaworld message
He needs help in real time.
R-e-a-l T-i-m-e. You.have.to.go.in.person.to.get.him.

Winc: Right! Let's do it! ::heading for the door::

Scratch: How? Where is he?

Winc: Oh. ::sheepish::

> **Jabbaworld message**
> The law knows that Toobe is underage so if you would use your fertile minds for something other than cybersex, you'd realize the media will pounce and there will be
> "CHILD PORN RING"
> written over all your foreheads.

Winc: Child porn?! Us?

Scratch: That's ABSURD!

Winc: Is Toobe in danger?

> **Jabbaworld message**
> Please grow up and smell the public sentiment. He needs to be taken from the temporary place to a more permanent place until all this blows over.

Winc: Scratch?

Scratch: Mmm?

Winc: Where *is* Toobe? Did I miss something?

Scratch: Oh, right. ::scrolling through entire chat session::

Winc: Maybe we're supposed to put our messages together like a puzzle again.

Scratch: You're so smart!

Winc has left the room.

Scratch has left the room.

Winc has entered the room.

Scratch has entered the room.

Scratch: OK, uploading coded message to Jabbawindow. 1-2-

Winc: 3! Mine's uploaded too.

> **Jabbaworld Message**
> Island
> Coney

Scratch: Coney Island! New York!

Winc: ::doubtfully:: That's where he is?

Scratch: Gotta be.

Winc: Wait, that makes sense! It's skateboarding heaven, of course he would go there.

Scratch: Then let's go!

END SCRATCH AND WINC ENTRIES

GWYNYTH DIARY ENTRY

As far as I can tell, there is still no plan, enthusiastic as they seem.

It sure looks like they're taking off . . . for here!

Not that they know where here really is.

Snagged this out from under the govt three minutes ago:

> **To:** FBCS All Hands
> **From:** Henderson, Enforcement
> **Subj:** Child abduction?
>
> ATTENTION: We have an unconfirmed report that perp Toobe may be under the influence of a cult of mind-control hackers, or an East Coast child pornography ring. Arrangements have been made to transport perp to Bellevue psychiatric for investigation upon apprehension.
>
> —H

END GWYNYTH DIARY ENTRY

08
HIDING IN PLAIN SIGHT

GWYNYTH DIARY ENTRY

FUNNY OF THE DAY

Comedy = Tragedy + Time.

—Many people

Toobe asked me to post one of his Funnies. Dear child. He stores them away like acorns. I have allowed him to send an email just now, heavily encrypted:

> **To:** Winc@<encrypted>
> **From:** Toobe@<encrypted>
> **Cc:** Scratch@<encrypted>
> **Subj:** Help?
>
> Guys, I gotta tell you, I'm scared. I'm safe at the moment but you wouldn't believe a memo I saw—about me!—from the cops. They're saying I could go to the looney bin. How did it get like this? I'm one of those Most Wanted doodes . . .
>
> There's no way you can answer this, but I hope I get to see you *soon* for real.

—T.

P.S. Just so you know this isn't some govt trick and that it's really me: Winc, Don't drop your Droors!

I'm working on a way to reach Toobe's father without being traced. The little one is safer here, and if it gives him some comfort to reach his friends, then more kibble to him.

His friends responded quickly and used one of my safe email bypasses:

To: Razorfun
From: Gyrl
Subj: Morphin' USA

Got it! They're gonna be looking for our friend the skateboardin' teenager, right? Let's morph him into something completely different!

You're gonna hate this.

We're all gonna hate this.

But we have to go real time, and if there's even the smallest chance they know or put together what we look like in real life, we've got to go the other way.

Oh, you and Toobe are so gonna hate this . . .

Let's make him a girl, and we'll be his parents! No one would notice us, we waltz right out of there, just a happy little family. (I'm assuming you can make yourself look like the parent of a 15-year-old.) You up for it?

—W.

To: Gyrl
From: Razorfun
Subj: Parents

::narrowing eyes:: Who's playing which character? I'm NOT saying I'm going along with this, I just want to know what you had in mind.

—S.

To: Razorfun
From: Gyrl
Subj: Depends on . . .

. . . your height. In their minds, fathers are tall and mothers are short-er, so that's what their eyes are gonna be looking for. I'm 5'10", how about you? ::innocently:: whoever's tallest is the father, the shorter one is Mom, was what I was thinking. Got a mustache? Going to shave it off? Grow one? Go to a costume store, hmmmmm?

::eyes twinkling::

—W.

To: Gyrl
From: Razorfun
Subj: You're *how* tall?!

Sigh. I guess I'm the mother. How did I *know* it would lead to this? I'm 5 . . . never mind what height I am.

—S.

To: Razorfun
From: Gyrl
Subj: You're so brave

::gently:: It was just an idea. If it's too much . . .

—W.

To: Gyrl
From: Razorfun
Subj: ::eyes twinkling::

Oh, what the hell, it's too outrageous to fail.

I tell ya, "drag" is a good name; the prospect doesn't appeal to me at all. But you're right, they won't be looking for a nuclear family. Ok, I'll meet you at the roller coaster. I'll be the one sliding around reluctantly on high heels and tottering towards a tall man with a mustache, possibly accompanied by a young female teenager. But what about our little Toober: Will he go along with this?

—S.

To: Razorfun
From: Gyrl
Subj: Amurican

He doesn't have much of a choice. He'll be our shining daughter, full of hope and promise and mascara. Can't wait to see you, and of course, what you will wear?! ::ducking::

—W.

To: Gyrl
From: Razorfun
Subj: IHOP

Oh, groan. Okay, but we need a bland, midwestern wash over the whole thing: We need to be invisible. No style, no glossy makeup.

I'll pick you up for our getaway. Gawd knows I won't be able to walk far in the kind of shoes I'm going to need.

—S.

P.S. You know, this is just another role. I mean, I'm nervous about meeting you in real time and all, but I love that we're going in drag. We won't be any different than hundreds of people facing their day in costume. Right? ::shudder:: I just hope this morph is as hard for you as it is for me.

To: Razorfun
From: Gyrl
Subj: This role

::smiling gently:: This role *is* hard for me, my love. ::softly:: I'm scared, but also relieved. We can put our theories to the test in real life, non?

—W.

To: Gyrl
From: Razorfun
Subj: I know you are but what AM I?

Test, that's a good word for it. I've realized it's fine whoever *you* are, I mean whoever you are is okay with me. But the idea of what each of *you* would then make *me* is tripping me out.

Look, depending on who *you* are, then I'll become one of the following: queer, a straight person, or a freak in some new way that I'm not a freak now. You know?

The hardest thing would be if you were a man. That would be the biggest stretch for me.

Also, nothing about the *content* of who we really are will change, but the *form* of us changes completely. Which I didn't think I cared about, but now I find that I do care (disappointing realization).

I used to dream about a better world that would make it easier to figure out who I was going to love. But that ain't here yet.

I guess none of that makes sense, maybe it'll just be moot when we finally meet. Wouldn't that be sweet?

::shakily, but determinedly::

—S.

Dress our young Toobe up as a girl! Oh, what fun! Time to get out the old paint pots and froufrou.

END GWYNYTH DIARY ENTRY

NARRATIVE ENTRY, JABBATHEHUT

The interior of the commercial airliner is a nice, soothing shade of green. Wally Budge needs soothing right now. He's out to head off his two perps at the pass. But soothing is not the wailing child across the aisle. Or the overlarge man seated next to him, perspiring a particularly vile cologne. Soothing is the text currently scrolling on his laptop.

To: FBCS Investigations
From: DevilsOwn
Subj: We're IN!

Greetings, missy copper. Yer friendly neighborhood hacker here, with good news.

First, to answer your question: no, I've never heard of any "mind-control cult of hackers." Maybe lay off the conspiracy theories?

BUT I'm in Winc's email database, and I was able to extract Winc's unread mail for you. Am I good, or am I better than good? This character sure gets around.

Thanks for the prompt payment. A pleasure to do business with you, darlin'.

—Dev

The good lieutenant winces at "darlin'," and reads:

Dear Winc,

Do you remember me? We met in the Disabilities Forum. My father says that if you are half as good as the police say you are that you'll get this message even if your mailbox is bugged.

Well, I sure hope you're reading this, and I also hope you are what I think you are, a boy in a wheelchair like me, because you give me so much to look forward to. I really think it's fun to be other things online too.

I am Registered, and so are my parents, but none of us believe the pornography or child abuse stuff they're saying about you because you never tried anything like that with me so thank you.

Your friend who likes you,

—Emilio Saldarriaga

On to the next missive.

Dear Winc,

Hey babe, remember me? ::wicked chuckle:: We got it on a couple of months ago. ::dangling long-handled spoon in front of your eyes to jog your memory::

Look, I just wanted to see if I could help—somehow. I know you're a dyke, even if those stupid cops can't figure it out. First time lesbian invisibility came in *handy*, huh?

Keep on doing what you need to do, girl. We're all proud of you for taking the heat. Speaking of heat . . .

::curling my finger between your collar and your throat::

Until we meet again.

—MstrssBoot

"What the hell did they do with the long-handled spoon?" muses Budge aloud. He reads another:

Dear Winc,

You are going right to HELL! You are so sick you make me and every good person I know want to throw up. And if you ever show anyone the log of the filthy things you made me do online with you, I will tell them that you did it not me so you might as well throw that log away and never show it to anyone ever.

—NCJes333@sen.gov

Amused and alarmed, Budge notes the address as one Senator Jesse Helms, one of the most vocal opponents of anything having to do with lesbian and gay people. But he figures no one deserves this next one . . .

DIE YOU FAGGOT WINK ASSHOLE-SUCKING HIPPIE SHIT, I HOPE THE COPS FUCKING TEAR YOUR FINGERS OFF

. . . and probably no one really deserved this one either . . .

Dear Mr. Winc,

We'd like to speak with you and Mr. Scratch concerning a made-for-television movie we're pitching. No promises, of course. But I think the climate is right, and you could walk out of this deal a very rich man. Please contact me soonest.

John Lancer, assistant to Barry Dillard

Paramount Television

Wally Budge stares out the window at the clouds. "Maybe they'll make me a very rich man for being the cop who catches them," he muses. One more hour of the flight, then the half-hour helicopter ride to Coney Island. Budge has finished Winc's mail and is reading his own, which isn't much better.

Lieut. W. Budge—

As legal liaison for Family Values Above All (FVAA), I wanted you to have an advance copy of an article we hope to have released in the Washington Post this Sunday.

We stand behind you, Lieutenant. Please call on us, and God be with you.

—Amos Rafferty, D.D., Esq.

Budge grunts once and scans the press release:

FAMILY NEWS

HARD-CORE CHILD PORN HITS INTERNET

By Matt Holloway, staff writer for Concerned Parents Digest

The infamous "Scratch" and "Winc" are currently at large, transmitting obscenity through interstate phone lines via the Internet. The case opens the eyes of the computer network industry, good Christians everywhere, and all concerned parents. There can be no denying the rampant and growing availability and acceptance of sexually explicit images and the eroding control of parents over the information their children take in.

Apparently Scratch and Winc are responsible for bringing rain to the desert, driving children away from parents, solving the problems of quantum physics and/or operating a huge contraband ring.

In other words, no one knows anything, but everyone is talking. Not that anyone is talking clearly, nor is anyone coming forward, and no one has got a shred of evidence. Even 60 *Minutes* has resorted to using passive terms such as "unnamed sources" and "it has been reported that."

There's a fractured photo of Toobe the gossip TV show uses every night: "Have You Seen This Child?"

Back in the office of the intrepid Wally Budge. He types:

To: Henderson, Enforcement
From: FBCS Investigations
Subj: URGENT: SEARCH PARAMETER MODIFICATION

Henderson: I've got reason to believe that juvenile suspect Toobe may be in the company of . . .

. . . two adults, or slightly older juveniles. They may be any race, any physical presentation. These adults or older juveniles are to be detained for questioning along with the kid.

No reason to believe there is any porn or mind control going on (where did you *get* that?), so the kid may need some talking to, but he surely doesn't need a shrink. I advise you to call off the men in the white coats.

Repeat: You are looking for a group of three or one lone white juvenile male. I'll be there in less than two hours. Hold for questioning any, repeat *any* suspicious-looking threesome that includes the suspected perp until my arrival on site.

Budge

He leans back in his seat and ponders the real problem. It isn't catching the buggers. It's what to charge them with. Failing to Register was made illegal by presidential decree, so it's a flimsy and untested law. If that's the only charge they've got, then any penny-ante public defender can merrily release them back to their hidey-hole homes.

END JABBA NARRATIVE ENTRY

09
NO TRACTION

PERSONAL LOG, JABBATHEHUT

I have procured a number of hysterical accounts of The Great Coney Island Rescue. This is the one I concluded as the most accurate—but at this point, who knows.

Scene: Coney Island

A tall man in a checkered sport coat, sporting a mustache and wearing unbearably cheap shoes stands with a young girl. She looks as pouty as most young girls in the presence of their parents. Soon they are joined by a plain, worn-looking woman.

END JABBA PERSONAL LOG

WINC JOURNAL ENTRY

I gotta say, Toobe looked adorable. I've only seen him in skateboard gear. But there he was, tottering on heels . . .

So sweet; then he asked me, "How did you know it was me?"

"Oh, I just knew," I said, smiling. I didn't want him to worry or be embarrassed so I made sure to add, "You look great. And you look like the kid I've loved forever. Most importantly, the cops won't know it's you at all."

Then I saw Scratch. Clearly a female, but looked odd somehow. Awkward, the gait not quite right, the clothes seeming to fit funny. I could see hir tottering on hir shoes, even though they were one-inch heels at most, and quite sensible. Charming.

I wanted us all to hug, but as usual Scratch was aware of what was happening around us, while I was only aware of the rush of emotion in knowing we were safe—at least for the moment—the three of us. In the riptide of that emotion, I realized crazily, "This is my family," and wanted to join hands with the two of them and swing round and round right there on the boardwalk. I laughed out loud, and Scratch was laughing too.

"Look at us," ze said. "The people I care about most in the world are right here, in real time! I didn't expect we'd look like this!"

That's exactly what I was thinking. It was like a simulpost, when we both would type the same thing online? Only there was no delay, and I was standing there, completely willing to stay like that forever. My Scratch!

Toobe was grinning, as if he believed that as long as we were literally surrounding him, he was safe. Scratch's eyes kept darting around, and sure enough, it did look like a number of dark-suited men were prowling, although none of them had looked our way, yet.

"We gotta go," Scratch said, jolting me out of the reverie.

"We're just a family at Coney Island, and now we're going to the car, okay?" ze added.

I felt this thump inside: We were nowhere near out of danger yet and could be surrounded by the Bad Guys at any minute. I couldn't begin to sort out whether ze looked like what I had imagined, but the feeling was the same; ze was making plans and I believed in hir and it was going to be all right.

Ze was having so much trouble in those low, low heels! But I didn't laugh. I just put out my arm and ze had no choice but to hold on to it for balance, and I'm pretty sure ze was grateful. I took slow, measured steps that were just long enough for both hir and Toobe. Nevertheless, ze grumbled with every lurch.

Toobe was laughing quietly. I'm sure he felt awkward as hell in the rather outré fishnets Gwynyth had supplied him, but (thank goodness for modern fashion) I'm sure he appreciated heavy combat boots and a backward baseball cap along with his skirt. He really did make a very pretty grrl. A little too much makeup, but Gwynyth was pretty smart with the application, all things considered.

We were walking out the main gate when damn, damn, damn . . . we were stopped by one of those men in the dark suits!

I remember turning to Scratch to figure out what to do. But instead of Scratch, this sweet woman was looking up into my face with all the warmth and confidence a . . . a man could wish for. I took a deep breath and so help me I responded in kind: I went into being Dad.

"Yes, officer?" I said. "Anything I can do for you?"

The "little woman" held on to my arm, and Toobe had no trouble at all looking like a very uncomfortable teenage girl.

The officer didn't do a double take. He didn't stare at us like any of us might be the "wrong" gender, and believe me I know what that stare looks like. He simply explained that he was sorry to bother us, but this was about—he lowered his voice so as not to offend my darling wife and child—the porn industry. They were to question any suspicious-looking threesomes. My brain was screaming, *Threesomes? They know?* But I got quite grave with him, nodding a silent signal of thanks for not speaking too loudly. My knees were shaking inside my baggy trousers.

Apologetically he said he needed to check my ID. I figured that was it—we were caught—but at that moment, I saw Scratch pinch Toobe's arm. Hard! And Toobe lets out a long "Owwwwww!"

Scratch, smooth as silk, glided up to the guard and in this hushed voice, said, "Officer, I'm so sorry, but my daughter is having her first . . . well, you know . . . her first little visitor."

The guy stared at Scratch, uncomprehending. So Scratch lowered hir voice again and said, "It's her first period, Officer. She's having her monthly time, and we need to get her to a bathroom. Now."

Well, the guard went pale, and Toobe went even more pale. I stared at Scratch with a mixture of pure disbelief and admiration, and then turned to the shaken guy with an apologetic look, who glanced at me real fast and waved us on through.

We found Scratch's car; Toobe dove into the backseat and started peeling off his fishnets immediately, yowling about the shackles of the opposite sex or some such thing, and I said, how do you think I feel, peeled off my mustache, and wiped off the makeup that was concealing the tattoo under my eye. Soon, we were all hysterically laughing, relief and joy and tension spilling out of us. I have never been so thoroughly happy.

W.

END WINC JOURNAL ENTRY

SCRATCH JOURNAL ENTRY

What a trip to see Winc take off that hat and see long hair spill down, and the mustache off, and those wise, wise eyes. Ze's taller than me and has the longest legs, I think that's what made hir look almost like a colt, kind of awkward. Then ze did that classic maneuver women do of reaching under hir dress to undo hir bra, but of course it was actually a roll of ace bandages that were keeping hir breasts down, and the juxtaposition of hir in that man's shirt with breasts all soft underneath them was so sexy. I thought, *oh, good, two women, that's what we are*. And started tripping on all that would mean, to me and to hir. But neither one of us knew the half of it.

—S.

END SCRATCH JOURNAL ENTRY

TOOBE ENTRY

Man, what a day. Wow. Meeting each other in real time. So, no surprise, they were just as lovestruck in real life as they'd been online. I guess the drag worked because we made it past the cops and then just sat in the car, stunned. I couldn't believe we were getting away with it. But instead of screaming away for a high-speed chase, Scratch said, "Okay, what gender are we all really? I mean, in real life?"

Silence in the car.

"Okay, okay," said Scratch, "I'll say what I am."

But ze didn't say anything, until . . .

"Why would that be the big question now, anyway?" ze said, more to hirself, looking out the window. "Not 'am I Jewish' or 'where do I live' or 'do I like to ride horses'? Why would the biggie be male or female?"

I felt my heart sink. I was sitting with my best friends, and they were about to talk about the gender thing. As usual, my mind just glazed over. "What does it matter?!" I wanted to yell, and I should have. Maybe it would have made a difference.

Plus we were still sitting in the car. Why weren't we escaping?!

"Okay," Scratch finally said, all the breath pushing out of hir in a whoosh. "I'm a girl, woman, crone, maiden, chick, bitch, cow, dyke, babe, butch, sweet-pea, white female person. This week I wish I looked more like Wesley Snipes and last week it was Garbo. Sometimes I wish my skin were a different color or that I was a wolf instead of a dumb human."

Ze kept looking down, but the words kept pouring out.

"I'm not afraid to walk down the street alone because I am all those things inside without thinking about it; then somebody calls my name—or rather, my sex—and I feel like I'm in a borrowed body, the body I was born into, easily recognizable to other people, but not to me. They want to sculpt it and dress it and reduce it and extend it but it just doesn't work for me.

"I'm a female," ze finished in a voice that trailed off. "And now my freedom's over." Ze looked over at Winc, who was quiet now.

Scratch added, "I haven't worn a dress in about twenty-five years. I'm thirty-eight, and in the last few years I've grown to love my face and my tits and, for some reason, my feet. I've heard 'ugly chick' in my head for so long it has no meaning anymore."

No way Scratch is ugly!

"Finally I started dressing and acting how I felt cuz it's my fucking life and I wasted a whole lot of time acting like it's someone else's." Ze paused. "Do you know what happened when I started doing that?" But ze wasn't really waiting for our answer. "Nothing. Except," and Scratch started blushing, "I got a whole lot more dates from women."

For some reason, I blushed too. We all sat together in silence for a while.

Winc took a deep breath and said, "Okay, since you're being so honest. Um. . . ."

"Wait!" Scratch asked. "What do you think about all that?"

"Well, maybe I'd like to know—who do you like to sleep with?"

My jaw dropped.

"I like to sleep with my teddy bear and my modem at this point," Scratch snapped.

"Stop it. For real, just say," Winc replied.

But Scratch talks in paragraphs, so I knew this would be long. But first ze turned to me.

"Sorry about this, kid. I promise I won't go into gory details. You okay?"

I nodded. Of course I was okay. But I'm glad ze does that. I feel safe with Scratch. Ze took a deep breath and spoke to Winc.

"I'm not sure what I am or who I sleep with. Not that I'm some fence-sitter, but right now, touching someone else's body—no matter what sex—is equally scary to me. I prefer the company of women, but sometimes it's as a man, so what does that make me? I have a mustache—I keep it in a jar—and an old fedora. Sometimes I go to a bar as a guy and buy drinks for people. Most times for women, sometimes for men. Gay men, mostly, but the point is I do it silently like there's a contract between me and the bartender that's as old as men drinking in a bar. It's amazing what you don't have to say if you look like a man. Then I go home and take it all off and stare at my body and am shocked that I don't look like James Dean or don't have a tail. It kills me sometimes that I don't have a tail. . . .

"I can't believe you asked that," Scratch added. "I can't tell you what I'm about sexually; I just arrived at being female. My kind of female," ze muttered.

"It makes a difference to me, that's all," said Winc, and ze didn't add anything else.

I've never heard that kind of thing matter to Winc before. Ze was being persistent in this way I'd never seen, like ze'd decided something.

Scratch looked at Winc, studying hir. "You're worried about how we'll do it?" ze said, kind of shaking hir head.

Winc stared out of the car window. "No! Yes! Look, this is getting too nailed down! Can't we just go back online now?"

Scratch smiled. They looked at each other. I felt like I was reading somebody else's mail and should get the hell out of there.

Right then, Scratch said to me, "I'm really glad you're here, dude. You're keeping me honest."

"Yes, exactly," said Winc, and they both looked at each other like everything was all figured out now. I was more confused than ever.

"I asked that stupid question," Winc said, turning back to Scratch, "because of that little problem we've talked about: Who we are affects how we will be with each other. Can we just get it over with?"

I wanted to be funny because of all this tension, so I said, "Hey, I'm a guy, and I'm 15! That's my story! Thanks for asking!" and they both laughed.

Winc took a deep breath and said, "I think what's important is to figure how to keep Toobe safe right now."

Well, sure that was important, but Scratch and I looked at each other, both knowing Winc was stalling. Scratch is cool; ze let Winc stall. Then ze said, "I think we just stick together." I agreed, and we all went silent again.

I thought it was time for Winc to tell hir story, so I said, "Maybe you could start with how you know me, Winc?"

"Right. Okay," Winc mumbled. Ze took another deep breath.

"Toobe's father and I went to college together. Matter of fact, we were in the same dorm. Same dorm room."

Scratch said, "Uh, huh."

"Dorm rooms weren't coed then, Scratch," Winc added, eyes glued to the road. "I've known Toobe since he was born. I taught him to skateboard. We skateboarded all over the place. But I wasn't happy, except maybe when I was with you, Toobe, because you never really cared what I was. When Toobe came over one day, and I was dressed like . . . like I always wanted to dress, he didn't even notice; he just wanted to go skateboarding. He's always been like that. In some ways, he saved my life. He didn't care that I decided to become a woman. I used to be a man, Scratch. Up until about a year ago."

Silence in the car.

Scratch didn't explode or do anything like I guess Winc thought ze would.

"Wow," ze finally said. "This is funny. I mean, so ironic!"

Winc said kind of weakly, "Yeah. So, here we are, the all-American family."

Winc kind of touched hir own face like a girl, which I saw Scratch catch out of the corner of hir eye. Scratch was smiling and trying to say something, but it came out in a whisper and just sounded like *wait a minute, give me a minute*. Then all of a sudden, Winc goes, "Could you drive, please?" We were still sitting in the parked car.

For some reason, that set Scratch off, like a delayed reaction, maybe.

"Oh, right!" ze exploded. "Gonna really act like the girl, now?"

Everybody was stunned, especially me. But Winc was real careful.

"It's not that, Scratch. I don't have a driver's license. Ever since my change, I've kept meaning to get a new one, but when you apply, they ask you for birth ID, and . . ." Ze shrugged.

Scratch seemed really embarrassed. "I'm sorry. I think I'm a little tripped out." Ze finally pulled out into traffic. "So, you're a woman."

"Thank you for saying that. Thank you so much. But actually," Winc said, kind of pulling hirself away from Scratch and closer to the door, "I don't think I can really say that either."

Scratch looked totally confused. I could tell ze would have said something if Winc had said, "Yes, I'm a woman," but now ze didn't know where to go.

"So, um, what would you say you are, then? We came up with some cool theories, but you do have to choose something, don't you? Well, I guess you don't, if we're really going to reject the two sexes—"

"Scratch? Can I keep talking? I wasn't finished—"

"Oh jesus, I'm sorry. Yes."

We rode on in silence while Winc regathered for a short moment, but it felt like forever.

"All I knew was I was not-boy," Winc finally said. "Since kindergarten when they lined us all up."

Scratch nodded.

"It was like gravity pulling me," Winc continued. "To the other line. From then on, I just knew I wasn't a boy. The more boy things thrown at me, the more weird I felt. So, with only two choices, I thought I must be girl."

"That sounds so familiar," Scratch said.

Winc turned in hir seat to look at Scratch for a minute. There was a question in hir eyes.

"I didn't realize women went through it too."

Scratch looked like ze was about to fire something off, but Winc held up hir hand.

"Please. So about a year ago, I had the surgery, and—"

"We're kinda jumping the story a little, aren't we?" Scratch interrupted again.

Winc sighed almost impatiently.

"I went through a whole lot of painful years crossdressing, feeling like a freak," ze said in a hurry, trying to rush through that part. "I met some transsexuals, I read everything I could get my hands on, I decided to become a woman. Snip snip. It was done. Then I went online, and realized I loved being everything. Including wolves and lions . . . and tigers and bears, oh my."

"So . . . ?" Scratch started slowly. Winc smiled a little.

"So now I'm saying I may be neither," ze said. "Not a man. Probably not a woman. Seems like the most honest thing to say."

"Whoa. Okay." Scratch threw hir head back against the headrest. "So you were socialized as a man, you have no idea what it's like to be a woman, except online you can come off as one when you want. This is textbook; I know everything about this conversation. But . . ." Ze shook hir head stubbornly, like ze had to go through with the thought, even if it wasn't pretty. "It's not going down real well, this story of yours. Because I'm making the wonderful discovery that I'm as bigoted and uptight as your average asshole."

"You're not bigoted, Scratch," Winc said. "This is hard."

Winc was going someplace else, someplace just a little farther away. I don't think Scratch saw it, but I did.

Scratch kept driving and shook hir head. "Look, it's like all of a sudden you're another species. Being female is its own thing; so is male. You say you're not a boy, but I have to say, you're not a girl either."

"I know that, Scratch; that's what I just said." Real calm, real quiet.

"Right, you did. I'm having a hard time relating to no-gender right now. I mean, in person. I mean, sitting here right next to you. Also god, you're beautiful, I've been thinking that, and I haven't said it so now I have. Fucking beautiful. But what the . . . no gender?" Scratch sat very still then, eyes on the road. Ze gathered up hir thoughts like fish, you could almost see the net.

Scratch continued, "If you're a woman trapped in a man's body then . . . then I don't know what that means. I want to ask you a million questions to see if you match some kind of internal test I've got set up for people like you. . . ."

Ze shook hir head again, as if trying to bodily throw out the half-formed thoughts.

Winc studied hir fingernails, turning them this way and that. Ze didn't jump all over the "people like you" remark—ze sure could have.

Scratch doubled down. "On the other hand, I've never met people like you—not that I know of, anyway." Ze looked lost again. "All the thoughts inside me, like that you're not a 'real' woman, not like I am, all those thoughts are bigoted and ignorant. . . . As if I'm a 'real woman,' hah!" Ze trailed off. Finally ze said, "I do NOT like what I'm thinking! How can I be thinking this?!"

"How can you be thinking what, exactly?" Winc said back softly. I thought ze was so brave, cuz even I didn't want to hear how Scratch answered.

"Men can do any fucking thing they want to. Now they even want to be women, and sure enough, they're doing that too! Why the fuck do they have to take every fucking thing in sight?"

Scratch looked shocked at what ze'd said. Even from the backseat, I could see hir cheeks were flushed. "No, that's not what I mean. Let me try again. You're not a woman or a man and . . ." Ze was muttering. "Talk about no traction. . . . How the fuck do I relate to you?"

"Like you always have," Winc said in that tone that sounds so reasonable.

Scratch winced before starting again. "All right . . . now I'm looking at you, studying your face for clues of manness. If we were walking down the street, what would people think of you?"

"You mean what would they think of you?" Winc said, real quick. "Isn't that what you're really concerned about?"

There was one of those terrible pauses that kept filling up the car with already-breathed air.

"Look," Winc went on, "I don't have answers—"

"I know that, goddammit!" Scratch interrupted. "I know you're the person I fell in love with online, and nothing has changed since last week!"

"Fell in love with?" I knew Winc would never let that one pass, and ze didn't.

Scratch was sputtering. "Okay! Yes! I fell in love with a . . . with a . . . ze!"

We all kinda laughed a little, even Winc. Felt like there was more air in the car again. I just had to pipe up from the backseat: "You get used to it, after a while."

"Oh, easy for you to say, little dude," Scratch said, but I could tell ze wasn't really mad. "Winc, I have one more question. Why are you presenting yourself as a woman if you're saying that's not who you are?"

Winc and I looked at each other and then down at our clothes. Winc fingered hir necktie, still trying not to smile. I held up my fishnets.

"You know what I mean! Why are you—"

"But that's just it, Scratch," Winc said quietly. "Today I look like a man . . . tomorrow I may look like a girl cheerleader."

Scratch and I laughed a little again.

But Winc went on. "It's because I've had the chance to do all that with you—online—changing from one thing to another to another to another . . . that's given me the courage to do it in real life."

Winc looked at Scratch in this really funny way, hir mouth all crooked and hir eyes kind of lit up, and ze said real quietly, "I like it, Scratch. I like girl. It feels right. It's fun. I just like walking through the world that way."

Which made Scratch sputter again. "The point is, the point is . . . the point is that what I'm facing here is a monster of my own creation!"

Winc stopped smiling then. "Oh thanks, that feels real good," ze said.

"No, I mean I'm always mouthing off about how useless gender is and how we'd all be better off without it and now I'm sitting next to someone whose gender is 'optional,' for lack of a better word. Freaks me the fuck out!"

Winc got that look back on hir face. "You're awfully cute when you freak out," ze said. "Did you know that?"

"I'm serious! What are you? And yeah what does my attraction to you make me? If I thought I had to worry about that before . . ."

Winc kept smiling, and I kept watching Winc. If ze wasn't worried, I wasn't.

Scratch was still sputtering. "This is just what I dreamed of. And I hate it! Now if I become a genderless person, too, then we can be a nice happy couple, but the fact is I'm not. I'm a woman; I was raised to be a woman. I've made myself into a whole different kind of woman than I used to be. You were raised to be a man, and then you became a woman, and now you're saying you're not either. Then of course the question is, what's a woman?"

"And what's a man?" Winc shot back, just like I knew ze would.

"I don't know!"

Winc looked out the window, away from Scratch, and said, "Right." A few miles went by in silence. "It seems to me that your consternation is about how you're going to behave now, with me."

"Yeah. Well, it's not just behaving for other people, it's behaving in a physical space with you."

"But wouldn't that be a problem for anybody after they meet in person? I mean, how do you feel about Toobe now that you've met him?"

Scratch shrugged. "He's a guy. I mean, a person with a gender. I can relate to him." Ze swore under hir breath. "I can't believe I said that."

There was a long silence. Then Winc went on in that calm voice, "Yes, but Toobe is also very physical right now, which is different than email Toobe or chat room Toobe. You have to take that in: maybe he has an annoying habit that you never had to deal with online."

I added helpfully, "Yeah, I'm generally annoying in real life."

Scratch craned hir head around to look at me. "Yeah, Toobe. Now that I think of it, it's weird that you're so . . . near. You both are right in my face. Not like I'm a hermit or something, but all the sensory input from new people, in person, makes me a little crazy."

At which point ze pulled the car off to the side of the road, got out, and walked around on the busy street. We sat inside, me fidgeting and Winc being very still. Finally Winc called out the window.

"Darlin', remember we're on the lam, here."

So Scratch ambled back to the car and started talking like there hadn't been any break. She pulled out into the traffic. "Men invade other people's territory like splashing into still water and scattering all the creatures into oblivion. Then they look around and see the environment's changed and they say, what happened? They stock the pond with more creatures, but only ones like themselves, and the rest of the population disappears and then the pond dies and they wonder why."

"I love how you stretch your metaphors, hon," said Winc. "Always have. And I agree. I hate that about men too."

"Then why can't you just be a better man! Stretch the borders like I did! Why do you have to come over to this side of the fence and plow into this water?"

Winc finally looked over at Scratch. "That hurts. I'm really trying to stay with you on this, but it doesn't include your hurting my feelings just because you're angry. You're talking to me as if I'm one of the bad guys, and the fact is—"

But I interrupted, cuz something finally dawned on me: "Nobody is."

Winc answered, "Well, dear, there are bad guys out there. There really are."

Winc turned back to Scratch. "I don't know about all men, all I know about is myself." Ze looked very flustered.

Scratch sat there while Winc composed hirself.

Winc spoke carefully. "I never was happy or felt like myself when I was stuck in 'man.' It wasn't that I was running wildly into becoming 'woman,' when I look back at it. I was running wildly away from man. At the time, there just wasn't any other place to run to."

Scratch's face got all soft, and I could tell ze wanted to say something, but Winc said, "Please. You're asking if I could just be a better man. I guess, in a way, that's what I've done. This is it. This is what a better man looks like to me. And the only way for me to be a better man was to scrape off all the man stuff—the stuff we both cringe at—and become woman. Then when I found out that didn't work either, I've had to scrape off all the woman stuff and be . . . whatever the hell is left."

Scratch covered hir head with hir hands, like ze was trying to crawl into a cave. Ze was steering with hir knees, which made me a little nervous.

"Wait a minute," Scratch said, hands back on the wheel. "Can we go back to this 'better man' stuff? I mean, why couldn't you change? Leave behind 'prick' or 'jerk' or 'arrogant asshole.' Pick a different option."

Scratch looked around for the words again. "What about 'sensitive guy,' 'great father,' 'loving husband.' You know, those kinds of guys."

"Scratch, I'm well aware of the options in that category."

"So maybe you could make yourself over without . . . without ripping off women! Men can be great; it's when they take from other people that they get so obnoxious!"

"Like time and power and physical space, uh-huh. . . ." Winc was nodding hir head.

"Right!" Scratch shouted. "Women have redefined 'woman.' You can bet they got some shit for it too. Why can't men do that?"

Winc sighed and nodded. "They should. Don't you think I've been racking my brain about that? All my life? Here's all I know. Can you hear this for a minute?"

"Of course." Scratch turned to Winc, and hir voice was all quiet. "I don't like feeling this way."

"That's a lot of why I love you," Winc said simply. "And of course I love all of you." Winc's eyes were still sad. "Let me try this," ze went on. "Maybe 'better man' was just too hard for me to define. Maybe the only solution was to join the other category, the one that's got some hope."

Scratch looked calmer than ze had for a while. "You mean abandon the category of man altogether? Like maybe it isn't a category worth saving, the way it's defined now?"

"Yes, maybe that's it."

"Because it's such a fucked-up category and doesn't even work that well for men themselves?" Scratch looked like a kid in my classroom.

"Exactly, dear," Winc said. "I enjoy femme, Scratch. I enjoy just being in your butch company. I enjoy lots of things when you're being lots of things."

Scratch's expression was this weird combination of wild-eyed and calm at the same time. "That's really incredible," ze said slowly, staring at the dashboard. I watched to make sure ze looked up at the road again. Ze did. Finally.

"That's subversive!" Scratch said, and started muttering. "That really blows my mind, and I think I'm freaking out again."

Winc shrugged. "I can't imagine trying to work from inside 'male' again. I can't imagine what it would take. I don't think I could do it."

But Scratch's eyes were all lit up. "I always say when men get in my space that they're invading. But maybe they really want to be women. Well, maybe not women, but not men either. Maybe we're all not-women and not-men! Traction again!"

Winc smiled for the first time in a while, but ze still looked kind of distant. "So you're saying there should be only one category or no categories at all?"

Scratch nodded.

"Yeah," Winc said. "That's a good one."

Right then, the car started to sputter and cough. Out of gas. Unbelievable. Then something really funny happened . . . Scratch and Winc said to each other, at the exact same time:

"I can't believe you let the gas run out. Just like a guy!"

They looked at each other and cracked up, then said, "Simulpost!"

Scratch pulled the car to the side of the road, and I chose that moment to say I was hungry—it seemed as good a time as any. All I'd been eating at Gywynth's for five days was tofu!

There was a diner across the street. Winc realized we had to get back into drag if we were going into a restaurant. Scratch and I groaned, and I complained about having to put the fishnets back on. Thank gawd Winc said I didn't have to.

Back went Winc's mustache; I could see how ze used to look when I was growing up, but ze still looked like someone completely different and now I could also see how Scratch looked . . . funny . . . in that dress, something not quite right. I'm still not sure if it was cuz I knew ze was a woman who never wore that stuff, or if I was still getting used to seeing hir in the flesh after imagining hir online.

So we all trooped to a diner across the road, proper family that we were, walked in, sat at a table, and looked at our menus. The waitress came over and our jaws all went slack, and I swear we all just stared at her shirt. She was wearing an "I Like Scratch and Winc" sweatshirt! I had to think of something cuz it was zombie-town at our table, so I whined "I'm hungry" in a high voice.

It worked; they both looked up at the waitress's face and flapped their menus around. Then the waitress turned to Winc and asked 'him' what we were having, ignoring me and Scratch, right? And Winc, I can't believe this, Winc sat up straight, and cleared hir throat, and stroked hir mustache, and in this way deep, grown-up guy voice, said to Scratch, "Honey, what are you having?" I thought Scratch was gonna pee right there, but then Scratch ran with it. Ze got all sweet and smiley and said to Winc, "Oh, you order for me. You always pick something nice."

Then Winc almost lost it. But ze went completely into "Dad-ordering-us-breakfast" mode, and the waitress walked away like nothing was strange.

Then it was silence again until our food came. All three of us tore into it.

"I want to get back to something you said, Scratch," said Winc around a mouthful of waffles. "About sensory overload."

Scratch, who I swear looked one minute like everyone's mother, and the next like some guy in drag, and the very next minute, well, strong and proud, got all quiet and nodded, so Winc kept talking.

"It ties in with something I was saying, about the courage you've given me—online. See, I did want to be a woman, Scratch. I really, really thought that was the answer for me, because all my time being boy and man—it was all acting. Then I finally made that change, and I had become . . . well, a woman . . . it still felt like I was acting."

It was weird hearing all this come from a doode with a mustache.

"Too many rules on both sides of that gender fence, and I just don't get along well with rules."

Scratch looked a little more like what I think ze really looks like then. "So online," ze said, "you got to escape?"

Winc nodded, then Winc took a deep breath.

"I wouldn't call it escape. I fell in love with you a lot of ways, Scratch. I loved being boy to your riot grrl. I loved being nasty gay man to your nasty gay man. I even loved you when you were a vampire, and I was your supper. I fell so deep and hard when we were Frankie and Johnny. . . ."

I felt embarrassed but hoped at least what ze was saying would maybe save this whole thing.

Hir voice trailed off, and Scratch's eyes got a little wet, and ze just nodded some more. Winc went on. "What I'm realizing now," ze said, "is that I was falling, but with a safety net beneath me."

Winc was getting sadder and sadder, but ze kept talking. "I was finding a way to be all the different mes I could be, with you. But it wasn't with all of you, not really. A lot of it was in my head. It wasn't really you. It was the you I wanted you to be."

Ze just stopped and looked down and took another bite of hir waffle, but I don't think ze was hungry. Scratch took up the slack.

"So you were becoming who I wanted you to be?"

"Sort of."

Scratch looked disgusted with hirself.

"I wanted to be those people too," Winc went on. "I loved that no matter who we became, you were right there with me. We both had the safety net. I . . . I didn't have to worry about looking like a freak to other folks. And you didn't know you were with a 'freak.'"

Right then, the waitress came back and asked Winc if "the table" wanted more coffee. So Winc responded in this girly voice ze usually uses now, "Thanks, hon, yes please," and the waitress just stared at hir, poured the coffee quick and got outta there.

"You're a freak?" Scratch said when she was gone. "You think you're the only one? Don't you know I'm one too? Why do you think there's so many of us online? Not just queers, either, but lots of people are freaks out there."

Ze looked around the diner. "I mean, out here."

Winc looked kind of surprised but didn't say anything. Ze had a kind of "tell me more" look in hir eyes.

"Every time I walk outside, I kind of hunch up. People think butches look so tough, but we're . . . bracing," Scratch finished, real quiet.

Winc was crying now; ze just nodded. Then excused hirself and despite what was happening I hoped ze would remember to use the right bathroom!

When ze was gone, Scratch looked at me and asked if I thought ze was being a jerk. Scratch is so cool that way, asking me what I think, but I could tell ze was really confused, even hurt. Not just by what Winc was saying, but by what ze must be feeling.

So I said, "Nah, you're not a jerk. I think you're just scared. When things change so fast . . ." I shrugged.

"Yeah, I guess that's it." But Scratch sounded kind of doubtful.

Then Winc came back and slid back into the booth.

"I don't want this whole thing to get into who used who, okay?" Winc said. "It's a two-way street." These walls had shot up around hir—spooky.

Winc continued. "I know that I fell in love with you. I learned a lot about who I am and how I want to be in the world. I learned I could be a lot of things with you, and figured maybe I could really be that way. I could be anything, anyone, everything, everyone, all of me. With you. For real."

Scratch looked at hir; maybe something was about to happen, but right then, I had filled up too much, and I just busted out crying like a little kid.

Scratch reached across the table toward me. "Oh, man, Toobe, I'm sorry. Jesus, I . . . we'll be alright, Toobe!" Ze looked at me, then looked at Winc, then put hir head in hir hands.

Winc reached hir arm around me. We held still, just like that.

Finally Scratch said to Winc, "I don't see how it's going to work in the real world. There's so much involved. I wish I was bigger than I am, but I guess I'm just not."

Winc got that other smile on hir face then. Someone else's smile. Ze sat way back in hir seat. "Then I guess I should say it's been nice to meet you," ze finally said, "and have a good life."

I felt like I'd been hit with a jolt from a million light sockets. But Scratch didn't move.

"Oh, that's very Ingrid Bergman, my friend, but this isn't the movies," Scratch said in a kind of drawl. Ze was grinning! And kept right on talking.

"Don't you realize that we're just getting started? Don't you realize we're at some kind of precipice, instead of stuck inside some theory!"

I didn't really get what Scratch was talking about, but I did like the grin. Winc looked surprised too, but ze still had a guarded face.

"What do you mean?" ze asked, kind of huffing up. "I wasn't being dramatic, I was—"

"I know, but darlin', you're not the only one with the good lines here. What about my freak status? My idea of a good time would be to walk off into the sunset with a woman, a wolf, or my computer. Not a husband. But probably not a wife either."

"Oh, so I'm messing up the dream because I'm not a real woman?"

Scratch winced big. "I don't think that's what it is. I came here ready to deal with your being a guy, to being straight and narrow all over again. I'm still stuck on what I'm going to be now. When the thought of being a straight anything makes me want to choke!"

They looked at each other. Then Scratch looked back at me.

"Oh, Jesus, Toobe, this must be awful for you, pal. I mean, Mom and Dad are fighting. I'm sorry. I really am."

I got kind of mad, then, but I still didn't know why I was crying. "You're not Mom and Dad! You're Scratch and Winc. I don't know why that's not good enough for you!"

Scratch swung hir head back at Winc like a gangster. "He's hit it on the head again, you know dat, shweet-hawt?"

Winc just said "Yeah," eyes all misty and clouded and really beautiful too.

They just sat there, a kind of truce, I think, or at least an agreement not to pick at this gaping wound that looked like it would spew all over the place again.

Then Scratch looked up at the TV on the wall of the diner, and there was a story about us! There was Coney Island, there were cops, there were walkie-talkies, helicopters, and an anchorman doing a standup and everything!

You wouldn't believe how fast somebody with a mustache can get his check. We were outta there.

END TOOBE ENTRY

10
THREE BLIND MICE

NARRATIVE ENTRY, JABBATHEHUT

Lieutenant Wallace Budge crumples up the empty popcorn bag in his lap. "Tell me again," he says very patiently, the kind of patience that makes an underling nervous, "exactly what you saw. Just one more time for me, please."

The uniform in front of him takes a deep breath. "We hadn't gotten your memo yet, sir, so all we had to go on was a young white male, adolescent, or some threesome including a young, white . . ." His voice trails off.

"Yes, I understand. Go on," says Budge, oh-so-courteously.

"So we go to Nathan's, like we'd been advised."

Budge is on him like a hawk. "Nathan's? Why Nathan's?"

"Umm . . . we were hungry, sir, and our dispatcher said they had the best damn hot dogs. And they do. I've never tasted such good—"

"Uh-huh," Budge interrupts. "So you're at Nathan's. And did you see a threesome fitting the description they've got at the gate?"

"What? The guy, his daughter, and his wife?"

"Yes, those would be the ones."

"Yeah! But sir, you said they were criminals, and that the minor would be a young boy! We were going pretty fast, looking at all these people. There was a very suspicious-looking threesome, let me tell you!" The cop rocks back on his heels a bit.

"Is that right? And why were they suspicious?"

"Well, one was young, and the other two were older, and the young one was white, the other two were Black, and they had sweatshirts on."

"I see. Thank you, Officer, that's fine."

"I'm sorry, Lieutenant, we just didn't—"

"Right, I understand," says Budge, the last drops of patience dripping out of him like hot oil from an overheated engine. He heads to the gate, where a nervous security guard directs him to a security cam monitor. Endless bad footage of black-and-white figures dances on the snowy screen. He scans forward as Budge watches. And watches. And then sees them: the Scratch and Winc and Toobe family. One's playing the father, one the mother, and sure enough, there's Toobe buried under a young girl's guise. Looks uncomfortable as hell.

"Did you stop these three?"

"Well, as a matter of fact, I did, sir." He starts to look pleased, then checks himself. He did let them go, after all.

Budge can't believe his own good behavior. He simply looks up, eyes encouraging. "And?"

"Well, they looked normal enough, and they were in kind of a hurry."

Budge swivels his head around like an old dog. "A . . . hurry?"

"Well, yeah. The young one was having her first time, you know? Her monthly. The mother says they have to get her to the bathroom. Kind of embarrassing. I didn't know if there was gonna be some kind of . . . accident or something."

Budge smiles for the first time that day, but it's not a happy smile; in fact, it resembles something more like a grimace.

"I can see why you might not have pursued that line of questioning," is all he says.

"Yessir."

Budge crumples up the nearest thing to him. It's a paper ashtray full of butts.

"Aw shit."

END JABBA NARRATIVE ENTRY

GWYNYTH DIARY ENTRY: AS SEEN ON TV

Three bedraggled outlaws are now draped over various of my overstuffed furniture, their eyes glued to the television. We are watching instant replay coverage of the hunt in the park.

Fortunately, our outlaws sped off in that car, losing any tails that might have been chasing. Chasing tails! Hah! As far as I can tell, they just drove in a great big circle because now they're back with me.

My worst fears were confirmed when I saw a huge net of uniformed police converging on the amusement park, not thirty feet from my own home. Perhaps I was rash to carve my lair out of the warehouse space beneath the roller coaster. No, they've not found any of my doorways . . . they won't find us here. Especially since the cops think they drove off into the sunset.

In any case, the pigs at last fled the scene, leaving behind them the jackals of the press. There they were, their prey clearly my young charge, whose photograph they persistently flash every chance they get. Just when I'd despaired the whole ruse was up, the three of them came bursting through my door, looking for all the world like some sitcom from Hades. Cats scattered everywhere.

Why no one picked them up is beyond me. Their disguises had slipped considerably, and they were flushed with the chase. They were laughing and crying and hugging me, though two of them had not met me before. None of them have commented on my beard. Perhaps they realize that, at this point, they've no room to cast stones.

END GWYNYTH DIARY ENTRY

TOOBE ENTRY

Awesome! All clear! Gwynyth says we can stay here 'til the heat dies down. Winc even called my dad to let him know I'm okay. Whoops, good idea, I forgot about that. He was relieved I was with Winc; he trusts hir completely.

Gwynyth says I can be online again; I just have to use all her tools. When we got to her house, it was like some bizarre family gathering. Only I liked all of them.

And Gwynyth's going to teach me a lot more about her "craft," as she calls it. She's a phone phreak too.

We were on TV! Cops swarming all over the place. Then the guy talked to the press, the guy I saw in that photograph that time he caught me online. Must have been an old one, cuz he looked grayer now, and his face was like some action hero, all craggy and pockmarked. Both Scratch and Winc said at the same time, "Kinda sexy."

They looked at each other in surprise for a second. Then they cracked up. Then their fight started again.

First, Winc pointed out that Scratch's theories about everybody just being human weren't working since ze obviously couldn't handle Winc.

Then Scratch saw that Winc was getting dressed back in women's clothes and said, "I thought you were going to be neutral, a no-gender creature."

I was beginning to feel less scared and more tired of it all. They sounded like little brats! Gwynyth told me it was a good sign when that happened, but I didn't get it.

"They're running out of steam, child," was all she'd say.

END TOOBE ENTRY

GWYNYTH DIARY ENTRY

To: Jabbathehut
From: Gwynyth
Subj: Three Blind Mice

Toobe calls them The Mighty Morphin' Ninja Turtle Rangers. I call them "The Three Stooges." Whatever they are, they are safe from any immediate danger. Thank you for your caution as to my privacy, but I am quite delighted at present.

Still I'm concerned that the Police State has added "Kidnapping" and "Corruption of a Minor" to the growing list of non-charges for the other two. It's all over the media and the Net. They must go their separate ways. They had no *overt* objections to spending time away from each other.

Poor children! I'm sorely tempted to intervene with a lovers' spell, but I've lived this long without resorting to one of those, as well you know.

Will write more as it surfaces.

—Gwyn

P.S. I won't be charging you for any of this. I haven't had this much fun since the day we hacked our way into Fort Monmouth and left all those pictures!

P.P.S. Have rerouted my phone lines to appear as located in Six Flags Amusement Park in California. That should keep the hounds at bay. Monterey Bay. Hahaha! See what I did there?

END GWYNYTH DIARY ENTRY

TOOBE ENTRY

Gwynyth's got this cool beard! More than I can grow. I noticed Winc looking at it a lot. We haven't had a chance to talk in private yet; it's been too crazy.

Everybody was bouncing around, reacting to all the stuff we'd just been through. Gwynyth shed some light on Jabba's ways, how she "never deals in possibilities," only sure things. I told Scratch and Winc I needed them to be with me. It helped to see my friends. That even seemed to make them feel better.

Scratch and Winc are going back home, but Gwynyth's giving them cool bypasses to avoid detection: all leading back to amusement parks around the country, and there are hundreds of them! I made the mistake of asking Gwynyth why amusement parks, and she got out this album with postcards and photos of every single fun park in it, and lots of close-ups of the roller coasters. A whole album full. It took a couple of hours, but her stories made it fun.

As they were getting ready to leave, Scratch was calmer again. "Okay, just tell me," ze said to Winc. "If you're big on not being a woman or a man, why do you wear women's clothing?"

"I've answered that question every way I can! What do you want me to do, break out singing 'I Enjoy Being a Girl'? Look, Scratch, just how far do you think I'd get if I let my beard grow and walked around in a dress?"

Gwynyth snorted at that one, but she didn't say anything. Winc must've heard her, cuz ze went all red but kept talking. I never knew Winc had to shave!

"Or maybe you'd rather I wore men's clothes and a mustache but you could see my breasts?"

Scratch looked like one of those surreal pictures where light shines down on somebody from out of the sky.

"Oh, man," ze said. "You speak truth, my friend."

Then Scratch shared what it was like to walk around on the street in anywhere but a big city. Scratch was dressed as hir normal self I guess, with jeans and a T-shirt and boots.

"They'd kill me," Scratch said, nodding. "And they'd kill you."

END TOOBE ENTRY

To: T. Sparrow
From: Drew
Subject: Read this . . .

Hi Dad,

Talk me down? Here's an excerpt from Toobe's journal (above)—that cool little kid I was telling you about. That was about a conversation from 30 years ago about the dangers of being gender nonconforming in public. Makes me so sad and so fucking mad. Even 5 years ago I would have said things are better now, but they're worse. They're worse.

Yer kid Drew

11
GOOD COP, NO TRACE

NARRATIVE ENTRY, JABBATHEHUT

"Walls?" Shelly calls over to Lieutenant Budge.

"Yep?"

"It's a theme," she murmurs, checking several screens.

"Whaddya mean, theme?"

"They've been on all these bypasses, which is why it took Typhoid Mary so long to find them. All the so-called locations have the names of amusement parks."

"So?"

"So, find the amusement park, find the location. Typhoid Mary found New York, that would mean . . ."

"Coney Island!" Budge erupts.

"Exactly, handsome."

"So that would mean . . ." Budge struggles with his thought. "That would mean that other amusement park that popped up, what was it?"

"Six Flags in California," comes the reply.

". . . is not where they are. But . . ." and here he gives a raspy chuckle, "Henderson doesn't know that."

"Ooh, Wally, that's evil!" But she's purring.

At last, he will have Scratch and Winc himself. Now all he has to do is invite them to a room to have a little chat. Separately. For the classic game of "guess what your accomplice told me."

END JABBA NARRATIVE ENTRY

TOOBE ENTRY

FUNNY OF THE DAY

> Toobe, Scratch, and Winc are living underground with an entire computer node at their fingertips. They are safe, protected by a group of foreign legionnaire types prowling the premises. Be on the lookout for repeating patterns: waterfall references, pronoun deception, and good sex. 54% of the Young Libertarians Alliance has enjoyed congress with both Scratch and Winc, and a few conversations with Toobe. Please report all sightings to this node, as we vow to protect the fugitives to the best of our ability.
>
> —*Dennis*

It's good that they're on our side, but it's all lies and they don't know what the fuck they're talking about.

Scratch and Winc have each gone back to their own caves to nurse their psychic wounds. They are still not speaking to each other. It's been over a week. I got back to Gwynyth's with no trouble.

I can see why it'd be hard when somebody suddenly becomes a *he* or *she* if you've known them in the free zone of *ze*. They each blame themselves for the fight. Perfect for each other. Gwynyth still says not to worry; they need this time to think. If they could meet in some chat room, I think they'd be fine. But they refuse.

And Winc and Scratch still write to me.

Here's just one of the letters Scratch has sent me:

To: Toobe
From: Scratch
Subj: Dummy

Toobe, my man, I'm an idiot. I asked for something, I got what I asked for, and now I'm running away from it. Not to whine, but it ain't a great time in the world to be unusual, and as you have seen for yourself, I'm anything but usual.

I'm not one of the cool kids, I wear big shoes, I sleep with whoever turns me on but mostly only online. I'm in love with somebody who looks like a woman but kind of looks like both. What a dream come true, eh? What did I do with that? Took a great big breath, and ran the fuck away.

Easier to be a freak all alone, at least you're carrying your own suitcases. When you've got someone else with you it's less lonely but your feelers extend to them now, you get protective and controlling and anxious and worried.

I'm back in my stupid apartment, just like I wanted. There's dust over everything, real-time sunlight streams in, illuminating all that is dingy. Instead of a happy Spring feeling, it merely points up the pitfalls of the Real.

I miss hir. I wouldn't have even noticed this crummy apartment last week. I would have jumped online and talked to my Winc.

Am I nothing without interacting with another? Me, who loves to be alone more than anything? Now that I'm *there* I don't truly know who I am.

I am Scratch to the mailman, Scratch to the woman I buy cigarettes from, and Scratch to Winc. To you. To Gwynyth even. And without them I am Scratch to myself, whoever the hell *ze* is: stubborn, boring, unwilling to stretch, unable to make connections fire in my brain, unable to even pee without commenting on it.

Big talker all right.

Me, scared of this person? Smoky eyes and a laugh like music even when it was shaking with fear?

Me, not willing to walk down the street with a creature whose gender slips like a failing clutch?

Me, with the short hair and the wide hips and the mannish walk, the one who makes the bad guys uncomfortable and the ladies curious?

Me, what exactly do I have to protect?

—S.

END TOOBE ENTRY

NARRATIVE ENTRY, JABBATHEHUT

Wally Budge is nervous. This is his first face-to-face with the entity known as Scratch.

***** You are in room "White Flag" *****

Scratch: ::drumming fingers on tabletop:: You're late!

Ms. Budge: Let me guess: You're not really on the Santa Monica boardwalk, are you?

Scratch: What's it to you?

Scratch: And what makes you think I wanna talk?

Ms. Budge: If I were you, I'd want to know as much about who's chasing me as I could.

Scratch: OK, here's a starter. I thought you were a guy.

Ms. Budge: Look, it was a screwup when I Registered, OK? I *am* a guy.

Scratch: Whatever you say, Miss Thing.

Ms. Budge: Ha ha. You haven't been hanging out with your pal recently, have you?
Scratch: Why the hell are you after us?
Ms. Budge: Don't you read the papers? You're America's Most Wanted.
Scratch: Yeah but why?
Ms. Budge: All right, good place to start. No matter what you say, the law says I can't hold you to it anyway.
Scratch: Oh, gee, now I'll tell you everything you want to know.
Ms. Budge: Hey, give me a break, will you?
Scratch: ::softly:: you're after me, Mister, why should I give you a break?
Ms. Budge: OK, OK, just answer me this . . . please.
Scratch: ::heavy sigh:: Oh, ga.

Budge is about to ask what "ga" means but turns to his dog-eared manual instead. Christ, the sign deaf people use for "go ahead." He makes a note: cross-reference "Deaf."

Ms. Budge: Are you now or have you ever been involved in any kind of trafficking in pornography?
Scratch: No!
Ms. Budge: Thought not. OK, next question . . .
Scratch: brb.

Scratch has left the room.

Ms. Budge: Damn!

He looks up "brb" in the manual. Scratch will "Be Right Back."

Scratch has entered the room.

Ms. Budge: Hey, where'd you go?
Scratch: Just checking to see if this is being traced. Good cop.
Ms. Budge: The best. I'm being straight with you, Scratch.
Scratch: Uh huh. Next question?

Ms. Budge: Are you now or have you ever been involved in any kind of trafficking in the distribution of illegal access bypass code?

Scratch: Define illegal.

Ms. Budge: Ha! Good thief. OK: bypassing Registration. That's technically a crime, and I can charge you with it.

Scratch: I refuse to recognize "Registration." Sodomy isn't recognized by the govt either, but it's done, isn't it?

Ms. Budge: Um, OK. All right—last question, and it's the tough one. Are you now or have you ever been involved in hurting the kid in any way?

Scratch: What kid?

Ms. Budge: Toobe. The kid. The boy.

Scratch: ::face steaming up, red as hell:: You guys got nasty minds. I'd do *anything* for that "kid."

Ms. Budge: OK, calm down. I had to ask.

Scratch: Where the fuck do you get your info? Why aren't you going after real bad guys, like politicians and rapists?

Ms. Budge: My job is to go after you.

Scratch: So bypassing Registration is my "crime"? You've been chasing us for something you "suspect"?

Ms. Budge: I can get you on illegal trafficking of code, but the laws on that are so fuzzy, you'll probably get off.

Scratch: And how do you get off, sir?

Ms. Budge: I don't understand your question.

Scratch: Forget it.

Ms. Budge: Look. No one can prosecute you, let alone convict you. Come on in.

Scratch: So your only job is to chase people you suspect of keeping to themselves, and maybe just maybe committing crimes online, which is an unreal world in which nothing that happens is real.

Ms. Budge: Afraid it's better than that.

Scratch: Yeah?

Ms. Budge: We've got warrants out for you and Winc.

Scratch: Why?

Ms. Budge: You were the one in the cute flower print dress at Coney Island, am I right?
Scratch: No, I was the big Black dude you're so afraid of in your dreams.
Ms. Budge: If you keep hiding out I'm gonna have to add "Resisting Arrest." I won't like it, but I'll do it.
Scratch: Why are you talking to me if you have a warrant?

He doesn't have an answer to that. The screen scrolls blank after Scratch's question.

Scratch: I think you want to know something else.
Ms. Budge: You interest me. You're something/someone I don't have a handle on.
Scratch: What's so mysterious? brb.
Ms. Budge: Why do you DO this? DAMN! He's gone again.

Scratch has left the room.

Scratch has entered the room.

Scratch: Good cop, no tracer.
Ms. Budge: Told you. It's just me and you.
Scratch: Tell me: Is there a crime in having different IDs?
Ms. Budge: There's no legal precedent for that, no.
Scratch: So why go along with it then? Do you really believe we're breaking the law?
Ms. Budge: Too much around me changes all the time. I like things stable.
Scratch: That's why you're a cop. Good guys, bad guys, real clear lines.
Ms. Budge: You think because I like things nice and slow and predictable I'm a bad guy?
Scratch: No, I'm saying cops love black and white. Sorry, pal. Some good people break the law, some bad people are real sweethearts.
Ms. Budge: Hey, don't start talking to me about criminals with hearts of gold.
Scratch: I don't think your heart is really in this investigation.

Budge pauses as he notices they have both typed the word "heart" at the same time.

Scratch: Hey, Ms. Budge, do you know what a simulpost is?
Ms. Budge: Huh? No. What is it?
Scratch: Forget it.
Ms. Budge: I spoke with your buddy just the other day.
Scratch: Which buddy?
Ms. Budge: I need to tell you, Scratch, he's not going to last too long.
Scratch: Who?
Ms. Budge: Don't play cute. Winc.
Scratch: What about Winc?
Ms. Budge: Winc's flighty, doesn't have the stamina to keep running. You know I'm right.
Scratch: We're not running. We're living. Don't you get that? Why does that bother you guys so much?
Ms. Budge: Your life is starting to run mine, and that bothers me.
Scratch: I'm so sorry.
Ms. Budge: Come on in, Scratch. Bring Winc with you. I'll get you a fair deal.
Scratch: A fair fucking deal for what? We did nothing wrong!
Ms. Budge: My point, exactly!

Budge cringes at the burst of honesty, cursing himself for typing it.

Scratch: If you know we did nothing wrong, then stop the chase.

Again, he has no answer.

Ms. Budge: Look, this thing has gotten a lot bigger than you and me.
Scratch: Uh huh.
Ms. Budge: And if I don't bring you in, someone a lot nastier is going to.
Ms. Budge: That's a fact.
Scratch: They're gonna "bring you in" too.

Ms. Budge: Huh?

Scratch: If it's bigger than us, then you're a flunky.

There is another pause at Budge's end.

Scratch: ::softly:: You don't even believe in what "the law" is doing this time, do you?

Ms. Budge: I believe in justice. You broke the law with those codes. You're breaking the law by evading arrest, and you broke the law by refusing to Register.

Scratch: You chickened out, bub. I was never told, to my face, that I was wanted. I never evaded anything. So why bother, dear?

Ms. Budge: Why bother with what?

Scratch: Don't you think the Reg process is just a wee bit inadequate? Considering that you are currently trapped in a female identity?!

Ms. Budge: I told you to cut that out. Of course it's flawed. But if the laws fall apart, there's going to be a lot of people hurting a lot of others.

Scratch: Oh, don't give me that law crap. I can tell you have a bigger brain than that.

Ms. Budge: Gee, thanks.

Scratch: Well, that's a pretty big flaw, getting your identity "wrong." You know when they check your office accounts they'll report your female profile? And send you the "appropriate" mail?

Ms. Budge: I know. You should *see* the ads I'm getting.

Scratch: ::sweetly:: I bet.

Ms. Budge: Tell me this. Since you don't like that neighbor of yours. Why don't you just shoot him? Fuck the law, right?

Scratch: Jesus fucking christ! How much of my mail do you read?

Ms. Budge: All of it . . . dear.

Scratch: You fucker.

Ms. Budge: I don't like it, but it's going to get worse if you don't cooperate.

Scratch: You motherfucker pervert, reading other people's mail . . .

Ms. Budge: Grow up, Scratch, you're in the big sandbox now. It's the only way to find you.

Splattered, Budge thinks to himself. That's the word he's heard about this kind of online chat. *I'm splattered.*

Scratch: Look, let's cut the crap, OK?

Ms. Budge: Winc is going to crack faster than you, and he'll bring you with him.

Scratch: You don't know shit about Winc, it's obvious.

Ms. Budge: I know more about Winc than you'd like to hear.

Scratch: ::waving hand impatiently:: You want me to fill in the blanks. But filling in blanks just creates more rigidity. More ways for people to become "illegal." Those rules and categories turn into a juggernaut, hammering over people like me. Forcing genders, forcing identities, forcing Registration. And ultimately? That juggernaut runs right over you, too, my friend. The only ones left will be pod people.

Ms. Budge: What are you talking about?

Scratch: To follow a law just because it's a law is not good enough.

Ms. Budge: I don't give a fuck whether you Register or not . . .

Scratch: All I did was refuse to Register. And now you say you don't give a fuck?

Ms. Budge: I AM NOT DISAGREEING WITH YOU!

Scratch: Huh?

Ms. Budge: I'm not saying what you're doing is right or wrong. I'm saying right now it's against the law. And it won't be cops judging you, it'll be a jury of your peers.

Scratch: My peers are too fucking scared of people like you.

Ms. Budge: I know, and I really wish to hell you weren't scared of me.

Scratch: You know what? I'm *not* scared of you anymore. It's liberating as hell. Maybe it's because you're less threatening as a "woman"!

If Budge could type what his own sputtering sounds like, he would. The thought crosses his mind to send an all-purpose Private Message to everyone online: "I AM NOT A WOMAN"

Scratch: Look, Budge. If this is bigger than both of us, then you can't cut me any deals. You have no power here, be gone.

Scratch: I'm outta here. But it's been great talking to you.

Ms. Budge: Wait, Scratch . . .

Scratch has left the room.

Ms. Budge: Aw, great . . .

END JABBA NARRATIVE ENTRY

TOOBE ENTRY

To: Toobe
From: Winc
Subj: Oh, ouch

::softly:: Hey there. I just wanted to know if you're safe and well. Please let me know, soon as you can.

Have you heard from Scratch? Don't tell hir I asked. Ze needs some space just now, space that doesn't include me. But if you could pass any word back, I'd appreciate it.

Wanna know something funny? I thought Scratch was going to be a guy! I was all set to be the little woman in his life. ::sigh:: Next time this sort of thing happens, slap me!

The real world has become more and more threatening. Have you been reading *half* the stuff they're saying about me and Scratch? I start crying, it scares me that much. Which prison would they put me in, Toobe?

Not joking here. In England, they put gurlz like me into the men's prison, even after surgery. I don't know what they'd do to me *here*, because all my paperwork still says boy. I'm too freaked to go to the corner for Diet Pepsi and Cheez-Its, it's rice-cake city in my apartment. With peanut butter. Even the Pakistani family who runs the corner store is now asking if "Missy Winc" is the same Winc everyone's talking about. So . . . ::deep breath:: I'm getting out of Dodge.

Out of my neighborhood, out of the whole damned state. By the time you get this, I'll be "return to sender, address unknown."

Cyberspace is the one place I found to splatter into all of who I am—free—so I'll just stay there. Been doing a lot of surfing these past few days, in every kind of identity, but never my own; that's under reconstruction.

I miss you. I miss Scratch. No . . . I miss what Scratch has been to me, with me, online. I don't miss who ze turned out to be. But I miss something, someone.

Love you, hope you're well. Say hello to Gwyn for me, will you?

—W.

If they would just talk. Winc thinks Scratch is rejecting hir when ze's only just thinking, and Scratch thinks Winc is all of a sudden just one person, instead of all the ones ze's known for a while.

END TOOBE ENTRY

NARRATIVE ENTRY, JABBATHEHUT

Meanwhile, Winc has graciously accepted Lt. Budge's invitation to chat.

Online Host

***** You are in room "White Flag" *****

Winc: ::standing outside the lion's cage, peering in at the strong handsome lion wearing a badge:: Howdy!

Ms. Budge: Thank you so much for talking with me.

Winc: Any time, darling.

Ms. Budge: You don't sound like a man.

Winc: Why *thank you*. I'm not being a man today. Are you?

Ms. Budge: I am a man.

Winc: Cute screen name. Get you many dates?

Ms. Budge: It was a mistake in Registration. I assure you I'm Lt. Budge, a man.

Winc: ::purring:: Oh I doubt that, but we'll let it ride. What do you want?

Ms. Budge: What do you mean you're "not being a man today"?

Winc: ::eyes sparkling:: You haven't done your homework.

Ms. Budge: Ah, I see. But why *do* you change around so much?

Private Message to Ms. Budge

> **Winc:** Please feel free to use your Private Messages, dear. They're so much more intimate.
>
> **Ms. Budge:** I'll try, but this is still fairly new to me.
>
> **Winc:** ::slow smile:: How sweet!

Winc: Is *that* what you want to know? Why I change? ::laughing delightedly:: Try it yourself!

Ms. Budge: I'd rather hear it from you.

Winc: What is it you want to hear? What I'm wearing, right?

Ms. Budge: No, no, no. I wonder if you know that the law is after you?

Winc: ::smiling softly, opening top buttons of my blouse:: The law? Whatever do they want?

Ms. Budge: Jesus, lady. That's not what this is about. We've been talking with your friend Scratch.

Winc: ::rubbing a hand over my stubble, fixing my tie:: Hey, buddy, watch who you're callin' a dame!

Confused, Budge simply doesn't answer.

Winc: ::smiling gently::

Weakly, Budge types:

Ms. Budge: Okay, you're pretty good at that.

Winc: ::purring:: The best you'll ever meet.

Ms. Budge: I guess that's why you're so good at phone sex, right?

There is a long pause from the other end.

Ms. Budge: You're awfully quiet now . . .

Winc: When did you talk with Scratch, asshole?

Ms. Budge: Oh, the lady has a mouth. Recently.

There is another long pause. Budge worries he's driven him/her away.

Winc: Well, good for you. Did you get hir autograph? Or a blow job?

There's that word again, "hir." Maybe Winc doesn't even know what sex Scratch is? He makes a note on his dog-eared manual.

Ms. Budge: What's the matter, have a fight?

Winc: Fuck you.

Ms. Budge: Look, let's try another tack.

Winc has left the room.

Ms. Budge: Damn!

He remembers the Private Messages.

Private Message to Winc

Ms. Budge: Winc, please come back, I want to talk with you. I'm sorry.

Winc: Hold on . . . I'm checking something.

Winc has entered the room.

Winc: No tracer, huh? Good cop.

Ms. Budge: Of course not. Can we start again?

Winc: ::sitting down across from you, blouse still open to reveal just a soft curve, leaning forward::

Ms. Budge: You can check a trace that quickly, eh?

Winc: ::softly:: I can do lots of things, darling. What do you want?

Ms. Budge: Are you aware there is a warrant for your arrest?

Winc: On what charges?

Ms. Budge: Well, they may or may not be true, but there's evidence enough for us to arrest you. So can I ask you a question or two, to clear this thing up?

Winc: ::laughing lightly:: Be my guest.

Ms. Budge: Are you now or have you ever trafficked in pornography on the Internet?

Winc: ::leaning forward, resting my hand on your knee:: As a participant?

Ms. Budge: Selling or loaning pornography to minors and others.

Winc: ::stroking your knee absently:: No, not that I can recall, officer.

Ms. Budge: Have you done any harm to the kid?

Winc: Excuse me?

Ms. Budge: Have you trafficked the kid Toobe in porn or otherwise corrupted him?

Winc: Oh fuck off, sewer brain!

Private Message to Winc

Ms. Budge: Excusez moi?

Winc: ::melting into the floor in a writhing mass:: Yessssssssssssss . . . talk French to me, you hot thing, you!

Budge rocks back in his chair violently. Recovers, then types again. He repeats the question, back in the "room" where he feels safer. In English. What compelled him to speak French, he wonders?

Ms. Budge: I'm sorry, could you answer that question. We're concerned for his welfare.

Winc: Just a *little* question first? ::trailing my finger gently up your leg::

Ms. Budge: First you answer: Did you hurt the kid?

Winc: Is your dick so small that all you can think of is hurting other people so you feel big? ::sweet smile::

Ms. Budge: I take it that's a no.

Winc: Bingo.

A new Private Message zaps his screen:

Private Message to Ms. Budge

SubRobert: ::shivering:: I *knew* you'd be online again, Mistress. I've been searching all over for you!

Ms. Budge: Huh?

SubRobert: Don't you remember me? I sure remember your handcuffs.

Ms. Budge: BUZZ OFF! I'M BUSY!

SubRobert: Oh . . . Private Room, huh? Can I lick up what's left over?

The trembling detective punches IGNORE.

Ms. Budge: All right. What *your* question? (I'm sorry for my poor typing.)

Winc: (Typing with one hand always does that.)

Ms. Budge: Cut that out! I'm being straight with you, sir or madam.

Winc: ::laughing:: My question is simply this: What law have I broken?

Ms. Budge: Have you ever distributed illegal bypass codes?

Winc: Yes indeedy.

Winc has left the room.

Again, Budge tries the pleading tone, but it's starting to wear thin.

Private Message to Winc

Ms. Budge: Please, Winc, can we talk some more?

Winc has entered the room.

Ms. Budge: Where did you go?

Winc: ::smoky voice:: Maybe I slipped into something more comfortable.

Ms. Budge: Look, I'm not trying to come on to you! I'm just trying to understand you.

Winc: ::pouting:: Don't you find me a *little* bit attractive?

Ms. Budge: Why don't you come on in, we can make a deal. I don't think any of the charges will stick if you do.

Winc: ::softly:: I'm waiting for an answer . . . don't you find this . . . me . . . attractive? Come on now . . . really, just a little?

Ms. Budge: Scratch has told us most of what we need to know. We just need a few blanks filled in before we move in on you.

Winc: ::folding arms across my chest, mouth shut::

Ms. Budge: I see. You can make this easy. Just turn yourself in. I can make a deal for you.

Winc: ::sighing:: You're no fun at all. Ever get told that?

Ms. Budge: Yeah, I'm afraid I do. Sorry, not my job to be fun. Perhaps if we meet you could teach me.

Winc: ::laughing gently::

Winc: In. Your. Dreams. Copper.

Ms. Budge: I'm sorry, that was inappropriate.

Private Message to Ms. Budge

> **Winc:** ::purring:: Of course it was, darling. Don't worry your pretty little head about it. Way ahead of you . . . always will be.
>
> **Ms. Budge:** Thank you. I think.
>
> **Winc:** So what did Scratch say?
>
> **Ms. Budge:** Scratch told us you would be much more cooperative. Guess you aren't speaking right now, huh?

Ms. Budge: Your mail is very interesting.

Winc: ::tossing my hair off my face, smiling:: You read all of it, huh?

Ms. Budge: Yes. All of it.

Winc: Did it get you hard?

Ms. Budge: Actually, no. Is sex all you think about? Is that what this is about? You're sexually frustrated?
Winc: Uh huh. That's all I think about. That's all I am. What did Scratch say, exactly?
Ms. Budge: That you were weak and you'd tell us what we need to know because you're eager to please.
Winc: You're so full of shit.
Ms. Budge: Am I?
Winc: Scratch would *never* say anything like that.
Ms. Budge: Are you sure?

There is a long pause.

Winc: Tell me Scratch's words. His exact words.
Ms. Budge: Just come on in. Scratch has already cooperated. So you don't think he'd do that, eh?
Winc: ::smiling:: No, I don't think he would.
Ms. Budge: I assure you, he talked with us. We already have enough to bring you in, why not just do it voluntarily?
Winc: Well, you tell him from me that his dick is even smaller than yours, and that I'm outta here. Tell him I said that, OK?
Ms. Budge: I'm sure I'll pass that on.

Winc has left the room.

Private Message to Winc

Ms. Budge: Winc, please come back. We were doing so well.
Winc: Oh, go suck your boss off like you've always wanted to.
Ms. Budge: Damn!

Just as he starts a probably futile trace on Winc, a message flashes:

URGENT! ACCEPT ME NOW!

Puzzled, he abandons the trace attempt, pushing the ACCEPT button, only to have the following appear:

Paid Advertisement for MS. BUDGE:
This is your opportunity to make hygiene history!

****

Many career women like yourself have written us, asking for a new, more absorbent, more easily insertable feminine hygiene product.

WE HAVE RESPONDED TO YOUR CALL. Click here to receive your free sample of MINIMAX, designed with the career woman in mind . . . and body.

Ms. Budge has left the room.

Wally Budge lifts his eyes to catch the latest "Headline News Alert" and smiles.

NO FLAGGING DOWN SCRATCH & WINC
(AP)

Over 50 Law Enforcement agents gathered at dawn at Six Flags Amusement Park in California, where a "reliable tip" told them they could expect to find Scratch and Winc. They found some of the nation's best rides, but no cyberfugitives. Chief enforcement officer, Phillip Henderson, had no comment.

RELATED ARTICLES:

"Government Search: Roundabout, or Merry-Go-Round?"
"Nighttime Talk Show Hosts Rip into Government Hunt."
"Geraldo at 4:00: Identical Twins Who Have Had Cybersex with Scratch and Winc."

END JABBA NARRATIVE ENTRY

TOOBE ENTRY

I must get a few hundred of these a day:

> **To:** Toobe
> **From:** Blaze@Hardcopy.com
> **Subj:** Article
>
> We're very eager to hear from you, sir. We can go to press at a moment's notice should you give us an interview. I've gotten the go-ahead for $100,000, as you requested. We've got everything else, we report on the Scratch and Winc story every night.
>
> Please get back to me asap.
>
> —Blaze Selder
>
> Producer, *Hard Copy*

Man, these people are sly. I never requested anything! They just started with a $25,000 offer, then more. Not answering.

Things have escalated, really spooky. Something I learned from my dad about the '60s is that once somebody gets to be a hero, they get shot. I don't want that. All I want is for my two friends to talk to each other again.

And for the law to find somebody else to fry.

END TOOBE ENTRY

12
THE QUESTIONS

NARRATIVE ENTRY, JABBATHEHUT

The esteemed Undersecretary LaBouchere has summoned Lieutenant Wally Budge to her office for one overdue dressing down.

"MS. BUDGE?! Do you KNOW they're laughing at us? Everyone! Did you KNOW that Letterman is intimating that you and I are LESBIANS?

"You don't get it, do you?" the undersecretary continues. "Screw 'procedure'; this has got nothing to do with that. It's got nothing to do with Scratch or Winc either. There's an epidemic out there, Lieutenant. Scratch and Winc are symbols."

He has suspected the same thing but had no idea she'd pegged it too.

"They're catalysts," she tries again, searching in the air for something that will somehow get through to him. "Everyone is falling into line; they've all begun to resist Registration. Do you know what that means? Have you any idea why there's a Registration? We are letting down our end of the bargain, Lieutenant."

He is genuinely confused—what bargain is that?

"Let me spell it out for you, my friend. Registration is tied to advertising, advertising is tied to government. It's all a partnership. And," she sputters, "Scratch and Winc are messing up the whole thing! Of course it's ridiculous, but that's not the point. We need to get back to real police work. Whatever it takes."

Lieutenant Budge shuffles back to his office, sits down, and leans way back in the creaky chair.

"Ooh, you don't look good, Walls," Shelly murmurs as she quietly steps in to join him. "She was pretty mad?"

"How dumb could I be?" he growls. "I should have known why they were going over my head. They made the ol' proverbial deal with the devil."

"Sure looks like it, Walls. I'm so sorry."

END JABBA NARRATIVE ENTRY

TOOBE ENTRY

FUNNY OF THE DAY

Surgery happy USA

Don't you think it's kinda weird that you can just go pay a surgeon to break your nose, suck out fat from your hips, stretch your face tight over your skull, or add dangerous globs of saline to your breasts, but . . .

If you want to change your genitalia you have to live as the 'opposite' sex *before* the change (just a mite dangerous in this culture), go to therapy, and play the nice girl/boy and get *permission*?

I bet if I looked in Big Brother's closet I'd find stacks of porno magazines . . . all of it Chicks With Dicks.

—*Yer friendly, neighborhood Winc*

Was just remembering what Winc told me about the beginning of hir transition. Ze had to "live as a woman" while ze was starting hormones. Ze really looked kind of "in between" for a while there. That's like going out in drag against your will. Ze had to do that for an entire year before surgery. They told hir to make up a whole childhood as a little girl, so no one would suspect ze was once a guy. Ze said that being in therapy for being a transie (hir word for transsexual, not mine) was the only therapy where they encouraged you to lie.

END TOOBE ENTRY

To: Editor, They/Them magazine
From: D.I. Drew
Subject: Word choice

Hi Asa,

You're right to ask—I too wondered if "transie" would be offensive, but turns out "transie" was coined by Sandy Stone, that great pioneer of transgender studies. People in her circle on the West Coast used it, but it doesn't seem to have made it across the country very far. I bet Winc was a friend of hers!

You're also 1000% on point about the chilling similarities between Registration in 1995, and the algorithm/gatekeeping/data mining we have today. Though the whole idea of Registration failed thanks to our heroes, it was replaced by something more insidious. There's no need to track people because we freakin provide all our data voluntarily!

Cheers,

Drew

PS: Our two heroes are so frustrating. Apparently, Gwynyth felt the same . . .

GWYNYTH DIARY ENTRY

Scratch is burying hirself online, having asked me to help hir lurk without being detected.

Winc lights from room to room, never staying long enough to have a real conversation.

I want to shake them both! I'm about to side with the child and tell them they've had enough time.

The boy does *not* like that I refer to him as "the child" and has taken to calling me "the old lady" in retaliation. Very well . . . henceforth, I shall call him "Toobe." Though now that I think of it, he could call me "the old witch" and he'd be spot on.

Ah. I see a new chat room has popped up in my Safe area. I won't eavesdrop, but at least they're talking. Fingers crossed.

END GWYNYTH DIARY ENTRY

WINC JOURNAL ENTRY

***** You are in room "Questions" *****

Scratch: Okay, let's say I've got the music right: I love you, I want to be with you somehow, but the lyrics are still fucked up, I have questions that are stupid but I have to ask them of *somebody*. It might as well be you since you're the reason I'm asking them.

Winc: What do you mean, "I love you"? *Heck* of a thing to open with, but beautiful music yeah. I guess I've got nothing to lose by answering as honestly as I can, and maybe even something to gain.

Your questions prolly won't be stupid. Questions are brave.

And I love you too.

Scratch: Why do so many transsexuals wear too much makeup and look like they're about twenty years behind the time fashion-wise?

Winc: Answer: Not that I can answer for EVERY transsexual, but a lot of us have fantasized about our transition for a very long time. When we finally get a chance, we often pick the clothes that were popular at the time we really started our journey. Teenage years. So when I started, I kind of looked like Anjelica Huston in the '70s.

Scratch: Do you still have facial hair?

Winc: ::groaning:: Yeah, I do. I have to scrape my face every day. It's a sore spot with me (literally!). But electrolysis is *so* expensive: $40–$80 an hour. And the average number of hours needed is around 200–300. I'm lucky, my estrogen stuff seems to slow down the growth-rate of my face hair. ::wincing:: Should talk with Gwyn about how she can just let hers grow and grow! Anyway, I can go for a little over 24 hours with a passably smooth face.

Scratch: If you were het before, are you lesbian now? Or did your sexuality change too and now you're a straight woman?

Winc: ::slow smile:: Who wants to know?

Are you flirting with me again? ::laughing lightly::

I've always been attracted to women romantically and sexually, and those are two different attractions. I've always been attracted to men sexually, but never romantically. What does all *that* make me?

When I was being Man, I figured I couldn't *really* be a real woman because I was *attracted* to women, and real women are all attracted to men. (So, lesbian types weren't real women either) I didn't have that heart-zing for men (like I did for you).

But I *tried* getting involved with men. Spent a whole period of my life picking up guys, and I was a guy, right? I'd pick up these men, well, I'd let them pick *me* up, and they'd take me to their homes, late at night, and we'd lie down on their living room floors, and I'd suck them off. I liked doing that. A lot. But we always had to be quiet, because their wives were sleeping in the next room or upstairs. You know I'm not making this up.

Am I a straight woman now? No way! I'd still like to have sex with a guy, using this new equipment I have (You do know I had genital surgery, right?), but it's scary. Guys scare me. So, no, all that said, I guess I'm not straight.

Scratch: Do you tell people you used to be a boy even though you weren't really, in your mind?

Winc: ::gently:: Scratch, I *was* a boy. No in-the-mind about it. I was a boy, and later I was a man. I think that mind-body-spirit is so tightly woven that you can't say anything like "I wasn't really a boy, in my mind." At least *I* can't—it's just not my story. I was a boy, and I hated it. I was a man, and I hated it. I changed my body, and I changed my mind, and now my spirit feels so much more free!

Yes, I come out to people I want to be close to. And now you're going to ask why didn't I tell you from the start. Because we agreed not to say anything, and whatever you were being online, you kept bringing out the girl in me, the femme in me, even when I was trying to be boy or man, and I loved that so much, and then I got scared again that you would freak if you knew.

But I did tell you as soon as we agreed to tell each other.

Scratch: Did you wear your mother's clothes when you were little?

Winc: ::smiling:: What kind of transsexual textbooks have you been reading, hon? Only one time when I was about five or six. It felt really taboo to me, very wrong. I mean, that was Mom, not Woman. That was wearing Mom's clothes, not women's clothes. I made my own clothes to wear, though, from towels, old blankets, drapes, whatever, when I was a little kid.

Scratch: Did you have to learn how to "be a woman" in terms of mannerisms and attitude, or was it already there?

Winc: Had to learn. It's all learned, isn't it? Look at how uncomfortable you were in being Mom at Coney Island, darling. That's how I spotted you from across the park. You never learned that girl stuff, and I'm so glad you didn't. But wait, maybe you did learn and you rejected it? That's a question for you. I'll add it to my list.

Scratch: Do you miss your dick?

Winc: ::hands on hips, tossing my head back defiantly:: Let me tell you a thing or two about what happened to my dick, darling.

First, the docs cut it open like they were filleting a fish. Then they scraped out all the spongy stuff, they turned it inside-out, and they poked it up inside me—like when you turn a sock inside-out.

So my dick is still there, technically. It's just in another, more palatable shape. I have an innie now, not an outie.

::laughing merrily:: No, I don't miss it. I never hated my dick, though. I hadda lotta joy with that thing. It was sweet, in a vulnerable way. I loved making myself come with it. What I hated is what it made me in the eyes of everyone else: a man. What I've been learning with you is that gender is as much how people relate to you as it is what you feel, and all these people were relating to me as a man, and it was all because of this thing hanging down between my legs, so . . . snip snip. Happily gone.

Scratch: Do you have all female parts and do you come?

Winc: ::eyes sparkling:: Female parts? When did we become such a prude, dear heart? I have a surgically-constructed vulva, vagina, cervix, and clitoris, if that's what you want to know. I have no internal stuff like uterus and ovaries.

But wait . . . what exactly are female parts? I know some terrific women with dicks, and some truly manly men with pussies. And no, you can't ask me if female = woman and male = man. Well, you can ask me but then you'll have to watch my brain fry. Right in front of you.

Do I come?

::softly:: Yeah, I can. I do. I have with you.

Scratch: ::blushing:: Okay, well then.

Hope these questions are okay. The more I ask my questions, the more I recognize myself. And yes, I had to learn how to act female, too, and I was born one.

Now, please ask me the questions you've got.

Winc: Okay, first a confession. I lied to you a little bit. I knew about butch and femme before seeing that online board. When I was first trying out my girl stuff, I would get myself dressed to the nines, what anybody in their right mind would call femme, right?

Of course right. Now I want to tell you a story.

In the early days of my transition, I would go out to lesbian bars. It was women only, and I felt more safe there than I'd ever felt anywhere in my life. I was too scared to try to pick anyone up, or to let someone pick me up. But there was this one bar I used to go to and sit and have a drink, watch, study, learn. I couldn't really relate to all these young bar bunnies, not physically, but the *life* they had! The exuberance! I wanted that. Alas, there I was, this tall gangly, older man/woman. They weren't very gentle with me. Can't say I blame them, not in hindsight. I was awfully defensive.

Anyway, I finally got up the courage one night to go upstairs, where the bathroom was. And the bathroom was just off a room filled with all these older women, sitting there in shirtsleeves and ties, some in T-shirts, some in muscle shirts, and always a couple of women in flannel shirts. They were sprawled out in comfy chairs, and, hon, their eyes lit up the minute I walked into the room. I'll never ever forget that moment. They were all butch, and they were happy to see me.

This one sweet butch said, "Hell-l-l-lo, sugar, come have a seat." And she stood up for me, so gallant. I sat there, and it was a dream come true. They bought me drinks, we danced, I watched them play pool, they showed me how. I choked on one of their cigars, they laughed, but not *at* me.

That was pretty much the moment I first realized I could be happy as girl, with butches. I went back up there as frequently as I could. Then, like most of the girl bars in the city, that one closed down, and there was nowhere else to hang out, not that I knew of, anyway. That's around the time that Toobe taught me about this online world—where I met my favorite butch of all time.

Scratch: Wow. Good story. Proud of butches for how they were with you.::going back into the laboratory, or is that to the drawing board::

I know that the outside world, and most lesbians nowadays, smirk at the concept of butch/femme. They smirk at us. But they're not looking closely, because butch/femme is . . . deep and powerful. Whatever it is. Fuck what people think, if it works. (Although obviously I'm not a classic butch, born too late and never got trained right!)

Winc: You're surprising me again. You keep doing that, I love that about you. But I'm just going to ask you my questions and see what that leads to. ::deep breath::

Winc: Why do most lesbians have such short hair? ::gently:: Why do *you*?

Scratch: The better question might be to ask a lot of men why they *don't* have long hair. They'll probably tell you it's a pain in the ass to keep up. Most straight men I know love long hair on women, so straight women grow it. Me, I don't have to.

Winc: Are you *trying* to look mannish? Pass for "man" in the world?

Scratch: Ouch this hurts. What is mannish anyway? I've been asking myself this since I was 9 and my mom told me to put on a shirt when I went outside. So much shame followed, that what I wanted to be and act like was reduced to wanting to be "like a man." And that was bad of course. So it's taken forever to simply say that I love being a woman. There's more ways for women to look than what's offered in "fast-food fashion." Sometimes I wear eyeliner because it looks cool. When I get dressed in the morning, I'm going for comfort, power, and sometimes armor, but never to hide.

Winc: People stare at you like they stare at me. How do you deal with it?

Scratch: Lately I tell myself they stare because I look so damned good. (Okay, this works about a tenth of the time.) Why would I want to look like everyone else?

Winc: Why do lesbians insist on "women only" spaces? Isn't it just hiding away?

Scratch: It *is* kinda like hiding away and it feels great. Any guy can tell you how fun it is to sit in a bar with his male buds and watch TV. It's a breather from dealing with the "opposite" sex. He just doesn't have to put up a bunch of signs advertising where to do it. My question is, as a former man, can you tell me why do men want to go into women-only spaces, or why are they offended by them? Why do they think it has anything to do with them at all?

Winc: What do you mean by "men"?

Scratch: Right. ::laughing:: Um, like straight frat boys coming into women's bars.

Winc: You know, I have no idea. I never wanted to do that when I was living as a man. I do know what you mean, that a lot of straight men go into those spaces. ::shrugs::

OK, this is a hard one for me to ask you. Why do women in women-only spaces refuse to admit transsexual women?

Scratch: That answer is changing even as I speak. And this is just MY answer. You couldn't find a more "it depends on who you ask and what space it is" question if you tried. First of all, I've never "refused to admit transsexual women." In fact it was my discomfort with the whole thing that made me actually talk to transsexual women. I felt so protective of my new lesbian space that I thought that's all who should be allowed. Until I thought for a minute. Then someone tried signs that said "women only," but there are obnoxious dykes who sure could ruin the vibe so I couldn't really stick with that. Before any of us actually talked to a real live transsexual woman, it was this vague fear of being overtaken by "maleness." But also? There are many "women-only" spaces that *do* admit transsexuals. It's the ones that don't that get all the attention.

The best tip I got was from a transsexual woman who said, "why not just put 'no transsexuals' on your fliers?" I was all offended and then realized she was right. By saying "women only," we really were trying to make a policy about being exclusive. At one event someone came up with, "if you can put your dick in a drawer, and slam that drawer, then you are welcome." But that was directed only at transsexuals who hadn't had surgery, which not everyone wants or can afford. All that made me realize how stupid it was. I mean, if you want such an exclusive club, just create a private party and invite whoever you want. Don't plaster it all over fliers.

Winc: First good answer to that question I've ever gotten. Thanks.

Okay next . . . I know that no sexuality is pure. There are always some tickles and surges of lust for people of the "wrong gender." What do lesbians do with their attractions to men?

Scratch: The great taboo. The younger generation's doing better than mine on it. I still get very attracted to men. I used to go to bed with them even though I called myself a lesbian. But sex with men was always the same, and I never cared about them emotionally, they just don't interest me. Now I just enjoy my attractions but don't act on them. To hell with people who think that's being attracted to the "wrong" sex. That's where all our struggles started, right?

Winc: What was it like for you, growing up? Were you a tomboy? Did you hang with the guys? Play sports?

Scratch: I was definitely a tomboy. Fortunately so was my mother, so I got to stay tomboy longer than most girls. But then she got freaked out and thought I'd end up being a girl who couldn't get a guy. She started girl-ifying me.

One day at school I went out to play kickball and only the boys were there! I looked around for the rest of the girls on the team and finally found them in the bathroom. They were playing with makeup and showing off their newly shaved legs. It was like some dog whistle had called them and I never heard it.

I started doing it, too, so I'd be normal: stockings, skirts, high heels . . . which I hated but figured something was wrong with me. When I came out as a dyke, my girlfriend said if I didn't like makeup I didn't have to wear it; I haven't since.

But there are lots of lesbians who wear skirts and lipstick, etc. Because they like it. "Femme dykes" are never noticed as lesbians. It's a particular thorn in their sides, because they're always getting come-ons from guys; a lot of lesbians don't notice them either. They're caught in the middle. It's like they're invisible. They call it "femme invisibility."

Winc: The $64,000 Question, Scratch, and it comes in a lot of parts: Why were you attracted to me? What turned you off about me?

Scratch: I was attracted to everything. Not a damn thing turned me off.

Winc: Awwwwwww.

I guess those are my questions for now.

I'm getting on with my life, surfing and avoiding the law. Oh! Speaking of which, that Lt. Budge thinks you're a guy.

I need some space, Scratch. Oh I hope to see you from time to time when these wounds are healed. No, I'm not being Ingrid Bergman, just realistic. I love you.

Scratch: Space is what you want, space is what you have with all my love.

Oh . . . Budge is convinced you're a helpless sweet thang, so we must be doing something right. Motherfucker. Did he try to play you off me? Tell you I told him everything? You *know* I'd never, right?

I love you. I love you.

END WINC JOURNAL ENTRY

NARRATIVE ENTRY, JABBATHEHUT

A weary, wary Wally Budge stares disconsolately at the message. Shel said she got it from her connection at ACI, and that Budge should read it. OK, Budge is reading.

To: Undersecretary LaBouchere, Bureau of Census and Statistics
From: Robert Blaine III, Allied Consumer Industries
Subj: No Registration/No Money

I'll dispense with the amenities, Margaret, and cut to the chase. We are in deep brown sauce. Permit me to summarize:

Registration has ground to a complete stop. Rubes everywhere are Registering as variations of "Scratch" or "Winc," and *that* has begun to foul up our database.

E-ads are being ridiculed to the point of ineffectiveness. Don't get me wrong, when ads get ridiculed, people remember them. But this is different: ads are being *ignored*.

Go find the Scratch and Winc page. A grassroots campaign has been mounted: "If Scratch and Winc Don't Need It, Neither Do I."

And I thought this was America.

Direct email campaigns are failing. People aren't signing up for giveaways. They see that they don't have complete access to the Net, but only to areas our demosurveys indicate they would enjoy.

The punters are demanding COMPLETE ACCESS. Have you any idea what a mess that would be? And why do you suppose they want complete access, when most of them can't even use their microwaves correctly? Because Scratch and Winc have full access. And they're using illegal bypasses, which your department cannot seem to stop!

Lastly: If Scratch and Winc are not behind bars in five days, we're pulling all funding for the Internet.

Yours truly,

—Robert Blaine III, Esq.

Budge closes his eyes for a moment. They had a point. Hey, he shit-cans every ad that comes to him. Shelly does the same thing. But tossing ads away has nothing to do with Scratch and Winc—it's common practice. Even before the Internet. So why are they hanging it on these two jokers?

Then it hits him. They're trying to stick Scratch and Winc with their own fuck-ups. All that money—public funds, corporate grants—sunk into the Net as the ultimate advertising medium. And it flopped beyond belief. Scratch and Winc are taking the rap. So insisting on Registration is the desperate move to recover their losses. But even Registration isn't going to last. People are smart.

END JABBA NARRATIVE ENTRY

To: Drew
From: T. Sparrow
Subject: Come down off that ledge

Yes, that is sad. Now you can't even say a word near your phone without an ad popping up. We need smart people with good hearts now more than ever.

Love,

Dad

SCRATCH JOURNAL ENTRY

To: Winc
From: Scratch
Subj: Us, Midnight . . .

I'm a bear of little brain. I can't remember what our particular isms or differences are, and I don't care. I'm furious at this Budge character. I miss you fierce. I miss Toobe, I mean, the old way we used to write to him. So much to teach him, so much that he teaches us. Lately my letters to him have been whiney.

I feel such love for you, my friend, my lover, my fellow traveler. Your vulnerability is overwhelming sometimes, until I realize it is my own. There's no support for outlaws, even among ourselves. Your path is so lone, as is mine, and we cannot help each other, any more than we do in comforting words. Nevertheless, we still return to relating, to the realizations, albeit alone.

As more people get online, I'm sad that when I try to connect to people as someone without a gender, or without a specific sexual preference, just me, gender-free and loving whoever comes along, I get blank faces. Tinged with fear and judgment.

It kills me how one choice instantly obliterates others. As a grown-up, when I must make choices, I watch possibilities slip away. My inevitable reaction is to turn inward, to write, to confide sometimes.

It's all the same thing—the connectedness of spirit, a capacity we're born with, and either spend our lives denying or searching out to the farthest corners.

I want that connection, to see and be seen, with someone. The point is, Winc, you do see. That's worth everything to me. More than any of my ignorance or fear of change. I miss you. Have you had enough space now? Can we meet? Please.

Thanks for listening, my love. Goodnight.

—S.

To: Scratch
From: Winc
Subj: Was reading some Zen stuff, and my brain fried . . .

Chuang Tzu taught that the mousetrap exists for the sake of the mouse: once the mouse has been caught, you can forget the trap.

He further taught that words exist for the sake of their meaning: once the meaning has been grasped, you can forget the words.

And the fool in me extrapolates that identities exist for the sake of relationships: once the relationship has been established, you can forget the identities.

Now here I yam, looking for someone who's forgotten identity . . .

So?

—W.

To: Winc
From: Scratch
Subj: My brain with fries to go

Yes!! Me! Me! Take me! I'm forgetting identity! Trying anyway!

—S.

END SCRATCH JOURNAL ENTRY

GWYNYTH DIARY ENTRY

Word has gotten out that the orphans of the cyberstorm have various safe havens online created by none other than moi. Not good. If the "good guys," as Toobe calls them, can find those two, then someone else can too.

I'm sure I can put together a white light spell that'll blind anyone who makes the mistake of looking in my direction.

But hackers are afoot, breaking down bridges as soon as I build them. Winc has been tagged and needs extra links, which still don't hold very long.

Note to myself: Collect more sage.

END GWYNYTH DIARY ENTRY

13
HEAT

FUNNY OF THE DAY

We've pretty much come to the end of a time when you can have a space that is "yours only"—just for the people you want to be there. Even when we have our "women-only" festivals, there is no such thing. The fault is not necessarily with the organizers of the gathering. To a large extent it's because we have just finished with that kind of isolating. There is no hiding place. There is nowhere you can go and only be with people who are like you. It's over. Give it up.

—*Bernice Johnson Reagon, talk given at the 1981 West Coast Women's Music Festival, 1981*

SCRATCH JOURNAL ENTRY

To: Scratch
From: Winc
Subj: Make it or take it

I guess you can know now: Trenton, NJ is my home sweet home, I moved here from New York after it got too expensive. You see, I was quite the flamboyant fixture on the Lower East Side, but I'm also a private person. Everyone knew my name, said hello to me on the street, gossiped with me in all the shops and corner stores—but no one knew a thing about me. Queer culture was all around me, but I didn't hang out with anyone. You and I have different ways of being private, darling. On the bright side: even after moving down here, I kept my job. ::lopsided grin:: You can do phone sex from *anywhere*.

It's pretty fucking bleak here after NYC. The streets are so narrow, and flamboyancy is not an option. So I'm stealth. My face tat makes folks look twice, and I've made a couple of old ladies cross themselves when they see me.

Look, you didn't do anything wrong. Neither of us did. This whole thing is making me think deep, and that's always good. I have a tendency to put on a great big smiley face, like all the best circus clowns. I'm just too tired to put on a big ol' smiley face for you, my love.

::sigh::

Why does it matter so much to me, how you feel about me, what we are to each other? Haven't we been discovering that we can be anything we choose? But I'm hurt because it's finally clear to me that this stuff *is* a choice, and you talk real good but you're not choosing me.

::looking out over the row houses::

I just know I'll move back to New York. It's just a matter of time. Time! I've spent so much time trying to be what I was second-guessing you'd want me to be that I never bothered to figure out what I want from you. I'll work on that one now.

Yours in High Treason,

—W.

To: Winc
From: Scratch
Subj: Stuff

I don't see where it says in the instructions what we gotta be.

Overwhelmed by the endless defining of ourselves. Why do it anyway?

The snap judgments I make are to protect myself.

This online space creates a village square where people can actually talk to one another. But we also have the freedom to contemplate what someone says and not be considered rude if we don't respond at all! That's an amazing freedom.

Winc, this weariness and grief is making me miss you. The you I know. I just want to fuse with you, to connect.

This separation between us hurts.

—S.

P.S. Re: Treason? What?

END SCRATCH JOURNAL ENTRY

To: D.I. Drew
From: Editor at They/Them magazine
Subject: Two rabbis go into a chat room

Kudos.

I find that their chat room style with each other is visceral—I can feel their bodies. So different from their emails, which are a more intellectual level of conversation. It's like listening to two rabbis discuss the Talmud. You probably already know this word but it's one of my favorites: "sapiosexual."

Thanks,

Asa

SCRATCH JOURNAL ENTRY CONT'D

To: Scratch
From: Winc
Subj: Grief

The separation between us hurts me too.

You ask why do we endlessly define ourselves. I hadn't framed our romps that way before. I've been thinking of it as identity surfing. I like the endlessly part.

Why? How about because it's so much fun? Yessssss, but fun for fun's sake gets old after a while. However, fun that's tied to enlightenment? Oh, man. I think it's the old thing of peeling the layers off an onion. We keep looking for the heart of who we are.

—W.

P.S. Re: Treason. It's official, hon. You and I are conspiring to overthrow the government of the United States of America. ::tossing hair:: Or didn't you know?

END SCRATCH JOURNAL ENTRY

TOOBE ENTRY

No way Scratch could have read the announcement; ze doesn't know how to access things very well. But it's everywhere:

A Public Safety Announcement
from
the U.S. Government Bureau of Census and Statistics
presented with the cooperation of your local Internet Service Provider
and the Alliance of Consumer Industries
◊

Regarding suspected criminals
and known Registration evaders
"Scratch" and "Winc."
◊
Suspected activities have resulted in the formal charge of conspiracy to overthrow the government of the United States of America.

This is an act of High Treason, punishable by death.

☠ WARNING ☠

Any attempt to provide aid to or harbor the persons of "Scratch" and/or "Winc" will automatically carry a similar charge of conspiracy.

We apologize for the interruption, and we thank your local provider for their assistance in making this public safety announcement available to you.

End: PSA #427

END TOOBE ENTRY

NARRATIVE ENTRY, JABBATHEHUT

He's reading the PSA for about the thirteenth time.

"Aw, shit."

Digital memos are piling up. He's not answering them.

To: FBCS Investigations
From: Henderson, Enforcement
Subj: Where are they?

We can be mobile with thirty minutes' notice. So, where are they?

—Henderson

. . . and . . .

To: Ms. Budge
From: Undersec'y LaBouchere
Subj: Green Light

Attached warrant for the arrest of Scratch and Winc. Do it.

. . . and probably the most disturbing one, causing the small hairs on the back of his neck to stand up . . .

To: All Bureau Personnel
From: Undersec'y LaBouchere
Subj: Protocol

A large number of citizens are using the screen names "Scratch" and "Winc" in varying combinations. e.g., Sccratch, Wink, Wincc, etc. We must assume these citizens are sympathetic to the anti-government sentiments of the perps.

In accordance with the Gingrich-Helms Free NetSpeech Act, the following safety precautions are hereby invoked and operative:

Any persons with the screen names "Scratch" or "Winc," or any derivative thereof, may be located, detained, questioned, and/or held for any reason, whether necessary or not, on charges of aiding and abetting the overthrow of the government of the United States of America.

All websites or newsgroups, all chat rooms private or public, with topics including or referring to Scratch or Winc may be monitored openly or by stealth, and subject to immediate closure.

Let's do what we get paid to do.

—L.

END JABBA NARRATIVE ENTRY

SCRATCH JOURNAL ENTRY

Private Message to Frankie

Hotdog: What up?

Frankie: ::purring:: G'morning . . . still sleepy eyes.

Hotdog: R u m or f?

Frankie: ::mischievous eyes:: Ah, darlin' . . . I've made an oath never to tell.

Private Message to Frankie

Johnny: Hey, dollface.

Frankie: YOU!

Johnny: Yep! We're safe for the moment. Wanna join me?

Frankie: I'm, um . . . entangled just now. But yes yes yes wanna join you. Hang on.

Private Message to Frankie

Hotdog: R u wet?

Frankie: ::laughing lightly:: Takes more than the question to get me wet, love.

Hotdog: Heh heh.

Frankie: Oh darlin, I want you so bad but my husband and three children just trooped through the door, back from the mall. Gotta dash. 'nother day!

Private Message to Frankie

Johnny: ::looking at you evenly:: We're live. We happened into this sector at the same time. Come to me.

Frankie: ::biting my lip:: Where?

Johnny: Private room "heat"

Frankie: ::nodding:: Be right there.

Online Host

***** Frankie has entered Private Room "heat" *****

Error: There is no host in the room.

Frankie: ::peeking in the door::

Johnny: No idea who Error is!

Frankie: ::shivering:: Everything like that is making me paranoid.

Johnny: I know. Me, too. I'll check it out, brb.

Johnny has left the room.

Johnny has entered the room.

Johnny: bak. It's Gwynyth's Safety protocol!

Frankie: ::weak smile::

Johnny: ::smilin' back::

Frankie: Scratch, I . . .

Johnny: Yes?

Frankie: Nothing.

Johnny: Look. I got one word for you, OK?

Frankie: Yeah?

Johnny: Hypothermia.

Frankie: ::blinking:: Is that supposed to be romantic?

Johnny: ::slow grin:: Want to know what it means?

Frankie: ::leaning back:: Uh huh.

Johnny: When a person gets hypothermia, it's very difficult to revive them. You have to take them to the hospital and work on them all night long, because there's nothing to replace body heat easily. ::deep breath::

Frankie: ::watching you, listening::

Johnny: In the mountains, when a hiker gets too cold ze's got maybe half an hour until ze's frozen. So the only thing ze can do is hope to find another person.

::pushing on::

That other person gets into the sleeping bag with the cold one, they have to both be naked, and they wait. Sure enough, the heat from the rescuer heats up the frozen person. Almost instantly. They have to stay together until the person's heat comes back to normal.

Frankie: You're making me cry.

Johnny: I was frozen, Winc. You warmed me up. I want to stay in the bag with you.

Frankie: ::loss for words::

Johnny: Um, ::talking rapidly:: it's my favorite story. I've loved it since I first heard it from a crusty old ice climber.

Frankie: ::reaching my arms up around your neck::

Johnny: ::holding you close to me:: ::breathing you in::

Frankie: ::moving softly into your arms, crying crying::

Johnny: ::stroking your hair::

Frankie: Missed you missed you missed you.

Johnny: Samesamesame.

Frankie: ::willing my heat around the two of us::

Johnny: ::relaxing into you:: I used to bore people with that story, never had anyone get it.

Error: Window closing.

Johnny: We got to go. But now we're . . . we're all . . . you know?

Frankie: ::fiercely:: I know. We are. And we're *gonna* be.

Johnny: <--- loves when you get fierce.

Frankie: ::growling, extending claws::

Error: Window almost down, dearies. ::waving sage around the room::

Johnny: Wow! Gwynyth's personalized touch! And she's not even here!

Frankie: ::laughing:: Guardian angel!

Johnny: Bye, love. We'll find each other, OK?

Frankie: ::nodding::

Frankie: Scratch?

Johnny: ILY.

Yes?

Frankie: ::softly:: Simulpost.

Johnny: I figured.

Error: Window closed. Communication stopped.

END SCRATCH JOURNAL ENTRY

TOOBE ENTRY

They were, as usual, oblivious. They were being called traitors! Do I nag them? Will they deal? Gwynyth still says to wait, but she got a tiny smile when I told her they were talking again. Tiny smile on her means a big one on other people.

END TOOBE ENTRY

NARRATIVE ENTRY, JABBATHEHUT

Let the rest of the Bureau roust up the folks named Ssscratch or Wwwinc. Wally Budge is reading some very interesting correspondence, forwarded by one of his hackers.

BEGIN FORWARDED TEXT:

To: HoneyDew
From: Vina
Subj: Is that you?

Please forgive me if I've reached the wrong mailbox, but I'm looking for Winc. The real Winc. We heard that this is one of your screen names. I represent a group called The Coalition, and we need to locate Winc ASAP.

—Vina

With a satisfied grunt, he adds "HoneyDew" to his database and chalks up another entry for "The Coalition." Patterns, patterns. Now we're talking. Familiar territory at last. He feels like a cop again. The next message, however, isn't so satisfying.

To: Ms. Budge
From: DevilsOwn
Subj: Progress, BUT . . .

We've got some leads. But something *really* weird is happening. Someone is pulling all the Scratch and Winc clones offline. Is that you? If it is, STOP IT! We've been using them to determine genuine leads.

And do you know about The Rally tonight at the Scratch and Winc Website? DON'T mess with it, okay? We'll have it wired, and we're counting on at least one live lead attending.

—Your everlovin' Devil

Now ain't that a kick in the pants? He forwards it to Shel, then calls her.

"Did you get that message from my hacker?"

"Yeah. I'm lookin' at it right now."

"How do I tell Her Ladyship to lay off all the Scratches and Wincs?"

"Heh, that came out funny," she purrs.

"Ha! Yeah, but seriously, Shel, how do I tell her to leave all the websites and newsgroups alone?"

A pause, then, "Leave it to me. Dinner tonight at Antonio's. You're buying."

"Shelly, if I had a nose full of diamonds and rubies, I'd sneeze them all achoo."

END JABBA NARRATIVE ENTRY

14 THE EMAIL HEARD 'ROUND THE WORLD

To: Editor at They/Them magazine
From: D.I. Drew
Subject: Coupla notes

You may notice "LGB" to indicate a queer group below. That's historically accurate: the T wasn't recognized nationally until 1998, and GLAAD officially added Q in 2016.

Cheers,

D.I. Drew

FILE UNDER: MISC. COMMUNICATIONS

To: Winc
From: Scratch
Subj: Invites

I don't know if you've been getting mail, but mine is full of offers. They usually make my skin crawl, but I kind of liked this one. What do you think?

> **To:** Scratch
> **Cc:** Winc
> **From:** Coalition of LGB Folks
> **Subj:** Help us?
>
> What you're doing is very important. We've noticed that you refuse to say exactly what sex you are, and that makes us believe that you believe your sex is outlawed. If that's the case, we are your family.
>
> As a coalition of lesbian, gay, and bisexual people, we know how it feels to be marginalized. We have all had to deal with issues of sexuality in our lives, and we think it would be terrific if you could publicly announce that you identify as one of us.
>
> There are so few role models for us, and now that you have everybody's attention, we think it would be wonderful if you could come out and give the movement a shot in the arm. It would mean so much, especially to all our youth.
>
> (signed by all members—LGB Coalition)

What say you? I'm kind of mixed. I could call myself queer, not being your average Straight Amerikan, but I'm seeing that nobody much is.

—S.

To: Scratch
From: Winc
Subj: The Coalition

I got one too. It rang true. Wouldn't it be kind of exciting to help?

Let's find out more! Like which letter applies to us!

—W.

To: Winc
From: Scratch
Subj: Hermit crab

Whoa. Stop. Never mind. I don't think I want to do that.

I don't know what I was thinking. I don't do groups well. People's IQ levels drop when they're all together in a room. Something about processing one idea until every member gets it or something. Then they'll start writing manifestos to sign, and I'll object to maybe one little sentence, and then they'll have to discuss *that* and then send it back to us . . . signed off by six people. ::throwing up hands:: Then one of us will be wearing a fragrance somebody's allergic to, or someone will say they can't abide flash cameras because somebody has epilepsy, and they'll have to vote about whether we can attend or not, etc.

Let's just write them a long letter saying thanks but no thanks.

—S.

PS—Well I claim L for lesbian, or maybe B for butch. Kidding. I guess you can too. At least sometimes you can. ::laughing, ducking::

To: Scratch
From: Winc
Subj: Yes indeed you are

Oh, I hadn't noticed that about groups, but you're probably right. But I think we might be having an impact. Maybe we *are* in a position to do something.

—W.

PS—I want my own letter. T . . . for transgender . . . would do.

To: Winc
From: Scratch
Subj: (Nice to talk again)

Do something about what?

—S.

PS—I wish there were a letter we could both claim.

To: Scratch
From: Winc
Subj: (Yes, indeed it is)

People are getting pissed off, have you noticed? This week I got letters from Star Trek clubs, a disability rights organization, the right to bear arms people, and a million others. They all think we're role models!!

If we seem to speak to all those people, maybe we *should*!

—W.

PS—New letter. Yes.

To: Winc
From: Scratch
Subj: (Oh, good)

I got letters from the Rainbow Coalition, the Latina Hermanas group, on and on and on.

What do you mean, speak to people? What would we say?

Let's go chat.

—S.

To: Scratch
From: Winc
Subj: Armed rooms

Meet me in room Arms.

—W.

***** You are in room "Arms" *****

Winc: See what I mean? Maybe we didn't intend it, but we stand for something.
Scratch: ::waving hand impatiently:: People are bored. We're just the latest thing to hit the charts.
Winc: I don't think so. And while I respect your cynicism, *I* think you secretly hope something will come out of this.
Scratch: Come out of this? What do you know about what I secretly think?
Winc: ::hiding a smile:: You're sputtering. It's a sure sign I've hit a nerve.
Scratch: ^&*(()#@!
Winc: Uh huh.
Scratch: OK, so I hope they all fucking turn off their computers, stop buying stuff, and refuse to Register. What's so bad about that?
Winc: ::laughing:: Nothing. What do you mean turn off their computers?
Scratch: Ghandi's idea: Home Rule. If we stop using the damn things, they'll have to stop with the invasions. What's driving them anyway? Moneylust. Never mind how much they're getting already, they always want more.
Winc: They?
Scratch: Same old They.
Winc: I think it's a different They this time, dear.
Scratch: Government, advertisers, online providers—all They to me. Do you think They make any distinctions about different kinds of users? Like this group is white females or that one is Black disableds or whatever?
Winc: I suppose not.

Scratch: They look at money. Not whether we have it, but whether we'll spend it. Poor folks get more marketing shit leveled at them than anyone else.

Winc: But the govt says this is about porn trafficking or hurting innocent children.

Scratch: Still comes down to $.

Winc: ::thinking:: When we refused to Register, and then other people didn't either, ACI swarmed all over all of us, and so did the feds.

Scratch: Right!

Winc: Tell me, why *didn't* you Register?

Scratch: Oh, well. ::heavy sigh:: I don't do connectivity well.

Winc: Connectivity? You're all about connectivity. I for one can vouch for your limber and lubricated connectivity.

Scratch: Oh not that! But thank you. No, I mean: driver's licenses, traffic tickets, library cards, memberships, taxes. I might build a whole philosophy out of resistance, but the truth is . . .

Winc: ::still listening::

Scratch: That's it. No big philosophy. No noble reasons.

Winc: ::covering my mouth::

Scratch: I knew you'd laugh. And you? Why didn't *you* Register?

Winc: Kind of similar. Nothing noble.

Scratch: Yeah?

Winc: Third question in the Reg form. Sex:__________.

Scratch: ::blinking:: Why not just put female? Or whatever you wanted?

Winc: It's not that easy. I'm still male on my driver's license, birth certificate, etc.

Scratch: Oh. Come to think of it, that's about where I gave up, too.

Winc: I take it you don't want to be the Coalition spokesperson.

Scratch: I'd fuck it up.

Winc: But I think your other idea is good.

Scratch: Which one?

Winc: The strike.

Scratch: Oh, that was just an example.

Private Message to Winc

Toobe: Orlio is going to send me stuff from The Rally!

Winc: You're not risking going are you????

Toobe: ::snort:: I'd be nabbed. Gotta be careful.

Winc: Okay cool. Whew!

Winc: No, I mean it, we should strike.

Scratch: Yeah, right. How would we get everybody to do it?

Winc: ::looking at my mailbox, looking at yours:: I think we could get the word out.

Scratch: Email them all?

Winc: Email a few, word will spread.

Scratch: You have a lot of confidence in our popularity.

Winc: Scratch, I think I understand you a little better now. You don't stay in touch with the world a whole lot, right?

Scratch: Well, sometimes. Some people. Some groups.

Winc: Right, well, at present they're staying way in touch with you. And me.

Scratch: ::thinking::

Private Message to Toobe

Gwynyth: Young man, hast thou not been online a mite too long?

Toobe: Just a little longer? Please?

Gwynyth: Hmm. I'll have to readjust some spells. OK, but *you* change the litter boxes tonight.

Toobe: ::groaning:: It's a deal.

Winc: So tell everyone we don't think the Reg process is fair, it only reduces who we want to be, who we *can* be, blah blah, and then see if everybody wants to join in.

Scratch: What if it doesn't work?

Winc: Then it doesn't work. Can't hurt! Just ask everybody to stop using their computers for a day?

Scratch: ::excitedly:: They should say something before they sign off. Something about themselves, about who they really are. Some true thing, not about what they buy or what kind of B.O. they have.

Winc: Yes. YesYesYes

Scratch: Let's tell this LGB Coalition first. They'd get it.

Winc: Perfect! You want to write the letter?

Scratch: OK. Who *you* gonna tell?

Winc: Well, I think I get this software/hardware thing better than you, no offense.

Scratch: Oh, no, it's true. You know everything!

Winc: ::laughing:: Non non, darling.

Scratch: You do!

Winc: So I can write an announcement from both of us, and send it all around the world.

Scratch: Wow. ::shyly:: Do you really think anyone would give a damn?

Winc: Scratch, I have six letters from CBS News alone in my mailbox.

Scratch: Hmm, so do I. I thought it was advertisement offers.

Winc: From a news program?

Scratch: Oh.

Private Message to Winc

Toobe: Orlio's at The Rally! Hundreds of people there!

Winc: Yikes!

Winc: For very real connectivity reasons, are you Windows or Mac? I'm on an old Mac Classic. You?

Scratch: You're going to laugh again.

Winc: No, I promise I won't. Tell me.

Scratch: I use a Tandy, an old one from Radio Shack. It's a laptop, but they weren't even called that then.

Winc: When?

Scratch: Oh, 1988–89, when they were invented.

Winc: Don't tell me it's the kind that uses disks for all the programs. No hard drive? *That* one?

Scratch: That's the one.

Winc: :X

Scratch: You said you wouldn't laugh.

Winc: Not laughing! It's sweet! How did Gwynyth set you up with all the bypasses then?

Scratch: Why do you think it took so long? She treated me like some fossil in a museum!

Winc: Scratch?

Scratch: Yes?

Winc: I love you.

Scratch: ::ducking head:: I . . . love you too. I've missed you.

Winc: Me too, you. Let's just move on. OK?

Scratch: ::setting jaw:: OK.

Winc: Besides, ::tossing hair:: we have a cause!

Scratch: We do?

Winc: ::tapping my foot::

Scratch: Oh, right, we do! OK, off to write letters!

Winc: Goodbye, sweetie.

Scratch: Bye!

END MISC. COMMUNICATIONS

NARRATIVE ENTRY, JABBATHEHUT

As promised, a certain clever law enforcement member, possibly named Shelly Dunlap, managed to find the actual law regarding the harassment of citizens. Until there is some kind of law governing the Internet, basic rules of publishing and communications will stand. Hence the following memo makes its rounds quickly among all law enforcement agencies:

> All FBCS personnel are to disregard the previous memo implementing the Gingrich-Helms Free NetSpeech Act, effective immediately, and until further notice. There will be no harassing of citizens online, and no shutdown of websites or newsgroups. Any sites or newsgroups that have been shut down are to be unlocked and reopened immediately.

"Hey, Wally, good news," Shelly says as she shows him the announcement on her screen. "Not only have the rights been reinstated, but apparently some civic-minded citizen of these United States found out about the memo and blew the whistle to the ACLU."

"What?!" exclaims Budge. "How'd they find out so fast?"

"No idea, Wally," Shelly says, perhaps a tad too quickly. "But it seems the ACLU has mounted a mass lawsuit, number of parties unlimited."

END JABBA NARRATIVE ENTRY

GWYNYTH DIARY ENTRY

48 hours until Mercury goes retrograde.

All systems are up. Where is everybody? Could our young lovers have hit on the goof of the century?

END GWYNYTH DIARY ENTRY

To: Editor at They/Them magazine
From: D.I. Drew
Subject: . . . heard 'round the world

Hi Asa,

My high school civics teacher made us memorize the famous "How does this strike you?" email. Did yours? I remember being so inspired. And all the anthems that followed, tens of thousands. So here it is, now in context—

Drew

GWYNYTH DIARY ENTRY

To: All Our Friends
From: Winc@PalisadesPk.NJ.com
Subj: How does this strike you?

Hey, hello. We hope you're well.

I'm writing for both Scratch and myself. Can't make this too long because some people would rather we took up residence somewhere with no windows. The two of us have been blown away by all the letters we've been getting. We can't answer them because of tracers. But we want to say thanks so much.

It's been a really weird time for both of us, especially now with this charge of High Treason. After they get us, who are they going to target *next*? So, we came up with an idea:

We want to call a general strike, an online shutdown for 24 hours, to let the govt know they can't get away with tracking us online, and Big Business can't tell us what to buy. Obviously there's a whole lot of support for this way of thinking, more than anyone realized, and we should let our helpful govt know that *our* eyes are on *them*.

The deal would be for everyone to sign off and shut down at once. Not forever, just a day. March 15, 1995. Beware the Ides of March, and all that jazz. Everyone goes to the website jumping_off dot com and posts their own version of a farewell, an anthem, or even just a fuck you. Everyone writes their own. You can sign it or not. More powerful if you do, but it's up to you.

Every single user: no matter what you use to get online. The only ones left online will be the govt, and let's see how much fun they have talking to themselves, without us to spy on.

We hear there's a rally online tonight. Maybe you could talk about it there? Obviously Scratch and I won't be able to be there, but maybe this is something to do?

{{{Netfriends}}}

—your everlovin' Scratch and Winc

P.S. We were thinking 24 hours starting 8 a.m. Eastern time, March 15. That's the day after tomorrow.

Romeo and Juliet are planning their strike for the precise moment Mercury goes retrograde. How wonderful!

END GWYNYTH DIARY ENTRY

TOOBE ENTRY

I hate when adults are right. I would've snuck into The Rally if Gwynyth hadn't threatened me with permanent kitty litter duty. If I'd gone, it would have ended in tears, just like she warned. It all started fine. Way fine. See this report I got from Orlio.

To: Toobe@Farm Reports.org.Monsterride.santacruz
From: Orlio@aol.com
Subj: Comin' Down!

I'm not making it up when I say everyone in the *world* is here! We're all in rooms called "The Rally," You know how when there's an overflow in one room, another one gets created automatically and it's called, "The Rally 2"? Well each room maxes out at 500 attendees, and now, I'm hanging out in "The Rally 1029." Heehee.

There's newspaper reporters; e-zine types; a whole group of deaf people; people from role-playing game rooms; people with multiple personalities. It's like a street fair. People selling Scratch and Winc T-shirts, buttons, commemorative dinner plates, and I'm not kidding: Scratch and Winc holsters!

END TOOBE ENTRY

Sample "true accounts" of Scratch and Winc encounters

BarBun: Scratch is the best online lover I've ever been with!

HotHead: Too right there, grrl!

BarBun: Uh huh! Knows how to take time, build things up.

HotHead: She knows what fingers are for!

BarBun: She?

HotHead: Huh?

BarBun: He.

HotHead: She.

BarBun: He.

HotHead: Scratch is all grrl, you spritzhead!

BarBun: ::tossing hair:: I know a real man when I see one, you tramp!

Tale2Tell: Winc and I switch a *lot*! I love that about hir.

Barnabus: Aw, that's sick!

Tale2Tell: No. You get to be everything, not just one thing.

Barnabus: ::cautiously:: What exactly does that mean?

Tale2Tell: Guess you'll just have to go explore, Barnabus. ::kiss::

NARRATIVE ENTRY, JABBATHEHUT

Wally Budge and Shelly Dunlap know it's bad the moment they pull into the parking lot. Every light in the place is burning except Budge's office. Like a Christmas tree with one bad bulb.

"Ohhh," Shelly laughs. "Look what you started!"

Her laughter is infectious, as always, and Budge starts chuckling—he can't stop until he reaches his desk. Every alarm and whistle on his computer is flashing or beeping, demanding "read me, read me!" Wearily, he reads:

> **To:** Ms. Budge
> **From:** Undersec'y LaBouchere
> **Subj:** Excuse me, but . . .
>
> I'm so sorry to disturb your dinner, Lieutenant, but I just received this little item, and I'd *really* like to answer it soon.
>
> —L.

To: Undersec'y LaBouchere
From: Director of Small Budgets, office of POTUS
Subj: Confidential

Madam,

I hope you are well.

Things are getting out of control. In-baskets are jammed with nothing but mail about Scratch and Winc. The allegations are alarming, as is the increasing number of people claiming to be Scratch and Winc, and the resulting disrespect they are paying to their targeted advertising, as evidenced by the sharp rise in rude return emails.

Margaret, please have a look at the attached list of suspect events, crimes, threats, and heroics.

We want to know does it all come down to the two prime suspects?

1. who are the real Scratch and Winc,
2. where are they, and
3. how much of this dog's breakfast is true.

Answers. Now.

Yours truly,

DSB, Office of POTUS

POTUS! Wally Budge's eyes do a cartoon bulge as he reads down the list of events, crimes, threats, and heroics attributed to our stalwart cyberfreaks, his eyes growing wider as he proceeds from plot to theft, prank to lurid sexual exploit, and finally to a list of a dozen suspect organizations, each claiming responsibility for the outlaw antics.

He dashes off an email to the undersecretary.

To: Undersec'y LaBouchere
From: Ms. Budge
Subj: Allegations

Ma'am: The White House can't be seriously thinking these two goofballs are *doing* all this, can they?

—B.

Of course they can be thinking that. Why not? Everyone else is thinking it. He stabs at the well-worn DELETE button and starts again in a vain attempt to dismiss the ridiculous theories.

He settles on a placating return email, then presses SEND, shaking his massive head. Enough foolishness. Time to be a cop.

His phone rings; he picks up. There's that throaty laugh. He starts to grin.

"Hello, Lieutenant. I had to ask you, maybe you could trap them in a chat room?"

He's grinning ear to ear now.

"Where would I ever be without you?"

"Without me? You'd be up to your neck in trouble and paperwork."

END JABBA NARRATIVE ENTRY

15
HIPPIE CHICK

TOOBE ENTRY

Winc uses "splatter" to describe playing two or three or more different identities all at the same time. Like when you're in a bunch of Private Messages at once, in a bunch of different personas.

But right now splatter means all my worlds in collision. My dad's mad at the advertising and the invasion of privacy. Orlio's all excited about The Rally (still going on), and Gwynyth is making "incantations" over her altar. Who'm I supposed to be with all that going on at the same time?

Plus so much mail to me and S&W. What is the obsession with us?

Coney Island scammers must be making megabucks on those T-shirts, and the coaster still rattles the walls of my room every day. Funny, I've gotten used to it. My dad says the cops tracking us for such a stupid reason is "an old struggle in new surroundings." This may not sound very cool, but I just want to go down to the beach with him for an ice-cream cone, right now.

Anyway: The Rally's been going on for almost twelve hours; Scratch and Winc are chatting somewhere, Jabba has gone silent, Gwynyth's hyper, bustling all over, muttering a lot.

"Sense of purpose."

"Guides be with me."

"Uranus well-timed."

Stuff like that. More later.

END TOOBE ENTRY

GWYNYTH DIARY ENTRY

The strike reminds me of ancient gatherings, where all responded to some unseen signal and met in the woods by the moon. Venus is so lovely this time of year.

The strike is to begin in under twenty hours. What will I do for a 24-hour absence of electronic activity?

Resolution to myself: clean house.

The tribes are gathering. Haven't had this much fun since we all got naked in Central Park and passed out flowers to the cops! Speaking of cops, where are they?

END GWYNYTH DIARY ENTRY

SCRATCH JOURNAL ENTRY

To: Winc
From: Scratch
Subj: Update

The Coalition is excited about the Strike. They're gonna put together a statement. What coalitions do best!

Have you seen the Gender Board? Abuzz. ::tearing up:: It's happening:

Post: Gender Board

I read that 90% of intersexed infants are surgically altered at birth.

I was furious but one thing relieved me: at least we've found each other instead of wondering if we're alone.

"Intersexed" means hermaphrodites in this context. I didn't even think of that possibility!

—S.

The dragnet was closing in. But guess what America's most wanted were doing. Hee hee.

***** You are in room "The Shore" *****

Winc: ::sitting on the beach, watching the waves, turning to you and smiling::

Scratch: Hi.

Winc: ?

Scratch: It's happening.

Winc: ::carefully:: It? ::folding arms around knees, watching the water::

Scratch: ::waving at news bulletins:: The rally. The buzz. The happening.

Winc: ::nodding:: Momentum's building!

Scratch: I wanna hide. Have I mentioned I don't do crowds well?

Private Message to Scratch

Toobe: Thousands and thousands of people at The Rally, you guys (I'm double PMing you).

Private Message to Winc

Toobe: Thousands and thousands of people at The Rally, you guys (I'm double PMing you).

Scratch: I have a question. Hope it won't offend. Can't censor anything right now.

Winc: It's fine. What?

Private Message to Winc

Toobe: They're all talking about you!

Private Message to Scratch

Toobe: They're all talking about you!

Scratch: Acccccckkkkkkk!
Winc: Don't worry, hon.

Private Message to Toobe

Winc: Great news, honey! But a little overwhelming just now. Can you hold off a bit?
Toobe: Sure thing! I'm sorry.
Winc: No, I really want to know, but Scratch is a little publicity-shy.
Toobe: ::smacking forehead:: I forgot about that.

Winc: ::continuing to stroke your hair, listening::
Scratch: How can you be so womanly, when you lived so long as man?
Winc: ::blinking::
Scratch: Offended? ::please hoping not::
Winc: ::smiling:: Offended? No, flattered. Let's see . . . I think it has to do with my phone sex, believe it or not, and . . . ::shyly:: Zen. Gwynyth rekindled my practice.
Scratch: ::snuggling in:: Zen?
Winc: When they do a gender change, a lot of people layer a new gender over the one they had. Like putting on a mask, or a costume. You're not really changing. I think the deal in a gender change is to destroy yourself utterly . . . to get to a point of zero, nothing . . . and then you can create from there.
Scratch: Like art.
Winc: Right. There's an art to um . . . doing, or performing gender.

Excerpt: Online Rally

Luger7: No special rights for homosexuals.

Vina: This isn't about homosexuals!

Scratch: I *guess* I'm happy we're getting rally reports but jeezuz can't they stop for a minute?

Winc: I think Gwynyth set them to share with us so we'd be inspired.

Scratch: Oh. Not that last one though. ::stroking beard:: Were you creating from zero before or after surgery?

Winc: Definitely after. Before, I was just like everyone else, racing for what we all thought was the finish line.

Scratch: Thinking your journey would end as you came out of anesthesia . . .

Winc: Yes, exactly.

Scratch: So did you say, fine, I'm a girl, now what? And then, uh oh, what's a girl?

Winc: Sort of . . . It was less than a year after my surgery that I talked with some women and they asked me how could I be a woman like them? Other women said outright that I am simply and only a castrated male.

Scratch: No way! ::flatly:: I don't believe your womanliness is created . . . It *is* you.

Winc: You are the sweetest thing ever. But riddle me this, Batman: what's womanliness?

Scratch: Touché.

Winc: ::grinning::

Excerpt: Online Rally

MikeM666: Newbies die!

RainBeau: Hackers suck!

Success: Oh, for chrissakes

Scratch: ::Putting my head on your lap:: Overwhelmed at the juggernaut.

Winc: ::stroking your hair:: People were ready to do *something*. If we hadn't started a strike, someone else would have. But y'know what's cool?

Scratch: No. What's cool?

Winc: Whether they know it or not, this people's strike started with you loving me, and me loving you.

Scratch: All I could think of was you, your cyber-lap.

Winc: ::shaking my head:: You always make me smile, always know how.

Scratch: I feel messed up: I can fuck you, I can put you on your knees, but lie in your lap? Biggest risk of all.

Winc: Then thank you for trusting me like this. So much.

Scratch: ::sigh:: Is this where we cue the music?

Winc: Yep, and the sun sets slowly in the West.

Excerpt: Online Rally

StLouis7: No NRA freaks!

StLouis7: Militia monsters!

Shooter: Fuck you!

Scratch: Quite exhausted kitten now. But feel more calm.

Winc: Glad to hear it. ::happy sigh:: We'd better get going, then, huh?

Scratch: ::nodding:: Thanks for putting me back together.

Winc: I just sat here . . . you did the hard part. You go first.

Scratch: Why do *I* leave? ::grumbling::

Winc: Because you leave first, and I stay here waiting and that's how it works.

Scratch: ::sighing, burying my head in you::

Winc: ::holding you tight::

Scratch: O . . . K. Good night.

END SCRATCH JOURNAL ENTRY

NARRATIVE ENTRY, JABBATHEHUT

(Note: My brilliant friend has created a safe chat room for Scratch and Winc to meet the erstwhile Lieutenant Budge. But all he knows is that it was created by a mysterious "SysOp," a term meaning "system operator" of any given Internet service.)

Wally Budge is putting one and three together. Find the evil SysOp, find Toobe. Find Toobe, nab Scratch and Winc. Find SysOp guy, pay dirt. Ten hours until the strike.

END JABBA NARRATIVE ENTRY

GWYNYTH DIARY ENTRY

Evil, am I? Guy, am I?

END GWYNYTH DIARY ENTRY

NARRATIVE ENTRY, JABBATHEHUT

The following "communication" has appeared on every screen of every single online user.

A Public Safety Announcement
from
the U.S. Federal Bureau of Census and Statistics
in cooperation with your local service provider and Allied Consumer Industries

Subject: Net Strike Rumors
Reports verify that the source of the alleged "Scratch and Winc Strike Document" is in reality a teenaged drug dealer
". . . trying to have some fun."
The United States government strongly urges all citizens to IGNORE talk of a Net Strike. It is a bad practical joke.
Please LEAVE the RALLY Website NOW
and enjoy your time on the Net.
We are working to ensure this sort of mischief does not reoccur.
REPEAT: Talk of a "Strike" is all a practical joke.

One by one, hundreds of people have begun leaving The Rally.

At the same time, Budge's virus, the infamous Typhoid Mary, zeros in on Scratch, Winc, and Toobe. Budge and Shelly are watching the virus and celebrating.

Around this time, the SysOp cryptically writes: "Time to enable the StickyBomb."

"Uh-oh, handsome, we may have started celebrating too soon."

"How's that?" Budge looks up warily.

"That SysOp thingy is also taking out your hackers!"

"What? You mean, like zapping them off the Internet?!"

"Looks like it."

"Okay okay, not worth it, we don't need a war with this SysOp."

He thinks for a minute.

"Can we tweak the Mary thing to just disable Scratch, Winc, and Toobe's computers, and not fry them?"

"Sure thing, Walls," Shelly says, and her red fingernails fly over the keyboard. "There." She sits back, satisfied.

"Thanks, Shel."

"No problem, Walls," comes the reply.

END JABBA NARRATIVE ENTRY

GWYNYTH DIARY ENTRY

I'm having a little fun with the brave lieutenant. Poor dear. As soon as the DISABLED button is selected, a message from that sly ol' SysOp pops up:

> **To:** Ms. Budge
> **From:** SysOp (oooh, what an archaic word!)
> **Subj:** Peek-a-boo, I see you!
>
> Ten little hackers,
>
> Working on a fix.
>
> Four met a kitty-kat.

Now there are six.

Very kind of you to choose Disable over Destroy. But do mind your step, dearie. Remember, I see you when you're sleeping, I know when you're awake, etc. etc.

—SysOp—

The wolves are at bay for the moment.

Perhaps it was foolish, but I couldn't resist flicking the nose of the chief wolf himself. Now he's answered, and we are actually having a lively little interchange.

To: SysOp
From: Ms. Budge
Subj: Re: Peek-a-boo, I see you!

Dear Sir or Madam,

I'm guessing you already know who I am and who I work for. I'm also guessing you know where Toobe is. And where his two buddies are. I want you to know I'm on their side. I want them to give themselves up and come in on their own. It'll be a lot easier for them if they do. Truly, there's no way anyone can make these charges *stick*.

I'm not totally Net-stupid. I'm guessing you could cybersquash me like a bug with the flick of your little finger. Please don't do that. I'm looking for them, but I'm not their enemy. They need me on their side. At least let me meet with them.

So how about you help me call it all off? It'll save the US taxpayers some money, and they've paid a hell of a lot for this investigation so far.

Thanks.

—Wallace T. Budge, Lieutenant

Investigations, FBCS

Oh, call me an old softie, but I answered him:

To: Ms. Budge
From: SysOp
Subj: Yer ass is MINE, copper

Ha! I've always wanted to say that. Please forgive me.

Since it seems you learned some manners from your mother, I'll not "cybersquash" you as you so quaintly put it. But I remind you: I'm watching.

AND THIS I SWEAR BY CODE AND BY CRAFT:

If you so much as touch one hair on their precious little heads, I shall become the Fury whose name only your nightmares shall dare whisper.

SO BE IT.

Peace and Love,

"SysOp"

END GWYNYTH DIARY ENTRY

NARRATIVE ENTRY JABBATHEHUT

The two of them are staring into the screen. Shelly speaks first.

"Your SysOp is a woman."

"Huh?"

"That's a mama lion you're dealing with; she's protecting her cubs."

"But Typhoid Mary can disable her, right?"

"Right. Typhoid Mary is gonna disable anything that gets in her way."

"Wow. Shelly, I . . ." He flaps his hands vaguely.

"You what, big fella?"

"Um, you, well. I feel . . . I just . . . You are so swell. I mean when you . . ."

She watches his shoulders heave with a sigh.

"I know, hon, I know." She kisses him on the cheek, her scent lingering.

END JABBA NARRATIVE ENTRY

TOOBE ENTRY

Oh noooooooooo. When the govt lied that the strike is a gag, people started leaving The Rally in droves!

It's all coming apart at the seams. Collapsing.

I hate stupid grown-ups who believe anything that scares them. I hate it when people flap their mouths instead of their ears. Too much like school. And Orlio—I can just see his face, like a kid who just learned there's no Santa Claus. Look what's happening:

Shooter: It's a damned lie! The govt *always* lies!

Brknstck: Maybe not always, Shooter. Personally, I think it does sound like some drug dealer's prank.

AWESOME: No way, Brk . . . I *met* Scratch. Good sense of humor, but not mean. I believe it.

FredMan: Fine, Awesome . . . *you* sign off at 8 a.m. I'm not!

Brknstck: Me neither, Fred. My online time is too self-affirming. I'm not going to throw it away on some joke.

HotHead: *You're* the joke, don't you see that? ::fuming::

Tom: No strike! The strike's a joke!

Dick: Yeah! No strike! The strike's a joke!

Harry: Oh fuck the both of you. I stand with Scratch and Winc.

Private Message to Toobe

Orlio: Heyyyy Toober, people are dropping out of The Rally left and right. Have to ask you . . . *was* it all a practical joke?

I wish I could hug Orlio. But I did let him know it's no joke. Probably too late.

END TOOBE ENTRY

NARRATIVE ENTRY, JABBATHEHUT

In the chat room mysteriously created by "the evil SysOp," Budge finally gets to meet his fugitives.

Scratch has entered the room.

Scratch: Hello, cop.
Ms. Budge: Hello, Scratch. Where's your pal?
Scratch: On hir way.
Ms. Budge: Do you taste all her food before she eats it, too?
Scratch: Don't try "Divide and Conquer." It didn't work last time, it won't work now.
Ms. Budge: You're quite right.
Scratch: So what the hell do you want, Ms. Budge?
Ms. Budge: I need to know if you and your partner in crime are in any way connected with any terrorist groups trying to overthrow the govt?
Scratch: Ah, same ole . . . I thought you had something new today.

Winc has entered the room.

Scratch: Careful, Winc, he's already started on the wrong foot.
Winc: ::sweeping grandly into the room:: *Has* she now?

Private Message to Winc	Private Message to Scratch
Gwynyth: He's got hackers tracing your phone lines. What would you like me to do?	**Gwynyth:** He's got hackers tracing your phone lines. What would you like me to do?

Ms. Budge: ::raising my hands:: Sorry. Can we talk, please?

Winc: ::purring:: Oh look, Scratch, she's being nice!

Scratch: ::evenly:: OK, lieutenant. Talk away.

Private Message to Gwynyth

Winc: Should we be scared?

Gwynyth: Not this very minute, no.

Winc: Phew! Thanks *so* much! I wanna talk with him.

Gwynyth: You want to stay on, then?

Winc: Uh huh, please?

Gwynyth: Then so you shall.

Private Message to Gwynyth

Scratch: What should we do?

Gwynyth: Winc wants to stay on and talk.

Scratch: Cool. Me, too!

Scratch: ::checking address book:: Nope, no terrorist groups here!

Winc: ::peering over Scratch's shoulder:: Ze's right, officer . . . no terrorist groups there at *all*!

Ms. Budge: Haven't you heard the charges against you?

Scratch: Oh yeah, corrupting minors, getting our modems in a twist, etc.

Winc: ::softly:: I don't think that's what she's talking about, Scratch.

Ms. Budge: He, dammit! I'm a he!

Scratch: ::Yawn:: What're the charges?

Ms. Budge: You are currently being charged with High Treason.

Scratch: Whoa! ::looking over at Winc:: Did you know this?

Winc: ::hands on hips:: I *told* you that.

It's the whole conspiring to overthrow the govt thing.

Scratch: ::turning to Budge:: Do you honestly think that's what we're doing?

Winc: ::sweet innocent smile at Budge:: Li'l ol' us, officer?

Ms. Budge: High Treason is punishable by death in this country.

Scratch: I hate when that happens.

Winc: ::folding arms across my chest:: Well, we didn't do it.

Scratch: Yeah, right, we didn't do it.

Ms. Budge: Will you two stop clowning for one minute? This is very serious. We have evidence.

Winc: What evidence?

Scratch: What evidence?

Winc: ::looking over at Scratch fondly:: simul . . .

Scratch: . . . post.

Ms. Budge: You two are inciting a riot. Instructing your cohorts to sign off is evidence of insurrection.

Scratch: Ah, what a load of crap. We made a suggestion.

Ms. Budge: That's considered . . .

His hands freeze on the keyboard. Beside him, Shelly is holding her breath. The message onscreen from his hacker says that they have roughly traced all parties to their physical locations. Wally Budge suddenly realizes he doesn't know what to say.

Scratch: Cat got your tongue?

Winc: ::leaning across the table toward the handsome officer, allowing cleavage to show:: Something distracting you, officer?

Ms. Budge: Why do you pull that shit with me?

Scratch: Maybe she'll go for this: ::straightening my tie:: Can I buy you a drink, hon?

Winc: ::leaning back, stroking my mustache, watching Scratch pick up the pretty girl cop::

Ms. Budge: Why do you have to play at being something else?

Winc: ::blinking:: Why not?

Ms. Budge: Why not just be yourselves?

Winc: ::gently:: Maybe this *is* ourselves. All of our selves. Maybe it's fun.

Winc: Maybe that's all there is to it, Occifer.

Ms. Budge: You said you're innocent. So come in and let us help you.

Scratch: Will they give us room service? A parade?

Winc: ::warily:: Who's "us"? You and your little squirrels trying to trace us?

Wally's hands fly back off the keyboard as though he'd received two hundred volts.

Shelly's massaging his shoulders.

"Just keep them online, Wally. Hang in there."

Ms. Budge: If you two could try to be serious for a moment—

Scratch: We're dead serious, Ms. Budge.

Winc: Damned serious here, Mister. What about those squirrels?

Ms. Budge: What squirrels?

Scratch: Oh, don't play dumb.

Ms. Budge: ?

Private Message to Scratch

Toobe: Get the hell outta there!

Scratch: Why?

Winc: We know you've got hackers all over us. You lost four and you only have six left.

Scratch: Besides, if we were to come in, *you* wouldn't be in charge anyway.

Ms. Budge: None of this would be necessary if you would just cooperate.

Scratch: You don't sound very convincing.

Private Message to Scratch

Toobe: They're arresting people at The Rally!

Scratch: What? Bouncing them offline?

Toobe: No! Arresting them at their houses!

Scratch: Jesus.

Ms. Budge: I mean it.

Winc: ::turning to Scratch:: He means it.

"Wally," Shelly's saying, "it's Henderson on the phone. There's been a new development."

But Lieutenant Budge is deep in conversation with his perps, self-righteous indignation making him type fast for once.

Ms. Budge: I know what is right and what is wrong. And I know my job.
Winc: ::gently:: You know all that? Do you know what *we* are?
Ms. Budge: No. I mean, yes. You're wanted criminals.
Winc: No. Who are we, what are we?

Private Message to Winc

Scratch: Winc! Did you get the message from Toobe?
Winc: No. I'm flooded with other messages. What'd he say?
Scratch: People are being arrested at the Rally. I mean, in their *homes*.

Ms. Budge: My job is to locate and apprehend you.
Winc: Really, that's all we are to you? That's all you think of us as?

Toobe has entered the room.

Toobe: You guys! I didn't get any answer from you, and I mean it, they're arresting everyo . . .
Ms. Budge: You!

Toobe has left the room.

Private Message to Scratch

Winc: Tell me you're kidding.
Scratch: It's true!

Scratch: Listen you fucker, what's this about arrests?
Winc: Scratch? Arrests? You mean it?
Ms. Budge: What?

Private Message to Toobe

Winc: Are you OK?

Toobe: I'm OK, but I'm outta here fast.

Winc: Go with care. We'll talk later.

Toobe is no longer online
and did not receive your last message.

Scratch: I mean it. I'm gone. You're a fuckhead, Budge. I was actually starting to like you.

Ms. Budge: Wait. There's no arrests, it's got to be a rumor!

Even as he types, he catches Shelly's grim face out of the corner of his eye.

Private Message to Scratch

Winc: That fucking . . . I'm speechless.

Scratch: Sign off now!

Scratch has left the room.
Winc has left the room.

"Damn!" He lights a cigarette with shaking hands.

"It's true, Wally. They've made over sixty arrests nationwide in the last thirty minutes."

His jaw drops.

"Did Lieutenant Henderson happen to mention who he might be arresting?"

"He said they're insurrectionists," she answers. "And you already have two cigarettes going, babe. I don't think you need that third one."

He looks down at the match he's holding and blows it out with a puff.

"Well, I'll be damned," he says. "Thanks for doin' what you do."

"Oh, there's lots I could do, Lieutenant."

END JABBA NARRATIVE ENTRY

TOOBE ENTRY

Oh man, oh man, oh man. I just got this from Orlio at The Rally.

To: Toobe@<encrypted>
From: Orlio@<encrypted>
Subj: Every nightmare you've had

Doode, this is *scary*. I was in a rally room and people started dropping off the line, right? We thought it was a node overload, but look:

BarBun: Hey, where'd Thesman go?
FredMan: I'll call him live. brb.
Hanzoo: So, you guys gonna strike?
HotHead: Well, I was, but now I don't know.
FredMan: bak! I . . . this is TERRIBLE! They've arrested Thesman! They think he's conspiring with S&W. They came to his fucking HOUSE!
BarBun: ::firmly:: That does it. I'm pissed.
Hanzoo: What can we do? Lodge a complaint?
BarBun: Let's go ahead with it.
FredMan: The strike?
BarBun: Yep.
FredMan: Yes.
Hanzoo: Me too.
Azazello: What about online shopping, BB?
BarBun: I'll deal.
HotHead: Go, grrl!

See what I mean, bean?
They're actually arresting people! Duck!!

Orlio

To: Orlio
From: Toobe
Subj: Quack! I'm ducking!

Doode! No! Scary fer sure. Hey, be real careful not to mention . . . our two friends in any chats or they'll come after you too. Stay safe.

Toobe

I didn't hear anything from Orlio for over an hour, and then this!

To: Toobe
From: Orlio
Subj: There's a place . . .

Hey my man,

I hope this is okay but I told my dad about people getting arrested. He is pissed! He was ranting about freedom of speech and Persecuting the Youth and all kinds of other stuff. But he agrees that your friends are in danger, so they can use his office in Manhattan if they want. It's super high tech, looks super low tech, and they can dink around online safely. Watch the Strike, Rally, whatever, from there. Hope it's okay I told him.

Sending you the address encrypted and swizzled a million different ways.

Orlio

I love my pal!!! Okay, so I encrypted and re-encrypted his message, and sent it on to Gwynyth. She wrote back: "The witch hunts have begun. Like they even know what a witch is."

Shrug. So I asked her to please encrypt it again a million times before sending it on to you-know-who so they can get to that address.

END TOOBE JOURNAL ENTRY

NARRATIVE ENTRY, JABBATHEHUT

Budge struggles to keep up with the emails pouring onto the screen. He fires off one of his own to his boss.

> **To:** Undersec'y LaBouchere
> **From:** Ms. Budge
> **Subj:** They are NOT connected!
>
> Ma'am: I don't know who authorized Henderson's Kristallnacht, or on what evidence, but Scratch and Winc are operating *apart* from any gang. See attached logs as proof.
>
> —B.

Another window pops up.

> **To:** Ms. Budge
> **From:** DevilsOwn
> **Subj:** Grim Reapings
>
> Okay, Ms. Cop. We got their towns located just before they jumped offline. And I lost three more men.
>
> Winc is in Trenton, New Jersey.
>
> Scratch is in Dingmans Ferry, PA.
>
> We can't narrow it any further until we get them back online, and unless they're complete duncewads, they're not coming back.
>
> Tread softly, lady. I've grown fond of you.
>
> —Yr devil

It goes like this every time, he reminds himself. Halfway through the pursuit, it always looks too dark to see. He types:

To: DevilsOwn
From: Ms. Budge
Subj: As Ye Sow . . .

Sorry about your lost buddies. That's part of the job. You're a good man, Dev.

Now, get me those street addresses. I'm doubling your bonus right now, and I'll double it again when you get the perps.

I want you online. I want you everywhere. If they so much as sneak a byte out of the Net, I want you on them like gnats on rotten fruit.

—Budge

SEND! And yet another window opens.

To: Ms. Budge
From: Undersec'y Sec
Subj: Your recent memo

Dear Ms. Budge: The Undersecretary thanks you for your concern in this matter and assures you that she has every bit of confidence in you to do your job in such a manner that would make your government proud.

Sincerely yours,

—Ronald McVey

U-Sec Sec

He's wondering how to attach a paper bag full of dogshit to his next memo, when one more window opens up.

To: Ms. Budge
From: DevilsOwn
Subj: Double our treasure, double your fun

> Yes ma'am! But I'm no man, ma'am.
>
> ::wide grin::
>
> When this is all over, if you ever get up to NYC, let's me and you meet up at the Cubbyhole. Ladies only, my lady.
>
> —Devil

Wally Budge sputters.

"That's nice—she thinks you're nice," offers Shelly.

END JABBA NARRATIVE ENTRY

TOOBE ENTRY

That bastard! Budge started arresting people! He says it's not him, but I'm starting to believe my dad that all cops are pigs.

People started dropping out of The Rally like a scene from Jaws. Little heads pulled under the water. Scratch and Winc were talking to Budge, for gawdsakes, at the time. Do they have any idea how close they were?!

END TOOBE ENTRY

NARRATIVE ENTRY, JABBATHEHUT

Shelly is reading the thread over his shoulder.

> **To:** Henderson, Enforcement
> **From:** Ms. Budge
> **Subj:** Confirmed Locations
>
> Scratch positively confirmed in Dingmans Ferry, PA. Winc in Trenton, NJ. Street addresses to follow ASAP.
>
> —B.

To: Ms. Budge
From: Henderson Sec
Subj: Re: Confirmed locations

Ma'am, Lt. Henderson has asked me to convey his thanks and his regrets that he cannot act on this information as his task force is now operating independently, ref FBCS Charter&Code Ch. 6, Sec 114, Para 12, SubPar c.15.

—Sgt. Anna Pepper

Sec'y to Lt. Henderson

and this . . .

To: Undersec'y LaBouchere
From: Ms. Budge
Subj: I need 24 hours!

Ma'am, I have them located down to the city. Give me 24 hours!

—B.

To: Ms. Budge
From: Undersec'y Sec
Subj: Your recent memo

Dear Ms. Budge,

The undersecretary thanks you for your concern in this matter and assures you that she has every bit of confidence in you to do your job in such a manner that would make your government proud.

Sincerely yours,

—Ronald McVey

U-Sec Sec

"Shel, have I been reassigned? To some dumpster?"

END JABBA NARRATIVE ENTRY

WINC JOURNAL ENTRY

Private Message to Scratch

Winc: Did you see what I just saw?

Scratch: What?

Winc: It was a cartoon: a little hippie chick parading across the screen.

Scratch: Oh, that. Sure. Doesn't show up that well on my Tandy, but I saw it.

Winc: OK.

Private Message to Scratch

Winc: Scratch?

Scratch: Mm?

Winc: The hippie chick just went back across the screen, and . . .

Scratch: Yeah?

Winc: She waved at me!

Scratch: Cool!

Private Message to Scratch

Winc: Scratch, the little hippie chick is making me nervous.

Scratch: Huh?

Winc: She keeps walking back and forth.

Scratch: Wait a minute. Are you saying she doesn't *belong to you*?

Winc: ::hands on hips:: I should say not! Look at those *shoes*!

Scratch: ::looking:: Right.

Private Message to Scratch

Winc: The hippie chick is ba-ack.

Scratch: I figured it out! Must be one of Gwyn's guardian angels.

Winc: Of course!

Private Message to Winc

Gwynyth: The little hippie is not mine, my dear hearts, but I'm watching.

Winc: Anything we should do?

Gwynyth: Nope.

Private Message to Scratch

Gwynyth: The little hippie is not mine, my dear hearts, but I'm watching.

Scratch: It's a spy!

Gwynyth: Yup.

Private Message to Winc

Scratch: Um, the hippie's got company.

Winc: I see! What *is* that?

Scratch: Beats me. Looks like a dandelion with wisps sticking out.

Private Message to Winc

Gwynyth: Don't be alarmed if you see my StickyBomb. Whatever you do, don't touch her!

Winc: StickyBomb?

Gwynyth: Dandelion crossed with sludge and quicksand.

Private Message to Scratch

Gwynyth: Don't be alarmed if you see my StickyBomb. Whatever you do, don't touch her!

Scratch: ::blinking:: I don't think I get it.

Gwynyth: ::wryly:: Hopefully, they won't either.

Scratch: Ah.

Private Message to Winc

Jabbathehut: You must get offline. Email for you both in the usual manner.

Winc: Right!

Private Message to Scratch

Jabbathehut: You must get offline. Email for you both in the usual manner.

Scratch: Right!

END WINC JOURNAL ENTRY

TOOBE ENTRY

Three minutes later. They're back online, talking with each other! Can 15-year-olds get gray hair?

Scratch has entered room "City That Never Sleeps."

Winc has entered room "City That Never Sleeps."

Winc: You not sleeping too good, honey bunny?

Scratch: Let's talk private, Peanut.

Private Message to Scratch

Winc: Hippie chick's back.

Scratch: I see her, and Gwyn's StickyBomb.

Winc: It's a showdown! What *is* a StickyBomb?

Scratch: If you hit it, you get stuck, which of course makes you angrier, so you hit it again, you get more stuck, until you can't move.

Winc: You're so smart!

Scratch: Gwynyth is.

Private Message to Scratch

Winc: Whoa! Did you see that?

Scratch: What?

Winc: Hippie chick took a swing at the StickyBomb and now she's *stuck*!

Scratch: Just looks like a bunch of Xs and Os on my screen. Keep me posted.

Winc: ::purring:: Of course.

Private Message to Winc

Winc: Every time Hippie touches the thing she gets stuck. ::cracking up::

Scratch: Xlnt!

Private Message to Scratch

Winc: Hippie's down for the count!

Scratch: Her words are comin' out all garbled!

Winc: Don't you just love Gwyn?

Scratch: Glad she's on our side.

Private Message to Gwynyth

Scratch: Hey, we think you're great! Thanks for the StickyBomb. She won!
Gwynyth: ::chuckling:: Not bad for an old broad, huh?
Scratch: ::leaning back, grinning:: Not bad. Period.

Private Message to Gwynyth

Winc: We love you, Gwyn! The hippie chick is *covered* in stickiness!
Gwynyth: Love you right back, dear. Wait until she brings that sludge back "home!" Ha!

Scratch: So, I'll see you in Manhattan? ::dancing to imaginary swing band::
Scratch: Get it now? City that never sleeps?
Winc: ::looking into your eyes:: Manhattan.

Scratch has left the room.
Winc has left the room.

END TOOBE ENTRY

NARRATIVE ENTRY, JABBATHEHUT

A woebegone and bedraggled Typhoid Mary is struggling beneath a mess of clinging . . . something. Thick, sticky. Quicksand? Wally Budge doesn't know the Internet, but he knows trouble when he sees it.

He picks up his phone and dials.

"Shel, it's me. Whatcha doin'?"

"I'm still researching the Bureau code to find out how Henderson snagged this case out from under you."

"Check my screen. Are you seein' what I'm seein'?"

"Oh gee, Wally, yes."

"It's bad, right?"

"It's worse. Listen. Whatever you do, don't touch that mess with your cursor, okay? It's the mother of all viruses, and if you touch it, your entire database is gonna make the La Brea tar pits look crystal clear."

Budge carefully removes his hands from the keyboard. "Um. . . ."

"I'll be right there, hon."

Carefully, Shelly takes over, using keystrokes instead of the mouse to move the cursor farther and farther from the ugly steaming mess in the middle of the screen.

"I'm going to try this thing, cross your fingers, Walls."

Budge grunts.

"Okay. Isolate . . . Delete . . . Execute . . . Escape," Shelly breathes. Removing her hands from the keyboard with a flourish, she stares at the screen.

"That's all I know to do, Walls. Let's hope to hell it works."

END JABBA NARRATIVE ENTRY

SCRATCH JOURNAL ENTRY

Scratch: Winc, one more thing, I know we gotta go. I'm horny as hell.

Winc: ::glancing down at you::

You don't hafta tell me that, sailor. I can see for myself.

Scratch: I'm gonna see you soon *and* we're doing something dangerous: That combination is sexy as shit!

Winc: True. ::dropping to my knees::

Scratch: It's why I like gayboyz: the complete intrusion of sex into everything; they can't keep their dicks out of it.

Winc: Nope, they can't. ::leaning my head on your thigh::

Scratch: The rude insistence of it . . .

Winc: ::kissing your thigh gently::

Scratch: ::desire welling up:: I love you.

::softly::

I love you, Winc

I love you, Digqueer

I love you, whatever your boy-name was.

I love you, Frankie, and Tasha Yar.

Winc: ::tears filling eyes::

Scratch: Bye, dollface.

Winc: ::softly:: Bye handsome

END SCRATCH JOURNAL ENTRY

NARRATIVE ENTRY, JABBATHEHUT

Midnight. The building is quieter now.

Budge's hands are tied. He has no authorization to move in. Poor slobs. Henderson doesn't use kid gloves.

The phone rings.

"It's Shel."

"Yeah?"

"It's about your being taken off this case."

"Yeah?"

"I found a loophole."

"Aw, Shel."

"Get ready to be happy."

END JABBA NARRATIVE ENTRY

16
SIGNING OFF

PERSONAL LOG, JABBATHEHUT

I rather like my young friend's habit of posting a thought for the day, though many were somewhat pedestrian. I shall continue the tradition, but from a somewhat loftier plane:

FUNNY OF THE DAY

> Anyone who can be proved to be a seditious person is an outlaw before God and the emperor; and whoever is the first to put him to death does right and well. . . . Therefore let everyone who can, smite, slay and stab, secretly or openly, remembering that nothing can be more poisonous, hurtful, or devilish than a rebel.
>
> —*Martin Luther* (1483–1546)

It is with great difficulty that I note that some Internet systems are actually closing down entire nodes, not to mention millions of people personally signing off altogether.

But, back to the cops chasing Thelma and Louise. . . .

END JABBA PERSONAL LOG

NARRATIVE ENTRY, JABBATHEHUT

A train is speeding northward along the Northeast Corridor. Wally Budge's personal hacker, DevilsOwn, has intercepted an address in Manhattan where Scratch and Winc are headed this very minute. An office belonging to—Budge checks his notes again—a friend of Toobe's, screen name Orlio.

Budge pauses, thinks. "Whoops, guess there's no point sharing the address with Henderson, since he is working so very independently now." This has given Budge no end of satisfaction and one of the biggest smiles of his career.

He has no choice but to capture his perps himself.

Lieutenant Budge is surprised to note that, even though it's close to one in the morning, nearly every seat is taken. Talk is animated. Several boom boxes are tuned to public radio affiliates and AM talk shows, making conversation difficult.

"Isn't radio use illegal on board a train?"

In the next seat, Shelly Dunlap turns to him and smiles.

"Not during a national emergency."

"Oh, yeah." He grins. "That." He brings the portable radio closer to his ear, then goes back to his laptop to the email he'd downloaded before boarding.

To: Ms. Budge
From: Henderson, Enforcement
Subj: Assignment

I don't know how you wormed your way back onto this case, but don't get your hopes up. I'm keeping you as far away from them as I can.

What I wanna know is who or what tipped you to the National Emergency clause. You got a friend upstairs who knew that'd get you back on the case? Well I got friends upstairs, too, so keep your nose clean.

—Henderson

He looks up from his laptop.

"I don't know how you managed that, Shel, but I'm grateful."

Shelly laughs lightly and punches him gently on his arm.

"Stick with me, gumshoe. We'll go places."

And indeed, thanks to that little National Emergency subparagraph, the entire staff of the Bureau has been sent around the country to stake out nodes that hadn't shut down yet. One of those nodes would lead them to Scratch and Winc, went the reasoning. Except, of course, no one else knows about the office in Manhattan.

One by one, the commercial, public, and private enterprises have gone offline. It wouldn't be cynical to assume that this decision was made in an effort to hold onto customers.

It's well past midnight when Lieutenant Budge looks out the window at the crowds of people waiting to get on board the train. *Damn! If this strike is gettin' to crowds of folks in Trenton, it's got a reach. Izzat why everyone is so damned cheerful? In the background, an endless series of announcers from the National Public Radio Network are going on about how many nodes have shut down, how many people are estimated to have signed off already. Jesus, they might pull this off. But I know where you are now, and here I come.*

A faltering voice from just behind him pulls Wally out of his reverie.

"Lieutenant Budge?"

He swivels his head to find himself inches from the face of some kid in his early twenties.

"Who wants to know?" he asks gruffly. Ever since his "television debut" at the Coney Island debacle, people have come up to him on the street to say hello.

The young man goes beet-red. "It's me, sir. Francis Norton."

Wally's puzzled. Shelly leans in close and whispers, "Your communications chief, Lieutenant."

Wally nods but continues to stare at the nervous young man. "What was your job before this assignment, Norton?"

"Hard copy routing and expediting, sir."

Wally blinks. "You work in the mail room?"

The young man's wince is painful to watch.

"Yessir. But we don't call it that anymore, sir."

"What is it you want, Agent Norton?"

The young man's face flushes with shy pride at the lieutenant's use of the title.

"Well, sir, you asked me to tell you when we were halfway there.

"We are, sir.

"Halfway there."

It was a near parody of earnestness.

"Thank you, Agent Norton. Carry on."

Wally and Shel share a crooked smile.

He looks back out the window. What a motley crew. All of them leftovers, just like him. All of them sent up to the front lines, just like him. Thank you, National Emergency.

"Thank you, Shel."

"You're welcome, Walls. You're always welcome."

END JABBA NARRATIVE ENTRY

GWYNYTH DIARY ENTRY

I am delighted to include a bit of chat that was risked just before Romiette and Julio finally got offline:

***** You are in Private Room "Serifos" *****

Gwynyth: I had a feeling you might be lurking until the bitter end.

Jabbathehut: ::eyebrows raised::

Gwynyth: I thought you might like some company.

Jabbathehut: Madam, I do not lurk.

Gwynyth: Of course you don't, dear. You are very busy, I know.

Jabbathehut: Purpose of this intrusion?

Gwynyth: Oh, slide down off that horse, you old fart. I'm just making contact.

Jabbathehut: Forgive me. I'd forgotten the social convention.

Gwynyth: Well, you can learn again, it's very easy.

Jabbathehut: I have had no reason.

Gwynyth: I know, dear, I know. And someday maybe you'll tell me why.

Gwynyth: I don't just think of you as a genius, you know.

Jabbathehut: Nor I, you . . . as well you know.

Gwynyth: I miss you.

Jabbathehut: I confess to happiness, being here in the ever-diminishing cyberspace—just the two of us.

Gwynyth: Three of us, dear.

Jabbathehut: Three?

Toobe has entered the room.

Jabbathehut: ::gruffly:: Very well, then, three of us.

Toobe: Better make that five.

Jabbathehut: ::lifting an eyebrow:: Five?

Winc has entered the room.

Scratch has entered the room.

Jabbathehut: ::sighing heavily:: Five.

Winc: Oh yay, it's a family!

Gwynyth: ::suppressing a smile:: *Jabba Knows Best*?

Toobe: *The Jabba Bunch*!

Scratch: ::eyeing Jabba's scowl:: *Mama Jabba's Family* ::ducking::

Jabbathehut: ::utterly speechless::

Jabba signed off immediately, of course, but if you can tell such a thing onscreen, I think the old dear might have been secretly pleased.

END GWYNYTH DIARY ENTRY

NARRATIVE ENTRY, JABBATHEHUT

Pennsylvania Station, New York.

New York will be the next station stop.

Finally. Wally checks his watch: It's stupid o'clock. Four-thirty in the morning. This train has been like a goddamn party for the past four hours.

"Wanna round up the troops, Shel?"

"Yes, Lieutenant." She grins.

The agents were easy enough to spot. They were the only ones sleeping in this lively crowd of revelers. Wally Budge leans over to the woman seated across the aisle, vaguely wondering if she's one of his "men," since she doesn't seem to be chatting like all the other lamebrains around him.

"Pardon me, ma'am, I couldn't help notice you weren't joining in the festivities here."

She turns to him slowly, strawberry-blond waves falling down across her right eye. She's smiling.

"Is that a crime, Officer Budge?" Husky voice, kind of Lauren Bacall. He's always liked Lauren Bacall.

"Heh-heh," he laughs nervously. "Saw me on television, huh?"

"And who in the entire country hasn't, officer?"

He shakes his shaggy head. "Yeah, I suppose. Do you have any idea why everyone's so happy? It's a national emergency, after all." Damn, her legs go on forever.

She laughs lightly. "Well, Lieutenant Budge, I suppose it's like getting a day off from school. People are actually talking with each other—without keyboards and monitors. They're not stuck in their houses."

"And you?"

The train is pulling to a stop.

"Oh, I'm visiting an old friend in the city."

She shakes her hair out of her eyes, revealing a waterfall tattoo dropping from her right eye down to her cheekbone. Wally can't stop himself from asking. He points awkwardly at the tattoo.

"So, you're a Winc fan, huh?"

This is Pennsylvania Station, New York.

She raises her hand, drawing a long, slender finger down the length of the design. Smiles into his eyes.

"Who in their right mind wouldn't be a Winc fan, officer?"

She's up in the aisle now, pulling a bag down from the rack above her seat. Wally Budge is up in a flash, standing by her side. She turns to him, startled.

"Yes?" She's got a good four or five inches on him.

"Let me get that bag for you, ma'am."

A slow smile, her head inclined just slightly. He feels like a teenager.

"Why, thank you, officer." With a small laugh and a wave, she's through the door and out on the platform.

A tapping at his shoulder. It's Shel, amused.

"Lieutenant Budge? The troops are ready to disembark. Best put your tongue back in your mouth, your eyes back in their sockets, and wipe the sweat from your brow."

"Shel! You know I only got eyes for you."

"Here, your tie's crooked."

END JABBA NARRATIVE ENTRY

GWYNYTH DIARY ENTRY

True Romance, take two.

> **To:** Gwynyth@<encrypted>
> **From:** ScratchnWinc@ecotech.com
> **Subj:** Checking in, as you requested
>
> We're ba-a-a-a-a-a-a-ack! NYC! Can you believe it?
>
> First, I've got to tell you that I sat across the aisle from a certain lieutenant the whole train ride up here. I held my panic down all the way from Trenton. Even made him blush.
>
> Okay, so our plan seems to be working! I waited outside the address Orlio gave us, and it's about 5 a.m., right? Just a few people out walking. The streets belong to the delivery trucks.
>
> This kid comes up to me, eyes popping out of his head, and he says, "Winc?" I say, "Orlio?"
>
> He's laughing, and he says "Wow, you really *are* a lady!" And I say "Sometimes, dear." And he keeps laughing.

We're only there a few minutes when suddenly there's Scratch at the curb in that silly car. Ze leans out the window with a crinkly grin and says, "Hey, Dollface, kept you waitin' long?" Swoon. Ze must've broken every speed limit getting here on time.

"Gwynyth's Guides are with us! There's a parking space!"

I shake my head in disbelief.

Orlio can't get over Scratch.

"Oh man, that is so cool: You're gay!"

Scratch keeps smiling, glancing at him all gruff-but-not-really, and finally says, "Sometimes, dear." I swear!

Right, so just as he said he would, Orlio's dad let us into his loft at this office called EcoTech, then he and Orlio went home, and now it's just the two of us, cozy as can be.

See you and Toobe soon, yes?

—ScratchnWinc

END GWYNYTH DIARY ENTRY

TOOBE ENTRY

Well shit. All nodes have gone down except one (plus Jabba's). That guts the strike. Technically. But people are still out in the streets celebrating!

I can't believe their stupid plan is working. I love them.

END TOOBE ENTRY

GWYNYTH DIARY ENTRY

Balls of fire! Scratch and Winc are actually sitting together in the Manhattan office of EcoTech, in the node room, typing to one another side by side (Winc's idea of an icebreaker, I imagine). The two of them seem quite oblivious to the law closing in, having now pegged them to NYC.

***** You are in Private Room "Hee Hee" *****

Winc: ::sleepy smile:: Good morning.

Scratch: Check this out! Dueling computers!

Winc: ::blinking:: You seem very awake.

Scratch: Way!

Are you reading the "Scratch and Winc" board?

Have you missed me?

Do you have enough stuff to read?

Read this: ::uploading::

Post: Scratch and Winc Website
It's working, it's working! Very few nodes left!
Signing off now!

—Alternative to Loud Boats Node, San Diego

Winc: Do you know you make me happy beyond words?

::shaking my head:: Delighted to see this side of you.

Scratch: So many sides. So happy to see you!

Winc: Me too you! ::softly:: Why are we typing then?

Scratch: We're shy. And we have to keep activity on this line.

Winc: ::dimly:: Still haven't had any coffee yet, dear.

Scratch: When all the nodes shut off we'll be the only ones left!

Winc: You seem pretty happy.

Scratch: Hysterically happy!

::measuring happiness::

85% cuz you, 30% cuz rebels with a cause.

Winc: Your math needs some work, sweetie. Know what?

Scratch: ::stopping short:: What?

Winc: When you're happy, you tell stories.

Scratch: Hmmm, guess you're right . . .

Winc: Lovely to see, darlin'. You're full of joy.

Scratch: Joy's got me picked up by the holes like a bowling ball.

Scratch: You wanna hear something else?

Winc: Always.

Scratch: ::demonstrating:: I put my fingers inside your cunt, then I put two more in your ass, then I rock you back and forth and up and down and then I kiss you and then I pick you up and you come and then we are happyhappyhappywackos!

Winc: ::gasp:: Yeah, that's sort of what I had in mind . . . like that . . .

Scratch: Then Razorfun comes in all dark and scary and cuts you and then we bleed all over naked bodies and roll around in the daisies . . .

::circuits crossing and jamming::

::Technicolor explosions::

Winc: You are so sweet.

Scratch: . . . and then Scratchgrrl jumps into Winc's riotboy arms and we slamdance around while I pull his cock and then Digqueer trips us up and we fall down on the green grass with all kinds of wet stuff and lots o' flowers . . .

Winc: Scratch. I am so glad you're back.

Scratch: Back ain't the half of it.

You may fear you've created a monster . . .

Winc: ::purring:: You have always been my favorite monster.

Scratch: Do you think we should be logging this?

Hard to recreate hysterical joy . . .

Winc: ::rolling my eyes:: Been logging for hours. It's bound to be someone's idea of history someday.

Winc: But I'm a little scared of going offline.

To be with you face to face again.

I can feel the warmth of you next to me.

::carefully keeping my eyes glued to the screen::

Scratch: Yeah, me, too. But there's no other way but forward.

We gotta be together for this last thing.

::using all my willpower to keep fingers on the keyboard::

Scratch: I'm sorry I was gone so long, must have been very difficult for you . . .

Winc: ::nodding, smiling gently:: Made sense, though.

Look how long it took to get to know each other, not just in surfing, but . . .

I go away too, just not quite so noisily as you

Scratch: I know. Too much stimulus. So I just shut down.

Winc: Understand.

Scratch: Trying not to think about you on the floor . . .

red marks on your back . . .

Winc: ::moaning::

Scratch: Oh damn, it's like I heard you really do that!

Scratch: You've got to protect yourself from my going away.

I have NO idea when it's coming . . .

Winc: Sighing. It's all part of love.

Winc: Didja hear that?

Scratch: I sure did, sugar pop.

Scratch: ::slight grin, continuing to type::

Wanna get you all wet, always want to get you all wet and messy . . .

Winc: Wanna be on my knees in front of you.

Scratch: }->

Winc: Is that a picture of Razorfun?

Scratch: Uh huh.

Winc: Wanna press my face against your boot.

Scratch: Wanna slap that face and kiss that face and slap it some more . . .

Winc: You know I really wanna feel you slap me.

Scratch: You know I really wanna mark you with me.

Winc: Wanna be yours.

Winc: Scratch?

Winc: Scratch?

Scratch: Guess what?

Winc: NO! ::small voice:: g'bye?

Scratch: Yeah, we should do our signoff soon.

Winc: ::gulp:: Right you are. ::waving::

By goddess, I hope the heck they learn to talk in real time.

END GWYNYTH DIARY ENTRY

NARRATIVE ENTRY, JABBATHEHUT

6:00 a.m., Manhattan Monday, still no traffic. No early-to-work types rushing to their offices. A gaggle of government types stand on the sidewalk, holding cups of sticky-sweet concoctions from the Papaya King. They're all listening to Budge hold forth about his days as a beat cop. Only Shelly Dunlap notices that he keeps shifting his eyes to the EcoTech building, up to the fifth floor, where one light is burning.

"What're we waiting for, Wally?" she whispers.

"For Henderson to wake up and give us the damned go-ahead," says Wally. "Even though he thinks we're on a false trail. Can't say I acted without orders. Until then," he grins, "we wait."

He looks over at his shabby crew.

"Hey, you guys. And gals. Have I told you the one about busting the pickets at the abortion center in Chelsea?"

To: ScratchnWinc
From: Jabbathehut
Subj: Errant nodes

There appear to be only two nodes left online. One belongs to some kind of gun-rights group whose last message was "we don't know how to turn it off." The last node is mine. I assure you I will continue to operate as usual, as it is not my nature to be a joiner of any kind. Please excuse that inconvenience.

Fighting God,

—J.

To: Jabbathehut
From: ScratchnWinc

Subj: Naughty nodes

Gun rights? Wow. And um, did you know that if we all go offline you'll be the only one left? Could you please consider taking a holiday for 24 hours? We wouldn't really count you among the strikers, but it would make everything perfect.

—S&W.

END JABBA NARRATIVE ENTRY

GWYNYTH DIARY ENTRY

I might have to agree with Jabba about people's short attention spans. Having had 10 minutes of no activity, Scratch and Winc goofed around online and, incredibly, discovered the Allied Consumer Industries database file. Perhaps because there were hardly any nodes online, it was easy to discover? How do they DO these things?

END GWYNYTH DIARY ENTRY

SCRATCH JOURNAL ENTRY

OMG, we found *the* database with all the Reg info, all the answered Reg forms!

I got off on just looking at it, but Winc went right in. Ze said Jabba had taught hir a few codes, and ze just started hacking away until ze was in. Fuck!!!

First thing ze tried to do was delete the whole thing, but it kicked hir out a few times. Ze found another backdoor and we got to the database spreadsheet itself, which showed all those stupid Reg questions we hated about Registration.

Then we got another note from Jabba.

To: ScratchnWinc
From: Jabbathehut
Subj: Confirmation

There being only two nodes left makes you extremely vulnerable to actual capture. Since the gun-rights site is in SF and mine is in NYC any fool would know you're in one or the other.

F.G.,

—J.

Right. So back to the spreadsheet: We skipped down to the third question, our favorite one to hate:

Sex: M/F

Annnnnnd, I go . . .

—CLICK—

And the whole column was selected, easy as pie! Saying that out loud made Winc announce that ze wanted some pie. Obviously punchy by then, bored out of our skulls but wired from all the waiting, adrenaline, and the sex we weren't having. We put our fingers together and hit the DELETE key as one, fully expecting a big old nothing.

We didn't really know what we'd done, but it went sorta like this:

Winc: Wow, it's an hourglass.
Scratch: What does that mean?
Winc: It's thinking.

—pause—

Scratch: Wow, it's still thinking.

Every time we looked back at the screen, the hourglass was still there. And the little lights blinking on the console. S L O W L Y.

Meanwhile, in came another memo from Jabba:

To: Scratch/Winc via bypass
From: Jabbathehut

Subj: Neatness

There is one more node left besides my own, the gun-rights site. Not a blocker, but one likes clean, smooth lines in one's patterns.

There appears to be no means of having your little action work, so long as this node is open.

—J.

It always fucking goes this way. One stupid little scared clutch of people fuck it up for the rest of us. All they had to do was shut down for 24 hours. But no, as if taking a stand on something, anything, would fucking kill them.

What else could we do? We had to sign off. Winc says to be patient.

END SCRATCH JOURNAL ENTRY

TOOBE ENTRY

To: Jabba
From: Toobe
Subj: Just please

::looking at you straight in the eyes:: Please help us. Isn't there something you can do about that last node? I guess I'm asking you again for help, which I know I've done too much lately. But it's really important.

—T.

To: Toobe
From: Jabba
Subj: Just please

You are compelling, my friend. My fish tanks are sparkling. I have made my temporary conduit safe from the bored antics of its two occupants.

By my calculations, the feds will be at their door by 8am.

END TOOBE ENTRY

GWYNYTH DIARY ENTRY

At last, I've finished my signoff anthem:

AND THIS I STATE:

I started getting cranky back when they shuttered the Coney Island Freak Show and put up a McDonald's. Let me tell you—there weren't many places left for a bearded lady to work.

Memories:
"Can I help you, sir?"
"Look at the man in the dress, Mommy!"
"Sorry, this land is for women only."

I have always found refuge in my computer. Next to my cats, that ornery pile of chips and circuits was the most forgiving creature in my life. I plied a thriving trade in online tarot readings. Until my site was hacked, and suddenly men were signing on for cybersex. Gave the damn fools a tarot reading anyway, and they never knew the difference. Ka-ching for me.

I flourished, built vast domains, for all who entered to explore, experience, and emerge enlightened. I had one lone companion who could match me in my speed and desire for all things techno.

My friend and I built cyberworlds and romped as playmates, inventors, artists. We were there when Tim first proposed the idea of using hyperlinks to create a "web of information." It wasn't long before we came up with HTML. Ah, great days. Never did we meet face-to-bearded face. And then one day twelve long years ago, my friend simply disappeared.

I was suddenly alone in an empire of zeros and ones. I built and fortified my secret cyber-fortress. I practiced my Code and my Craft, waiting to discover my raison d'être. I missed my large friend.

Now, after twelve years of virtual and quite real solitude, I have three new friends who've gazed upon my furry face and never blinked an eye. It's been worth the wait. And lo, of late my brilliant friend and I are speaking again. All this because my three new friends needed us both so badly.

Oh, you can call it chance.

You can say it's Fate.

I call it the power of an open heart.

Now I know the reason for my cyberpowers.

I know the reason for my understanding of the Craft.

And the reason for my beard.

From this day forward, I pledge my life to opening my strong arms to all my family members everywhere. By Code and by Craft, I do.

SO BE IT

This is me, signing off. Plus all my cats.

—Gwynyth

END GWYNYTH DIARY ENTRY

PERSONAL LOG, JABBATHEHUT

To my . . . what can only be described as shock, the strike seems to be working. In all honesty I never thought it would get this far.

END JABBA PERSONAL LOG

SCRATCH AND WINC JOURNAL ENTRIES, COMBINED

Okay, this is us signing off.

We can't wait anymore to see if the last node changed its mind.

Question authority ain't the half of it.

Question everything.

We don't have any advice, just big hearts and no common sense, and we hope nobody gets hurt in all this.

Until we can meet again,

Digqueer/Luvboyz
Frankie/Johnny
Leilia/Karn
Spoiler/StarfleetFT
Mythter/Gyrl
Spike/HoneyDew
Scratch/Winc
We luv you, buh bye . . .
—ScratchnWinc

We grabbed the elevator down and were outta there.

END JOURNAL ENTRIES

NARRATIVE ENTRY, JABBATHEHUT

8:00 a.m., and he's tired of waiting for the goddamned elevator, even though it's slowly headed down. Wally Budge is out of breath from climbing five flights of stairs. He heads to the node room of EcoTech Technologies. He's grinning ear to ear, though. Henderson's tone of bitter resignation over the phone had made it all worthwhile.

"They're not in San Francisco, Budge. They must be at your site."

"Is that an order to search the premises, sir?"

Henderson had simply hung up the phone, and Budge started issuing directives.

His dirty dozen, as he has come to regard them fondly, swarm through EcoTech like ants at a picnic. He knows he's just missed them. Shelly Dunlap looks up from one of the monitors.

"Got something interesting here, Wally. It's the master database for the Registration. They tapped into the ACI master file!"

"How? Never mind. What'd they do to it?"

Shelly pauses before answering.

"Well," she says slowly, "they've given it a command it can't comply with."

He lifts a craggy eyebrow. "What does that mean?"

"It means," she says, "there's gonna be no more database, no more Registration, no more online marketing, and . . ." She pauses.

"And?"

"And you won't have to be Ms. Budge anymore."

"Well, ain't that a pleasant surprise."

The two of them stare into the screen for a few moments.

"Those two little idiots won't find anything important, will they, Wally?"

"Nah, they hit delete. But we've got them. On my home turf. I'll have them in custody in less than two hours."

On the screen before them, the hourglass sits squarely in the middle of the screen.

END JABBA NARRATIVE ENTRY

PERSONAL LOG, JABBATHEHUT

There is only the gun-rights node left, and my own of course. No strike. Well, not unless I tap this little button here. The button that someone there should have tapped but didn't know how. When oh when did activism become the bureaucracy it was founded to take down?

::flicking my wrist::

And the node is disabled.

My own node is easy as well. For me that is.

::flicking my other wrist::

All this wrist flicking has made me weary.

Viva la revolución and goodnight!

END JABBA PERSONAL LOG

17
SHOTS FIRED

To: Editor, They/Them magazine
From: D.I. Drew
Subject: Anthems

Hi Asa,

As we all learned in school, against all odds the internet shut down. But imho one of its biggest obstacles was its biggest achievement: cooperation. Every single node eventually shut down, even the last few holdouts. Also uplifting were the range and depth of people's signoff "anthems." Here's one I really loved.

Cheers,

D.I. Drew

ZINE EXCERPT

PISSED OFF, NOT GONNA TAKE IT ANYMORE

. . . a strong suspicion and even distrust has replaced the growing hope that Registration would bring more options, not less. But anyone who has had obnoxious ads hurled at their screen names can tell you it's annoying to fend off campaigns for hair replacement implants when you're trying to find a law library, or worse, when you're taking the occasional cyberstroll as a different persona, even as a different gender. The joy of the Net is its freedom.

Update: NPR
Radio On-Scene Report, KRUW Wichita
There's a different feel to this crowd. I've never seen such diverse groups of people here in Sedgwick Park. In one corner, people are using sign language, in another, young people with pierced noses, purple hair, and big combat boots are talking animatedly. Every age is represented, and every color of the human rainbow; it's phenomenal. Like a demonstration, but with no agenda, no speeches, and no discernible cause. Just . . . joy.
Rap Shoopman, NPR Youth Reporter
Shoopman: Amid all the people celebrating what looks like the actual shutdown of the Internet, there is a very serious raid going down. Feds and local cops are stationed wherever a false Scratch and Winc sighting led them. A car traced to Scratch is currently parked outside a Travelodge. Police have been preparing for action in this area, having focused on Times Square and Madison Square Garden, while other SWAT teams were camped out at City University and SUNY. This is Rap Shoopman, reporting for NPR.

SCRATCH JOURNAL ENTRY

Winc and I went for a drive, just aimlessly cruising around. But then we saw a group of people shouting that suddenly all nodes were down! No idea why! The strike worked! We looked at each other, and then I pulled over. I ran into a coffee shop, and when I came out I saw Winc looking at me through the car window like ze'd always ridden in there with me. Like some movie. The sun was still in its early morning place, making everything feel new. Winc was smiling at me, the light right behind hir hair. I jumped in the car and handed hir coffee, and we were off, for who knows where, but we were going.

We got a few blocks and all that relief and tension flooded through me, and it went to my crotch. All of a sudden I had to get my hands on hir, my Winc. I looked over at hir all shy but later ze said it was more like sly. There was this cheap hotel right in front of us, so I screeched into the parking lot.

We were in the room and I was swimming in desire, totally aware that ze was real, not online—big as life, hir body warm and real and right up close. With even the slightest touch, it was like electricity zapping me. Ze said it was the same for hir, like we needed to take an hour for every inch of skin, but we had no time and the electricity was fierce. I was swooning, actually swooning, a word I'd never understood until that moment, but I couldn't breathe and I was dizzy and all I could do—all I wanted to do—was hang on. I knew, right then, that despite all my great philosophizing, it was hir gyrl stuff that turned me on right then, hir breasts and hir smell and hir hair and hir eyes looking at me so womanly and open and ready for me. Ze was female. I wanted hir.

I'm not even sure I got all our clothes off, but it was a fast, furious, glorious fuck—I felt I could eat hir bones with my teeth and smash our skin together so it would never come apart. We tore up that room, with the radio blaring about the strike, about "Scratch and Winc" who sounded like the totally made-up cardboard heroes they were. We fucked when the stupid commercials came on, and then we took a shower and practically broke the door fucking in there.

I splattered: Even though I had to conquer the hell out of hir and tell hir all those dirty things in my head and vulgarize hir and bring out hir want and need and crave, at some point we became this one passionate body that didn't have a name or a sex or a place that was anchored down anywhere; we were us, juice and blood and kisses.

Until we heard on the radio about the police swarming, at which point . . . well, we got the hell out of there.

END SCRATCH JOURNAL ENTRY

PERSONAL LOG, JABBATHEHUT

To: All who care to listen
From: Jabbathehut
Subj: My signoff statement (I refuse to call it an anthem)

It is not in my nature to be public in any manner, nor to join the activities of others, as organized efforts are at best mediocre and lack creativity. However, I have been unwittingly infected by the desperate idealism of those I have come to regard as friends.

It's been a good 12 years since I retired to my lair, driven here by forces of evil in part, but mostly of cruelty and chance. Such is the nature of God, a malevolent fellow who appears to suffer the same boredom many of us do in these uncertain times. I doubt I shall surface again, at least in this guise, as my conduits have become far too known to far too many. So, a farewell attempt at self-revelation.

Many years ago, I loved fiercely. She was intelligent and beautiful, and blessed with a ferocious determination I had not seen before nor since.

And then, she was gunned down, for no other reason than we lived in the United States and she was caught in a random crossfire. As one is. Here at least.

At her side was her best friend, who was also shot, succumbing to her injuries later. That equally random fact saved my life. Because my beloved's partner in death had left behind a young son and a husband. Quite simply, they needed me.

"John," the little one's father, is a sensitive sort; it was all I could do to keep him feeding the dogs and shaving himself each morning. You might say that little "Toby" saved us both, with his wondering eyes and quick heart. He asked us innumerable questions, gave endless and irritating hugs, and possessed an insatiable curiosity that perhaps appealed to this battered ego of mine. Once I was assured that his father was skating on all wheels, I retired to this peaceful room with my fish and electronic spiderwebs.

We've kept in touch, and it does not surprise me that Toobe—as he has come to call himself—should be a part of a movement so large, successful, and chaotic.

And later, at my side, was of all things a Witch, a Pagan, and like myself, a lifelong citizen of the fabled Isle of Lesbos. Over the next four years or so, we built empires, she and I . . . our collaborative artistry has awakened again!

But it was some time at three this morning that I realized it was Toobe who had saved me, not I him. And so, when I discovered one node still functioning, I decided to end my own strike against the world and at least facilitate the wishes of my beloved charge.

It was quite simple to arrange an electronic soldier to attack the node. In a matter of minutes, the last node shut down.

Fighting, but perhaps not God any longer,

—J.

END JABBA PERSONAL LOG

SPECIAL ON-SCENE REPORT FROM RAP SHOOPMAN, ARCHIVAL TRANSCRIPT

Shoopman: Scratch and Winc came out of the hotel, and they sure didn't look like fugitives. One's short, the other tall, they had their arms around each other, looking kind of spacey. They seemed to be in no hurry to get to their car, which they drove perhaps a block before they were stopped. All of a sudden, they were surrounded by police, and they looked absolutely stunned.

Now, get this: They were stopped for a traffic violation! I'm not making this up. Scratch had a fistful of old parking tickets now gone to warrant—the plate was already in the system. The officer on duty immediately saw the connection to America's most wanted and called for more backup. And then, well it all went to comedy.

The government agents pushed through the crowd to reach the scene. The NYPD was yelling and waving their arms at the government cops to lay off their collar. In the confusion, no one was watching Scratch or Winc, who were sitting there in the car, spaced out.

As I'm talking, the local cops and the feds are at some kind of bureaucratic standoff, and no one has approached the car.

TOOBE ENTRY

I'd been in touch with Scratch and Winc, but suddenly they were offline, doing what, I have no idea. Once everything started coming down, I just wanted to be with my dad. I hugged Gwynyth goodbye quickly (her not so quickly), hopped the train, and when I got off at his stop, there he was. I felt better immediately. We had to know what was going on with all my pals, so he and I nonchalantly walked the few blocks down to the EcoTech office. A bunch of people were partying in the street, plus there were some reporters. My dad and I blended into the crowd, and we just hung out. It was great watching everybody mill around in the street!

END TOOBE ENTRY

SCRATCH JOURNAL ENTRY

We were so dreamy we could hardly stand. Hey, you would be too if you'd just had that kind of fuckfest. Aw man, if I'd had my antenna up I never would have let us walk out of that hotel.

Goddamn parking tickets. Do they have nothing better than to go after people with parking tickets? Did you know when a cop sees the warrant in the database the arresting officer has no idea if it's for illegal parking or murder?

I got this flash of jail, then my stomach went totally cold when I realized it would be worse for Winc. Hir license still says male, so she wouldn't be sent to a women's prison. Totally fucked. All I could think of was to run. We quietly slipped out of the car and took off down the alley like our shoes were on fire. NO ONE WAS WATCHING US!

Yeah, I know I just yelled that. But really, all the cops were just standing there, yelling at each other, so we got a head start before someone noticed. I really thought we were going to make it. Then shots behind us, like firecrackers only louder. Then Winc fell down. They fucking shot Winc!

END SCRATCH JOURNAL ENTRY

To: Editor, They/Them magazine
From: D.I. Drew
Subject: Who's what where?

Hi Asa,

I had to study more than a few archives to figure this out: At this point, Toobe is with his dad, Scratch and Winc are staggering around near the EcoTech building, and Gwynyth and Jabba are in their respective lairs.

Cheers,

Drew

TRANSCRIPT: NPR ALL THINGS CONSIDERED, SPECIAL EDITION

Shoopman: Apparently shots were fired at Scratch and Winc just moments ago, when they tried to run after a routine traffic stop connected them to a warrant for Scratch's overdue parking tickets.

Officers had been instructed to proceed with extreme caution. Nevertheless, one officer drew his weapon and fired. It is not known at this point if anyone was hit, but for all intents and purposes, Scratch and Winc are still at large.

This places the balance of the hunt-and-chase in the hands of Lieutenant Wallace T. Budge of the Federal Bureau of Census and Statistics . . . the man responsible for the Coney Island fiasco only weeks ago. His was the first in a series of fruitless government raids on the nation's amusement parks. We will keep you posted as we await further developments.

SCRATCH JOURNAL ENTRY

I didn't give a fuck what happened next, I just wanted Winc to be right where ze was, lying in my arms. The cops were nowhere to be seen. I don't think they knew they'd hit hir because ze just kept running. I didn't even know until ze fell down, and I thought ze'd just tripped.

Suddenly there was absolutely no hurry. I remember a watery beam of sunlight somehow peeking its head over the tops of the skyscrapers. We found a little hollow in a pile of cardboard, me leaning against a brick wall with hir collapsed into me. I could feel hir blood, sticky and hot against me, like I'd always imagined. But not this way. Not this way, no!

Ze was murmuring how much ze loved me and looking into my eyes. I got all panicky and yelled, "No! No!" I knew ze was blissed out beyond all comprehension, hir little self happy to be lying in my arms, frozen for all time, just like that, with me.

"How I always wanted it to be," ze said.

And hir eyes were so near, so deep and changing colors every five seconds to a shade more beautiful than the last. I knew it was a perfect moment, too, but I also got really pissed—like I always do when I feel everything's going down the path of least resistance without trying to change itself into something better.

I got pissed at hir and the police and the Net and people and subways and cars and skyscrapers, and even my beloved NPR. I practically hauled Winc to hir feet and made hir walk, willing some hospital or medicine man or something to be around the corner. My survival instincts kicked in: Just get out of there. And obliterating everything else, all our silly fights and misunderstandings, it was like this big cartoon dialogue balloon appeared over the two of us that said: live, Winc, just live.

END SCRATCH JOURNAL ENTRY

TRANSCRIPT, NPR SPECIAL EDITION

Shoopman: Well Bob, it's a mass of confusion around here. Impossibly, the fugitives appear to have slipped away.

All I know is that at one point an officer took some shots as they fled down the alley, and the taller of the two fell to the ground. We have to assume it was a result of having been hit, but I'm not sure of that, either, because when the smoke of the general confusion and hollering cleared, the two had vanished. And they're gone, Bob, just gone.

SCRATCH JOURNAL ENTRY

Winc was having a lot of trouble walking, so we took a break, sitting up against a pile of boxes in an alley, hir back against my chest, my hands doing their best to stop hir bleeding. Ze looked so pale.

Then I looked up and saw him. Standing just a few yards away at the mouth of the alley. He wore a shabby suit, good shoes but worn to hell. He was so close, I could see his nicotine-stained fingertips.

I knew who he was; of course I knew. If he'd spoken I would have recognized the voice. We locked eyes for one of those long moments. My mind started formulating some acknowledgment, a warning, a thank-you, a quip. But there was only that silence, Winc and I looking at him, him looking at us. Then, he turned away. Yes, he did.

He walked very fast, very deliberately to the other end of the alley. He went up to the crowd of cops, but I didn't panic. I took my time, getting Winc to hir feet, adjusting hir against me, and kept walking the other way.

Down the alleyway, I heard him, and he was telling the others he'd seen us. I could see his thumb stabbing the air, and then I heard him bark the classic line.

"They went thataway."

He never looked back at us, but he kept his gaze steady on his retreating troops. Then he, too, was gone. I heard his footsteps following the others, and then it was very, very quiet.

We were alone again, Winc and I, and I knew there was no place else I'd rather be, nobody else I wanted to be. We were together, alone, as we'd always been, and that was enough. Hip to hip, we walked slowly, me half holding hir up, my Winc, bleeding hir life into mine.

END SCRATCH JOURNAL ENTRY

TOOBE ENTRY

I can't even type this. I saw them, ran to them. Like slow motion. But . . .

Winc!

Scratch and Winc were running. I heard these shots, and then I saw Winc fall. And ze was bleeding way bad.

My dad held me back, kept saying it wasn't safe, telling me they'd be okay. Right!

Then they kissed each other. Usually I don't like looking at people kissing, but this was such a lovely kiss that I couldn't stop looking.

And I had no idea if this would be their last kiss ever.

I just fell into my dad's arms.

Love,

T.

END TOOBE ENTRY

To: Editor, They/Them magazine
From: D.I. Drew
Subject: The end?

Hi Asa,

This is where the story that everyone knows ends. Despite my conviction that someone must know what happened to Winc and

Scratch after that fateful day, I've failed to find a reliable source. That said, there's one more installment of this tale.

Cheers,

D.I. Drew

Nearly Roadkill: End Note

Dear Reader,

The whole world's gone mad, I tell you, upside down. I am the storyteller become the story.

I set out to tell a story about the mad, crazy, queer, sexy love of (quoting Toobe here) ". . . two idiots who don't know anything. One's confused, and the other's a ditz." This love brought the Internet to its knees. End of story, right? The two of them escape through some back alleys in New York. Winc's bleeding, but Scratch has got hir, and they're limping off into the sunset. The End.

But no! There has been a plot twist . . . or three. So, here's the rest of the story, brought to you by me, D.I. Drew, your friendly neighborhood nonbinary journalist. I'm the nerd behind the "Nearly Roadkill: Scratch and Winc" series, published here at *They/Them* magazine. I still have two huge questions: What happened to Winc after the big chase, and where are the lovebirds today?

There are no definitive answers to these questions. Every scholar I talk to today has their own theory, but back in 1995 after the shutdown, all the usual suspects went strangely silent on the subject. No one was talking. Not Toobe, not Jabba, not Scratch or Winc. The mainstream media covered the political story surrounding the Internet shutdown, but the love story of Scratch and Winc got lost in the process. Only the tabloids were talking—in their usual fashion.

I Was Winc's Gay Lover!

Pregnant Transsexual Man Claims: It Was Me and Scratch and the Couple Next Door!

or

Scratch Becomes Luddite, Is Spotted Living in the Desert as a Bearded Lady

The following scenario is not proven fact, but it's plausible. I've pieced it together from some of the more rational theories, blog posts, docs, chat logs, bulletin boards, and the few eyewitness accounts I found using the Freedom of Information Act.

Warning: it's sad as all fuck.

NEARLY ROADKILL, THE EPILOGUE

Scratch is sitting in an ugly green hospital waiting room. The clock on the wall measures the seconds, going tick tick tick tick tick tick.

Down the hallway, through the swinging doors of an operating room, one harried ER surgeon, her nurse, and an altogether too tired anesthesiologist huddle over a patient.

"Damnit, we have to crack her open."

In the waiting room, Toobe is seated next to Scratch. Toobe is back in his regular clothes but has kept the eyeliner.

Tick tick tick tick tick.

"Scalpel."

"Scalpel."

"Sponge."

"Sponge."

"Sternal retractor."

"Scratch," Toobe is saying, "I'm scared for Winc."

"Me too, little buddy. Me too."

Tick tick tick tick, for about an hour. Open heart massage—for twenty-five minutes. Then comes that sound, that terrible sound we all know when a patient has flatlined.

"Time of death, 12:39."

A nurse walks slowly down the hallway from the OR to the waiting room.

"I'm so sorry, Mr. Scratch," she says. "The doctors did everything they could, but it wasn't enough to save her. Winc's gone. Oh god, I'm sorry, is that Ms. Scratch?"

Long, awkward, heartbroken silence.

Scratch and Toobe sit, slack-jawed.

And that's that.

Winc, the peoples' hero, cyber rebel, gorgeous queer, died. I'm so sorry, but you read that correctly. I really wanted this to be a happy ending, romantic that I am. But I've got hospital records saying a "Jane Doe of transgender experience" checked in in critical condition with gunshot wounds on March 15, 1995. No other records found, which is still typical today.

So . . .

Did the feds kill Winc?

Did Scratch ever recover? Is Scratch alive today?

I went round and round on this until I realized: Toobe! He would know! It's been thirty years since this all went down. Scratch would be sixty-eight today. Winc would have been seventy-five. But Toobe was just a kid back then. What happened to him? It all comes down to Toobe. If he hadn't been so diligent about documenting every detail—if he hadn't pulled everyone together the way he did—no one would have had a clue about Scratch and Winc, or their great love story.

Find Toobe, find answers. But I could find nothing current—no trace of him in all my searches. No social media presence at all.

My dad works in tech, and he has connections. I know a lot of his pals, so I asked around, and a friend of a friend of a friend agreed to trace back the IP address of Toobe's last posts from all those years ago. I ran it, and something went wonky because it came up as my dad's address. Ha! I got punked. Well, screw that. I asked the guy to be more careful and to run it again.

And guess what? Toobe's IP traced back to . . . My. Father's. House.

What the everloving f—?!?!

"Hey, Siri."

"Mmm-hmm?"

"Call my dad."

"Calling Tobias Sparrow."

Well *that* set off all *kinds* of bells and whistles in my brain. My dad's name is Tobias. Tobias. *Toobe*.

Ring.

Ring.

"Hello?"

"Dad."

"Hey! My favorite detective inspector!"

"I love you too. But this is really important."

"Sure thing, punkin'. Shoot."

"Y'know that Scratch and Winc story I'm working on for *Them*?"

"Ummm, you mean the story you've been working on for what, a year now? That story? Sure, kiddo, what's up?"

"I'll get right to the point. Why does Toobe's old IP address lead me to your door?"

Dead. Fucking. Silence. And then . . .

"Oh man, listen . . . I can't talk right now. Hang tight. Give me an hour, and I'll get back to you."

And he hung up.

I called him back, but it went to voicemail.

Six times, it went to voicemail.

But in exactly one hour, the doorbell went ding-dong.

NEARLY ROADKILL, THE REALLY FINAL EPILOGUE

Right, so my dad is standing in the doorway.

"Hey D.I."

"Hey . . . Toobe."

He winces but gamely follows me into the living room.

"Okay, you got me," he says. "But I have a great reason."

Over the next hour, he tells all about the NDA the government made him sign in exchange for dropping all charges related to selling illegal bypasses. According to the terms of the agreement, he was not allowed to speak about any of the events that led up to the Internet shutdown. To anyone, not even any of the other players. But, over the next thirty years, he was able to develop a tunneling technology so he could talk to Scratch and Winc and Jabba and Gwynyth without getting caught by government surveillance.

"Wait a minute. Winc?" I ask. "You said Winc? Winc's alive?"

"Oh yeah," says my dad casually. "Alive and kicking. And when you first told me you were gonna work on this story, I told the two of them."

I sit down. Then I stand up. Then I sit down again. I don't know whether to be mad at him or hug him.

"I seem to have that effect on people," he says, looking down at his feet.

He tells me that all three of them were bound to silence by the NDAs.

"But we wanted you to get the whole story, so we, well, um . . ."

My antenna goes up. "You what? You what, Dad? Or should I call you Toobe?"

He sighs and summarizes:

Apparently, when I showed such interest in the story, he contacted Scratch and Winc so the three of them could find the best chat logs and journals, direct messages, and all the good stuff that painted the true saga of Scratch and Winc.

I feel all the air go out of me.

"So my super-sleuthing skills were bullshit? You fed me everything? What about the chatbots? The Jabba archives? I know for a fact my FOIA (Freedom of Information Act) requests netted some great stuff."

"They did, they did," he answers. "Seriously, D.I. Drew, it was your super-sleuthing skills that unlocked all the information; we couldn't just hand it to you, or to anyone. We've been wanting to tell this story for the last thirty years, and we couldn't. It would've meant prison. But you found this story, and you told it. And now that it's out in the open, we can be too. So thank you, Detective Inspector. Your reporting set us free."

I'm only somewhat mollified and still so curious.

"But didn't I out you, break your NDA? With this story?"

"No, that's the beauty of it. I checked with my lawyer. Once it's out in the open, there's nothing to hide."

"So Winc's alive," I finally manage to say, "and you've been in touch with both of them all this time."

"Yep! As you'd expect, they're cyber-activists, founding members of the Electronic Frontier Foundation, and both senior staff at Wikipedia. Winc has a job training large language models—she's so good with that stuff. Scratch can't stand the idea of AI. She spends her time tending goats."

"Goats?" I stammer. "Scratch is a goatherd?? And they're both 'she'? Shut the front door!" It's all too much. But before I can say another word, the doorbell goes ding-dong. I open the front door to find a tall, slender person with long red hair, boho chic, and a faded waterfall tattoo falling from one eye.

"W-W-Winc?" I manage to croak.

"Hi-eeeeee," she says with a smile.

"Hey," I reply weakly.

In my head, I'm saying Oh my god. Oh my god. Oh my god. And what comes out is "I love you guys!!!!! I mean hello! I'm Drew. I'm Toobe's kid, and I just found that out, and I wanted to tell your story, I wanted to do you justice, you have become my heroes, I . . ."

Winc gently raises her hand.

"You did a great job with our story."

I gape at her.

Winc continues, "We've been reading it out loud to each other as each installment comes out. Thank you by the way, *They/Them* magazine."

"I have so many questions!"

"May I come in? I can't come in 'til you invite me. Mwah-ha-ha!"

"But, but—is Scratch? Where? Are you still—"

"All in good time, m'dear," says Winc. "Ooooh, I've always wanted to say that!"

I step back and do something like a bow, I think, and with a sweep of my arm, welcome her into my home. How corny! And there we are. Me, "Toobe," and Winc.

And then it hits me. My chance to finally get some answers.

"Wait a minute! Wait a minute! You were shot, Winc! You were bleeding—a lot! How . . . ?" My question trails off as Winc raises a well-manicured hand.

"Well, that's a complex story, Drew," she says, "I'll wait to tell it until everyb . . . the right time," she adds cryptically. "How about we get to know each other just a little bit first?"

At just that moment, the front door goes ding-dong.

"Saved by the bell!" Winc says brightly.

I open the door wide and there stands a short, solid blonde with the best short haircut I've seen in a long time.

"S-S-Scratch?" I stammer yet again.

"Come on in, babe!" Winc shouts from the sofa. They stand with their arms around each other, looking for all the world like a genderqueer Penn and Teller, except good-looking in a way that only queers can look no matter their age. They're hot, and they're in my living room. I'm stunned.

And then I smell it. I look around surreptitiously, wondering what's died in or under the house. Or whether my dad hasn't showered in a while. Winc notices.

"Ah, don't mind her, she's been tending her goats," she says. "Judging by the smell, it was Carter today. They're all named after Democrats."

"Oh no, it's fine!" I'm so embarrassed—I must have wrinkled my nose.

"Seriously, not a problem, I'm not offended," laughs Scratch. "I was just so excited when I got the text from Toober here."

"Toober." Ah, right. My dear ol' dad. Scratch has this grin; it's . . . infectious, and I find myself grinning back at her. Sigh.

But then I'm not fangirling anymore, and I'm back to D.I. Drew, journalist detective of truth and justice and matters of the heart. And Scratch and Winc are right here in my living room! "I have to ask. . . . In my piece, I got as far as your getaway and you limping off together into the sunset. THEN what happened?"

"We might as well tell, Scratch," Winc says, looking lovingly at Scratch.

"I'll start," says Scratch, sitting down right there on my carpet. "I live with Winc about half the time; the rest of the time I raise goats and get my sanity back."

"Hey!" says Winc. "I make you insane?!"

"Where you live makes me insane!"

"Well, your goats make me insane!"

"My goats are my sanity!"

"Well, then they're not helping!"

The two of them crack up—they've had this "argument" before.

My cat's sniffing Scratch. I don't think she's ever sniffed goat before. Scratch dangles a sly hand on the floor in front of her and picks up talking to me.

"I still use computers a little. I have no electronic connection to the Internet most of the time, and I upload my work to a file transfer system."

"It's not called that anymore, Scratch," says my helpful dad.

"Whatever. Anyway, I just edit stuff and send it back to people who pay me. 'Life' is Winc and my goats. Wanna see some pictures?"

"As for me," Winc interrupts quickly, "I still love tech, what can I say. But don't let Scratch fool you. She's still active in the Electronic Frontier Foundation."

Scratch is active on my carpet, rolling around with my cat who has really taken a liking to her.

"And I'm working with the most amazing AI," says Winc. "I can actually train it to search out social media algorithms that are designed to hook kids into this or that terrible thing."

"Right!" says Scratch, rubbing the cat's belly. "And then we expose them as bad guys!"

Chicken doesn't let *anyone* touch her belly.

Scratch continues more seriously. "If you ever wonder if greedy bastards know what they're doing, they do. They totally and completely do. Same old greed, new tools."

"She's right," said Winc glumly. "You know the book *The Chaos Machine*?"

"I love that book," I add. "But, Winc, you have to tell me: how did you not die?! I mean, please tell me?" I am a dog with a bone. But she waves me off.

"Oh, that's a long story," she says. "I wanna talk about *you*. Look at you, you're all grown up and out loud genderqueer!"

"Nonbinary," I correct reflexively. (Fuck, I can't believe I'm correcting the real live Winc about gender!)

Winc catches my eye, and her eyes are smiling.

"My apologies," she says. "We never had a word for what we were being back then, and now there's so *many* words! So you're nonbinary."

"You're defining yourself by what you're not," laughs Scratch, still down on the floor with the cat. "I love that."

I give Scratch a thumbs-up and continue, determined to be the journalist here, not the subject. "You two were pioneers in virtual fluid embodiment of postmodern gender theory. Where do you stand on that now?"

A moment's silence.

"Words, Drew," says my dad. He's always good at pulling me back from the edge of academia. I start over.

"I would've thought for sure you two would be in the middle of all the conversations going on now," I say. "I've searched for you in all the gender discussion corners of Instagram, TikTok, Twitch. . . ."

Scratch sighs. "Yeah, no."

I look to Winc, but her smile says *I'm sorry*.

"What?" I ask, officially confused now.

"We just don't talk that much about gender," says Scratch with a shrug.

At the same time, Winc says, "Gender isn't our favorite thing to talk about."

And yeah, they look at each other and say, "Simul-talk," and laugh.

"Well, I mean of course we talk about gender," says Scratch. "Just not publicly. Or rather, just like we used to, in small, private chat rooms."

"And safe!" Winc chimes in. "People are still so mean to each other. Sometimes it's just silly, like who's a man, what's a woman, and why you hafta be one or the other."

"Or both, or neither," adds Scratch.

"Or any, or all of 'em all at once," agrees Winc.

It's not like they finish each other's sentences exactly. It's more like they build a conversation together. Just like in those chat rooms. So cool. But I want to push them on this.

"You're saying gender policing is crueler today than it was thirty years ago?" I ask, my mind racing with examples to the contrary: Today, trans kids have role models, books to read and movies to watch, Internet and IRL support groups. We have language for every aspect of who we are. Isn't that progress? As if she heard my thoughts, Scratch continues.

"Ah, yes, no, you're right," Scratch ventures. "I don't know what to call anyone without having a conversation first. Which is actually just what we dreamed about! That's kind of cool; you have to actually talk to someone. To learn who they are."

"*Exactly* what we were hoping," adds Winc. "But we thought the meanness would go away. Naive, I know. There's such a huge, strong, queer army out there now. Really fabulous when you think about it. They have to fight against book bans, anti-drag queen campaigns, legislation against healthcare for trans children, all that crap. Fierce!"

I can feel my chest kind of puffing up at being a member of the strong queer army.

"I love your cat," Scratch says.

"Mmm-rowww," says the cat, right on cue.

"Chicken," I say.

"No! She's a cat!"

"Her name is Chicken."

"Oh! Sure!"

Winc turns to me.

"For years, all of us outlaws seemed to be all knitted together into more or less a loving family. But now?" Winc looks pensive. "Nobody's giving anyone the benefit of the doubt."

"But we still have fun with identity," says Scratch.

"Only it's a lot more subtle," says Winc.

"We got into studying mindfulness together. The dharma path. Loving kindness and all that. You know, Zen," says Scratch.

"Yeah," Winc agrees, "but that was Zen, and this is Tao."

We all groan, and then the room gets quiet.

"I guess what we're saying is," Winc adds, "is we've kind of retired from being at the forefront of that particular struggle. But so glad other people are taking it on."

Winc turns to me. "So, who are you, Drew? How was it, being raised by Toobe?" Pointing to my dad.

And I guess that was it for gender. But then it hits me again . . . I'm talking with Scratch and Winc! And WINC's alive!

"Wait a minute! How did you not just bleed out and die? I checked hospital records; assuming you were their Jane Doe, you were in really bad shape. . . . So how—?"

Winc opens her mouth to answer, and yet again my goddamn front doorbell goes ding-dong.

"Well, this might be your answer," laughs Scratch slyly. Chicken jumps up, poised to run under the couch just in case it's a pack of snarling dogs out there. Scratch gets up in solidarity.

I walk to the door, all dazed and confused, open it, and standing there is a gorgeous silver-haired woman and a craggily handsome older man. And even before they speak, I know.

"Hi, I'm Shel. I think you know my guy, Wally."

So there I am, face-to-face with Wally fucking Budge. After all those months of trying to find them.

Of course I ask them in.

"That's a terrific series you're writing for *Them*," says Shel.

"Yeah, you've got good facts," adds Budge.

"Here's a fact I wanna know: how did Winc make it out alive?" I ask yet again.

"Oh, has no one told you, hon? For god's sake, they shouldn't keep you in suspense." Shel takes a breath, and out spins. . . .

NEARLY ROADKILL: THE (THIS TIME I MEAN IT) REALLY, WAY VERIFIED EPILOGUE

"Well," Shel begins, "I think when you last saw everyone, my hero here (she leans on Budge's shoulder) told the cops that Scratch and Winc had gone in the opposite direction. But what he won't tell you, because he's so modest, is that that was the moment of truth for him. When he saw even more cops arrive on the scene, he just couldn't take it anymore.

"As he watched his men run off in the wrong direction, he reached into his pocket, pulled out his badge, threw it on the ground, and stomped on it!" Shel chuckles her low chuckle.

"And then our hero—"

"Aw now, honey, I can tell it," Budge interrupts gently. And I don't think I'd ever heard such a smoky cigarette voice except in the movies.

"I didn't do much, really." He shrugs. "I just turned around and caught up to these two." He gestures with his thumb. "Figured I might as well, 'cause I'd been on their trail so long. Winc was lookin' pretty bad. . . ."

"But still good, if you know what I mean," laughs Winc.

Budge sighs and continues, "It didn't take much to convince them I was on their side. I took 'em to my car, drove 'em to the hospital, and checked Winc in as Jane Doe."

"Brilliant, eh?" Shelly purrs.

Budge smiles at her.

"And the hospital called me *a woman of transgender experience*," adds Winc with a smile.

I found that clue! My inner sleuth screams.

"And the doctors do the good job they often do, and now I'm alive and well as well can be," finishes Winc. "In the chaos of the ER, the staff was way overworked. Once I was up and running, well limping, they just sort of waved me out the door. No paperwork. So you couldn't find record of what happened to me."

I look around the room. Still kind of sputtering. Happily. "I can't believe it," I finally say. "A happy ending. Fer real."

"Happy ending!" exclaims Scratch, smacking her forehead with the palm of her hand. She takes out her phone (Android, of course) and starts tapping. "Gwynyth was right. She told me that we'd all be together in a room one day, and I should open this file and use password Happy Ending."

"Wait a minute, wait!!" I say. God I hate not knowing so much. "Gwynyth?!!!"

"Oh yeah, she passed on, some years back," says Scratch nonchalantly. "But you'd never know it, because she talks to me from the other side."

"I can vouch," Winc interjects. "We put our hands on the Ouija board and damned if it doesn't zing around like a cat possessed. Which I guess she kind of is. And what do you think Scratch and Gwynyth talk about, you might ask?" Winc says with a tight smile. "Cat food recipes. I swear."

"It's not just about that!" says Scratch indignantly. "We talk about lots of stuff."

I'm almost afraid to ask. "What about Jabba? Is she still around?"

They all laugh. "In a matter of speaking," says Shel.

I must look confused, so Winc says, "Jabba, being Jabba, created a bot of herself. You've probably run into her in your investigations. One of the first real algorithms actually based on a person, not a marketing technique. She shows up in all of our feeds from time to time, even on Scratch's phone."

"Yep, my phone too," says Budge. "Even though it kind of bugged me, that story she wrote about me."

"It was pretty accurate, though, Walls, wouldn't you say?" says Shelly sweetly.

"Yeah, I guess. . . ."

"So, it's like she's not even gone," finishes Winc.

"Anyway!" says Scratch. "Let's check the message from Gwynyth."

Scratch clicks the link, sending a signal out to all our devices and every one of them goes . . .

Ding-dong.

And then our screens flash.

HAPPY ENDING
FOR BUDGE AND SHEL!
HAPPY ENDING
FOR TOOBE AND DREW!

Even Wally Budge is wiping a happy tear or two from his eye. We hang out for a while, swapping stories (it's great to hear about my dad as a silly teenager), and finally Shel and Budge get up to leave. We all hug and promise to keep in touch.

"C'mon, sweetie," says Winc to Scratch, rising.

"Movie night tonight," says Scratch, scrambling to her feet. "Let's watch *Babe*."

"We've seen *Babe*, like twelve times," says Winc. "*Star Trek: First Contact*."

"*Dogs in Space*."

"That's not even a real movie!"

"Is too! It's a documentary."

—And this picture will be in my mind for as long as I live. There they were, the two of them, standing outside my apartment, as dear a couple as I've ever seen. Scratch waves goodbye, and I close the door. And my iPhone goes ding-dong and flashes the message:

HAPPY ENDING
FOR SCRATCH AND WINC!

I'm standing there with my dad. Toobe. I can see all the versions of him at once now.

"I'm so proud of you, hon," he says.

I just throw my hands up and hug him.

The End

(No, really)

THANK YOU

First and foremost, to the brilliant, smart, sexy, and creative people at Generous Press, Amber Flame and Elaina Ellis. What a terrific experience this has been. Thank you for your patience and dedication to this project, which you raised singlehandedly from the dead.

Kate: Thanks to our first editor thirty years ago, Amy Scholder; first reader and helpful tipster, Emily Harris; dear friend and agent for all these thirty years, Malaga Baldi; best pussycat, the ragdoll Sausage; and best friend and partner in life and love, Barbara Carrellas.

Caitlin: Thanks beyond measure to my partner and soulmate, Ann Pancake, for her first-reader labors, general genius, and encouragement, always. To John Sutherland for giving me lunch money by buying my very first copy in 1995, to the unwitting and innocent readers Julie Kelly and Mary Conor Gainer for stepping up and providing great feedback, the less innocent but terrifically fabulous Jenny Johnson for her unique and crucial perspective, and to Liz Rossi for sharing endless pain and glory—I could not have done it without any of you!

ABOUT THE AUTHORS

KATE BORNSTEIN is a trans icon whose pioneering books on the subject of nonbinary gender, *Gender Outlaw* and *My Gender Workbook*, are taught in six languages at hundreds of colleges. Kate's *Hello, Cruel World: 101 Alternatives to Suicide for Teens, Freaks, and Other Outlaws* propelled them into an international position of advocacy for marginalized youth.

CAITLIN SULLIVAN has written several plays, two and a half novels, and a comic book, and has worked as a journalist and the editor of *Seattle Gay News* for many years. She lives in a small rural town near a loud donkey and quiet cows.

Generous Press

Generous Press publishes lush, high-caliber romance fiction by brilliant BIPOC, LGBTQIA+, and disabled authors. We tell finely crafted, poetic, cinematic, messy, weird, hilarious, and swoon-worthy love stories—romance with a generous twist.

Titles by Generous Press + Row House Publishing include:

Someplace Generous: An Inclusive Romance Anthology
edited by ELAINA ELLIS and AMBER FLAME

Losing Sight by TATI RICHARDSON

Nearly Roadkill by KATE BORNSTEIN and CAITLIN SULLIVAN

Generous Press is built on joy and the conviction that all people should be cherished and free. Learn more at www.generous.press.